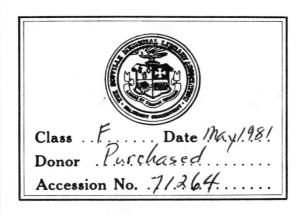

CANOPUS IN ARGOS: ARCHIVES

THE SIRIAN EXPERIMENTS

DORIS LESSING

THE SIRIAN EXPERIMENTS

The Report by Ambien II,
of the Five

ALFRED A. KNOPF   NEW YORK   1981

This is a BORZOI BOOK

Published by ALFRED A. KNOPF, INC.

Copyright © 1980 by Doris Lessing

All rights reserved under International and Pan-American
Copyright Conventions.

Published in the United States by Alfred A. Knopf, Inc., New York.

Distributed by Random House, Inc., New York.

Library of Congress Cataloging in Publication Data

Lessing, Doris May [date]

The Sirian experiments

(Canopus in argos: archives)

I.   Title.

PZ3.L56684SI   1980   [PR6023.E833]   823'.914

ISBN 0–394–51231–6   79–27710

Manufactured in the United States of America

First Edition

This is the third in the novel-sequence
CANOPUS IN ARGOS: ARCHIVES.
The first was *Re: Colonised Planet 5, Shikasta.*
The second, *The Marriages Between Zones Three, Four, and Five.*
The fourth will be *The Making of the Representative for Planet 8.*

Preface

The reception of *Shikasta* and, to a lesser extent, of *The Marriages Between Zones Three, Four, and Five* suggests that I should say something in the way of clarification . . . if I have created a cosmology, then it is only for literary purposes! Once upon a time, when I was young, I believed things easily, both religious and political; now I believe less and less. But I wonder about more . . . I think it is likely that our view of ourselves as a species on this planet now is inaccurate, and will strike those who come after us as inadequate as the world view of, let's say, the inhabitants of New Guinea seems to us. That our current view of ourselves as a species is wrong. That we know very little about what is going on. That a great deal of what is going on is not told to ordinary citizens, but remains the property of small castes and juntas. I wonder and I speculate about all kinds of ideas that our education deems absurd —as of course do most of the inhabitants of this globe. If I were a physicist there would be no trouble at all! *They* can talk nonchalantly about black holes swallowing stars, black holes that we might learn to use as mechanisms for achieving time-and-space warps, sliding through them by way of mathematical legerdemain to find ourselves in realms where the laws of our universe do not apply. *They* nonchalantly suggest parallel universes, universes that lie intermeshed with ours but are invisible to us, universes where time runs backwards, or that mirror ours.

I do not think it surprising that the most frequently quoted words at this time, seen everywhere, seem to be J. B. S. Haldane's "Now, my suspicion is that the universe is not only queerer than we suppose, but queerer than we can suppose."

The reason, as we all know, why readers yearn to "believe" cosmologies and tidy systems of thought is that we live in dreadful and marvellous times where the certainties of yesterday dissolve as we live. But I don't want to be judged as adding to a confusion of embattled certainties.

Why is it that writers, who by definition operate by the use of their imaginations, are given so little credit for it? We "make things up." This is our trade.

I remember, before I myself attempted this genre of space fiction, reading an agreeable tale about a species of highly intelligent giraffes who travelled by spaceship from their solar system to ours, to ask if our sun was behaving cruelly to us, as theirs had recently taken to doing to them. I remember saying to myself: Well, at least the writer of this tale is not likely to get industrious letters asking what it is like to be a giraffe in a spaceship.

It has been said that everything man is capable of imagining has its counterpart somewhere else, in a different level of reality. All our literatures, the sacred books, myths, legends—the records of the human race—tell of great struggles between good and evil. This struggle is reflected down to the level of the detective story, the Western, the romantic novel. It would be hard to find a tale or a song or a play that does not reflect this battle.

But, what battle? Where? When? Between what Forces?

No, no, I do not "believe" that there is a planet called Shammat full of low-grade space pirates, and that it sucks substance from this poor planet of ours; nor that we are the scene of conflicts between those great empires Canopus and Sirius.

But could it not be an indication of something or other that Canopus and Sirius have played such a part in ancient cosmologies?

What do our ideas of "good" and "bad" reflect?

I would not be at all surprised to find out that this earth had been used for the purposes of experiment by more advanced creatures . . . that the dimensions of buildings affect us in ways we don't guess and that there might have been a science in the past which we have forgotten . . . that we may be enslaved in ways we know nothing about, befriended in ways we know nothing about . . . that our personal feelings about our situation in time, seldom in accordance with fact, so that we are always taken by surprise by "ageing," may be an indication of a different lifespan, in the past—but that this past, in biological terms, is quite recent, and so we have not come to terms with it psychologically . . . that artefacts of all kinds might have had (perhaps do have) functions we do not suspect . . . that the human race has a future planned for it more glorious than we can now imagine . . . that . . .

I do not "believe" that there are aliens on our moon—but why not?

As for UFOs, we may hardly disbelieve in what is so plentifully vouched for by so many sound, responsible, sensible people, scientific and secular.

As for . . .

In this particular book I have created a female bureaucrat who is dry, just, dutiful, efficient, deluded about her own nature. A skilled administrator, she is; a social scientist. I could like Ambien II better than I do. Some of her preoccupations are of course mine. The chief one is the nature of the group mind, the collective minds we are all part of, though we are seldom prepared to acknowledge this. We see ourselves as autonomous creatures, our minds our own, our beliefs freely chosen, our ideas individual and unique . . . with billions and billions and billions of us on this planet, we are still prepared to believe that each of us is unique, or that if all the others are mere dots in a swarm, then at least *I* am this self-determined thing, my mind my own. Very odd this is, and it seems to me odder and odder. How do we get this notion of ourselves?

It seems to me that ideas must flow through humanity like tides.

Where do they come from?

I would so like it if reviewers and readers could see this series, *Canopus in Argos: Archives,* as a framework that enables me to tell (I hope) a beguiling tale or two; to put questions, both to myself and to others; to explore ideas and sociological possibilities.

What *of course* I would like to be writing is the story of the Red and White Dwarves and their Remembering Mirror, their space rocket (powered by anti-gravity), their attendant entities Hadron, Gluon, Pion, Lepton, and Muon, and the Charmed Quarks and the Coloured Quarks.

But we can't all be physicists.

THE SIRIAN EXPERIMENTS

SIRIUS-CANOPUS. BACKGROUND

This is Ambien II, of the Five.

I have undertaken to write an account of our experiments on Rohanda, known to Canopus in this epoch as Shikasta.

I shall employ the time divisions commonly used, and agreed on between ourselves and Canopus. (1) The period up to the first burst of radiation from Andar. (2) That between the first and second bursts of radiation—again from Andar. (3) From the second irradiation to the failure of the Canopus-Rohanda Lock, known as the Catastrophe. This third period is sometimes referred to as the Golden Age. (4) The period of subsequent decline. This account of mine will deal mainly with (4).

I shall not do more than mention the experiments before the first radiation, which are fully documented under Lower Zoology. During (1) Rohanda was damp, marshy, warm, with shallow seas hardly to be distinguished from swamp, and deep oceans kept turbid by volcanic activity. There was a little dry land. On this were a few land animals, but there were numerous varieties of water lizards, and many fishes. Some of these were unknown on other Colonised Planets, and on our Mother Planet, and we made successful transfers of several species. We also introduced on to Rohanda species from elsewhere, to see what would happen to them. All our experiments during (1) were modest, and did not differ from similar experiments in other parts of our Empire.

(2) The first burst of radiation from Andar was not expected. Both Canopus and ourselves were taken by surprise. We had kept a watch on the planet ever since the war between us that ended our hostilities. Because of the new situation we boosted our surveillance. The irradiation had the effect of abolishing some genera overnight, and of speeding evolution. The planet remained wet, swampy, steamy, cloudy, with the slow enervating airs that accompany these conditions. Yet new genera and species seemed to explode into life and existing ones rapidly changed. Within no more than a million R-years there were not only many varieties of

fish and reptile, but there were species that flew, and insects—both of these formerly unknown. The place teemed with life. It also soon became clear we were to expect a period of the gigantic. The lizards in particular showed this trend: there were many kinds of them, and some were a hundred times, and even more, their former size. The vegetation became huge and rank. Land and water were both infested with enormous animals of all kinds.

Throughout these times Canopus and ourselves conferred, when it seemed to either or both that this was necessary. Sometimes we, and sometimes Canopus, initiated discussions.

We always supplied Canopus with reports on our proceedings on the planet, but they did not *at that time* show much interest. This very important point will be gone into later. Canopus supplied us with reports, but we did not put much effort into studying them. Again, I emphasise that this is an important point, as will later become plain.

Canopus maintained a monitoring station during (2). We did initiate some experiments in various places over Rohanda, but these were mostly to do with sudden, not to say violent, growth; and since the planet itself was so generously supplying us with observation materials, we did not intrude ourselves very much. It was not a popular place with any of our scientists. Our Planet 13 once had a similar swampy and miasmic climate, and we already had considerable data.

For something like two hundred million R-years this state of affairs continued. Just as the previous, pre-irradiation characteristics seemed to be stable, if not permanent, so, now, did it seem that this watery pestilential place full of gigantic and savage animals would remain as it was. There then occurred, and again unexpectedly, the second burst of radiation.

The effects were again dramatic.

There was every kind of cataclysm and upheaval. Land sank beneath the water and became ocean bed; new land appeared from the seas, and for the first time there was high terrain and even mountains. Volcanic activity had never been absent, since the crust covering the still molten core was so thin, but now land and water were continuously convulsed. The mantle of cloud that had sometimes kept the whole planet in warm gloom for weeks at a time was rent tumultuously with storms and winds.

All the large species were destroyed. The great lizards were no more to be seen, and the forests of giant ferns were laid flat by the violent winds and rain.

There was a sudden cooling. When the convulsions lessened, and ceased, the planet was left transformed. In a very short time, much of the water was massed around the poles in the form of ice and snow. Some swampy areas remained but now earth and oceans were separated, and there were areas of dry land. That was of course long before the planet's axis had been knocked out of the vertical: before the "seasons" that contributed so much to its instability. The poles were cold. The area around the middle was hot. In between were zones of predictable and steadily temperate climate.

This was period (3), from which both Canopus and ourselves hoped so much, when conditions were as perfect as can be expected on any planet—and which was to last rather less than twenty thousand R-years.

It was at the very beginning of this new period (3) that Canopus invited us to a joint Conference.

This Conference was held, not on our Mother Planet, nor on theirs, but on their Colony 10, convenient for us both.

The mood of the Conference was one of confidence and optimism.

This is the place, I think, to say more about our relations with our eminent friend and rival.

I shall begin with this statement: that Canopus pioneered certain sciences, and in the opinion at least of some is still far ahead of us.

In my view the duty of a historian is to tell the truth as far as possible . . . no, this remark is not meant as provocation, though in the prevailing climate of opinion everywhere through our Empire, there are many who will see it as such.

For far too long our historians refused to accept the simple truth, that Canopus *was* the first to explore and develop the skills associated with what we all now call Forced Evolution. (I do not propose to enter here into discussion with those—I am afraid still quite numerous—people who believe that nature ought to be left to itself.) It was Canopus who began to look at species—or whole planets—from the point of view of how their evolution could be modified, or hastened. We learned this from them. That is the truth. We were pupils in their school. Willing—and not unworthy —pupils; willing and generous teachers.

That is why, when it came to sharing out Rohanda between us, we got the less attractive share. This was what fitted our position in relation to Canopus.

The critical reader will already be asking: Why this praise of Canopus when as we all know the story of Rohanda was one—to put it baldly—of disaster?

If Canopus was at fault, then so were we, Sirius. At that Conference on their Planet 10, we all assumed that if Rohanda had—to our certain knowledge—experienced very long periods of stability, two of them, both lasting many millions of R-years, then we might safely expect that this new period would similarly last millions of years. Why should we not? There are factors, which we all agree to call "cosmic," over which we have no control, and which may not be foreseen. All evolutionary engineering is subject to these chances. If we did not permit ourselves to begin any development on a newly discovered planet, or one that has become suitable for development and use, because of the threat of cosmic alteration or disaster, then nothing at all would ever be achieved.

Canopus, like ourselves, has experienced disappointment—and worse—in their career as colonisers. Rohanda was not the only failure. I am calling it a failure, though I know *they* do not—but it is no secret that I have been generally known throughout my career as belonging to that body of opinion that finds Canopus sentimental. Sometimes to the point of folly. What else can we call attitudes that are often uneconomic, counter-productive, wasteful of administrative effort?

What else? Well, I have learned that there are different ways of looking at things; though I do not yet share these viewpoints. That is, I hope, for the future . . . meanwhile, I am saying that judged from the immediate and practical view, Rohanda was not only a failure but perhaps their worst; and yet this was not at all or in any way their fault. And why should some of us be so ready to ascribe blame to Canopus, when we were, equally with her, ready to use

Rohanda for as long as was possible—for millions of R-years, as we then thought was likely to be the case?

The disposition of the land and seas was roughly, very roughly, the same as it is now. There is a central mass of land fringed with promontories, peninsulas, islands. Around it is a vast ocean, with many islands, some of them large. There are two continents, separated from the main landmass, and joined by an isthmus which has sometimes been submerged, and these are now referred to as the Isolated Northern Continent and the Isolated Southern Continent. Between the central landmass and the Isolated Northern Continent, looking west with their north pole at North, have been at various times, according to the rise and fall of the ocean levels, many islands, one of them at least enormous. But sometimes there has been only an almost islandless ocean.

Projecting southwards from the central landmass, of which its northern areas form a part, is another southern continent, now called Southern Continent I. (The Isolated Southern Continent is Southern Continent II.) Southern Continent I has sometimes been considered by geographers as part of the main landmass, since its northern parts have been so influenced by the easy migrations and movements to and from every part of the main landmass. But the southern parts have on the whole had such a different history that they are more usually classed as a different and separate continent. We, Sirius, were allotted in the share-out of Rohanda the two southern continents, including the northern areas of S.C. I, and any islands large and small lying in the oceans that we felt inclined to make use of.

More has to be said about the Conference itself.

It was considered a success. Remarkably so. Even though it was only one of very many conferences and discussions about the situations of a large number of Colonised Planets whose problems, in one way or another, we shared, everybody taking part felt that it marked a new level in co-operation. And the further it receded into the past, the more we were all able to see it had been extraordinary, and this not only because of the unexpectedly fortuitous new epoch on Rohanda. Committees, conferences, discussions, followed one after another through the millennia: it was to that particular one, on Colony 10, we were always referring back, as if there had been some particular and unrepeatable spring of life and vigour there we had not been able to approach again.

I am now going to say, with equal emphasis and confidence, that the Conference was a failure.

What Sirius understood of the resolutions, the agreements, *the verbal formulations*, was not the same as the understandings of Canopus. This was not evident then. It did not even begin to be evident for a very long time. It is not seen now, except by a small number of us Sirians.

By now it will have become clear, I think, that this report of mine is an attempt at a re-interpretation of history, from a certain point of view.

An unpopular point of view, even now: until recently, impossible.

Until recently, I have been among those who would have made it impossible: this I must say now, and clearly: I am not claiming that I am one who has been preserving an individual (and seditious!) view of history in secrecy, because of an oppressive conformity in the official way of looking at things. Far from it. If there is, if there has been, a minority of individuals who have in fact maintained a view different from the official one, then these will have considered me as a bastion of orthodoxy. This is not an apology I am making. We all see truths when we can see them. When we do, it is always a temptation to consider those who have not yet seen them as quite intrinsically and obdurately stupid.

In throwing in my lot with this minority—if it exists—I am doing so in the expectation of strong criticism—but not, I hope, of worse.

I shall deal at once with what I consider to be the root of the problem: that long-ago war between Canopus and Sirius.

It ended in a Truce . . . the anniversary of which occasion we still celebrate. The beastliness and horror have been formalised in tales of heroic exploits that we teach our young. The fact is that Canopus won this war, and, at the moment when they might reasonably have been expected to humiliate us and to exact tribute and retribution, they summoned our—thoroughly defeated—leaders, returned to us our Colonised Planets, which they were in a position to retain for themselves, informed us that we must stay behind our own boundaries, offered us co-operation and friendship, and announced that this agreement would be described as a Truce, so that we would not suffer ignominy in the eyes of our fellow states and empires.

A very long time later, and quite recently, I asked my Canopean friend Klorathy, head of their Colonial Administration, what he and others like him now felt about this magnanimous and high-flown behaviour, in view of the fact that we, Sirius, had never given them credit for it, but on the contrary had done everything to expunge from our history books, and even—apparently—from our memories, any hint that Canopus had won that war and had then behaved as no empire has ever—to my knowledge—behaved any-where. His reply was that "it was too early yet to say what the results would be and he preferred to withhold judgement."

I record this typically Canopean remark. Without comment. Without comment at this place.

I said earlier that Canopus had not shown much interest in the results of our experiments on Rohanda, or on any other planet, for that matter.

Just as we did not understand their attitude at the end of the great war between us, so we did not, do not, understand their indifference to our work.

This is because they, in their own work, have gone so far beyond us. They have never had anything to learn from us. But we have consistently interpreted their attitude as one of dissimulation, believing them to be pretending indifference, out of pride, while secretly ferreting out any information they could, even sending spies into our territories and making use of our work without acknowledgement.

Our set of mind has been one that has *consistently* led us into wrong judgement.

Let us take an example. That the Conference was on Colony 10 and that it was from here the colonisers for Rohanda were chosen was merely a coincidence. Yet we were all talking about the "cleverness" of Canopus in making sure that we met these vigorous and formidable people, so that we would not be tempted to overrun our boundaries on Rohanda. And this belief of ours, crystallised at the Conference—I was one of those responsible, and am in a position to admit to the harm done—continued on into our sojourn on the planet, influencing us in all kinds of ways. But it was quite simply nonsense: we had suggested their Planet 10 ourselves. This is the kind of error suspicion leads us all into.

There are many more examples I could give, but I will deal with the two main factors, or themes, of this Conference: that is, as we were affected. We supplied to Canopus outlines of the experiments we proposed, but did not see then—were not prepared to see!—to what an extent these were to be conditioned by what Canopus proposed to do.

That was at the beginning of the 20,000 years during which we were to profit by Rohanda's great time, under the influence of Canopus. It was not until later that Canopus decided to speed up her plan, because of her Planet 8, which was due to reach an untimely end because of unforeseen cosmic changes. Canopus was then thinking in terms of 50,000 and not 20,000 years, in which to advance the Colony 10 individuals to a certain level. She informed us that she planned two phases. First, a general heightening and consolidation of these Colony 10 volunteers up to a determined point. (That they *were* volunteers struck us then as laughable, though it was not long before we were employing the same policy, instead of conscripting.) This predetermined point—and we were offered full information and details—would be marked by what they called a "Lock"—that is, a synchronisation between Canopus and Rohanda that would bring the planet into harmony with their Empire as a whole. Harmony of a particular kind.

This, then, was the first theme, one unfamiliar to us at that time. Unfamiliar, I am going to risk saying, even now: for when we use words like harmony, good fellowship, co-operation—which we do plentifully and all the time in relation to our own Empire—we do not mean by them what Canopus means. At the Conference, being told that Canopus proposed to *develop* the Colony 10 volunteers, to *stabilise* them, to *make use* of their *evolution* to *advance* the Canopean Empire, what we understood from this was no more than the sort of development, stabilisation, evolution, advance, that we associated with our own territories.

The second theme was how Canopus proposed to achieve these

admirable results. For we were given—or offered, for we did not make use of this opportunity—all the information we wanted.

We did not accept because we were handicapped by being resentful, even though the general euphoria of the Conference succeeded in masking these unfortunate emotions. The northern areas were plentifully stocked with a certain species of primate. In parts these were already upright, using tools and weapons, with the beginnings of semipermanent settlement. This type of animal, at this level of evolution, is always of value, both for experiment and in training for simple tasks. There were none in Isolated Southern Continent II; and while there were some apes in Southern Continent I, they were at a low level of evolution, suitable for experiment, but of no use at all for work.

We saw Canopus "as usual" grabbing the best of everything, for not once did we remind ourselves that there was no reason we should ever have been allowed on Rohanda at all. It was not we who had discovered this planet.

Canopus told us that certain rapid and desirable developments of the Colony 10 colonists would be because of a "symbiosis" between them and the apes, and that the apes, too, would be benefitted. We saw this "symbiosis" in terms of a beneficial cultural exchange and, more specifically, as the superior immigrants being set free for higher tasks by using the apes as servants.

In short, the two main pieces of information, the bases on which the Canopean plan was predicted, were not understood by us at all. In spite of our being told everything. To emphasize this even more: now, looking back at the Conference, I can see that there was nothing *not* said, *not* made plain, *not* explained. But we misinterpreted what we were being told. And again, it is impossible not to ask, now, *why* Canopus set up the Conference in this way? To forestall reproaches of niggardliness? No! Knowing Canopus, this was not the reason. But they must have realised that we were not taking in what was being said, were understanding everything in our own way.

So why did they do it? It is only recently that I have had an answer to this question. The *beginnings* of an answer . . .

The end of the Conference was marked by all kinds of festivities and jollities. We were taken on trips to other Canopean colonies;

invited, "if we were in that part of the Galaxy," to visit them for as long as we liked—the usual courtesies.

Back on our Home Planet we Sirians lost no time. Planets in the healthy, vigorous condition of Rohanda were—and are—rare. We of the Colonial Service were all delighted and full of optimism. Incidentally, it was at that Conference that Rohanda acquired its name. Perhaps this is not the place—it is too soon—to remark that when the planet suffered its cosmic reversal, and ceased to be so pleasant, even if it did not lose any of its fertility, Canopus at once jettisoned the name Rohanda, substituting another, Shikasta, "the broken or damaged one," felt by us to be unnecessarily negative. This mixture of pedantry and poeticism is a characteristic of Canopus, and one that I have always found irritating.

Spacecraft had already thoroughly surveyed both Southern Continents, independently of Canopus. Our scientists had visited selected areas, and recommendations had been made. It was decided that Southern Continent I would be used mainly for agriculture. We had recently acquired our Colonised Planet 23 (C.P. 23) and had found it was well able to sustain large-scale settlement, provided it was supplied with food. This being part of the same solar system as Rohanda, and quite close, we had thought from the start of using one or other of the southern continents as an agricultural base. S.C. I was admirably equipped from the point of view of soil and climate. It was roughly divided into three zones, the middle one, equatorial, being too hot, but the other two, the southern part and the northern, useful for a vast variety of plants. We introduced several grain plants from both our colonised planets and those of Canopus and developed some indigenous grasses to supply grains and also developed locally-originating tubers and leaf crops. I was not directly in charge of this enterprise. Those interested will find accounts of S.C. I's twenty-thousand-year career as a food supplier for C.P. 23 in the appropriate documents. During this time, too, several laboratories were maintained on that continent, and a good deal of useful research accomplished. This was nearly all to do with agriculture and the use of indigenous and introduced animals. Our C.P. 23 flourished during this period. Its inhabitants originated on our Home Planet, all of first-class stock, carefully selected. None of their energies needed to be spent on feeding themselves, or on anxieties about their nurture; they had their attention free for mentation and intellectual activity. This twenty-thousand-year period was C.P. 23's Golden Age, when it achieved the position of Planning Centre for the whole of our Empire. The fact that it was short lived does not detract from this achievement.

I do not propose to say much more about the experiments on S.C. I. Nor shall I be giving full or even balanced accounts of our experiments on Isolated S.C. II. Details can be found under the appropriate headings.

I shall again say that the purpose of this record is to put forward a certain view of our relations with Canopus. There have been a thousand histories, formal and informal, of our experiments on Rohanda, but *not one* setting these in the Canopean context. This fact alone makes my point. What I say, therefore, about our re-searches will be chosen entirely from this point of view; and it must not be thought that the emphases given here would be those ade-quate from the point of view, let us say, of someone looking at the Rohanda experiments from a long-term view of their evolutionary usefulness. This particular epoch on Rohanda, short though it was, proved crucial in our relations with Canopus, both then and sub-sequently, and not only on that planet but generally. Which may lead us to ponder profitably on the implications of the fact that a short period of time, twenty thousand years, may turn out to be of more importance than epochs lasting millions of years; and that the small planet of a small and peripheral sun may have more influence than large and impressive-seeming constellations. I feel that this kind of speculation may throw light on the Canopean superiority to us in certain fields of endeavour.

In order to understand how our Colonial Service was thinking, it is necessary to sketch the situation in the Sirian Empire at that time.

Our technological development had reached a peak and had been established long enough for us to understand the problems it must bring. The chief one was this: there was nothing for billions upon billions of individuals to do. They had no purpose but to exist, and then die. That this would be a problem had not been foreseen. I shall at this point hazard the statement that it is usually the central, the main, consequences of a development that are not foreseen. What we had seen was the ending of drudgery, of unnecessary toil, of anxiety over the provision of the basic needs. All our efforts, the expenditures of energy of generations, had gone into this: a double or two-branched advance: one aspect of it to do with the conquest of space; the other, with the devices that would set us all free from toil.

We did not foresee that these billions, not only on our Home Planet but also on our Colonised Planets, would fall victim to depression and despair. We had not understood that there is inherent in every creature of this Galaxy a need, an imperative, towards a continual striving, or self-transcendence, or purpose. To be told that there is nothing to do but consume, no work needed, nothing to achieve, is to receive a sentence of death. The hapless millions, offered by their triumphantly successful leaders plenty, leisure, freedom from want, from fear, *from effort*, showed every symptom of mass psychosis, ranging from random and purposeless violence to apparently causeless epidemics and widespread neurosis. This period, known as the Sirian Dark Age, does not lack its historians, and I shall concentrate on its aspects that are germane to our theme. One was a phenomenon that became known as "invented usefulness." Once the cause of the general malaise had been understood, there were various solutions suggested, of which this was the first attempted: areas that had been relinquished to machines and technical devices were deliberately reclaimed. I will mention one example. Everything to do with the supply and demand of food, and household goods, had been mechanised so that the means in most general use everywhere in the Empire were vast depots, each one of which might supply a million inhabitants, needing no attendants at all. These were dismantled in favour of small suppliers, sometimes specialist suppliers, and the billions employed in this artificial industry were conspicuously happier than the idle masses. For a time. We had to take account of what is, so we know now, a law. This is that where the technology exists to accomplish a service or task or to supply a need, then if this is not used, because of humanitarian or other social reasons, there is no real or lasting satisfaction for the people involved in that sector. They all *know*, in the end, even if this realisation is delayed—

sometimes deliberately, and by themselves, in efforts of self-deception—that their labours, *their lives*, are without real purpose. And—in the end, if this is delayed—they fall victim to the same constellation of ills and general malaise. This is not to say that "invented usefulness" was not plentifully used; that it is not sometimes, in controlled areas, still used. As therapy, for instance; I will shortly describe an experiment on these lines.

Another phenomenon of the Dark Age was named, derisively and with unconcealed resentment, "pastimes of the rich." Few of our better-off citizens did not acquire for themselves land, where they farmed in the old style: "pastimes of the rich" were mostly in the agricultural area. Innumerable people everywhere on our Colonised Planets left their leisure, their controlled and planned entertainments, and regressed to a long distant past, with families working sometimes quite small plots of land, aiming at full self-sufficiency, but of course using the technical advances when this suited them. A favourite model was the ancient one of crops, animals, and workers as an interacting and mutually dependent unit. Such "farms" might not trade at all, but consumed what was grown. Others did set up trade, not only with each other but sometimes even made links with the cities where their products were in great demand—again with the rich. I do not have to say that the resentment against these "drop-outs" was due to envy. There was a time when it seemed as if there was not a male, female, neuter or child anywhere in our Empire who was not possessed with one idea: to get hold of some land, even by criminal means, and to retreat into primitive production. This period produced its literature, a rich one, which is not the least curious of our literary side products. This phenomenon, at its height, was not confined to *parts*, or *areas*, of planets, but whole planets were taken over, and sometimes even conquered, solely with this idea in view. Our Colonised Planets 19 and 22 were for several millennia agricultural paradises, with not a town to be seen and both consciously planned and developed to avoid the growth of villages larger than market-places for the exchange of goods. There were mass movements of mainly young people whose aim was only to reach either of these planets or to conquer a new one. These movements had all the characteristics of the "religions" that afflicted Rohanda in its period of decline and degeneration. To "live simply," to "get back to nature," seemed to nearly everyone the solution to all our new problems. But this phase, too, passed, when it became evident that these artificial schemes, these expedients, did not succeed in stilling the inner drive towards transcendence, both social and personal. There are still such farms, such ideas, in existence, but they have long ago been understood by everyone as pathetic regressions.

It was by then clear to us all that we needed a drastic decrease in population. To state this is enough to raise the questions that then ravaged us all. Were we saying that the conditions of our existence in our Empire were to be governed entirely by economic factors? That the lives of our peoples should be judged solely by the levels of our technical achievements? Of course it goes without saying that when the question was put like this, the answer was that the numbers of populations, and their ways of living, had always been governed by economic factors: all that had happened was that famines, floods, diseases, had been replaced by the consequences of technical development. Nothing had changed: that was the argument. No need to torment ourselves now about questions about the purpose of life, the value of the individual, and so forth. Had we pondered and agonised over the results of natural disasters? Yes? Had this done any good? No? Then why were we now prepared to agonise and torment ourselves over equally uncontrollable factors?

But that was the nub of the thing. We had seen ourselves, in bringing our technical achievements to such a pitch, as being in control, as exercising choice. Our thinking had been governed by this one idea. That we had abandoned chaos, and random decimation; that we had advanced towards conscious and deliberate controls.

To say that we were deliberately choosing to reduce our populations, *that this was a choice*, was simply not true, no matter how judiciously and carefully we were doing it. We had been forced into this position by our economic growth that had gone naturally from step to step—upwards. As we had seen it.

This debate went on for a long time, throughout our Dark Age, in fact, and while we were actively reducing populations everywhere. And has gone on ever since, in one form or another.

Thus did our technological advances announce to ourselves, to other empires, to anybody interested, that what governed the coming into existence, or not, of an individual, was work. Or the lack of it. And where would that end? Were we to refuse life to more people than we had work for? Surely that was ludicrous, absurd. We needed agriculturalists—these could never, can never, be dispensed with. We needed technicians of all kinds to do with the production of synthetics and foodstuffs and household goods. We needed some craftsmen. And there was necessary a small governing and administrative class. On our Home Planet, it was estimated that we could do very well with half a million people. At our population peak, our Home Planet had two billion people.

Again, it had to be recognised and acknowledged that we were not in control of what we did, for we were forced into what we did. And that our social programming was always a matter of compromises, of adjustments, of balancing one force against another. We had a very small area of choice, if that word could honestly and accurately be used at all.

This realisation affected some of our administrative people badly, resulting in depressions and psychological maladjustments of all kinds.

The populations everywhere, on every one of our planets, were drastically, but carefully reduced; while the philosophical aspects of the matter were left, temporarily, to the intellectuals.

There was a very long period while this was being done when there were blocs of vast numbers of people who had no occupation, and for whom occupation was made. This fact, too, is relevant to what follows.

Meanwhile, there were extraordinary and bizarre contradictions to be observed everywhere.

The idea of ourselves, not only on the Home Planet but everywhere, as people who had evolved beyond certain levels made it impossible for them to be asked to do some kinds of work.

I did not mention in the list of classes of work that had still to be done by people and not machines, some kinds of heavy manual labour, for which we had not found technical substitutes. Without using force, it was not possible to get any of our peoples to undertake these. In the early heady days of euphoria when we were so effortlessly and successfully—it seemed—surmounting every kind of technical obstacle, abolishing one by one the different classes of unpleasant and degrading work—so we called it—intensive propaganda had gone into adjusting and setting the minds of populations accordingly. When we reversed, or were prepared to adjust, our thinking, it was too late. It is easy for a skilled administrative class to change the ways of thinking of populations, but not easy to do it fast—not without all kinds of social upheaval. We found ourselves in the ludicrous situation where, with hundreds of millions of "surplus" people, we did not know where to find enough ordinary labourers.

We had evolved beyond using force: Canopus had shown us this path long ago. (By this I mean the use of large numbers of people, under duress, for tasks they found abhorrent or demeaning. This did not mean that we did not conscript for work that everyone agreed to find interesting—such as the Colonial Service.) It was not possible for us simply to round up the numbers we needed for mining, quarrying, building and so on, and then turn them into a prison population to do society's dirty work.

In the preceding remarks to do with our condition during that time, I have not yet done more than mention the space drive, which was the greater part of our development—indeed, the motor that governed all our technical development.

Our crisis had its own built-in solution from the beginning. It was to increase our space fleets, our space personnel, our programme for the conquest of space. Our situation was not a static one, not self-limited. Though it certainly did have its limits: the war with Canopus was a result of this sudden restless drive outwards. The devastation caused, the vast numbers killed, certainly solved, or postponed, some problems. I am speaking now dispassionately, and without submission to sentimental considerations: it had not been our intention to use this way of reducing our surplus populations—but that was the result; not our intention to ruin whole planets, so that much labour would be needed to repair them—but that was what happened. These were the *facts*. But the inherent productivity and resources of our Empire were such that all this damage was soon and easily—looking at it from a long-term view—put right. The real lesson of this war was that we were not to be allowed to trespass on Canopean territory. Certain parts of the Galaxy were out of bounds. This meant that the planets available to us, at our then level of technical achievement, were limited: we had already conquered, or at least surveyed, them all. What was necessary was an expansion of our space technology so that greater areas of the Galaxy would become open to us. This is what happened; but this story does not concern us here: only the aspects of it that help to make clear the general situation then, which was, to sum up: a deep and indeed permanent and incurable crisis due to technical mastery, which could be alleviated only by a continuous expansion in space.

I have now said enough to set the background to our experiments on Rohanda—which of course was only one of the planets being used in this way.

There are very few biosociological experiments that are not the result of natural development; whether they are set up deliberately or merely monitored as they unfold. Our first on Rohanda was imposed on us by necessity throughout and came definitely into the category of those that are observed during changes imposed by extraneous pressures.

I am starting with the Lombis, not because it was the first experiment but because it had long-term effects on the planet.

THE LOMBI EXPERIMENT. SOME OTHERS

Colonised Planet 23 needed to be made ready for the Thinkers . . . the reader may detect a note of derision in that phrase: but it is not my intention to detail social controversies of that long-past time: the criticisms of the institution of a planet devoted entirely to one function were certainly many, but these did not in any way affect it. It was a barren planet, waterless, all rock and sand and extinct volcanoes. Our activities there cannot be regarded as experiments, because we had long since perfected techniques for existing on such planets. We had to make structures that were self-contained, with their own climates and atmospheres. Once created, such societies needed very little maintenance. It was quite easy to grow food by hydroponic and other techniques, but these had proved to have their limitations. One was in the area of *grains*. There were other foodstuffs, too, that did not do well in these limited conditions. And it had been long established that while adequate for maintaining life, crops produced in water lacked an element that we only later isolated. But this subject can be studied under its headings. It had been decided that since C.P. 23 was close to Rohanda, which was so fertile, there was nothing to be gained by planning C.P. 23 to feed itself. The structures on C.P. 23 were therefore not as comprehensive and vast as they sometimes are on such planets; but they were large enough so that flying over it, the entire surface seemed to be covered by glistening silvery blisters: the domes of the controlled environment.

They had to be built. This involved the use of large numbers of ordinary labourers, not only for the putting together of the dome-sections, which were of course manufactured elsewhere—on C.P. 3, at that time specialised for this type of manufacture—but for clearing the ground, a formidable task on that uneven and rocky terrain, which needed hundreds of different types of machine. I have said that our many and varied populations all had been taught to consider themselves to have gone past this type of work and would not be induced to undertake it.

We had come up against a problem, central to the development of our Empire, which the Lombi Experiment was directly concerned with. It was this: as soon as we had colonised a new planet that already had on it an indigenous population, and even if these were at the beginning not more advanced than apes, or other types of animal, almost at once they saw themselves as defrauded of benefits and advances *that they were entitled to*. Over and over again we had seen this development. Our administrators would arrive on such a planet, and it could still be in a condition of first-degree savagery, and in no time at all, it was clear that a process of rapid social evolution had been begun, which might express itself in many ways, one of which was rebellions and revolts that at the start, and before we understood the causes, had to be put down by force. For it was then believed that this impulse towards self-betterment was due to crude envy and primitive emulation, and was regarded unsympathetically. It was only later that we saw that we were observing a force for growth that would constantly uplift and progress all the peoples of our Empire. It was *not* at all just a question of "they have such and such good things, and we want them, too," but of an irrepressible evolvement. Very soon in our career as the makers of Empire, we knew that if we established ourselves on even the most barbarous of planets, with the intention of using its inhabitants in various necessary ways for the good of our Empire as a whole, then it must be expected that in a very short time these savages would demand—at which point they would be freely given—all the advantages at our disposal. Our Empire could be regarded as a mechanism for the advancement of an almost unlimited number of planets, in different stages of development, towards a civilised norm. Towards uniformity?—an unwanted and undesirable uniformity? That is a different question; a crucial one, certainly, but not our concern here.

What we were considering, at the time Rohanda's new phase began, was why and how the mechanism worked that our mere appearance on a planet began this remarkable process. It was one that we found embarrassing, unwanted. We needed peoples at different levels. We already had billions of privileged peoples entitled to every benefit of technology. We did not want to discover, and then colonise, planet after planet of savages or semisavages who then, it seemed almost at once, would become privileged citizens. In short, we needed a reservoir or bank of populations whom we could use for ordinary, heavy, undifferentiated work.

We had recently found, and explored, Planet 24. This was in a solar system distant from both ours and Rohanda's: too distant to be conveniently incorporated in our Empire in a closely interacting bond. Visits would have to be infrequent, and strictly functional. But it was a productive and fertile place, with an atmosphere, and an indigenous population of animals of a common—and useful—kind. They were of simian type, using four legs or two according to need, were both vegetarian and carnivorous and extremely strong and vigorous. They had long but not overthick hair on their heads, shoulders, and backs, but very little in front. They were endowed with powerful shoulders and arms. They were squat, and shorter than any of the species we had discovered anywhere. Compared to the peoples of our Mother Planet they were a third of our height.

They lived in a variety of patterns, in tribes, smaller groups, in families, even as solitaries. They knew fire. They hunted. They were at the very beginnings of an agriculture. It will be seen that their main characteristic was adaptability.

It was decided that our technicians should from first contact with them adapt themselves to their level, their ways. There was to be no attempt at our usual practice of maintaining a clear-cut, well-defined level of Sirian living—which we did both as self-discipline and as an example. The problem was the physical difference. We chose Colonial Service officials from C.P. 22 who, because of their experience with backward self-sufficient agriculture, could be expected to find conditions on 24 at least recognisable, and who fortuitously were a small, stockily built people. They were instructed to approach the Lombis in a way that would give no indication of any sort of superiority in thought or practice. It was these researchers who established our knowledge of the Lombis.

Another controversy arose at this point. Previously it had been our practice to space-lift as many males, or females without young, as we needed. But not both. There had been disquiet at the inhumanity of this practice recently. I was involved in the widespread self-questioning: it was no longer possible for us to use newly conquered peoples without considering their emotional and mental, as well as their physical, welfare. To accommodate families on 23, and then on Rohanda, would add difficulties to our attempts, but would also enhance and widen the experiment. Our faction in the Colonial Service won the day. We defeated a compromise suggestion of taking sterilised females, and adopted a further compromise: of taking not equal numbers of males and females, but two-thirds males to one-third females. There were advantages to this: not least that it was something not yet tried by us before.

Fifty thousand of these animals were space-lifted to 23, where conditions contrasted in every way with what they had been used to, and both males and females were set to work to set up the space domes. This involved their working, to start with, in heavy equipment, of the standard type for such environments, which they could discard only when the domes were operational. This was not without interest: taking animals who had learned to spit meat over a fire, but not yet to use cooking pots, and putting them into space-age suits and machines. They were able, after instruction, to manage both.

Our technicians were always with them, on exactly the same level, eating as they did, deliberately refraining from any show of difference or superiority.

These technicians continued to be recruited from C.P. 22. This caused a good deal of unrest throughout the Service, though its necessity was appreciated: only 22 produced the individuals of a build approximating the Lombis'. Involvement in such experiments was always competed for. There was not enough to occupy our clamouring and idealistic youngsters. The term of service for the technicians was restricted to six months (Rohandan time) for two reasons. One was to give as many young people as possible their chance; the other was the contradictory one that none could have endured it for longer. To live on a day-to-day level with the Lombis was to regress to a past that our planets liked to think they had gone beyond forever.

During their time on C.P. 23, the Lombis were not pressured or indoctrinated in any way whatsoever.

Previously, our practice had been to find out the structure of belief on a planet, and then use these "Gods"—whatever form they took—in appropriate ways. For instance, we would have told the Lombis that their "Gods" needed them to perform special duties in distant skies. But as far as we could see, they had not reached the stage of gods and deities.

We told them nothing. Our technicians were among them on 24 for a time, without explanation—and none could easily have been given, within their language structure, which was primitive. When our spaceships descended on 24, they took the fifty thousand from different areas so that social patterns would not be too badly disrupted. On 23 they were simply told what they had to do, put into space suits already being used by our exemplars, shown where they were to eat and rest. When the first domes were up, they were given the use of them. All without any information beyond the utilitarian. The atmosphere on that planet inside the domes, strictly controlled, approximated that of their own. No physical shock could have been experienced on that score. Their food was also arranged with this in view.

It was much too soon to watch for signs of a demand for "higher things," for any such impulses in them were bound to be absorbed by these new habits of living they were learning. An immediate and expected development was fierce competition for the females, and a certain amount of belligerence.

Their term on C.P. 23 lasted five Rohanda years, during which they were supervised and instructed by the Planet 22 technicians, who were always changing, always lived exactly as they did, and who explained nothing at all of the reasons for what was happening to them.

Then these Lombis were all, again without explanation, space-lifted to Southern Continent I. Their task was the same: to create the physical conditions for others to use; but not controlled domes and environments, since this was Rohanda. As they arrived on the planet and were released from the spacecraft, our observers were there—but concealed from them.

The Rohandan atmosphere is not dissimilar from that of C.P. 24, but it has 5 percent more oxygen.

I have to record that the observers—among whom I was one—felt more than a little disquiet as the poor creatures emerged on to the grassy, watered plains. They had been for all that time—to them it must have seemed interminable—on 23, either within the domes, or outside working in their cumbersome space suits. There were skies inside the domes—but false skies, which they knew, since they had made them; there was vegetation, but none they had not put there; there was water that they had set moving. Here they stood on earth that was not all sand and rock and gravel, but was grassed and fertile, under real skies . . . as they came pouring down the spacecraft steps they let out hoarse cries of wonder and gratitude, and then flung themselves down on the grass and rolled there, and then clutched each other and—so it sounded—laughed and, when we looked closely at their broad, hairy faces through our powerful lenses, wept: we saw the tears roll. Tears are not part of our own functioning on our Mother Planet, but they are of some among our family of species. We had not known that these animals wept; no mention had been made of it. And then they danced, slowly, solemnly, thousands upon thousands of them, holding up their arms, lifting their ape faces to the skies and celebrating their joy at returning to—normality? Was that what they thought, we wondered? That this was their own home again?

So it turned out. They believed that they were home, since trees and blue skies and grasses and freedom from clumsy machinery and space equipment *were* their home; and did not realise for some time that this was not a part of their own planet but another planet.

When they did, they were not given time to develop negative reactions.

After an interval while they were allowed to rush about and to dance and to let out strange—and surely rhythmic—grunts and cries, a time while they were permitted to enjoy their freedom, they were again rounded up, divided into companies, and set to work. Forest had to be cleared for, first of all, settlements of our colonisers; and then when this was accomplished, wider tracts cleared for the planting of crops, and the siting of laboratories. When one station was ready with its buildings, its cleared fields, its laboratories, then the entire work force was lifted off again to another site further south. As soon as they left, but not before, since these animals were not to see creatures more evolved than themselves, the first contingent of agriculturalists came in from our Mother Planet. They had been chosen by lottery; such was the fierceness of the competition for this work, it was the only method that could be guaranteed not to cause resentment.

Ten different agricultural stations were established on Southern Continent I. These were enough not only to supply all of 23, but later there were plentiful supplies of what were luxury products, at luxury prices, for our Home Planet. The setting up of these took over a hundred R-years.

The average life of the Lombis was 200 R-years. As always, when establishing a species on another planet, the way this would affect a life-term was a major consideration. We had come to expect random and wild fluctuation at the beginning, and thereafter unforeseen variations in life-term. The Lombis were no exception. During the first few R-years, some died for no apparent reason (some race-psychologists classed these deaths under the heading of Mal-Adaptation due to Life Disappointment), and the young that were born seemed likely to be set for longer life-terms. There was also a quite unforeseen increase in height and girth.

When their work was done on Southern Continent I, they were not returned to their own planet.

This was because, during the period between their being taken off their own planet, and the end of their term on 23, another planet had been discovered, much nearer to Sirius, not dissimilar from 24, but with only very limited and lowly evolved life-forms. It was our intention to space-lift the Lombis to this planet— Colonised Planet 25—in order to establish on it this species, which, we hoped, would continue to be useful for general hard unskilled labour.

In other words, they were not to return home at all.

But it was not possible for them to be taken to 25 at once, because that was being used for certain limited and short-term experiments, and their presence there would be disruptive. They were therefore brought under my aegis, on to Isolated Southern Continent II, as an interim measure.

During their hundred years on S.C. I, they were in what can only be described as a social vacuum. They had not been allowed to glimpse any sign of Sirian general levels of culture. They had continued to be instructed—less and less, since they proved able pupils—by the C.P. 22 technicians, who never allowed themselves to be seen as superior in expectation to their pupils. They were not told why they were doing this work of establishing agricultural stations. Nor what happened on 23 after they left it. Nor what their destiny was to be. Some of their supervisors considered they were not capable of either asking questions or understanding the answers. Others disagreed. We took note of these comments but continued our policy, unmoved even by criticism that this whole experiment was brutal.

We were watching, closely, constantly, for signs of the familiar demand for more, for higher, for better. That was, after all, as much a purpose of their being put on 23 and then on Rohanda as the actual work they did. Meanwhile, they were set free on a particularly favoured part of Isolated S.C. II. Of course this was before the "events," the changing of the angle of the axis, the slight distancing of Rohanda from the sun. Everywhere on Rohanda was hotter then, proportionately. The southern part of the continent was ideal, a paradise—for once to use emotional language of course inappropriate to this report—and I have never seen anything to equal it. The conditions were similar but better than what the Lombis had known on 24: drier, more even, without extremes of any kind. They were given a large well-wooded, fertile plain, that had a central river and its many tributaries, informed they were not to stray beyond certain limits, and left entirely to themselves. Our monitors from 22 were withdrawn.

I and my staff were established well away from them in an inaccessible place among mountains that they had no reason to approach. They were not told that their stay in this beautiful place would have a term—and probably a short one.

I was at that time much occupied with other enterprises.

This was one: observing the healthy, invigorating climate of this continent, we thought it worthwhile to transfer on to it, though temporarily, some of those who were succumbing to the mental disorders, chiefly depression and melancholy, that characterised our Dark Age. We used it, in fact, as a kind of mental hospital, or asylum. The conditions were so easy, so little effort was needed to maintain life, that all we did was to space-lift those who wished to try the experience to parts of Isolated S.C. II—of course well away from the Lombis, and leave them there to make their own shelters of branches or grass. Food was brought across from Southern Continent I. They were not permitted to hunt or harm the animals, but were allowed to fish, within limits. The idea was a deliberate return to a primeval innocence, of a kind that did not need even to be newly invented or rehearsed, for this type of fantasy, too, had its literature, and its conventions, like old-time farming. What we were doing, in fact, was really a variety of tourism, but in ideal conditions, allowing highly civilised and refined populations to experience instead of observing. Yet they could observe, too—for one thing, all kinds of animals and birds unfamiliar to them, as well as the most attractive forests and rivers. This scheme was immensely popular. From everywhere in our Empire they clamoured to be allowed a sojourn on Rohanda. Our medical profession were enthusiastic. At its height half a million were living over the southern plains, for shorter or longer periods. But I have to record a failure. The original cause of the malaise that sent them to Rohanda was not touched. Doctors who worked among the unfortunates had to conclude that if melancholy and listlessness were sometimes palliated, then restlessness, feverishness, a hectic dissatisfaction, took their place. The scheme was classed as a mistake, and ended. No one was supposed to be left behind after the final space-lift, and officially this was accomplished, but after experience in many such projects, I believe that a few eccentrics and solitaries always manage to evade vigilance and creep away to make lives for themselves. So in a small way this experiment may have affected Rohanda.

There were many other short-term experiments and they absorbed enough of our attention to prevent us from doing more with the Lombis than make sure they did not stray off their terrain.

When we were told Planet 25 would shortly become vacant, this was rather before we had expected. We at once put on order a complement of 2,000 Planet 22 technicians. Our immediate problem must be obvious: it was essential that the technicians should be able to mingle with the Lombis on their level, but we did not know what that level now was, after nearly a thousand R-years. Before the 22-ers came, we had done enough work with binoculars and judicious near approach to have ascertained that they were outwardly at least not much changed. We put the techs in quarters near our head station. They had nearly all been involved with the moves of the Lombis from C.P. 24 to 23; from 23 to Rohanda; their sojourn on 23. There were no unexpected adjustments for them to make. But when the first investigative contingent of 500 went off, stripped of their clothes, carrying nothing, not even a little food, or a weapon, they could not hide discomfort. The 22 people do not have hair on their bodies, and have forgotten when they ran on four legs. But in my observation it is the moment when a species puts on garments, even the most vestigial, such as aprons of foliage or bark, that marks the transition upwards from beast; and this much more than standing on two legs. It is the birth of a certain kind of self-consciousness. To put off every bit of clothing was hard for these Planet 22 people, and they did not like being looked at by us. We respected their feelings and let them go off down the side of our rocky plateau unaccompanied: normally some of us would have gone with them part of the way. We did watch them for a time, though: this kind of observation being part of our task. Planet 22 people are more yellow than the dark Lombis, and they had been under the sun-machines; but they still were more dark yellow than brown. The company of wiry little people were soon lost to view among the foothills, and we heard no more of them for some days.

Messengers sent back to report on first encounters with the Lombis said not much more than that it was safe to send in the other 1,500, who duly set off, naked and discomfited.

The task of these 2,000 techs was to dwell among the Lombis and to assess them and what changes had taken place.

I shall now sum up their several reports.

The first 500 did not find it easy to locate the Lombis. When they did see some out on the plain gathering plants, and were observed, the Lombis ran to find cover and disappeared. It took days for the first encounter. None of them remembered, as individuals, their capture from their home planet and subsequent events. But they remembered as a race: this was the most important change: their speech had evolved. Not over the business of the day-to-day maintenance of life, but in this one direction: they had songs, and tales, that instructed them in all their history.

The second change was that they now had festivals, or feasts, at the time of the full moon, so that these songs and tales could be exchanged. This had unified these animals. On their own planet they had lived in all types of association, sometimes in small groups with no contact with others. But now every individual without exception was expected to travel in to a central feasting place once every R-month. This was not always the same, but changed, and was situated in a well-wooded place, with a river for hygiene and water supplies. Not only the regular festival or "solemn remembrance"—which was how their word for it translated; and the singing and storytelling; but the travelling to and from the central place had become ritualised and made the bonds that held this *new* nation together: for this is what they now were, according to our classifications.

They were, in any case, constantly on the move, changing their residences, their plant-gathering places, their watering places. Restlessness and fitful energy was their new characteristic. This was because they were using more oxygen than they had done on Planet 24. It was their chief *physical* change.

And here was a paradox, a contradiction. While never able to be still, always active, they nevertheless had become fearful and secretive. This characteristic was reinforced by the subject of their monthly rituals, which was, in various forms, their abduction from their home.

They had become a race of strong, indeed violent, contradictions. When first seeing our exploratory contingent, they hid themselves —because their history was of just such "strangers from the skies" who arrived among them, were friendly, and then ruthlessly kidnapped them. But "strangers from the skies" were what they expected to come again and rescue them . . . for they expected to be returned to their "real home in the skies."

They had, on their own planet, sometimes used leaves or hides as coverings, either for warmth or for ornament, but now all clothing of any sort was forbidden, and inspired terror, because the space suits of C.P. 23 were the worst of their memories. Even a young female balancing a few berries on her nose in play, or trying them behind her ears, or tying some leaves around her middle, or sheltering an infant in a pelt would bring forth a storm of chattering and scolding from any who saw her—as if they all felt that these were the first steps to the so-much-feared garments; the claustrophobias of the "little prison."

On 23, and while building the agricultural settlements on S.C. I, they had been supplied with simple foodstuffs, mostly cereals and vegetables. But these had been supplied and set before them and some had been cooked or processed—and they knew that prepared food was a "sign" of captivity.

In these two major ways, then, their advancement had been checked, and they were as naked as any animal in our Empire, and their food was as they gathered it or caught it. They had previously roasted their meat: now this was done only at feasts, as if it were too dangerous a thing for individuals to tempt fate with. To tempt "the skies" with . . .

Whereas previously they had lived in so many different ways, and quite casually and openly, unafraid of attackers, protected by their different associations, now they built rocky shelters for themselves, or leafy ones, always with great care—not for their comfort or warmth, but with one aim only: that they should not be easily visible. This was why our first attempts to locate them had been so frustrated.

Constant movement and activity—great festivals of thousands of animals all dancing and singing; and, at the same time, a terror of being observed and overseen.

The pleasant, easygoing, unsuspicious race of Planet 24 had become nervous, paranoid.

One of the changes had been expected by us.

Because of the disruption between males and females at the beginning, which took nearly five hundred years to disappear, the females had become the lawgivers, if not in fact, then in their view of themselves. The males were dominant in that they hunted, appointed sentinels and guards, saw themselves as protectors of the nation, but the women because of how they had been competed for at the beginning had all kinds of airs and graces, behaved as if mating were "a gift of themselves": and there were courtship rituals where it had to appear as if males were fighting for a female who at last and after long hesitation then "chose" one: and this even when the balances had been redressed and there was no competition for females. The females all had a rather bossy elder-sister manner, which was taught them by the mothers: this could even approach the regal, the gracious. These inevitable results of certain statistical facts do not cease to be risible because they *are* inevitable. . . .

But these poor animals aroused more pity than amusement among our technicians. We were approached by a delegation from them a few months after their acceptance by the Lombis. They all felt uncomfortable about what they were doing, which was to put into operation a plan that involved lying and deception. We had expected this delegation; the 2,000 Planet 22 technicians were being observed, in the same way as the Lombis were: it was necessary for us to find out if they were to be entrusted with taking the Lombis to Planet 25 and supervising them there when they expected to be returned home.

It is our experience that if you put two species together, after initial hostility they will begin to absorb each other's ways. If one is in a supervisory relation with the other, who are suffering hardship, then it is to be expected that a percentage of the first will sympathise with the second and make attempts to alleviate conditions—which result is often to be welcomed and encouraged—or to help efforts to escape. Under certain conditions even this second result is not always discouraged.

While we were making plans for adding companies of supervisors from another planet, which had not had contact with the Lombis, to the personnel who would transfer and police the Lombis, we were selecting 22-ers for further training in the arts of long-term judgement and assessment, and were putting the following points to them.

That conditions on Rohanda were better than on Planet 24.

That conditions on 25, while not perfect, could not be described as bad.

That it was no hardship to be a servant race—which admittedly was our plan for the Lombis—unless this race felt and resented their subjection, in which case the laws of our Empire made it inevitable that they would be advanced to a level they could sustain.

It was true this whole experiment was based on an attempt to keep, just for once, a race on a subservient level; but surely the fact that we had to make it at all proved our past good record.

Did they, the Planet 22 technicians, not think they might be sentimental instead of showing *true* benevolence—which always involved an overall view. . . .

To all this they respectfully but self-respectingly replied that they thought our arguments sophistry.

There was no need for them to say any more than one thing, to bring forward more than one basic fact: the Lombis had been free, living where they had evolved, and had shown all the characteristics of such races. Now they had all the attributes of slaves.

We enquired from them what they would like us to do. The reply was: to return the Lombis to their own planet.

Even though their return would most certainly disrupt the lives of the Lombis there, who were quietly evolving at their own speed, and who had forgotten them—they had not preserved any memory of the abduction of what had been a very small proportion of their number? There was no doubt at all that if we suddenly set down on Planet 24 this now well-cohered and self-sufficing nation, there would be sudden and savage war.

Was this really what they wanted us to do? If there had been wrong thinking on our part, then it was too late. Surely they could see this?

They did see it.

Of course, we knew what might happen: for in the circumstances it was to be expected. That we did nothing to forestall it was rooted in our improper attitudes to Canopus, and at the time we did not see anything wrong in these attitudes. Now, looking back—but if there is one thing I have learned, it is that it is not useful to say: If I knew then what I know now . . .

I will come to the defection of the technicians in a moment.

The Lombi festival during which our spaceships descended for the lift-off was a special one.

The site was a favoured place between rivers. It was relatively high, with thickly growing trees surrounding a small plain. The animals came in during the preceding few days and settled themselves under the trees in their groups. Our technicians were with them. Mating was encouraged at these times. The techs did not refrain. We had not expected them to: a mixture of these two vigorous and promising stocks was part of our plan.

The hunters brought in the animals for the feast, and the cooking trenches, with the spits over them, were arranged and tended by both males and females.

The singing and dancing began as the sunlight went and the moon rose.

First in groups around separate fires, and then in great revolving circles, these animals sang of their distant home and their longing for it; of their capture by the shining machines, of the place of imprisonment, where they had been confined in the "little prisons" or in the shining prisons where everything was false; of their second capture, and their return to "true breath and breathing, to the green earth, to the green hills"; of their labours under a foreign sun building "prisons" for invisible races whose presence they sensed, but whom they never saw; of their third capture by the shining machines, their being set down here "in this place where everything reminds us of our home but is not our home," and of how—on a day that was still to come—the shining machines would come again, and take them home to "the place that knew them."

Throughout this night of festival, our techs were singing and dancing and feasting, too. Well mingled with the others, so that they were always individuals who had become accepted by a family or a group, and never even in pairs, let alone groups, that could seem a challenge, these little yellow people, hairless though they were, did not seem so very different from that vast company of short, squat, brown, very strong apelike creatures bounding and prancing and wailing under the full moon.

I myself saw them from the "shining machine" that had picked me up from our headquarters, and was taking me back to our Home Planet where it would drop me off for a spell of leave.

I looked down on thousands of faces lifted in supplication to the skies, on thousands of raised arms, palms held outwards in a manner I had observed on so many planets! I was looking at a manifestation of the need for "higher things"—and thought that we had *not* foreseen how this innate and unconquerable need would develop in this way, with these creatures, safely channelled into nostalgia for "home," for "visitors from the skies," and so on.

They were singing about the shining machines as these descended. Drugged and entranced by a night of mass dancing and singing, they trooped willingly on to the spacecraft and were lifted off to C.P. 25. Their future development does not concern this history; but I shall describe a later visit I paid them.

Not all of them were there at that feasting place that night.

About 10,000 had been set down on Isolated S. C. II. And about 10,000 were taken off again. Yet their numbers had slightly increased, in spite of the inevitable deaths due to adaptation to the unfamiliar, if so beautiful, terrain. The technicians had of course known that the spaceships were to arrive and when. Some of the more disaffected had enticed away a few Lombis before the feast, telling them the shining ones were certainly coming, but they would be evil and would take them to a bad place. We lost 9 technicians, and about 500 Lombis. We did not mind this. What we had wished to forestall was that any of them should stay in that area, which we wanted to use for other controlled experiments—as far as such experiments can be controlled. We had therefore informed the technicians that all that terrain was to be used in a trial of certain diseases, so that they would move well away, with the

Lombis. We had done something else, too. Having carefully observed the more rebellious of the technicians, we had chosen two of them, told them we knew they intended to stay behind when the spaceships came, said we did not mind this, nor intended to stop them. But we would like them to undertake a task for us, for Sirius, who was after all—and would remain—their master, their friend, Sirius who had raised them from an animal status not in any way higher or better than the Lombis. We did not want promises from them; we were not promising them anything; we were not threatening them—but if it became possible for them to accomplish a certain task, then we would be grateful, and they would be playing a great part in our plans.

The names of these technicians were Navah and Hoppe.

THE SITUATION IN THE CANOPEAN AREAS. OTHER SIRIAN EXPERIMENTS

When the planet was shared out between us, many things were left unsaid, were implicit. One was that we would inform each other of what we did. This had always been done—within limits on our side, due to suspicion; and within limits on theirs because we could not understand Canopus. Another was that we would not interfere with each other. Canopus has not interfered with us. This I aver, from my position as one who can state this categorically. They have behaved throughout *honourably*. I use this word advisedly, in this place.

When Canopus "gives her word," she keeps it. This concept, which is foreign to us—again I must insist on this, as part of this history, which is being written as factually as I can make it—is one of several similar concepts, part of a general way of looking at things. If something is said by them, then it is the truth. If Canopus "gives its word," then this is kept, always, regardless of the inconvenience (and sometimes worse) to themselves. If Canopus "promises," then this is done. If Canopus offers aid, then this is the very best that can be given at that time in those circumstances. *Canopus is always and absolutely to be relied on.* I state this because it is the truth, and knowing full well the sort of reaction I may expect from certain of our historians.

We do not, many of us, understand this now; and we certainly had no idea of it then.

In short, we all believed that Canopus would try to trick us, as we intended to trick them. Not in any very important ways, or ones that would be damaging to them. It was all more in the spirit of youngsters who still find it amusing and clever to outwit each other.

I wanted to know what was going on in the Canopean part of Rohanda. That is what I had asked Hoppe and Navah to find out. It would be dangerous for them. They were very small people. The colonists Canopus had introduced from their Colony 10 were three times their size. Hoppe and Navah were yellow. The Canopus colonists were black or brown. There was no way the two spies could conceal themselves among these colonists. And we knew the ape species of the northern areas were, again, large, hairy, and organised in tribes that would almost certainly be hostile to hairless little yellow men. But it was my belief that Navah and Hoppe would enjoy the challenge; and in any case, they were not compelled in any way.

Now to anticipate. Twenty R-years later Hoppe returned, alone. Navah had settled in the southern part of Isolated Northern Continent, with a few of the Lombis. But Hoppe had travelled steadily north, a journey that took five years, while Lombis left the travelling party, in pairs and groups, and made settlements in favoured places.

They did not find any Canopean settlements. Later we found out there weren't any then. That continent was not the paradise S.C. II was at that time, but very hot, and in parts still swampy. Hoppe went to the north, and on the east coast found that the indigenous ape-people were travelling back and forth from the main landmass, by various types of boat, passing from one island to another: at that time that ocean was full of islands of all sizes.

Hoppe allowed himself to be made a prisoner by them. He was not ill-treated, but regarded as a curiosity and even as a pet.

On the western part of the main landmass he found the following facts.

One was that the Colony 10 colonists and the natives had started to increase in height. This I found easy to believe because the Lombis' height had increased by an R-span during their thousand years.

Another was that both colonists and natives were living longer, after an initial period when the colonists had a dramatically reduced life-span. This I believed, too, for the Lombis had shown signs of a longer life-span.

But the next fact was not believed by us, although Hoppe insisted on it.

It was that the colonists were living in settlements quite apart from the natives. These settlements were not makeshift, or arbitrary and casual, but were carefully constructed. Yet they were on a lower level than the cities of Colony 10. The natives, who had been at that stage so often found by us and by Canopus on many planets—just beyond the animal level, beginning to use fire, sheltering in caves and structures of branch and grass, sometimes covering themselves with leaves or pelts—were now in proper settlements, which were well made and sited, and they were being taught all kinds of crafts by the colonists. The colonists did not stay near the natives, but visited them for short spells while they imparted their information; then retreated to their own places, and only returned after an interval to see how their instruction had taken. No attempt was being made by them to use the natives as servants. So said Hoppe. So he swore.

Having found out all that he could, he begged the natives to let him travel back, island to island, to the Isolated Northern Continent, and they did. They were a good-natured species, and never harmed or threatened. Once there, he did not wait to argue with them, for he knew they would not want to lose him permanently, and he slipped away one night and travelled by himself southwards, where he was able to visit the colonies established by the Lombis, and he was much welcomed. I was relieved that Canopus had not set up colonies of their own on that northern continent, which was definitely part of their assigned territory; though of course I had planned to plead, if challenged by them, that the Lombis had escaped from one of our experiments—which was true after all.

As for what Hoppe had said of the relations between the colonists and the natives, I did not believe him, not being able to match with my own experience what Canopus had told us of their plans for careful, controlled, and scientific development—for the "symbiosis."

Hoppe felt that he had fulfilled his undertaking to me; and indeed he had. He went back north where he found a place in one of the settlements. I heard no more of him. The Colony 22 people are not long-lived and he could not be expected to come back within his lifetime.

But I was intrigued and curious about what went on up north. During all this time there were conferences between us and Canopus on various planets, and more than once on Colony 10 itself, but I did not find the information we were given adequate. For one thing, it reported such rapid progress of the Canopean plan I did not believe it. We were in the habit of exaggerating successes and concealing failures, and so we assumed that this is what Canopus also did.

But I couldn't leave it at that either. The next time one of our supply craft came from Southern Continent I, I asked its head operator to a consultation. I wanted a smaller craft, of the kind that kept liaison between the different agricultural stations on S.C. I, to visit enough of the central landmass to make sure of one fact: that the Canopean colonists and the natives lived in settlements at a good distance from each other. This was risky. Not because there was any need to expect more than reproaches from Canopus —certainly not reprisals—but because it would be a definite breach of our agreement. I reasoned, however, that it was unlikely settlements on the fringes of the landmass would ever have seen any type of aircraft, for we knew it was Canopean policy to visit their Rohandan settlements as seldom as possible. Besides, it was only a practised or expectant eye that was likely to see our modern craft, they were so fast, and because of the materials they were made of, almost invisible in certain lights.

The investigation was made, and the craft did more than actually fly over settlements to survey them; it landed, and several groups of both natives and colonists were watched from a distance. There was no doubt about it: Hoppe's report was true. Colonists were not employing the natives. I was ready to believe that this was because the natives had proved too backward to be employable, but this was not what our spy craft had found. On the contrary, even in the hundred years since Hoppe's visit, it seemed that the natives had advanced and were already using skills that they had been taught.

I gave the whole question a great deal of thought. Looking back, I have to credit myself with this, at least. But I concluded that the reason for the rapid evolution of the natives was something in the atmosphere of Rohanda. And that we had been unfortunate in our choice of both our Colony 22 and the Lombis. In this respect, not in any other: these two races may have been impervious to these peculiar and specialised Rohandan influences. When supply craft came from various agricultural stations on the other southern continent, I questioned the crew carefully about the personnel on these stations, who came from several of our Colonised Planets. But none had shown any marked evolutionary changes, whether for better or for worse.

I then concluded that it was the northern areas that must hold the beneficial influences, and I was bitter, believing that Canopus had withheld from us information about them so that we would not resent their claiming them.

It was this anger that was responsible for my next decision.

It will be remembered that Isolated Southern Continent II had no indigenous apes of any size; and that those on S.C. I were all very small and far from even standing on two legs. Our use of the Lombis and of the people from Colony 22 had been well enough as far as it went: but these were both such small races they were classified in our system as dwarves. I made a survey of all the races throughout our Empire, but at last wondered why I was taking all this trouble, when what I wanted lay to hand for the taking. . . . I instructed one of our fast liaison craft to make a reconnaissance of the Northwest fringes of the main landmass and then to direct a large cargo craft to kidnap an entire community of natives, without alerting the colonists who would then be sure to inform Canopus. After all, if our aircraft were not seen at all, the colonists could report only that the natives had gone—had probably decided to escape from a tutelary supervision unwelcomed by them. All this was done, and I was delivered an entire community of seventy natives, males, females, and young. They were treated at all times with kindness. We put them, not on the plain vacated by the Lombis, which was too large and was needed by us for other purposes, but on high wooded terrain not far from our own headquarters. There was no reason why they should not be aware of us; this experiment did not resemble that of ours with the Lombis. They at once made shelters for themselves of a quite advanced kind, using bricks of sunbaked earth, and well-dressed thatch for roofing. They showed no signs of distress at this arbitrary disruption of their lives but, on the contrary, were ready to be friendly and—because of their relationship with the Canopean colonists—to be taught. But while I forbade them to be used as servants or labourers in any way whatever—thus copying what I had understood of the Canopean experiment—I also forbade them to be made pets, or to be allowed inside our houses or to be taught any further skills, for it seemed to me that they had already been shown more than they could use. They knew, theoretically, for instance, about planting seeds and tubers for food, and about keeping animals for meat and milk, but were careless and forgetful in these, showing signs of letting aptitudes slide away from them altogether. Remembering that the settlements of colonists in the north were at a distance from their charges, and that contact was seldom, I believed I was following this example in not pressing our tutelage. At this stage the natives were slightly shorter than our own average height, at about seven or eight R-feet. They were upright, never descended to all fours, kept their dwellings clean, ate meat and vegetables and fruit, and milked a species of deer, but not with any system.

This little colony of northern animals was a most important factor of our relations with Canopus, and of subsequent developments on Rohanda. But this did not seem to us so at the time. Far from it. Yet we could hardly forget these creatures, who lived so close to us, always visible, and of much interest to us and our visitors in their comings and goings. They multiplied, but not very much; and their settlements spread, but never did more than cover the hills that were first allotted to them. Nor did we cease to monitor their development because this was where our preoccupation with Canopus and its work focussed. But while several thousand years passed, we were involved in many other experiments, all over this wonderful and rich continent, and these took up our attention.

I shall mention the one that did have an indirect effect on long-term Rohandan development.

Millions of females throughout our Empire, forbidden to produce young because of our population-reduction programmes, craved this experience while subscribing to a prohibition whose necessity they understood. We had more volunteers than we could ever use for our various eugenic attempts.

Prefabricated buildings of a high standard were space-lifted in from our manufacturing Planet 3, and placed on the terrain that the Lombis had occupied. These were filled with females, already impregnated, from various of our planets. The fathers had also been comprehensively chosen. Our need was to produce a strain that would adapt easily to widely varied conditions on different planets. While we were restricted by the nature of the conditions on our Mother Planet to planets that fell within certain atmospheric limits, these limits proved to be much broader than we had envisaged in the early days of our Empire. Species could learn to adapt: some much more easily than others. But our experience had been that if representatives of one species had adapted to certain conditions, then these did not necessarily take well to further adaptation. We wished to breed technicians who would be available for work on different planets, of differing atmospheres, sometimes with little or no time for adaptation or acclimatisation. These all-purpose, hardy, multifunctional technicians were in fact absolutely essential in certain outlying parts of our Empire.

The females on what we now called the Lombi plain numbered fifty thousand. They were supervised as much as was necessary to prevent them escaping, to supply them with first-class medical care, and to monitor the growth of their young, with the appropriate testing and analysis.

These females regarded themselves as favoured and privileged: indeed they were. They knew themselves to be of superb physical fitness and condition. They had been told by the highest among our Colonial Service, which is itself the highest function of our Empire, how much their services were valued. But in spite of all this, we knew a degree of watchfulness had to be maintained: this, the reproductive instinct, being the strongest there is, it could take —*had* taken, in the past—many surprising forms; and we did not want any of them escaping with their young when the time came to give them up. For they all knew that this must be when the young had attained five R-years.

This was one reason the breeding station was on Rohanda, which was a long way from our Mother Planet and visited by none except our craft and those of Canopus. (Or so we believed then—but of that later.) It would not be possible for them to escape either by spacecraft or out of the Lombi plain, for there were guards stationed all around a vast periphery, well out of sight, who had been trained in every manifestation of the maternal instinct in desperation.

The other reason this station was here, well out of the way, was that such experiments always aroused opposition. This phenomenon is so well known that I will do no more than draw attention to it. Even when females have volunteered for this type of service, even when the experiments are crowned with success, and the results are shown in new breeds and strains that fulfill everything expected of them and are heaped with honours, and whose functioning is remarked and followed with approval and admiration from everywhere in our Empire—even so there is criticism, and of a certain kind, which I have learned to recognise. It is always marked by a sharp painful note, or tone, that signals a feeling of *loss*—and not only a personal loss, not at all: this is why I for one have always taken pains to notice this cry, or protest, which is so much more than personal. I can only put it like this: that it seems as if—I do not see how we can conclude anything else—when such deliberate, controlled experiments take place, to produce definitely envisaged stocks or strains, it is felt—most deeply and profoundly, and by the most responsible and evolved of our peoples—that some other possibility may have been lost.

As if randomness and chance in themselves are a good and a blessing and even a means of acquiring something not yet defined. . . . I am stating my own personal opinion here, arrived at after much reflection.

This was the largest experiment in eugenics ever undertaken by us. Its success was due not least to the Rohandan atmosphere, the Rohandan isolation from other influences, our distance from the centre. When the fifty R-years of the experiment were over, and the breeding station finally dismantled, we congratulated ourselves that in that time not one of the successive inputs of females had escaped, and that we had not again contributed to the Rohandan species.

For five thousand R-years we did not investigate conditions in the northern Canopean areas: it will be remembered that we believed we had before us millions of years of a stable environment. We were informed that Canopus was sending a special mission, as they had reason to believe their plans were more successful than had been envisaged. The report of this mission was sent to us: it recommended the immediate implementation of something they called a "Lock."

Again it has to be emphasised that we did not understand the bases of the Canopean work. We did not know what this "Lock" was: though this did not mean we were not aware that there was regular contact between Canopus and Rohanda. But we assumed this was on the lines of the various types of electrical communication used by us with our own planets near enough for these methods. They also talked about "a degenerative disease," but without specification. These two concepts were not understood by us at all, until recently: are not understood now generally. We might have asked questions: Canopus was always ready to answer them. We might have asked *ourselves* questions, since we believed our technology was as advanced as that of Canopus. But we did not. The reason was the same: various forms of pride. What was in the body of the report inflamed us with disbelief and suspicion.

The natives who still enjoyed their well-supervised and comfortable lives so close to us were nowhere near the level described in the report on the northern hemisphere.

We had chosen disbelief—but not entirely, for again I decided on some investigations of our own.

It happened that at that time Ambien I was visiting me.

In our long distant early youth we had been aligned for the purpose of producing our allotted four progeny—that was before the reduction of general population levels. Ambien I had decided after our progeny were grown to enter into another alignment with a female who subsequently worked with me on various projects when we had reached general-service-age. The eight products of the two alignments had formed bonds of various kinds and, in short, the personal aspects of our lives had been satisfactory.

Ambien I had been on the committee that first considered what our work would be on Rohanda, and had been involved with it ever since. His visit to me was partly old friendship and partly investigative: I had not been back to our Home Planet for millennia: this was because I was thoroughly happy on Rohanda, enjoyed my work, and thought it too pleasant a place to abandon for service leave. Members of the Colonial Service, even members of the Five, visiting us for any reason always made excuses to stay. In short, Rohanda had become my home.

When we had had time to satisfy our accumulated curiosity about each other's doings, after what had been a good lapse of time, I asked him if he would undertake a spying mission to the northern areas. He agreed readily. More than once he had been in the teams that "opened up" new planets, and he had always enjoyed this type of rough dangerous work. We did not expect danger from this particular enterprise, but at least it would be a break from routine. He took a liaison ship to the extreme south of the central landmass, where he dismissed it. Altogether he was away ten R-years.

He travelled extensively over the central landmass, where there were everywhere settlements of colonists and natives, always positioned at short distances from each other. He went on foot, by boat, and sometimes by using suitable animals. Ambien I and myself are of course of the same general species, but his particular sub-species are broadly built, brown of skin, with straight black hair. I, being fair of skin and hair and very slight in build, could not go anywhere near the northern areas without discovery. But he, while being much shorter than the colonists—who were rapidly increasing in height, and were now twice the size of the original Colony 10 species—was rather taller than the natives, and could not hope to be taken for one of them. He at first avoided close contact with them, but seeing that he could not get the information we needed this way, approached them in settlement after settlement, and found no hostility at all—at the most, curiosity. At first he put this down to an innate good nature due to the favourable conditions they lived in, and lack of challenge. But then, though reluctantly, he came to believe they had visitors of other kinds. Not colonists, who were unmistakable because of their size. (They from this time were referred to as Giants by Canopeans, and I shall do the same.) If not colonists, then who? Was it possible the dwarf races of the Isolated Northern Continent had grown large and were making island-hopping journeys across that ocean? We were soon to learn differently: but it was this speculation that made him decide to visit the Northern Continent on his way back to me.

What he found everywhere on the central landmass corroborated the Canopean report. The native stock had improved so far beyond what they had been seven or eight thousand years before, it was not easy to believe them the same species. They were practising agriculture, understood the use of animals, and their dwellings were not only soundly built in well-planned settlements but were even being ornamented with attractive designs in sophisticated colours. They had begun to wear clothes, too, and these were well made and often dyed.

It was the Giants' settlements that could not be explained. They were living on a level not very much higher than the natives; and yet on Colony 10 they had evolved to the stage of advanced cities.

When Ambien I's survey was complete, he instructed the liaison ship to fly down over Isolated Northern Continent, to see what had happened to the Lombis and the stock from C.P. 22. But he could find no sign of them. We had a rough idea of where they ought to be, from Hoppe's information—but nothing. We concluded that they must all have succumbed to some epidemic, since there was no sign of settlement by natives or Giants either.

We had to come to terms with the facts about the Canopean work in the north. The captured native stock so happily living on their hillsides where they were always under our inspection could not be said to have regressed. They had not developed. They had abandoned attempts to care for and use other animals, but hunted skilfully and intelligently. They grew a few roots for food, but not grains. They picked leafy plants from the wild, but did not plant any. They wore animal pelts but no art was used in their preparation. The shacks and huts they lived in were adequate.

We did not understand what had happened to make the difference.

Again I was ready to conclude that the Canopean north was in some way better endowed, but Ambien I reminded me that the Giants actively instructed the natives on their visits, whereas we had pursued a policy of noninterference.

We decided to divide our stock of natives into two, and establish a colony of them at a distance from us, so that there could be no contact. This new colony would be energetically supervised and taught by us in the practical arts. Ambien I undertook this task: it was one he was particularly well fitted for.

He built himself a shelter in the new village, and settled down with them as an instructor.

This attempt was a failure. He was not able to teach them anything they could retain. That is, he taught them a variety of crafts, which they seemed to understand—but in a short time everything was forgotten. After a period of intensive work, he had to confess that the new colony was not much better off than the first one.

He did make further attempts during the next ten thousand years, goaded by the amazing results of the Canopeans, but they all failed. Meanwhile he was making more trips to find out what was happening in the north. Not only he, but others, too, whom we ordered from our Home Planet. We wanted individuals as near to the natives of the north as possible—no races in our Empire attained anything like the height of the Giants. Ambien I and these new experts again and again surveyed the north. Always, we believed, without discovery. Certainly without resistance.

Because of the number of spies we sent northwards, we believed that the Canopeans must be doing the same to us; and we were careful to spread rumours of the fierce and warlike nature of the southern hemisphere.

All this activity of ours during that period now makes me amazed and incredulous—as we are when remembering earlier cruder phases of ourselves. None of it was necessary. All we needed was to read, without suspicion and with an open mind, the material they continually supplied us and then to ask them questions. But it is always useless to bewail past mistakes.

During this period of ten thousand years, the reports by Ambien I and the others were increasingly amazing. There were cities being built everywhere, of a kind Sirius knew nothing about. The beauty of the cities on Canopus was famous, and we had always emulated them: to state the *fact*, which even now we are reluctant to admit. But these cities were built in remarkable shapes, of a mathematical kind. They were all different. The Giants and the natives lived together now. The cities were different not only in shape and size but in their qualities: Ambien I always said that it was not easy to describe what he could feel. On the islands, great and small, of the ocean between the Northern Continent and the main landmass were many cities, and the life on them was more advanced than any in our Empire. And we were talking about not only the Giants—whom we were certainly not surprised to find at this highly evolved level—but the indigenous stock whose unregenerate state we could see by going to the windows of our citadel and looking down: there they were, a lazy, amiable colony of—apes, for after all, that *was* all they were.

Why? It is not too much to say that Ambien I and myself and the others of our staff became obsessed with Canopus and their successes. I was, particularly. I had not seen what they described. But I did once insist on being taken in one of our fastest craft on a trip over the island-crammed ocean between the Northern Continent and the main landmass, and saw a very large island, that had on it a magnificent white city, circular, with many surrounding channels and causeways, and ships as fine as any we used anywhere riding in the harbours. This after only 5,000 years of the "Lock" that Canopus attached so much importance to.

Because of the primary intention of this account—Sirian relations with Canopus—and my emphasis on aspects of our researches that affected these relations, there is a danger readers may believe what is described here more or less defines these researches. I can only repeat that during the roughly 18,000 years of that ideal period on Rohanda, only a small part of our work had any long-term effect on Rohanda or on Canopus. During the 10,000 years we were so preoccupied with what went on in the north, we were also making full use of opportunities. I will mention one project, which lasted more than 10,000 years, involved nearly the whole of Southern Continent II, employed millions of our technicians from every part of our Empire, and which had no contact at all with, nor influence upon, our spying missions into the north, or Ambien I's attempts with the captured natives.

The paradoxical Sirian situation already mentioned had not improved: on all the older and long-established Colonised Planets were millions who had no employment nor hope of any, who knew that their deaths (which we of course did not hasten in any way whatsoever) would be a relief and a lessening of a burden on us all, and who were too softened and enfeebled by affluence for any but the easiest work, who had come to crave even the physical labour they believed to be beneath them—but who, when offered it, were not able to do it. For there was a period when we of the Colonial Service did in fact do our best to use these noisy and complaining hordes where we could on large-scale development projects. It was a failure. While demanding "any kind of work, no matter how rough"—most vociferously and tiresomely—when they were in fact put to this type of work their ingrained belief in their own superiority, their weakness of will, their self-indulgence, caused them very soon to slacken, or to manifest a large range of psychosomatic problems.

For a period of about 8,000 years, we had vast encampments all over Southern Continent II, where physical work graded to easy preliminary stages was created for these people, in order to fit them for the real work elsewhere on the newly acquired and still undeveloped planets that we were "opening up"—to use our term for the early phases of our colonisation. Our problem was that we did not want to disturb the ecological balance of Rohanda more than we had to. We did not want to destroy vegetation or animals. Nor to engage in plans that would scar or mar the earth. We had plenty of other planets whose natural endowments were suitable; but only one whose endowments were so lavish, fertile, beautiful. The food for these millions of apprentice colonists was easily supplied by S.C. I—whose agricultural stations remained successful beyond anything we had hoped for. But to supply them *work* without upsetting their environments was a different matter. It was, it had to be—invented. As each new contingent of, sometimes, many hundreds of thousands arrived from this or that planet, flown in by our giant transport craft, they were set to make their own housing and amenity buildings by using premade building materials. But this task did not take them long. And while so easy, involving very little real labour, they were already complaining that they were "demeaned" and "degraded." Yet each one was a volunteer, and had had explained to them that their sojourn on Rohanda was temporary, and for training purposes only.

I will make here an observation that was formed in that time and which I have seen no reason since to modify. It is that if a race or stock or species has once become enfeebled by soft living and a belief that it is *owed* easy living, then while *physically* such individuals may later adapt to a vigorous use of themselves, *mentally* this is almost impossible except for a very few of the more flexible. Self-pity will be their disease—a disease of the *will*, not of the flesh.

Once their settlements and camps were set up and operating, the real problem began.

The training work we created for them was of two kinds. One involved the local animals. Using varieties of deer, we bred adaptations of them, thus enabling our volunteers to become used to ideas relating to eugenics, which we used so extensively everywhere in our Empire, and also taught them how to choose and use animals for food and heavy labour. Of course the animals of Rohanda were all strange to these volunteers who had come from so many different planets, and the novelty assisted us in the task of keeping alive their interest and enthusiasm, for they became bored and indifferent very quickly: they all needed constant stimulus. We also set them to classifying and recording the species of plant life— this meant that they had to keep on their feet out of doors. They were sent off on long investigative trips, under careful supervision so that they would do no damage to the environment. But while this could not be described as hard work, it was too hard for most of them. So went our diagnoses at the time, and these were of course true. But I wondered then, and wonder now, if part of their lack of enthusiasm was due, quite simply, to knowing that this was work already done—for of course they had to know this. Although they were told—again—that this was preparatory training for their real endeavours to come on other planets, they did not have the appetite for it. Continually demanding that they be put to work on "the real thing" at once, complaining that they were being undervalued by us, because of these "easy and piffling" tasks, they failed to make use of the real opportunities they were being offered to accustom themselves to harder. They were quite unreliable, shiftless, and, in the end, unproductive.

They were returned to their own planets after all had been given a fair chance to show if they could match their actions with their demands. But we did not want to exacerbate their already poisonous discontent and therefore tried to soften this rejection of them in various ways, by saying that "real" work would be found for them later, and so on. On the whole it was felt that these attempts had not only been failures but worse: for when these millions found themselves back on their home planets, their complaints and discontents fomented uprisings and uproar of every sort, which were already quite enough of a threat. Our military strength had to be increased at a time when we believed that we could look forward to rapidly rising prosperity due to a welcome dismantling of our armies. Some of the more discontented planets became, for a time, not much more than vast prison camps. And yet I can say that every possible effort was made by us to alleviate the tragic situation of these unfortunates, the victims of our technical genius.

In the meantime an, alas, only too familiar situation continued: while these useless millions degenerated, we still needed vigorous and intelligent stock for hard labour on the planets that the same technical prowess was opening up.

What we had to do was to take from those planets recently settled species that still retained their native vigour, and were uncorrupted by soft living—as you can imagine, we were being extremely careful how we introduced our luxuries and our ease to these newcomers to our Empire—and after suitable training, use them to develop the new ones. We would choose from these planets stocks and species that seemed suitable, and train them not on their home ground but somewhere else. Rohanda was tried for a while, the empty settlements and stations of the failed experiment being put to use. The work given these more vigorous stocks was much harder than that given to the enfeebled ones. It was necessary to preserve a balance between retaining an ability for physical labour, while developing capacities for initiative and enterprise. What we did was to tell them they were to explore possibilities of developing fauna and plant life, without damaging their surroundings. The results were most gratifying and useful.

I remember a trip I made with some of my staff from end to end of Southern Continent II during this period, using a small fleet of our liaison craft. Flying north to south and up the coasts, and crossing the continent back and forth, it was over magnificent wooded terrain with vast peaceful rivers. But everywhere this sylvan paradise, populated by herds of peaceful animals, showed the settlements of the successful experiment. We landed day after day, week after week, among these representatives of species from our numerous colonies, all so different, yet of course all basically of the same level of evolution—for it is only when a species has got to its hind legs and started to use its hands that it can make the real advances we look for and foster. Furred and unfurred, with long pelts and short, with fells and tufts of hair on their backs and shoulders leaving their fronts bare, black of skin and brown, their faces flat and snouted and heavy-browed and with no brow ridges, jutting-chinned and chinless, hairless and naked, naked but with leaves or bits of skin round their loins, slow of movement and quick, apt to learn and not capable of anything but beast work . . . to travel thus from place to place was really an inventory or summing up of the recent developments of our Empire. This trip was pleasurable, and gave us relief from the disappointment of our recent failure with the northern captives.

All these species—some of them new ones to me; all these animals, and none of them incapable of adaptation, were nevertheless, when matched in our minds with what we were being told of the Canopean experiments up north and the amazing, the incredible evolution of the indigenous native species, fell so short that the two achievements could not be compared. We knew this. We discussed it and thought about it. We did not conceal the situation then; though later our pride made it something to be glossed over and then forgotten.

This entirely successful experiment on Rohanda—the teaching of so many different stocks to be good and flexible colonisers, which was making us so gratified and confirming our confidence in our Colonial Service—was nevertheless and at the same time a defeat. We knew very well that none of these animals we were teaching would evolve very much beyond what they were now, or not quickly: their capacities would be stretched, their skills added to, they would make use of their new opportunities. But it was out of the question that we could expect them to make the jump, and in a few thousand years, from their animal state to one where they would live in cities as fine as anything we knew on Sirius, and maintain them, and change in them so that they could hardly be recognised as the same species as our engaging and likable companions, the simians who lived on their hillside so close to our headquarters, and who were always such a pleasant source of entertainment and interest for us and our visitors.

The Canopean experiment had changed the native stock. Fundamentally.

This was the point.

Our being able to survey all these different kinds of animals all at once, and coming to terms with their possibilities and limitations, resulted in a stepping up of our already quite intensive spying in the north. We had spies, both as individuals and in groups everywhere. We used less and less disguise. This was partly because of the openness with which we were received. Partly because all the southern hemisphere was covered with our supply fleets filling the skies between Southern Continents I and II, and we could always excuse our presence by talk of forced landings. Partly because of a new factor.

SHAMMAT. THE END OF THE OLD ROHANDA

We were approached by emissaries from Shammat. It is not easy to believe now, but Shammat at that time was hardly even a name. Puttiora, the shameful Empire, was, of course, not ignored by us, if for no other reason than that we were continually having to fight off incursions on to our territory. Shammat was spoken of as some dreadful sun-baked rock used by Puttiora as a criminal settlement. At any rate, they were pirates, adventurers, desperadoes. We had certainly not thought of them as having reached the stage of technology, and we were right, for the craft that set itself down on the plain below our headquarters was a stolen Canopean space shuttle. Four Shammatans came up the rocky road with the confidence of those invited, or at least expected, and this arrogance was typical of everything they did. In type they were Modified Two. Head hair, localised body hair, teeth at primary animal level, well-adapted hands, feet used only for locomotion. They were therefore above most of the species, though not all, currently being trained by us for colonial work; but far behind the Rohandan native species as evolved by Canopus. Though we were wondering, as we entertained these extremely vigorous and energetic visitors who had about them every mark of the barbarian and the savage, if this after all so common, not to say basic, type everywhere throughout the three Empires we knew anything about—Canopus, our own, and Puttiora —would not, if put into contact with the Giants, become as advanced as the northern natives. For we had recently adopted the theory that it was the Colony 10 Giants who had the secret of rapid evolution of inferior species.

I will not waste time describing our encounters with these Shammatans. There were many, because they would not take our "no" as final. They lacked inner discrimination as to other people's intentions. What they wanted was this. They had heard of our experiments with deliberately breeding first-quality colonisers. They knew everything about these, so we had to come to terms with knowing that their spying on us had been as intensive as ours on Canopean territory. Shammat wanted to "take off our hands" some of our surplus females. There were very few on that horrible planet of theirs. Those they had were not "able to match demand." I cannot exaggerate the crudity of their thought, and their talk.

While we continued to refuse, for of course there was no question of submitting any peoples under our care to such criminal savages, and while they continued to arrive day after day at our door, as if we had not discussed everything already, a pretty clear and unwelcome picture of their activities was forming in our minds.

Shammat had been on Rohanda for some time, both sending down spaceships, though not often, and fostering a small colony that continually kept spies at work among the Canopean settlements. This was the explanation of the easy reception of our first emissaries: our visits had by no means been the first received by the

Giants and the natives. Whatever it was Shammat had wanted, they had not been given it. Our visitors were cunning and evasive, but not able to hide what they felt and thought. They were angry, no, murderous, because of blocks and checks received from Canopus. And it wasn't—from Canopus—females they had wanted, but something else. *What* this was we did not know, nor did we find out— for millennia, millennia! And we did not find out because we did not know the nature of Canopus, any more than Shammat did. But Shammat had suspected, had wanted, had tried to get—like Sirius. *And Shammat succeeded where we failed.* I am making this statement, here and now, without concealment—though certainly not without trepidation, nor without anticipating criticism—that Shammat the barbarous, the criminal, the horrible, that planet that for so long we cannot remember the beginnings of it has been a synonym for everything disgusting and to be despised: it was Shammat who found out something at least of the Canopean secrets. Enough to steal a little. And we, Sirius, the civilised, the highly developed, have *not* found out.

To return to smaller matters. We of course wanted to know why these pirates had not simply stolen females from Canopus, since a spacecraft had been stolen—if not more than one. We could only conclude that Shammat was afraid of Canopus, and afraid of us, too: believing that punishment would more likely follow theft of people than theft of things. Rightly. But there was more to it than that. These Shammatans, returning day after day, climbing up the road to our fortress headquarters, did so for the same reason we were so ready to listen to them: they wanted to find out what we were doing.

We asked them at one point why they had not simply kidnapped some of the indigenous natives—at this point we had to suffer conniving glances and grimaces, as fellow criminals—but saw that they wanted not the unevolved unregenerate stock but the new improved stock, and members of this they were afraid of stealing, since they were all in the new fine cities, where the Giants lived, too. They were quite remarkably shamefaced and shifty about this, and itching with greed. Why had they not stolen some members of our other species—both failed and successful—who had, at various times, populated the Southern Continents? But again, it was the same: all these different types and kinds and stocks and strains *were not good enough*. Not good enough for these nasty thieves of Shammatans, sitting there in their red jackets—Canopean ex-colonial uniform of centuries back; in their green pantaloons—Puttioran fashion, long outdated; their hide shoes made from some unfortunate animals somewhere. No, they wanted the best. Their eyes were fevered as they talked of the fine, handsome, healthy females in the glorious cities up north. And they talked lip-lickingly of "those females on Canopus—they've got yellow hair and blue eyes, so we hear. . . ." (This was untrue.) And all this while they ate me up with their eyes. I could see that their fingers itched to feel my hair and poke at my pale skin.

Shortly after these nasty visitors took themselves off—back to the northern areas, not to Shammat—we discovered that the females who had volunteered for breeding service had also been visited by Shammat. To the extent that some of the progeny were Shammatan. There had been plots to escape, with Shammatan help. These had failed. But it was now important to watch for Shammat characteristics among the new race of colonisers that we had been so proud of. Later still we had again to modify our conclusions. Some of the breeding females had in fact escaped. Their places had been taken by Shammatan substitutes. The escaped ones had gone to Shammat, taking a good supply of the very best Sirian genes with them. Some of these females had originated in our C.P. 7 of fair-haired, blue-eyed stock—Planet 7 was the birthplace of my mother. They had proved very popular on Shammat, and new supplies were being demanded. . . .

I now come to the end of this phase on Rohanda.

About ten thousand years after the Canopus-Rohanda "Lock," we were summoned to an urgent conference. Canopus had to announce disaster. Unexpected cosmic changes . . . failure of the "Lock" . . . total write-off of the poor planet for whose sake Rohandan development had been speeded up . . . degeneration and dislocation of Rohanda inevitable.

We were told to expect random and wild mutations and changes of every kind among our experimental species; advised to limit our attempts until these changes could be monitored and understood.

I have to admit that at first we believed this was a feint, a ploy.

Particularly as we did not receive reports of any increased activity in the north—for instance, no increase in visits by their spacecraft. But then, their visits had always been few, and this had reinforced our belief that the "contacts" they were always hinting at were to do with communications.

We heard that a single emissary had arrived and was stationed in a circular city in a region where there were many inland seas. This was Johor, an official then of junior rank. Soon after that, our spies reported that spacecraft had taken off nearly the entire complement of Giants from the north, though a few had escaped. Our spies then submitted reports that seemed contradictory, vague, even foolish—we understood that Canopus had not exaggerated the ill-effects that would be expected. We recalled our spies, though a few never returned at all, and shipped out the remaining experimental subjects. After only a few years, these were showing signs of a decrease in life-span and of a tendency towards rapid reversal to barbarism—but this particular phase of Rohanda is so well documented under Social Pathology that I shall not linger over it: it has become, after all, the classic case of sudden evolutionary reversal.

Our most urgent question was C.P. 23, which had been established as our Think-Planet—if I may be forgiven the flippancy at such a serious point in my story. It was completely dependent on supplies from Southern Continent I. We decided not to make alterations in our agricultural stations. It was necessary to increase our police establishment almost at once, for it was discovered that workers previously quite reliable had taken to pilfering, and then, slowly, to various kinds of criminality. Still we maintained our agriculture. Then something unexpected: waves of invaders from the area of the inland seas came sweeping down, destroying first the more northerly agricultural stations, but then penetrating further and further south. Who were these rapacious ones? None other than the natives brought to such a high pitch of civic and personal responsibility by Canopus. What it amounted to was that we would have to maintain armies right across the top of Southern Continent I. Full-scale and urgent conferences were held on the Sirian Mother Planet itself. Our military resources were already stretched to their limit by the unrest on many of our Colonised Planets. We had no alternative but to withdraw from Rohanda.

Other arrangements were going to have to be made for C.P. 23: its brief but glorious career was concluded, and the Thinkers were transferred elsewhere.

I went on a last survey of S.C. I, just before the end. Everywhere over this noble continent, similar to S.C. II, but even larger and more various, were our agricultural areas. Each little group of buildings was surrounded by vast fields over which our servicing and surveillant machines hovered, glittering in the sunlight: green and yellow and umber fields, and brightly coloured craft. The shining rivers . . . the infinitely variegated greens of the plantations . . . the irrigation canals . . . enormous transparent structures for hydroponics, and for general research . . . I cannot pretend that I enjoyed that final trip. Even then they were dismantling the stations, while the enormous craft of our Inter-Colony Heavy Transport Fleet were landing and taking off, loaded with these structures, and with the last of our crops. I flew over some stations that had already been evacuated. Our policy to disrupt the landscape as little as possible had succeeded. Nothing was left to be seen but some hastily harvested fields, that would shortly be reclaimed by jungle and forest, and some belts of introduced trees that were already Rohandan. The millennia of our occupation would soon have left no traces.

I was not feeling myself, and Ambien I was not well either. We put this down to disappointment at this check of our plans. Then all our team confessed to general malaise and low spirits. It became evident that our mental powers were being affected. There was nothing for it: I gave the order for us all to leave Rohanda.

Shortly after that, Canopus convened a conference, again on Colony 10. Rohanda was only one of the items on the agenda. At the time it did not seem more important than the others.

It has always seemed to me that this question of "hindsight" is not to be solved!

What I see now, looking back, is not what I experienced then, but are we to cancel out former, and more immature, ways of viewing things? As if they did not matter, *had no effect?*—but of course not.

Among the many interests Canopus and Sirius had in common at that time one stood out. The Colony 10 Giants, returned to their own planet and waiting for new work to be allotted to them, had suffered. Now twice the size of their former compatriots and evolved beyond them, they could not settle in their old ways, nor was Planet 10 able to accept them easily. Superiority is never easily tolerated.

There was no planet among the Canopean colonies that could usefully welcome the Giants. Not immediately. Having learned of the Giants' capacities, and believing of them that they could make —almost overnight, evolutionarily speaking—civilised races out of apes, we wished Canopus to "lend" us the Giants in order that they might teach our specialised colonists "their tricks." Yes, that is how we talked. There is no point in blushing for it now. Canopus steadily, kindly, gently, resisted us. It was not possible, they said. We saw in the refusal niggardliness; saw in it reluctance to help Sirius to advance beyond Canopus—saw in it everything but what was there. Formal application had been made to Canopus for this "loan" and it was the main item on the agenda, and the chief topic of all the informal discussions during the conference. There was ill-feeling on our side. Resentment. As usual.

The general atmosphere of the conference was low and dispirited. Canopus had been shaken by the Rohanda failure, and was made miserable, as they freely confessed, because of the fate of the unfortunate Planet 8, which they now could not save and which, even as the conference took place, was being abandoned, with loss of life and potentiality. And we Sirians were low, too, because of Rohanda. I cannot in fact remember a conference that had so little of the energy that comes from success; though of course it did not lack purpose and determination for the future.

For me personally the conference was important because it was there I first saw Klorathy, who led their team. It was he who supplied the occasion with what vitality it could aspire to. I liked him at once. He was—and is—a vigorous, abrasive, sardonic being who can always be counted on to alleviate the torpors and languors that attend even the best conferences. We were attracted, told each other so, in the way of course appropriate to our life-stages: both of us had our breeding-bond phases behind us. Ambien I also liked him, and we all three looked forward to many pleasant and useful encounters.

It was Klorathy who had to carry the burden of refusing us the Giants, and I recall his patience as he over and over repeated: But, you see, it is not possible . . . while we *didn't* see.

I can do no better than to get down the main points of the agenda as it related to Rohanda, in order to illustrate points of view then and now.

1 The Canopean-Rohandan Lock had failed—the basic fact.
2 That degeneration of various kinds must be expected—which we had already experienced.
3 That Canopus intended to maintain their link with Rohanda, some sort of skeleton staff, in order to maintain the flow at a steady minimum level.
4 As far as could be seen, the cosmic alignments that had caused this Disaster would not reverse for several hundred thousand years, after which there would be no reason Rohanda could not revert to its flowering flourishing *healthy* condition.
5 That (and this was to them—to Canopus—the most important factor in this summing up) Shammat of Puttiora had discovered the nature of the Canopus-Rohandan bond, and was tapping strength from it. And was already waxing fat and prosperous on it.

I can only say that, reading these words now, and remembering what I saw in them then, I have to marvel at my blindness.

Again, resentment was partly the cause. And also fear: There was much talk about the Shammat "spies," which Canopus claimed they had known nothing about. We did not believe this. But could not pursue it, for fear our own spying would come to light. . . .

It will be seen from these brief remarks that this was an uncomfortable, unsatisfactory conference. When it was dissolved, I could see nothing positive in it except my meeting with Klorathy, and since he was to stay on Colony 10 to assist the Giants in their painful period of waiting, and I was to return to Sirius, we had nothing much to hope for, at least immediately.

Sirius had not abandoned the idea of using Rohanda for experiments. It was a question of finding ways of doing this without harm to ourselves. A joint committee Canopus/Sirius was set up at the conference for this purpose. Again I was assigned to Rohanda, at my request, and with instructions by Canopus—called by us and by them *advice*—on how to survive the new discordant Rohandan atmosphere. We were told that if we were to build settlements in exactly this way and that—measurements and proportions prescribed to the fraction of an R-unit—and wore such and such artefacts, and ate this and that (there were long lists of such prescriptions), then we might work on that unfortunate planet, at least for limited periods.

To begin with, their advice was only partly, or halfheartedly, obeyed: bad results followed. We then took to an exact obedience. Success.

This obedience was more remarkable than perhaps will seem now. At that time it would have been difficult to find anything good being said about Canopus anywhere in our territories. Our tone was one of indifference at best, but usually derision. We were spying on them everywhere and in every way. We did not hesitate to outdo them when we could, often quite childishly, and even illegally. Any who doubt this may find what I say confirmed in any common chronicle or memoir of that time: we were not ashamed of our behavior. On the contrary. Yet we suspected Canopus of ill-feeling and delinquency towards us, and complained of it. At the same time, and while *apparently* having little respect for their prescriptions, for we mocked them when we thought this would earn us admiration, we nevertheless followed them, and to the point where the practices became second nature, and we were in danger of forgetting where they originated. Then we *did* forget—or most of us—and "the Rohandan Adjustment Technique" was talked of as if it were a discovery of our own.

For a long time, more than a hundred thousand years, we Sirians were more on Rohanda than Canopus was. *So we believed then.* It was because we told our spies to look for Canopean technicians by the same signs that we understood for our own necessities and behaviour. We did not know then that Canopus could come and go in any way than by spaceship—by ordinary physical transport. Did not know that Canopean technicians could exist on Rohanda —and on other planets—taking the outward physical shape of the inhabitants of any particular time and place.

For long ages Canopean individuals were at work on Rohanda

and we did not know it. Even now there are those who refuse to believe it.

But a few of us who worked on Rohanda came to understand. And I will come to a fuller description of this, in its place.

Meanwhile, my preoccupation with Canopus continued, and I was not by any means the only one. And this was for a specific and definite reason.

THE SITUATION IN THE SIRIAN EMPIRE

It is necessary for me now to make a general statement about Sirian development—a summary of history from the end of our Dark Age until the present. It will be argued that it is not possible to sum up several hundred thousand years of an Empire's history in a few words. Yet we all of us do this when describing others. For instance, how do we—and even our most lofty and respected historians—refer to Alikon, the long-lived culture that preceded our own on Sirius, before we became an Empire? "Alikon was a rigid and militaristic society, based on limited natural resources, whose ruling caste maintained power by the use of a repressive religion, keeping nine-tenths of the population as labourers, slaves, and servants. It ended because . . ." That is how we describe ninety thousand S-years of what we always refer to as "prehistory." To take another example. Colony 10 of the Canopean rule was once "Senjen, a natural paradise, a pacific, easygoing matriarchal society made possible by a pleasant climate and abundant vegetable and animal stocks." Senjen lasted for two hundred thousand years before Canopus decided it needed improvement.

No: the dispassionate, disinterested eye we use for other peoples, other histories, we do not easily turn on ourselves—past or present! Yet most societies—cultures—empires—can be described by an underlying fact or truth, and this is nearly always physical, geographical. Is it possible that our reluctance to regard ourselves as we do others is because we do not like to categorise our own existence as *physical . . . merely* physical?

The Sirian Empire has been preoccupied by one basic *physical* fact and the questions caused thereby since its inception: technology: our technical achievements that no other empire has ever even approached. . . . I write that statement without the benefit of "hindsight." That is how we have seen it until very recently. It is because of how we define (and many of us still do) *technology*. The subtle, infinitely varied, hard-to-see technology of Canopus was invisible to us, and therefore for all these millennia, these long ages, we have counted ourselves as supreme.

We now mark the end of our Dark Age at the point where "we got rid of our excess populations." As I saw it expressed in a somewhat robustly worded history. At the point, then, when "population balanced necessity." Ah yes, there are a hundred ways of putting our basic dilemma! And each one of these formulations, evasive or frank, can only mask something we have never come to terms with! To sum up our culture, then, as we so arbitrarily encapsulate others: "The Sirian Empire, with its fifty-three colonies, almost infinitely rich, well-endowed, fruitful, variegated, and with its exemplary technology, has never been able to decide how many people should be allowed to live in it."

There you have it. I touched on this before: how could I not? There is no way of even mentioning Sirius without bringing up this our basic, our burning, problem. . . .

The Dark Age over, we saw to it that our populations everywhere were reduced to the minimum level necessary for . . . *for what?* In our enthusiasm over our new concept, our new capacities of control, we set fairly arbitrary limits to population on our fifty-three colonies. Very low numbers were permitted to be.

What happened to those teeming millions upon millions upon millions? Well, they were not exterminated. They were not ill treated. On the contrary, as I have hinted—to do more than lightly sketch these developments would come outside my scope—all kinds of special schemes and projects were set up to soften their tragic fate. They died, it is generally agreed now—now that so much time has passed and we can look at those days more calmly —of broken hearts, broken will. They died because they had no purpose, of illnesses, of epidemics that seemed to have other causes, and during mass outbreaks of madness. But they died. It took fifty thousand years of our bad—our *very* bad—time, but at the end of it,

we were left with nearly empty planets, and everything open for us
—ready for a magnificent new purpose, new plan.

But, in fact, nothing had changed: *we still did not know how to
look at ourselves*. Our technology was such that our entire Empire
could be run with something like ten million people. That was what
was *needed*. If to run our Empire was our purpose, and nothing
else . . .

I shall not go on. Some people will say I have already said enough
about this; others that, if I were to pay proper and due respect to
our terrible basic dilemma, I should devote not a few paragraphs
but several volumes to it.

Well, myriads of volumes and whole ages have been devoted
to it—when our stage was, as it were, swept bare and empty, waiting for its appropriate dramas, what happened was that schools of
philosophy sprang up everywhere, and nothing was heard but their
debates, their arguments. . . . What was our purpose? they enquired
of themselves, of us, pursuing "the fundamental Sirian existential
problem."

So violent, lowering, unpleasant, became these debates that it
was made illegal to even mention this "existential problem"—and
that epoch lasted for millennia. Of course, there were all kinds of
underground movements and subversive sects devoted to "maintaining knowledge of the truth."

Then, as these became so powerful and influential they could
not be ignored, public expression of our inward preoccupation was
made legal again. At one time several of our planets were set aside
as universities and colleges, for the sole purpose of discussions of our
existential problems. This is how "the Thinkers" of 23 originated.

Meanwhile, sometimes our populations grew larger and sometimes smaller, and these fluctuations did not relate to how many
individuals were needed in order to operate our technologies, but
according to how tides of opinion flowed . . . if we wanted to, we
could have crammed our planets with billions of genera, species,
races—as they once had been. When we wanted, they could be left
empty. We could—and did—maintain some planets, for special
purposes, at very high levels of population and leave others virtually
unpopulated.

While all these variations on our basic problem were attempted, our space drive had been stabilised. We had discovered that no matter how forcefully we swept out into space, gathering in suitable planets as we found them, incorporating them into our general plan, we took our problems—or rather, our *problem*—with us. What did we need all these new colonies for? What was their purpose? If they had special conditions of climate, then we could tell ourselves they were useful—for something or other; if they had new minerals, or large deposits of those already known to us— they were used. But suppose we went on acquiring colonies and reached the number of a hundred . . . a thousand . . . what then?

As our philosophers asked, and argued.

We, the administrators, had been watching Canopus: she was not acquiring ever more colonies. She was stabilised on what she had. She had far fewer than we . . . she was developing and advancing them. . . . But that was not how we saw it then: I have to record that we despised Canopus, that great neighbour of ours, our competitor, our rival, for being satisfied with such a low level of material development and acquisition.

I now return to our preoccupation with Canopus.

CANOPUS-SIRIUS. KLORATHY

At the time of the ending of our Dark Age, which was not long after the Rohandan Disaster, Canopus had as large a population as we—proportional to the fact they had fewer planets. That was one fact: and they showed no disquiet at all about it. Yet their technology, though *apparently* inferior to ours, was certainly near enough to ours to pose the questions that beset us? When we raised these questions, our "existential problem," they were simply not interested. But at the time we saw this—as usual—as an example of their deviousness. When they were asked how they adjusted their population levels, the reply always was: "according to need" or "according to necessity," and it was a very long time—only recently —that we were able to *hear* "according to the Need. According to the Necessity."

Sirius knew far less about Canopus—and this on a purely material level—than Canopus did about us. I had noticed this long before: mentioning any one of our planets, Canopus always seemed informed about it: and we accordingly admired their espionage system.

We were always waiting for the time when we could catch one of their spies and say: "Look, you have broken your agreement, now we demand information in return." But we never did catch any of their spies. For the good reason that they did not have any.

And when we asked for information, it was given, and we did not trust in it . . . did not believe what we were told.

Shortly after the Conference on Colony 10, the one to consider the results of the Catastrophe, I was called by my Head of Department and was asked to develop my relationship with Klorathy: our liking for each other had been noted.

I was of course not reluctant. I did not have then, nor have now, any feeling that it is wrong to use a personal relationship in this way. I am a Sirian. This is what I am first and foremost. I am proud to be a public servant of Sirius. If there were ever to come a moment of conflict between my duty to Sirius, to our Colonial Service, and my personal feelings, I should never hesitate. But why should there be conflict? I have always put first what I conceive to be the *real* interests, long-term interests, of Sirius. And of course I took it for granted that Klorathy must have been approached by his superiors, about me—and about Ambien I as well.

I was asked to return to Rohanda, where Klorathy was shortly to pay a visit: so we had been informed by them. The fact that we *had* been informed told us that Klorathy was allotted the same role as I had been: we could regard ourselves as spies if we wished.

My whole nature was involved in my preparations for this meeting with Klorathy. I cannot separate the "personal" from the public aspects of myself here—not easily. There are times in one's life when it seems as if everything that happens streams together, each event, or person, or even an overheard remark becoming an aspect of a whole—a confluence whose sources go back into the past, reach forward into the future. Personally, there was a gap in my life because a boon-companion had recently died. Death is not something we think much about, we of the superior Sirian mother-stock, since we do not expect to die except from accident or a rare disease.

But this old friend had been struck by a meteorite travelling on the Inter-Planetary Service. While we saw each other rarely, since his service was on C.P. 3, we were in a rare balance of sympathies and even knowing that the other was *there* was a support to both. I frankly hoped that Klorathy might take the place of this boon-friend. Not least because he was from Canopus: there had been cases of real friendship between Sirians and Canopeans, but they were legendary: heroic tales were made of them and used to support in our youngsters the comparatively new idea that Canopus was an ally, not to be seen only as an old enemy.

But there was something about Canopus itself that . . . is the word *attracted?* me. No. Obsessed? No, there was too much else in my life to allow a one-sided preoccupation. I felt about Canopus that inward, brooding questioning, wondering, that one may some-times feel about a person whose sources of action, of being, seem distant and other—as if understanding this being may open doors in oneself whose existence one does not do more than suspect. Yet they are there . . . one knows it . . . one cannot—*may* not?—open them . . . but other people *have* opened similar doors in themselves . . . they operate on altogether different—*higher?*—levels of them-selves . . . if one understood how, one could come close not only to them but to that area of oneself that matches their higher other-ness . . . so one broods, ponders, questions, sometimes for long ages, about some individual who—one is convinced—is only part-glimpsed, certainly only part-understood.

It will be seen that Klorathy for me was very much more than just himself.

Ambien I was to travel with me and I was glad of it, for he shared something of my feeling for Canopus.

Before going north, we descended at our old headquarters to see what possibilities there might be for future experiments. The dis-covery that concerns this account was a change in the colony of natives whom we had left on their hillside. We had expected a degeneration, but found something we had not expected and could not at first interpret. The natives had become two distinct species. Some had remained physically the same, though more quarrelsome, and divisive, no longer living in a large and easygoing tribe, but in small family groups, or as individuals, each defending patches of territory, hunting grounds, caves, or rough shelters. They had sunk away from proper building, the cultivation of crops, the use of animals. The other kind, living close, using the original stock and continually preying on them in every way, snatching from them their kills in the hunt and their females or their children whom they might eat or use as servants, had changed to a position between Modified Two and Modified Three. They were upright, but occasionally rested their weight on the knuckles of their long arms; they were tailless; they had fur on their heads and shoulders but were otherwise quite hairless, which gave them a sickeningly lewd and obscene look—and they seemed motivated by an avid cunning that was in everything they did. It was this characteristic that made Ambien I and I exclaim at the same moment: "Shammat!"—what had happened was that the Shammat spies had mated with the natives and this was the result. It seemed to us that we were unlikely to see the remnant of the poor natives again, belligerent and suspicious though they had become; the new stock was banded together in a large obviously efficient tribe, superior in intelligence and in strength. The old natives had a look about them that we knew only too well: the subdued, paranoid, almost furtive air of a species that would soon die out from discouragement.

We took note that this new stock could be used by us, possibly, in our experiments and flew north. Passing over the isthmus that joins the Isolated Northern Continent with the Isolated Southern Continent, we saw that the land-bridge had sunk, leaving a gap of 50 or so R-miles. Sometimes this bridge was there, at some epochs, and at others not, and we were able to deduce that the gap had been there for a long time, because the new stocks on the Northern Continent had not infiltrated southwards.

We met Klorathy as arranged on a high plateau of raw red rock and sand, the result of recent earthquakes, overlooking lower fertile plains untouched by the quakes. Our aircraft came down side by side on the burning desert: we conversed by radio, and together flew off into the shelter of a high wooded mountain. The three of us conducted our first conference under a large shade tree, sharing a meal. It was a most pleasant occasion. We were all quite frankly examining each other to see if our impressions on Colony 10 had been accurate. As for myself, I was more than happy. Klorathy in himself was as lively and attractive as I remembered, but there was the additional bonus always felt in meeting with the superior ones of our Galaxy. After all, so much of one's time is spent with the lower races, and as interesting as the work is, as likable as these races often are, to meet one's equals is something to be looked forward to.

Klorathy was a typical Canopean Mother Planet Type I: very tall, lightly built, strong, a light bronze in colour, his eyes a darker bronze, he was not dissimilar from my Ambien I. And I was conscious that my own physical difference from them both was felt by them as an agreeable contrast.

We still did not know why we had been invited to this meeting —both Ambiens (as we often humorously refer to ourselves) had been speculating. I for one had been thinking most of all about the mathematical cities of the pre-Disaster phase. I had even been wondering if we hadn't imagined all that—to the extent of asking Ambien I again and again to repeat to me what he had seen of them. But he reiterated that he had never seen anything like those cities ever, anywhere. *Yet on the Canopean Mother Planet they had nothing so advanced.* I had asked Klorathy about this at the last conference, and he had replied that there was "no need" for this type of city or building on Canopus itself. I had believed him. When with Klorathy, one had to know he did not lie. When away from him, it was a different matter, and I had been wondering why he had lied. Together again, sitting with him there under the light fragrant shade of the tree, on soft spicy grasses, I had only to look at him to know that if he said that on Canopus (the Mother Planet) they had such and such a city, then it was true. He had described these to me, and they did not sound so dissimilar from those on Sirius. Agreeable, genial cities, planted with all kinds of attractive and useful trees and shrubs, they are places where one experiences well-being. But they are *not* built as those round, or starlike or hexagonal—and so forth—cities of the old Rohanda.

"*Why not? Why not, Klorathy?*"

"It's like this, Ambien II: cities, buildings—the situations of cities and buildings on any planet—are designed according to need."

Well, obviously—was what I was thinking.

I was disappointed, and felt cheated. I felt worse than that. I had not really, before actually meeting Klorathy, stopped to consider the effect it would have on our being together, that I could not say anything about what was so strongly in my mind then—the horrible new race, or stock, of beast-men on Isolated S.C. II. We had not told Canopus that we had had visits from Shammat, or that we had stolen without telling them some of "their" Natives, or that C.P. 22 technicians had escaped with some Lombis and had settled not far from here, or that we had so often and so thoroughly conducted espionage in their territories, or that Shammat had done the same . . . it seemed to me, sitting there in that delightful picnic spot, as if instead of being open and generously available to this new friend, as one has to be in friendship, my mind had bars around it: keep off, keep off . . . and there were moments when I could hardly bear to look into that open and unsuspicious countenance. And yet I have to record that I was also feeling something like: You think you are so clever, you Canopeans, but you have no idea what's in my mind, for all that!

No, there was not going to be any easy companionship between us, not really. Or not yet.

Soon we found out why Sirius had been invited to send representatives . . . when we heard, we could hardly believe it, yet what we had expected was not easy to say.

The remnant of the degenerating Giant race had proliferated and spread everywhere—over this continent as well. They were now half the size they had been, about our size—eight to nine R-feet tall, and were not as long-lived. They had retained little memory of their great past—not much beyond knowledge of the uses of fire for cooking and warmth and some elementary craftwork. They did not grow plants for food, but gathered them wild; and they hunted. From north to south of the Isolated Northern Continent they lived in large, closely organised tribes who did not war with each other, since there was plenty of territory and apparently infinite stocks of animals. The two tribes near here, near this spot, were called Hoppe and Navahi, and it was Klorathy's mission to visit them and . . . I missed some of what he was saying, at this point. For I could not tell him the origin of these two names, and I was afraid even of looking at Ambien I. When I was able to hear again, he was talking about some dwarves that lived in these mountains, and in other mountain chains, too, over the continent, and he was to visit these, for Canopus would like to know more about them. And assumed that Sirius would as well. I can only say that I recognised in this a sort of shorthand for much more . . . for how much more I will not say at this point: certainly it turned out very differently from what I then imagined.

Klorathy was wanting us to go with him into the mountain habitations of the dwarves. This would involve danger, since they had been hounded by the Hoppes and Navahis, and while he was known by them we would have to win their trust. He was taking it absolutely for granted that we would be ready for this: and Ambien I most certainly was, for he liked challenge. As for me, I did not want any association with what were bound to be no more than squalid little half-animals—but I assented.

THE DWARVES. THE HOPPES. THE NAVAHIS

We concealed the two machines as well as we could in a canyon, and walked forth boldly towards the mountains. These had not been devastated by the quake, though some rock falls had taken place, giving the mountainsides a raw disturbed look. Standing close against a precipitous surface we could hear all kinds of murmurings and knockings and runnings-about, and I was reminded of the termite dwellings on Isolated S.C. II—putting one's ear to the walls of one of these, having knocked on its surface or even broken a part off, one heard just such a scurrying, rustling murmur. Coming round the edge of this precipice, there was a low dark cave entrance, and Klorathy walked at once towards it, lifting up both his hands and calling out words I did not know. We, too, lifted our hands in what was obviously a gesture of peace. There was a sudden total silence, from which we were able to gauge the degree of the background of noise to which we had adjusted ourselves approaching the mountain. Silence—the sun blazing down uncomfortably from the warm Rohanda skies—heat striking out from the raw and unhealed rocks—heat dizzying up from the soil. Suddenly there was a rush of movement from the cave, so swift it was impossible to distinguish details, and we three were enclosed in a swarm of squat little people who were hustling us inside the cave, which we tall ones—they came up to our knee level—had to go on all fours to enter. We were in a vast cavern, lit everywhere by small flames, which we later found were outlets of natural gas, controlled and kept perpetually burning. Yet they were not enough to create more than a soft twilight. The cavern was floored with white sand that glimmered, and crystals in the rock walls twinkled, and a river that rushed along the cavern's edge flung up sparkling showers of spray. I had not expected to find this soft exuberance of light inside the dark mountain, and my spirits rose, and as I was rushed along by the pressure of the little people I was able to examine them. They were certainly less animal than the horrid new beast-men of the Southern Continent, but quite seemly and decent creatures, wearing trousers and jackets of dressed skins. Very broad they were, almost as broad as tall: and I was easily able to recognise in the stock the powerful arms and shoulders of the Lombis, and the yellow skins of the Colony 22 technicians. Their faces were bare of hair, under close caps of tight rough dark curls, and were keen and sharp and intelligent.

We were taken swiftly through several of such caverns, always with the river rushing along beside us, until we were deep inside the mountain—yet it did not feel oppressive, for the air was sweet and fresh. We were in a cave so enormous the roof went up above us into impenetrable black, and the illuminations around the rocky verges were only pinpoints of innumerable light. There was a cleared space in the centre, quite large enough to take a horde of these little people and ourselves, but small in proportion to the enormousness of the place. We were sat down on piles of skins, and given some food—hardly to the palates of such as we, though it was not without interest to be reminded of what was—what had to be—the food of all the lowly evolved planets of our Galaxy. Meat. A sort of cheese. A kind of beer. All this time Klorathy was keeping up talk with them: he seemed to know their language at least adequately. It was Ambien I and myself who puzzled them, though they were civil enough—for we were both obviously of different kinds from

Klorathy. They eyed us, yet not unpleasantly, and one of the females, a quite attractive little thing in her robust heavy way, begged to touch my hair, and in a moment several females had crowded up, smiling and apologetic, but unable to resist handling my blonde locks. Yet I, for my part, was looking around into the faces packed and massed all around, and remembering the Lombis —who had never set eyes on me or anything like me—and the Colony 22 techs, who had . . . a long, long time ago, far out of personal memory, in their time reckoning, but such a short time ago in ours. Did they have any sort of race or gene memory? We examined each other, in a scene of which I have been a part so very often in my long service: members of differing races meeting, not in enmity but in genial curiosity.

How were we able to do this—see each other so close and well, when the twinkling walls of the cave were so far distant? It was by—electricity. Yes. Everywhere stood strong bright lights, wooden containers that housed batteries: it is never possible to foresee what part of a former technology a fallen-off race will retain.

And they were that—reduced, I mean; under pressure, beset. . . . I was able to recognise it at once, by a hundred little signs that perhaps I wouldn't have been able to consciously describe. These were a people in danger, endangered—*desperate*. It showed in the sombre consciousness of their eyes, fastening on Klorathy, who for his part was leaning forward, urgent, concentrated on this task of his . . .

Later we were led off, I by the women, the men separately, and we slept in small but airy rock chambers. And next day the discussions with Klorathy went on, while I and Ambien I were taken, on our request, to see this underground kingdom. Which I shall now briefly describe.

First of all, it was not the only one: Klorathy said that not only all over this continent but in most parts now of Rohanda spread these underearth races. But they had not taken to the caves and caverns by nature, only from need, as they found themselves hunted and persecuted by races so much larger than themselves. Though not more skilled.

These caverns were by no means the habitations of brutes. They had been adapted from natural holes and caves, often the old tunnels of former underground rivers and lakes. Sometimes they had been excavated. Many were carefully panelled with well-tailored and smoothed planking. All were lit, either by natural gas or by electricity. There were meeting places and eating places, sleeping places, and storage caves and workshops. Animals had been captured from the surface world and brought down to breed and increase in this below-earth realm. There were birds, some flying freely about, as if they had been in the air. These were underground cities, under-earth realms. And they were all based on the oddest and saddest contradictions or predicaments.

This race had become skilled miners and metallurgists. Beginning with iron, they had made all kinds of utensils and then—finding themselves hunted—weapons. For a time, and in some places, they had made approaches out into the world to offer trade, and trade had often been effective. They exchanged iron products for roots and fruits and fresh supplies of animals for their chthonic herds. Then they found gold. They had seen it was beautiful and did not rust and crumble as iron did, but found it too soft for tools and vessels—yet it *was* so beautiful, and everywhere they made ornaments and decorations with it. Taking it out to the tribes now forming everywhere above ground—for these were more likely to be their neighbours than the people of the advanced cities, at first gold was a curiosity, and then, suddenly, was something for which murder could be committed, and slaves captured—the dwarves were chased into the mountains and whole communities wiped out. They fled deeper into the mountains, or went into further ranges, always going further, retreating, becoming invisible except for rare careful excursions to see if trade was possible again. Sometimes it was. Often, coming out with their heavy dark vessels and spears and arrowheads, their glistening gleaming ornaments, they would be ambushed and all killed.

Yet they always mined, since it was now in their blood, the skill of it in their hands and minds.

Yet, and this was the sad paradox that they did not fully see until Klorathy pointed it out to them: suppose they had never mined at all, would they have missed so much: Did their food depend on it? Their clothing? Even their electricity? Their clay vessels were beautiful and strong and in every way as good as their iron ones.

Suppose they had never learned how to melt iron from rocks, and gold from rocks—what then?

But it was too late for thinking in this way.

Finding themselves harried and hunted, these poor creatures had sent Klorathy a message. Had sent a message "all the way to the stars."

How?

Coming together in a great conclave, from every part of this continent, creeping along a thousand underground channels and roads, they had cried out that "Canopus would help them."

Two of them had made a dangerous journey to the middle seas. There, so the news was, were great cities. This journey had taken many R-years. The two, a male and a female, having crept and crawled and lurked and sneaked their way across a continent and then from island to island across the great sea, and then across land again, had found that upheavals and earthquakes had vanished the great cities, which were now only a memory among half-savages. The two had gone northwards, hearing of "a place where kindness and women rule." There they were directed to Adalantaland, where there was kindness and a wise female ruler, who had said that "Canopus had not visited for a long time, not in her memory or in that of her Mothers." The two had left their messages, obstinately believing that what Canopus had promised—for promises were in their memories—Canopus would perform. And though they had died as soon as they had delivered their reports of that epic and terrible journey, soon Canopus *did* perform, for Klorathy came to them.

Had come first on an investigational trip from one end of this continent to the other. Had heard, then, of the "little people" in the other continents, for oddly—or perhaps not oddly at all— emissaries from the "little people," hunted and persecuted everywhere, had made their brave and faithful journeys to places where they believed "Canopus" might have ears to hear their cries for help.

Klorathy had then summed up all this information he had

garnered, and pondered over it and concluded that there was another factor here, there was an element of savagery, of beastliness, more and above what could be naturally expected. It was the work of Shammat, of course, Shammat who Canopus had believed to be still far away half across the globe—not that its influence wasn't everywhere . . . but on the subject of that "influence" Klorathy was either not able or not willing to enlarge.

"What do you mean, Klorathy?—when you talk of *Shammat-nature?*"—and as I asked the question I thought of those avid greedy faces, those glittering avaricious eyes. "A savage is a savage. A civilised race behaves like one." At which he smiled, sadly, and in a way that did not encourage me to press him.

What Klorathy hoped to achieve by this present excursion into the realm of the dwarves was first of all to encourage them, saying that Canopus was doing what it could. Secondly, he said he would now go out to meet with the Hoppes and the Navahis and put it to them that to harry these most excellent craftsmen of the mountains was folly—better rather to become allies with them, to trade, and to stand together with them against the vicious children of Shammat who were the enemies of both, the enemies of everyone. Therefore, Klorathy asked them—sitting again in the vast cavern under its canopy of twinkling lights, on the warm white sand that the dwarves carried from the outside rivers to make clean shining floors for themselves—leaning forward into the low and immediate light of the electric handlamps: be patient. When—*if*—the tribesmen come offering treaties and trade, then see if ways cannot be found to do this without laying themselves open to traps and treason. For his part, he, Klorathy, pledged himself to do what he could. And so we left that deeply hidden and fantastic realm, with its race of earthy craftsmen, being escorted into the outer air and the blue skies towards which the dwarves lifted their longing and exiled eyes before fleeing away into the earth again.

Now we had to make contact with the tribesmen.

Their lookouts soon saw us as we walked across the rocky and raw landscape, with no aim except to be captured. Which we were, and taken to their camp. This was the usual functional unit of the Modified Two stage. Their skills were less than those of the dwarves, so soon to be extinct. They hunted, and lived on the results of their hunting, and had developed a close harmonious bond with the terrain on which they lived. In which they had their being, as they—as their religion—saw it.

They did us no harm, because they recognised in us something of the stuff of certain legends—all about Canopus. Always of that Empire, never of ours. I drew the attention of my colleagues in the Service when I returned home to the fact that even in territories close to our allotted portion of Rohanda, which might be expected to owe some sort of allegiance to us, to Sirius, it was to Canopus that their higher allegiances were pledged, were given. Why was this? Surely there was a fault here in our presentation of ourselves?

These Hoppes recognised us—all three—as "from there," meaning Canopus. So it was as honorary Canopeans that we were welcomed into the camp, and then as guests at a festival that lasted thirty R-days and nights, which Klorathy obviously much enjoyed. I cannot say that I did. But I recognised even then that the ability to become part of—I was going to say "to sink oneself into," but refrained, because of the invisible moral pressure of Canopus—an unfamiliar scene, a foreign race, even one considered (perhaps out of ignorance) inferior, is one to be admired, commended, and even emulated, if possible. I *did* try to behave as Klorathy did and as Ambien I was doing, as far as he was able. Klorathy feasted and even danced with them, told stories, in their tongue—and yet was able never to be less than Canopus.

And when the feasting was over, I was expecting something on these lines: that Klorathy would say to them: I have some news for you, some suggestions to make, now is the time for us to confer seriously and solemnly and at length, please make arrangements for a formal occasion at which this may be done.

But nothing of the sort happened. Klorathy, in the tent they had allotted to him, and we two Ambiens, in our tents, simply went on as we were, taking part in the life of the tribe.

And now I have to record something that I most bitterly regret, for it set back my understanding for a very long time. Millennia. Long ages. I missed an opportunity then. I shall simply say it, and leave the subject.

I was impatient and restless. I found these Hoppe savages interesting enough and I would have stood it all—the lack of privacy, the flesh food, the casualness and indifference to dirt, the thousand and one taboos and prescriptions of their religion—if I had known the ordeal would have a term. The other Ambien advised patience. I did not listen to him but went to Klorathy and demanded how long he proposed to "waste his time on these semibrutes." His reply was: "As long as it is necessary."

I consulted with Ambien I, who said he would stay with Klorathy, if "Klorathy would put up with him"—a humility that annoyed me—and I took our surveillance craft, leaving him dependent on Klorathy for transport, and flew up northwards by myself.

This was the first time a Sirian had *openly* travelled into Canopean territory. Klorathy made no attempt to stop me, or discourage me. Yet he did say, quietly, just before I left: "Be careful." "Of what, Klorathy?" "All I know is that our instruments seem to indicate some sort of magnetic disturbance—in my view it would be wiser to stay in the centre of a continent rather than anywhere at sea level." I thanked him for the warning.

ADALANTALAND

Millennia had passed since I travelled this way with Ambien I. From the height I was flying, the terrain mostly showed little signs of change, but there were areas sometimes several minutes flying time across (I was in a Space Conqueror Type III, long since obsolete) where below me was nothing but savagely torn and tumbled rock, stumps of trees, overthrown or shaken mountains. I remembered that the cities of the middle seas, which I had flown over with Ambien, had been shaken into ruin and wondered if this was in fact a particularly seismic time on this always precarious planet. Flying over the areas of islands and broken waters that had been, and would be again, the great empty ocean separating the Isolated Northern Continent and the central landmass, I thought I saw that some islands were quite new, as if they had just been upthrust from the ocean bed. The island that had been covered by that marvellous city surrounded by its great ships had been under the ocean and risen out of it again. It had some rather poor villages on it now. But I wanted to see that area of great inland seas again, and I flew over and around it seeing everywhere near the rocky sunlit shores, ruins and collapsed buildings, some gleaming up from under the waters. But the region of these seas was rich and fruitful and would soon again put forth cities, as it had done so often before. It was, however, discouraging to see how transient things were and must always be on this planet, and I fell into a state of mind unusual for me, of the generalised discouragement known by us Sirians as "existential problem melancholia." For what I felt was nothing more than the *emotional* expression of our philosophic dilemmas: what were the purposes of plannings, our manipulations, our mastery of nature? I was in the grip of a vision—as I hung there in my little bubble of a spacecraft, looking down at that magically beautiful place (for Rohanda was always that), the brilliant blue seas like great irregular gems in their setting of warm reddish soil —of impermanence, as if this little glimpse of a small part of a small planet was an encapsulation of the whole Galaxy that always, despite its illusions of great stretches of time where nothing much changed, nevertheless did change, always, and it was not possible to grasp a sense of it as lasting or of anything as permanently valuable . . . I hovered above that lovely but desolating scene for as long as I could bear it and then directed myself northwards again to Adalantaland, for I wanted to see what a peaceful realm run by women would be like on Rohanda in its time of rapid degeneration. Analyses of Adalantaland are plentifully available in our libraries, so I shall confine myself only to my present purposes.

It was a large island among several on the edge of the main landmass. While the middle areas of Rohanda at that time could be described as too hot for comfort, the northern and southern parts were equable and warm and very fruitful. It was a peaceful culture, rather indolent perhaps, and hedonistic, but democratic, and the line of women who were its rulers governed by "the grace of Canopus," which were a set of precepts engraved on stones and set up everywhere over the island. There were three main rules, the first saying that Canopus was the invisible but powerful lawgiver of Rohanda and would punish transgressions of its Rule; the second that no individual should consider herself better than another, nor should any individual enslave or use another in a degrading way; the third that no person should take more from the general stock of food and goods than was absolutely necessary. There were many subdivisions of these precepts. I moved freely over this well-governed and pacific land, and found these laws were known by everyone and on the whole kept, though the third was perhaps rather freely interpreted. I was told that the Mothers had other, secret, laws given them direct by "those from the stars." I was not considered as emanating from "the stars." It happened that in physical type I was not far off from the Adalantaland general type: they were mostly fair-haired people, pale-skinned, with eyes often blue, and on the whole tending towards a large build, and plenty of flesh. My height and thinness caused much concern for my general health. I spent time with the currently reigning Queen, or Mother, who lived no better than her subjects, nor was in any way set up over them. The focus of my special curiosity was one that could not be shared with them. I wanted to know how it was that this realm managed to be so well ordered, lacking crime and public irresponsibility, when these qualities were not to be expected of Rohanda in this time of a general falling-off. The beautiful and generous and genial Queen, or Mother, of course did not realise that this paradise of hers—for she and her subjects saw their land as one, and knew they were much envied by more barbarous races—was not an apex of a long growth from a low culture to a high one, but was nothing but a shadow of former greatness that lay on the other side of that Catastrophe, the failure of the Lock. There were hints in old legends of a disaster of some sort, and many to do with the "Gods" who were watching over them and "would come again." They had come in the time of this Queen's great-great-great-great-grandmother. From the description I recognised Klorathy. He had given fresh precepts, somewhat at an angle to those used previously; had—also—rebuked, and had strengthened in them their purpose towards the maintenance of their fair and smiling land.

And the secret laws? The Queen was not at all reluctant to share these with me; the only reason, she said, that they were not given out to everyone, and written up on the public stones, was that they were so precise and pernickety—yes, I recognised Canopus here!—ordinary people, preoccupied as they had to be with ordinary life, could not be expected to bother with them.

These precepts were the same as those given to us Sirians by Canopus, used by us and already considered as Sirian, at least to the extent that it was hard to remember their Canopean origin. I even remember a feeling of affront and annoyance at hearing the Queen describe the things as from Canopus, remember chiding myself for this absurdity.

The Queen took time and trouble to explain these regulations, which were all to do with what substances would protect and guard, how to use them, the times to use them, the exact disposition of artefacts and how and when, certain types of place to avoid and others to seek out . . . and so on. There is no point in listing them, for they were not always the same, but changed, and we had been told how to change them and in accordance with what cosmic and local factors.

But I noted that in what the Queen was telling me were inaccuracies. Slight divergencies from prescription. It was a disturbing experience for me to sit quietly listening while this competent and friendly lady explained to me the conduct that must be followed on Adalantaland to preserve health, sanity, and correct thinking, when I was using these same laws of conduct myself . . . but using them not exactly in the same manner. My observances were more likely to be correct, since I had only just left Klorathy, who checked them with me. Yet he had told me not to alter this Queen's practices; had not mentioned them. So I said nothing.

The Queen wanted to know what part of Rohanda I came from, and I spoke to her of the Southern Continents, of which she had heard. In fact her mariners had visited the coasts of both—this interested me, of course, and from what she said, it seemed that these coasts had been explored by them. But recently she had forbidden voyages far afield: there was disquiet and alarm abroad, had I not felt it? People had not spoken to me of their fears and forebodings? Well, if not, that was because I was a foreigner and it would be discourteous to spread such unhappy states of mind. But as for her, the Queen, and the other Mothers who governed this land, they felt that indeed there was reason to fear. Had I not heard of the great earthquakes that had swallowed whole cities down southwards? Of storms and tempests where normally the climate was equable. . . . So she talked, her great blue eyes, which reminded me of the seas I had been hovering over only a few R-days before, roaming restlessly about, worried, full of trouble . . . and I was experiencing a lesson in the *relative*, for she was in fear for *her* culture, *her* beautiful land, while I had recently been contemplating the destruction of planets, cities, cultures, realms—and flying over large tracts of earthquake-devastated landscape in a frame of mind not far off that used for contemplating the overthrow of termite-queendom, or the extinction of a type of animal for some reason or other.

I left Adalantaland regretfully and travelled slowly to the coast where I had left my space bubble, not wanting to leave this realm of such lush and full fields, such orchards and gardens, so many orderly and well-kept towns—and not wanting to say goodbye either to these handsome people. I was thinking, as I went, about their third precept, that they must not take more than they could *use*, for it seemed to me to go to the heart of the Sirian dilemma . . . *who* should use *what* and *how much* and *when* and *what for?* Above all what for!

THE "EVENTS"

The scene that I saw when I looked down from my space bubble, and the thoughts in my mind then are very clear to me: it is because after the "events," as soon as I knew that everything I had surveyed was chaos and desolation, I took pains to retrieve my mental picture of it all so that it was clear in my mind, ready for instant recall.

I could see a great deal: below me the fair and smiling islands of those blessed latitudes . . . on one hand the great ocean that spread to the Isolated Northern Continent, with its unstable family of islands, now all visible and alive . . . to the north, the little patch of ice and snow whose very existence showed the sensitive and exact nature of Rohanda's relation with her sun . . . southwards the coasts of the main landmass stretched—at first balmy and delightful, then rocky and parched—to the burning regions of the middle latitudes . . . and inland from these coasts, the vastnesses of the mainland itself, where I had never been, though Ambien I had. I longed to see them. Such forests and jungles were there!—so he said: he had darted back and forth across and about in his space-craft and even so advantaged had found it impossible to easily mark the bounds of these forests. The beasts in the forests!—such a multitude of them and such a variety of species, some of them even now unknown to us. And beyond the forests, on great plateaux lying under blue and crystal skies, the cities that Ambien I spoke of. These were not the mathematical cities of the Great Time, but were remarkable and amazing places, often with systems of government unknown to us, some of them benign and comfortable to live in, and some tyrannous and very wicked. There they lay, a day's easy journey in my little craft, and it seemed that Canopus did not mind my travels in their dispensation, and so there was nothing to stop my going there at once . . . nothing except my state of mind, which was most unpleasant, and every moment getting worse.

I did not know what was happening to me. We have all of us experienced those shadows from the future we call "premonitions." I was not unfamiliar with them. It seemed as if I was inside a black stuffy room or invisible prison, where it was hard even to draw breath, and from where I looked down on those brilliant scenes of sea and land that seemed to baffle and reject my sight, *because* of my state of mind. I kept thinking of Klorathy's warning . . . just as the thought formed that his warnings were filling me with some-thing I had only just recognised as terror, it happened. . . .

What happened?

I have been asked often enough by our historians, delighted that just for once they had an actual eyewitness to such an event. And I always find this first moment hard.

There was an absolute stillness that seemed to freeze all of the scene below me. The air chilled—all at once, and instantaneously. I looked wildly around into the skies around me, with their Rohandan clouds and vast blue spaces—and could see nothing. Yet I was stilled, checked, *silenced* in all my being.

Suddenly—only that is not the word for the instantaneous nature of this happening—I was in total darkness, with the stars swinging about around me. I was in starlight. And now the stillness had been succeeded by a hissing roar. I looked down to see if the scene under me had also been vanished away, and saw that I was in movement—my craft was being spun about so that I could not see steadily. Yet I was able to make out the coastlands of the main landmass, and the islands, one of which was Adalantaland. My mind was clear only in flashes—as if lightning lit a landscape and then left it dark. This is why I had no coherent idea *then* of what was happening. Moments of intense clarity, when I was able to work out that Rohanda had turned over on itself, as a globe in a decelerating spin may wobble over—an understanding that this need no more affect the tiny inhabitants on its surface than the microbes of a child's ball know that they are in violent and agitated movement as the ball is flung from hand to hand and bounced here and there, but continue complacently with their little lives— calculations of how this reversal of the planet might affect it . . . all this went on in my mind in those moments of brilliant thought, when that mind in fact worked at a level I have not known since, in between periods of black extinction.

I had no idea how long this thing went on, and can only say now that it was for some hours—so our astronomers have calculated. Suddenly—and again I have to emphasise that this word cannot in any way convey the feeling that the event happened in an order of time not Rohandan—I was back in sunlight. The scene below *did not change*—that is, not for a long moment. And then all at once, flick! just like that, Adalantaland vanished beneath the sea, and a whirlpool formed where it had been. My eyes drawn to that place, darkened in grief for the loss of those people, were neverthe- less aware that all around the periphery of my vision islands were vanishing, leaving their spins of water, or land was rising up—and sometimes islands would plunge under the waters and then almost at once rise up again, seeming to be settled there stable and perma- nent, and then, flick! they disappeared. When I was able to with- draw my immediate grief from Adalantaland, to gain a wider view, I was able to see that all over the great ocean the islands that studded it had gone. And have not come back again since . . . and that is when the Isolated Northern Continent became permanently isolated. Though of course I am using that word relatively: often

enough I have flown from one end of that enormous expanse of
waters, with its few and clustered islands, and remembered those
other times, and thought how at any moment those old islands may
rise again, bare, water-scoured, to begin their slow process of
weathering into fruitfulness and plenty. Not only islands were
vanishing or appearing—everywhere the earth of the mainland was
bulging up and buckling, and the waters were rocking and spouting
and sloshing about as they do when someone jumps heavily into a
water pool. There was a foul mineral smell. The scene grew wilder
as I watched—as I intermittently watched, for I was being spun
about and I could see only in flashes. Spouts of water miles high
rose into the air and crashed thunderously, land spurted upwards
like water, clouds formed in the skies in a swift massing process
that seemed impossible—and then poured down at once in rain.
Suddenly everything below was whitened: the rain had fallen as
snow, and I was in a blizzard being whirled about in shrieking
winds. And yet, immediately afterwards, the white had all gone,
warm rains had washed the snow away from the heaving spurting
boiling surfaces of the globe, and I saw that the ice of the pole
had gone, and where it had been was a spinning whirlpool—and
then the spin of the water was slower, was hardly there, a crust
was forming over it, and the white of the ice cover gleamed again,
and spread, was rapidly growing. Again I was in a thick snowstorm
that seemed to be weighing down my little bubble. I felt that I was
sinking down, was being pressed down, and then again—and with
that same unimaginable suddenness—a wind arose from somewhere and carried me violently off. Of course none of my instruments was working, nor had worked since the start of this violent
re-orientation of Rohanda. I did not know where I was being
sucked or pulled, but felt that it was not any longer in a vortex or
spin but was direct, in a straight line. And I was always inside the
thick swirl of snow that was like no snow I had ever seen anywhere
or on any planet. I knew I was being steadily pressed down by it
and readied myself for a crash. Now that I was able to be more
calm, because of this long steady drive onwards inside the storm,
without sudden twists or dizzyings, I was able to hear again: beyond
the dreadful hush of the snowfall and the howl of the wind that
drove me were the multitudinous sounds of the earth itself, groaning

and shrieking, moaning and grinding . . . this went on for some time, and yet, even as it did, there were sudden spaces or moments within this time when the opposite happened. I mean that I *suddenly* found myself in sun and wetness, clouds of steam arising everywhere and not a trace of snow to be seen anywhere under me: a water world, with spouts of water flung up to the height of my craft, lower now than it was, far too close to the earth, and in that space of—a few minutes? seconds?—I was able to direct my craft upwards, away from the heave and churn of the muddy steamy land under me. And then the snow descended again and the cold was intense and frightful. I lost consciousness, I think, or at least if I did not, the awfulness of the strain has blocked out my memory. For what I remember next is that I had come to rest, and the crystal shell of my little space bubble was hot and glittery with sun. I was beyond rational thought, or decision, and I opened it and stepped out— risking death from a change of atmosphere, though I certainly did not think of that. The sun was what struck me at first. It had a different look to it. Seemed smaller . . . yet not much. Seemed cooler . . . but was that possible? I wondered if I had been tossed off Rohanda altogether and had arrived on another planet. I wondered if the upheavals and tumultuousness had affected my senses . . . my ability to judge . . . even my mind. Yet I held on fast to my first impression, as one does to some idea, quite stubbornly and sometimes it seems almost at random, to steady one in a time of upheaval. I was holding on obstinately to the fact that the Rohandan sun had changed . . . *was* smaller. I was able even to reach out—unclearly and uncertainly—towards the truth, that Rohanda had been driven, or sucked, or pulled, further away from her mother-sun by this cosmic accident she had suffered, and I was with one part of my mind working out the possible results of this. Meanwhile, I was standing by my little crystal bubble on a high mountain that was still "normal" in that it had trees and vegetation on it, though everything leaned about or lay crashed on the earth. I have no idea exactly where this mountain was. I was looking out over a plain where the earth had been convulsed about, because there were cracks in it, some many miles in length, and sometimes miles across, and there were volcanoes and rivers of mingled lava and water opening new beds for themselves. I could hardly breathe for the sulphurous smell. And I had a queer dreamlike vision that lasted only a few moments, of herds of animals—some of which I had never seen, so strange and new to me that I could not believe in them . . . these were running across the plain between the cracks and the spouting geysers and volcanoes, crying out and screaming and trumpeting and raging, and the multitudinous herds poured around the base of the mountain and vanished, and I was left wondering if I *had* seen them, just as I was wondering if I *had* been in that snow, *had* seen the whole globe blotted out by snow . . . and even as I thought about the snow, again it fell—I saw that everywhere in front of me was instantly covered by thick wads of blue and green and yellow ice, which came to the foot of the mountain I was on, and began pressing and squeezing up the sides, with a groaning and a shrieking that echoed the sounds of the unfortunate animals who had fled past a few moments before. And again I was blotted out in thicknesses of snow, that almost at once swallowed up the space bubble so that I only just had time to climb into it and pull over the closure panel. And here I was, not in the dark, for the lights were working, but inside the dark weight of a snowstorm, and silence. Now that it was silent, I understood what an assault my ears had suffered. And I again—what? Slept? Blacked out? Went mad enough that I have no memory of it? And again I can give no idea of how long I was in there. Within the blizzard. Inside—not terror—for that had gone, been driven away by immensities of everything, but a suspension of any ordinary and reliable understanding.

When I was myself again and believed that the snow had stopped falling, and burrowed my way out of the bubble, and leaned on it, holding fast as one does to a solid place in water, because I was as it were floating in loose airy snow, I looked out over an all-white landscape, under a sky that was a light clear fresh blue, lit by the new, more distant, more yellow sun. I seemed to be clear in my mind, and functioning . . . I pushed enough snow off the bubble to free it, tried the instruments, found everything in order, and took off into this new air, which was so sharp and clean again, yet with a metallic tang to it, and flew interminably over white, white, a dazzlingly correct and uniform white, where all hollows and valleys had been obliterated, leaving only peaks that were of bare, scraped rock. But one had a clotted or furred look, as if encrusted with insects of a vast size; when I examined it, I saw a multitude of animals, every imaginable variety of animal, large and small, all in the attitudes of immediate death. They had been frozen in an instant where they had taken refuge from the floods, or the surging ice packs, or the oceans of snow. But on other peaks that I flew past at eye level, there were trees still upright, their branches loaded with frozen birds. And in one place I saw a glittering plume rising into the air just in front of me, and as I came near to it, found it was a geyser that had been frozen so fast it was hanging there with fishes and beasts of the sea solid in it. It sent out a high twanging noise, and snapped and crumpled and fell in a heap on to the white snowy billows below.

The great ocean where the islands had been was not frozen. I saw it then as I have seen it ever since. I was flying across the northerly part, and underneath me was water, where Adalantaland had been, as if it had never been. It was not that there were no islands left anywhere in those seas but that now they were clustered or fringed around the coasts of the Isolated Northern Continent on one side and the main landmass on the other—these last being the Northwest fringes that later played such a part in late Rohandan history.

I wondered that the ocean was not frozen. And even as I flew across the last of the waters before reaching land, I saw ahead of me that the snows were melting there—had already melted in some places, leaving floods and lakes and muddy expanses everywhere. By the time I did reach the mainland, and was flying into it, the snows had all dissolved in water . . . I was flying over a scene of mud and water and new rivers. I could not land anywhere, but went straight across the continent looking down at a soaked and watery scene whose changes I was not able to assess because I had not been that way before. When I reached the opposite coast, on another vast ocean, I was able to see that pressures of some awful intensity had squeezed higher the mountain ranges that run from extreme north to extreme south of the two isolated continents—if one were to imagine these continents shaped in some soft substance, like clay or sand, but on a tiny scale, as on a child's teaching tray, and then pressure applied by some force right down one side of them, so that they buckle up and make high ridges and long mountain chains separated by narrow gorges and highlands, so had those two great continents been affected, and I had to postulate all kinds of pressuring forces deep inside the substance of Rohanda, under the ocean; and the visible signs of these were in the vast waters muddied and full of weed, and crowding jagged icebergs, and a metallic or sulphurous smell. I floated southwards along these tortured mountains seeing how forests and rock and rivers had been heaved up and down and toppled and spread everywhere until I reached the south of the Northern Continent and turned sharply inland to seek out Klorathy and the other Ambien. Again, I was not familiar with the terrain, but could see that, while everything had been soaked, so that lakes and sprawling rivers stained brown with earth lay everywhere, and the landscape was all mud, all earthy water, all swamp and fen and marsh, yet there were expanses of forests that had not been overturned and mountains that seemed intact, if shaken. And in fact it turned out that the southern continents, partly and patchily frozen and soaked and shaken and squeezed, had come off much better than the northern areas, and had not been entirely devastated. I travelled on in clouds of steam that whisked up past my bubble and made turbulence that tossed and spun me, so that I felt as sick as I had done in the tempests of the great disaster, and all the blue Rohandan skies were coiling and churning with cloud. This had been a high, dry, sharp-aired landscape, and it would shortly become so again—yet I descended to where I had left the others through baths of warm steam. They were still there. On a wet muddy plain surrounded by the mountains of the dwarves were the tents and huts of the tribes, and splashing through mud and shallow lakes, the savages were dancing: were propitiating their deity, the earth, their mother, their source, their provenance, their protector, who had unexpectedly become enraged and shown her rage. And so they danced and danced—and continued to dance on, through the days and the nights. When I joined Klorathy, he was exactly where I had left him, seated in the open doorway of his tent, apparently unoccupied, watching the dance of his protégés. And Ambien was near him.

We told each other our experiences: mine more dramatic than theirs: they had been briefly visited by tempests of snow, which had been dissipated almost at once by floods of rain, the earth had shaken and had growled and creaked, some of the mountainsides had fallen and there would be new riverbeds running off the plateau to the oceans.

We pieced together, among us, the following succession of events. The planet had turned over, had been topsy-turvy for some hours, and then righted itself—but not to its old position: Klorathy's instruments, more sensitive than ours, told him that the axis of the earth was at an angle now, and this would mean that as this angled globe revolved about its sun, there would no longer be evenness and regularity in its dispositions of heat and cold, but there would be changes and seasons that we could not yet do more than speculate about. The planet was slightly further away from its sun, too—the Rohandan year would be minimally longer. Many kinds of animals were extinct. The level of the oceans had sharply dropped, because the ice masses of both poles were much enlarged and could be expected to increase. Cities that had been swallowed by the waters before in previous sudden changes would be visible again . . . islands that had vanished under the waves might even be visible, glimmering there in shallower seas . . . and perhaps poor Adalantaland, that vanished happy place, might ring its many bells close enough under the surface for voyagers to hear them on quiet days and nights—so we talked, even then, when we were surrounded by mud and swamp and flying clouds of steam, and the catastrophe was already receding into the past, becoming yet another of the sudden reversals of Rohandan condition. But when I used the word "catastrophe" of what had just happened—a not, after all, inconsiderable happening—Klorathy corrected me, saying that the Catastrophe, or, to use the absolutely accurate and correct word, Disaster, meaning an unfortunate alignment of the stars and their forces, could only properly be applied to a *real* misfortune, a true evolutionary setback, namely, the failure of the Lock. I have already hinted at my impatience with Canopean pedantry. As I saw it. As I sometimes even now cannot help seeing it.

I remember my meek enquiry, which was I am afraid all impertinence, to the effect that *some* might consider recent events catastrophe enough to merit that word, and remember Klorathy's smiling, but firm, reply that: "if one did not use the exact and correct words then one's thinking would soon become unclear and confused. The recent events . . ."—I remember I smiled sarcastically at this little word, "events"— ". . . did not in any fundamental way alter the nature of Rohanda. Whereas the failure of the Lock, and the Shammat delinquency, had affected the planet and would continue to affect it. That was a catastrophe, a disaster. This was unfortunate." And he kept the pressure of his bronze or amber gaze on me, making me accept it.

Which I did. But I was raging with emotion. I thought him cold and dispassionate. I was thinking that a being able to view the devastation of a whole planet with such accurate detachment was not likely to be warmly responsive to a close personal relationship: at the time, that my own personal concerns were being intruded by me did not strike me as shameful, though it does now. I have already said that "hindsight" is not the most comfortable of possible views of oneself or of events. The mention of Shammat affected me—I knew of course that it was all guilt. But while I was clear in my *mind* that our Sirian delinquencies and deceptions that I could not confess to had caused barriers between me and Klorathy, my *emotions* expressed this in anger and a growing irritation with Klorathy, even a dislike. . . .

I left him and went to my own tent, which was set on a high rock, damp but at least not saturated, and sat there by myself, looking down on the weird scene—the savages dancing and singing, on and on, in the splashing brown water and the mud, illuminated by a moon that appeared fitfully among the tumultuous clouds, and vanished amid the mists and fogs. Ambien I came to talk to me. He was conciliatory and gentle, for he knew how I raged and suffered.

He had wanted very much to leave, before the *events* that we were not to call a catastrophe. He had become bored with the inactivity of it all. The life of the savages went on, hunting, and curing hides, and eating their stews and their dried meat, and making clothes and ornamenting them. And Klorathy stayed where he was. He did *not* lecture or admonish them. What had happened was that the head man came to Klorathy one evening and sat down and finally asked Klorathy if he had visited the dwarves, and if there was anything that he could tell them—the savages. And Klorathy answered saying that he had indeed visited the little people and that in his view . . . explaining how he saw things. And then the head man went off and conferred, and days went past, and then he returned and asked again, formally, sitting on the ground near Klorathy, having exchanged courtesies, if Klorathy believed the dwarves could be trusted to keep agreements if they were made—for in the past, so he said, the dwarves had been treacherous and had spilled out of their underground fastnesses and slain the tribes, both men and animals . . . and Klorathy answered this, too, patiently.

What was happening, Ambien I said, was that Klorathy did not make any attempt to communicate what he thought *until he was asked a direct question*—or until something was said that was in fact a question though it was masked as a comment. And Ambien I then went to Klorathy and enquired if this was indeed a practice of Canopus: and whether Klorathy expected to stay there, living on as he did, with these savages, *until they asked the right questions* . . . and if this was Klorathy's expectation, then *why* did he expect the savages to ask the right questions?

To which Klorathy replied that they would come and ask the necessary questions in their own good time.

And *why*?

"Because I am here . . ." was Klorathy's reply, which irritated Ambien I. Understandably. I felt irritated to the point of fury even listening to this report.

Anyway, Ambien I had wanted to go, but could not, since I had the Sirian transport with me. He had in fact gone off to visit the dwarves again, by himself, another colony of them—a foolhardy thing, which had nearly cost him his life. He had been rescued by the intervention of Klorathy, who had only said, however, that "Sirians as yet lacked a sense of the appropriate."

Then had begun the "events" that were not to be described as more than that.

At last, I had arrived back, and he, Ambien I, could not express how he had felt when he saw the glistening bubble descend through all that grey steam, because he had believed me to be dead. And of course it was "a miracle" that I had survived—to use a term from our earlier epochs.

We stayed together that night, in emotional and intellectual intimacy, unwilling to separate, after such a threat that we might never have been together again at all.

We decided to leave Klorathy.

First, having pondered over what Ambien I had said about questions, how they had to be asked, I went to Klorathy and asked bluntly and directly about the Colony 10 colonists, and why we, Sirius, could not have them.

He was sitting at his tent door. I sat near him. We were both on heaps of damp skins . . . but the clouds of steam were less, the earth was drying, the thundering and trickling and running of the waters already had quietened. It was possible to believe that soon these regions would again be dry and high and healthy.

"I have already told you," said Klorathy, "that these colonists would not be appropriate. Do you understand? Not appropriate for Sirians, for the Sirian circumstances."

"Why not?"

He was silent for a while, as if reflecting inwardly. Then he said: "You ask me, over and over again, the same kind of question."

"Why don't you answer me?"

Then he did something that made me impatient. He went into his tent and came out with some objects—the same things that Ambien I and I had been supplied to maintain our balance on this difficult planet.

I at first believed that because of the recent "events," certain changes in our practice were necessary, and I readied myself to take in instruction, since I knew that exactness was necessary here, and that it would not do for me to overlook even the smallest detail. (I had told him—and heard his dismayed yet patient sigh—about Adalantaland falling off in this respect, how they had not maintained the care needed to make these practices work.)

I watched what he did. Certain kinds of stone, of natural substance, some colours, shapes, were laid before him and handled and ordered. But I was watching very carefully and saw that he made no changes in the ritual I had been using.

"So nothing has had to be changed?" I asked, knowing my voice was rough and antagonistic. "Not even the recent *events*, and the distancing of the earth from its sun, and all the other differences, are going to necessitate changes in what we have to do?"

"No," he said. "Not yet. Though perhaps later, when we have monitored the exact differences. In climate, for instance. And of course the magnetic forces will be affected. . . ."

"Of course," I said, sarcastically, as before.

He continued to handle the objects, precisely, carefully. I watched his face, the amber, or bronze face, long, deeply moulded, with the strong eyes that were so closely observing the movements of his hands.

And I continued to sit there, arms locked around my knees, watching, maintaining a dry tight smile that was all criticism, and he continued patiently and humbly to manipulate his artefacts.

I did not understand him. I thought this was a way of putting me off, of saying wordlessly that he would not answer me.

As I formulated this thought, he said: "No, that is not it. But if you want to understand, then I suggest you stay on here for a time."

"For how long?" And answered myself with, "For as long as necessary, I suppose!"

"Yes, that's it."

"And what sort of progress have you made? Are the savages and dwarves in an alliance? Are they ready to stand against the Shammats?"

"I think it is likely the dwarves have been sealed into their caves, and that we may never see them again."

The way he said this made my emotions riot. The end of a species —a race—the end of the Lombi strain on Rohanda and the 22 technicians.

He said: "Well, we have to accept these reverses."

"Then why are you staying on? The reason for your being here is gone—swallowed by *the events*."

"The tribes are still here!"

"So you are not with them just because of the old hostility between them and the dwarves?"

"I am here as I often am with all kinds of peoples . . . races . . . species, at certain stages in their development."

I did understand that here was a point of importance: that if I persisted, I would learn.

"You want me to stay?" This was a challenge: deliberate, awkward, hostile.

"Yes, I think you should stay."

He had not said: "Yes, I want you to stay."

I got up and left him. I told Ambien I that I intended to leave. And in the morning, having said goodbye to Klorathy, we took off in our space bubble. We surveyed, rapidly, the ravages of the "events" on both southern continents, and then went home to our Mother Planet.

THE LOMBIS. MY THIRD ENCOUNTER WITH KLORATHY

For some time I had little to do with Rohanda, which was judged by our experts as too much of a bad risk, and I was allotted work elsewhere. This was, too, the period of the worst crisis in Sirian self-confidence: our experiments everywhere, sociological and biological, were minimal.

The populations on our Colonised Planets were at their lowest, too.

As for me, I was pursuing thoughts of my own, for I could not get out of my mind the old successes of Canopus in forced evolution, and while whole strata of our Colonial Service and nearly all our governing class were publicly asking: What for? I was wondering if they would give room to such emotions (but they were called ideas, as heart-cries of this kind so often are, and the more so, the more they are fed by emotions and sentiments) if they had been able to watch, as I had done, creatures not much better than apes transformed into fully civic and responsible beings within such a short time. I shared these thoughts with Ambien I, with whom I was once again working, but our Empire was less tolerant then than it is now—or so I believe and hope—and the kind of social optimism that inspired me was classed in some quarters as "shallow irresponsibility" and "sociological selfishness." This may be the right place to remark that I had long since learned that if one is entertaining unpopular ideas, one has only to keep quiet and wait for the invisible wheels to turn that will bring those ideas back as the last word in intelligent and forward-looking thinking.

Meanwhile, I got on with my work. It happened that I was in that part of the Galaxy where the transplanted Lombis were on Colonised Planet 25. I had not thought of them from the old time to this; but I made a detour from curiosity. It could be said that the whole Lombi experiment had been inutile. They had been carefully preserved from any contact with more evolved races, except for very rare reconnaissance trips by Colony 22 personnel to see if it were possible to keep a certain pristine social innocence that might be of use in "opening up" new planets. Yet we had nevertheless ceased to colonise new planets in the total—may I say reckless?—way that had distinguished our policies up till then: we acquired a new possession only after long and careful assessment. Our interest in the Lombis continued to the extent that we wished to monitor the possible development of evidence of a craving for "higher things." From the spacecraft I made contact home to ask permission to make a small experiment of my own: it would not have been given me if the Lombis had not virtually been written off as useful material.

We had sent no technicians there for over a thousand S-years. Their life-spans had remained at roughly two hundred R-years. This meant that as individuals they could have no memory at all of visitations "from the skies."

I ordered a rapid survey of Planet 25 sunside and nightside, at maximum speed so that we would not be observed as more than a meteorite—we were not visible at all on sunside when moving— and then, having chosen a populous area, hovered in full view for some hours, while crowds collected.

I made as impressive a descent from the aircraft as could be devised. Unfortunately I had no formal wear with me on this working trip, but I devised a long cloak of some white insulation material, and made the most of my not exactly profuse yellow hair —it is not that I have ever wanted to be more hairy or *furred* than I am, but the yellow or gold-haired species always evoke awe, because of our rarity. I floated to earth from the spacecraft, and saw a multitude of the poor beasts fall to their faces before me with a deep and sorrowful groan, which did touch me, I confess, accustomed as I am to the awe so easily evoked in uncivilised races.

I had prepared all kinds of suitably vague replies to possible questions, but found that once I had said I had "come from the skies" and was their friend, that was enough: awe is a great inhibitor of intelligent questioning.

They remembered—or their ceremonies and songs and tales did—"the shining ones," and what dread they still kept from the old time on the other planets, I stilled by the most solemn promises that I would not take any of them away with me when I left.

And what was it they were so afraid of being taken away from? The reply to that is ironical . . . is sad . . . is a comment on more than just the situation of the Lombis . . . my so long, my so very long career in the Service furnishes me with several similar situations . . .

But first a general comment on their customs and mores.

They had not evolved much; any more than had the parent stock on Planet 24.

The prohibitions against covering themselves, and eating cooked and prepared food had not vanished, but had reversed; it was now for their ceremonies that they had to be naked and eat raw meat and roots and fruit. They lived as before in various types of crude shelter, hut or cave; they hunted; they wore skins; they used fire. Their basic unit was the family and not the tribe: this seemed to be retarding them. At least, as I travelled about that planet, which was adequately endowed with plant and animal life, though meagre compared to other planets—Rohanda, for instance—I was comparing these animals with the savages of the high plateaux whom Klorathy had thought it worthwhile to instruct: and such was the contrast that I was wondering for the first time if the superiority of those others was due to something innate, *a superiority of a different kind and classification* to those we Sirians could use, and which Klorathy and officials on his level would be able to measure? The point was that the Lombis had no capacity for development, or seemed not to have.

I was examining these short, squat, half-furred creatures, with their immensely powerful shoulders and arms, living in their groups of three, or four—up to seven or eight, but no more—each group jealously suspicious of its patch of hunting ground, its wild fruit trees, its sources of roots and vegetables, able to mingle with other groups only on ritual occasions when they all crowded together— and remembered with admiration things that I had scorned. Where were the customs that can make even hundreds of individuals a mutually supporting and culturally expanding unit? Where the intricate ceremonial dances? The finely worked garments with their fringes, their ornamentation, the delicately used feathers? The necklaces of carved bones and stones? The instruction of the young through tales and and apprenticeship? The specialisation of indi- viduals, according to innate talent, into storytellers, craftsmen, hunters, singers? Where was . . . but I could see nothing here anything like the skills and knowledge of the Navahis and Hoppes.

Now I come to what was painful and pitiful in their situation. How often as I travel from one of our Colonised Planets to another am I forced to remember the *natural* advantages of Rohanda, with her close and shining moon, her nightside that is crammed with brilliant star clusters?

This planet was a dark one, by nature and position. No moon here. The Lombis must have had somewhere in their gene-memory the knowledge that nights could be lit with infinite variation from a star hanging so close it seemed like a creature, a living being— and changing from a full and bright disc to the tiniest of yellow cracks one had to peer towards and watch for. . . . The Lombis had known what it was to wait for that moment when a sun seems to slide away into dark—and then up flash the stars, giving light when a moon is *temporarily* absent.

Not only was there no moon, but the nightside looked out into an almost empty sky—black upon black. In one or two places there was a faint sprinkling of light, stars far beyond our Galaxy, more like a slight greying of the night. And their sun was small and distant compared with the rumbustious Rohandan sun from which one may have to shelter, even now when it is further away than it was.

The Lombis' "shining ones" were now these infinitely faint and nearly invisible stars. Their old festivals of the full moon took place once a year, when a vast windy plain became filled with groups of these animals who travelled long distances to be there— and they stood in their family groups, lifting their flat sorrowful faces up to their black night, and sang of "shining ones."

And their sun was a "shining one," too, but their worship of it was ambiguous and double, as if it was an impostor, or tried to claim more than was due.

When our spaceship descended, a crystal and sparkling globe that evoked from them memories or half-memories buried in them by their environment, it was as if an original primal light had suddenly appeared to them. Oh, those black stuffy nights . . . those interminable unaltering nights, that seemed to settle on the night-side with the sun's disappearance like a physical oppression. A complete black, a heavy black, where a fire burning outside a cave or inside a leafy shelter seemed to hold back a felt and tangible pressure of darkness. I have never experienced anything like night on Planet 25. Never been on a planet where nothing could be done after sunset. In the daytime the Lombis ran about, and attended to their sustenance, but at night they gathered with the first sign of the sun's going into their groups and pressed together around their little fires, cowering and waiting for that moment when a rock, or a leaf, would emerge greyly from the thick black and tell them that once again they had survived the extinction of the light.

I left as soon as I could, making a dramatic exit from the planet, which they took on their faces, thanking me for my gracious appearance to them and my love for them. Yet I had promised nothing, told them nothing, given nothing: so easy it is to be "a high shining thing"!—and, speeding thankfully away from that oppressive place, I was remembering the apes on Rohanda under Canopean tutelage, and again my old dream, or if you like, *ambition* revived in me, and I wondered if I could not persuade Canopus now to part with some of those skilled colonists, the Giants: after all, a considerable time had passed.

If nothing could be improved in the Lombis, what was the point of keeping them as they were?

I sent in a report on my return home, reminding my superiors of the Lombis' remarkable physical strength: this was on the lines of what they would have expected from me. Meanwhile, I decided on guile, but nothing beyond what I believed then, and believe now, to be legitimate: only a question of interpreting my standing orders rather more liberally than would have been expected of me.

Our relations with Canopus had been limited for some time, because of our cutback in colonial development.

I summoned a meeting of my peer group, the Five, reminded them that it was our policy to maintain full liaison with Canopus, and asked permission to apply for a rendezvous with Klorathy: after all, it had come from them, originally, though of course the idea had been in my mind, that I should maintain contact with Klorathy. The fact that it had not led to anything then, or did not seem to have led to anything, did not mean there could never be benefits for us. I felt no enthusiasm in them, but I had become used to being the odd one out among the Five, always slightly at an angle to current norms of thought. They did not criticise me for this: it was recognised to be my role, or function. Nor did they actively discourage me now, beyond saying that since Canopus could not solve her own problems, she was unlikely to contribute to the solution of ours. This was in line with our attitude at that time; the thriving planets of Canopus, her busy trade routes, her enterprise and industriousness, was being classed by us as "superficiality and lack of experiential and existential awareness." I quote from a learned journal of that time.

The invitation I got from Klorathy was to meet him on their Planet 11. I was first gratified, since I had long wanted to see this planet that we had heard was "important" to Canopus and unlike any other known to either their Empire or ours. And then I found myself succumbing to suspicion: why Planet 11 and not Planet 10? For Klorathy must believe I was still after his Giants!

Their Planets 10 and 11 were neighbours: planets of the same sun. I even thought of making a landing on 10, with the excuse of power trouble, but decided to go on, and the first thing I saw on 11 was a group of Giants walking from the terminal to a hovercar. I told myself that I should put aside my readiness for suspicion: but wondered if Klorathy's plans for me to see the Giants here, at work and occupied, was another way of refusing me. By now I had got into my own hovercar.

What I could see from the windows was a flat featureless landscape, greyish in colour, under a greyish sky. The sun was pale and large. As I looked, the sun plunged out of sight. A reddish disc appeared over the opposite horizon. A moment later, close to it, came a smaller bilious green disc. These two moved fast across a lurid sky, giving me a sensation of whirling rotation. Looking out made me feel queasy, so I read the information sheet on the wall.

It said that this planet was a well-lit one, with two fast-moving moons, and its nightside well starred. It had no seasons, but had zones of differing climatic conditions, being generally warm and mild with extremes of cold only at the poles, which were left uninhabited. Visitors should not be surprised to find that most long-term inhabitants wore little or no clothes. They might find they needed more sleep than usual, this being the most common reaction to the fast alternations of light and dark. They would probably lose their appetites for a while. Adaptation might be slow, but a longer acquaintanceship with the planet would . . .

As an old hand at interpreting these benign messages, I resigned myself to an uncomfortable time. And in fact fell asleep, for when I woke up it was day again, and we were still skimming over a grey-green surface, under a grey sky. I was looking for something on the lines of the mathematical cities of old Rohanda: on a new planet I was always on the watch for them: they had perhaps become something of a fixation with me. My mental picture of the Canopean Empire included planets covered with these fabulous, these extraordinary cities. I knew there were none on the Canopean Mother Planet. . . . *But why not?* I had asked Klorathy, one evening among the tents of the savages, where I might see these cities and he said: "At the present time, nowhere." What I saw now was nothing but a dreary sameness, with at more or less regular intervals rough dwellings like sheds, which I supposed to be some sort of storage shed. And then I saw that outside some were

Giants, and had glimpses of a type of creature that did not attract me at all.

Just as I had understood that these dwellings were what I could expect to see on this planet, and that there were probably no cities, the hovercar stopped suddenly, near one of the structures, and Klorathy came out of it. It was a single-storey building, flat roofed, surrounded by a type of low rough greyish grass, which was clearly the characteristic vegetation. As I entered the place, dark descended again.

I and Klorathy were alone in a rectangular room, painted white, which was a relief after the dim colours of the sky and the landscape, lit by lines of soft wall lights that automatically came on and went off as the daylight and dark alternated outside.

Because we were alone I at once began to hope for the exchange of understandings that I associate with real companionship, but it was not to be. My set of mind forbade it: it was defensive, and critical; and my physical state forbade it, too, for I was feeling sick and a little giddy.

This shack, or shed, had in it some low seats and a table. The window apertures and the doorway had screens that could be pulled over them, but they were open now and Klorathy said at once: "Better if you do not shut out the outside: otherwise you won't get used to it."

I submitted. I sat down. On the table was a meal. Klorathy said I would feel better if I ate at once, and I tried to do so, but could not get a mouthful down. Meanwhile, he ate and I watched. The food was standard galactic fare.

We were sitting opposite each other, the low table between us. He was smiling and easy, I on my best official behaviour, because it was a way of holding myself together.

I remember thinking that connoisseurs of the contrasts so plentifully offered by the Imperial experience would have found the sight of us two piquant: Klorathy, the bronze man, so strong, well built, solid, with me, who am usually described—affectionately and otherwise—as "a little wisp of a thing," with my yellow locks and my "luminously pale" or "unhealthily pallid" skin—as the case might be. A good deal of our art, the more popular forms of it, dealt with such contrasts, which are found endlessly entertaining, particularly when suggestive or openly sexual. I am not above finding it so myself! But at the time I wanted only to lie down, and in fact, did drop off to sleep suddenly, and woke to see through the apertures, in the full Planet 11 light, contrasts rather stronger than anything I and Klorathy could provide. There was another shed not far away, and outside it two Giants, twice Klorathy's size and nearly three times my size, one a totally black man, shining in the pale lemon glare, the other a rich chocolate brown, both virtually naked. I had always seen them clothed, because during conferences everyone made sure of being well clothed, regardless of the local climate, for the sake of giving least offence during occasions that were always quite rich enough opportunities for annoyance or criticism. They were magnificent men: I have never seen anything like them. But they were in a group of creatures half their size, who seemed like frail and pale insects—that was the impression they made on me.

As I looked, the dark swallowed everything, and almost at once the two moons appeared, large and small, lighting everything with a strong yellow glare. Their colours seemed different from when I had seen them in the hovercar, and again I dropped off to sleep, with the strain of it all, and when I woke it was light, and Klorathy was outside, talking to a group of the "insects." They were not much different in plan from the physical structure common throughout our Galaxy.

They were in fact not very short, being taller than myself, but seemed so, because they were so extremely thin and light in build, and of a silvery-grey colour that made one believe them transparent when they were not. They had no hair on their tall domed heads. Each hand—and it was their hands one had to take note of first— had ten very long fingers, nailless, giving the impression of bunches of tentacles always in movement. They had three eyes, quite round, bright green, with vertical black pupils. There was a pattern of nostrils—simple holes—in the centre of their flat faces, three, or four or even more. No nose. And no mouth at all.

I was glad that I was able to examine them from a little distance, and even more glad that Klorathy was not there, because I have never been able to overcome an instinctive abhorrence for creatures dissimilar to my own species. This has been my greatest single handicap as a Colonial Servant. Attempts to overcome the weakness have cost me more than any other effort, such as learning languages and dialects, and having to acclimatise myself to places like this Colony 11, with its rapid rotation that one could feel and its violent alternations of light.

Despite my repugnance, I was able to watch Klorathy's lips in movement and his animated face, but could not see how *they* talked, with no mouth. After a time the same two Giants rejoined the group and Klorathy came in to rejoin me.

I could see no sign in him of repugnance.

Without speaking, he pulled the low seats to a window, and we sat side by side and observed the two Giants and the "insect people."

As I was thinking this unflattering description of them, and looking at the tentacles that seemed to flow around them and in the air around their heads, Klorathy said: "You are wrong. They are more highly evolved than any but one of our peoples."

"More than the Giants?" I could not help sounding sarcastic, the contrast between the noble and handsome black men and the "insects" was so great.

"They complement each other," was the reply.

And he looked at me, leaning forward to impress on me the force of his amber gaze.

I could not prevent myself sighing—it was impatience, and also tiredness. This atmosphere was exhausting—not the chemical balance of it, though it had slightly less oxygen than I was used to, but suddenly again the sun had gone, and now there was one moon shining blood orange this time, and then appeared the little moon, a sort of greenish colour, and the scene we had been watching, of low greyish grass, the two enormous black Giants, and the cluster of the others, was lit by a horrible reddish light, and the Giants seemed to be made of blood, and the shapes of the "insects" were absorbed, and all I could see was a mass of waving tentacles. I abruptly left my seat and turned my face inwards.

I said, "I don't think Colony 11 suits me." And tried to make it humorous.

He said nothing and I asked: "And you?"

"I spend a good deal of time here."

"Why?"

"At this time, for our present needs, this planet is important to us."

I understood that this reply was specific, and contained information that I wanted—had been reaching out for. But I felt ill and was discouraged; my strongest thought was that if after so many ages I still could not control an instinctive response to creatures physically different, then it was time I gave it all up and retired!

"It is not the physical difference as such," said Klorathy.

"Well then? I suppose they talk with their tentacles?"

"No. Their tentacles are sensors. They sense the variations in the atmosphere with them."

"And I suppose they use telepathy?"

We had no races in all our Empire who were telepathic, but had heard there were such races, and believed that Canopus had several. I was being sarcastic again, but Klorathy said, "Yes. They are telepathic. The Giants talk like you and me. The others in their own way. The two species get on well enough."

"And they have no mouths." I could not help a shudder.

"Have you not noticed something quite unique about this planet?"

"No. All I know is that it makes me feel very sick indeed, and I am going to leave it."

I looked out again. The moons were in the sky, but the sun was, too. The moons, sunlit, were faintly green and yellow in a grey sky, and each sent off a glow of illuminated gases.

"Wait just a little."

"There are no towns. No cities."

"And there are no crops growing. Haven't you noticed?"

"Ah! The Giants have given up eating!"

"No. We import enough food for them. But the people here do not eat."

"They live on air," I expostulated.

"Exactly so. Their tentacles assess the ingredients of the air and they breathe it in according to what is available at any given moment."

I absorbed this. It gave me a dismayed, cold feeling. It is not that I am, as our saying goes, eaten by my food, but it does not come easily to imagine life without any at all.

"And the Giants are teaching them, as they did the apes on Rohanda?"

"No. I told you," he said gently. "They are a balance for each other. Together they make a whole."

"In relation to what?"

As I said this I realised I had come out with a real question: one that he had been waiting for me to ask. At once he replied: "In relation to *need.*"

And my disappointment made me snap out: "Need, need, need. You always say need. What need?"

He did not reply. While I was wrestling with *my* need to formulate the right question, I fell asleep again, and when I woke up the moons of Colony 11 were absent altogether. The stars were many and bright, though, and I stood looking out into the night, feeling soothed and comforted, but not for long, for soon up sprang the larger moon, and the light was green and metallic and very unpleasant, and I decided at that moment to leave. I could not see Klorathy.

On the table was a large white tablet, and on it Klorathy had written: "The exact disposition of usefulness of this planet according to Need will change in twenty Canopean days. If you feel able to stay until then, I think you should. If not, then perhaps you may care to meet me on Shikasta (Rohanda, if you insist) in the city of Koshi on the eastern side of the central landmass. I have ordered the hovercar to take you to the space-port if you want."

It was waiting. I got into it, shut my eyes so as not to see any more of this nauseating planet and had thankfully left it before there could be another descent of its lurid and always different night.

Twenty Canopean days make a Sirian year. I attended to some other tasks and then went to Rohanda.

KOSHI

Instructions from Canopus—"may we be permitted to suggest"—arrived well before I left, and there was plenty in them to make me think. First, there was a change in the protective practices, or rituals. A sharp one, greater than any previous change. I had begun to take for granted certain basic usages that did not alter—nor could, I had thought—but now everything was different. I will not trouble to detail these practices, which were to change again and again thereafter. But it was emphasised that these were of importance, that their exact and accurate practice was vital, and that I should not be tempted to alter them, not for any reason at all, nor at the behest of any person whatsoever, no matter his or her apparent credentials. I am underlining here what was underlined. Certain artefacts were provided for my use. Secondly, I must remember that the planet was now under the domination, for all apparent purposes, of Shammat, and I must be on my guard: this was particularly true of the cities on the eastern part of the central landmass, and Koshi was as bad as any of them. Thirdly, I must remember that the planet, since its axis had been set on a slant, had seasons—Canopus believed that one of our own planets had seasons?—and this had much affected the general temperament, already, of course, thoroughly perverted since the Catastrophe of the failure of the Lock. Fourthly, the predominant stock was now a mix of the old giants and the old natives, with admixtures unplanned and planned from other genes (was that a reminder of my deceptions and errors, I had to wonder), and this hybrid, though physically vigorous, was nevertheless psychologically affected because of a sharp reduction in general life-span, and resulting dislocation of expectations for a certain life-span, and the fact. Fifthly, I should remember that a symptom of the general worsening and corruption was that females had been deprived of equality and dignity, and while I would be able to enter Koshi as a traveller without attracting too much attention, once there I would have to choose my role with the greatest possible care. . . .

There was a good deal more, too. I made a detour to visit our Planet 13 that had climatic seasons. How did Canopus know so much about us? Again I was prompted to brood about a wonderful espionage system with equipment beyond anything we could imagine. Planet 13's disabilities were a result of a hotheaded, and to my mind irresponsible, phase of our early Empire. The counsels of maturer minds in our Colonial Service had been unable to prevent a decision to propel a certain planet, then in orbit with several others around a vast gaseous planet, away from its station there, and into orbit around 13, a rich and fruitful planet, where it could make use of 13's natural resources of water and food to balance its own barrenness. The point was that this thoroughly dreary little world was loaded with every kind of desirable mineral. It was not that I—and my faction—did not want, just as much as the hotheads, to get our hands on these mineral riches but that we were not prepared to go to such lengths, take such risks. I maintain still that *we* were right: they that *they* were . . . The propulsion of 14 was a success. It arrived to take up its orbit around 13, again a planet's planet, but its "pull" caused cataclysms and catastrophes on 13, disturbing its balance, and making it slant on its axis. There were various species of animal on 13, none particularly attractive, but I have always believed in and supported policies that cause as little damage to indigenous races as possible. The upsets on 13 wiped out millions and completely changed the patterns of fertility —I see that I am talking like Klorathy, when he referred to the horrific cataclysms on Rohanda as the "events." As far as *we* were concerned, these unfortunate effects on 13 were enough to prove our policy correct: but there is no arguing that 14 has been producing minerals enough to supply all our Empire ever since.

All I wished, during my stop on 13, was to check briefly on the effects of continual, often violent, climatic change, sometimes from extreme heat to extreme cold. My account of this stopover, which turned out differently—and more dramatically than I expected— will be found in the records, entitled "Under a Punishing Moon."

It is enough to say here that I learned all I needed about these continual variations.

When I arrived over the designated area of Rohanda and looked down, it was with the thought that somewhere here I had been buffeted and swept about in the blizzards and torrents during the "events"—and that below me must be the mountain peak where

I had rested in my space bubble and seen the fleeing herds of animals and heard their sad, lamenting cry. Now I could see a dozen great cities on a vast plain that was coloured green from its grasses, and deeper green where forests spread themselves. But the grassy areas were showing tints of brown and ochre, and I saw at a glance that deserts were threatening—and was able to diagnose at once that these cities were doomed to be swallowed by the sands. As I have seen often enough on some of our own planets, before we became the skilled administrators we now are. I yearned, as I hovered there in my Space Traveller, to simply descend, give the appropriate orders, see them carried out—and then be able to rejoice that these cities, which looked healthy enough from this height, would live and flourish. It gave me the oddest feeling of check and frustration to know that I could *not* do any such thing!— that I must keep quiet about what I knew, and must allow my long experience to remain unvoiced. It is not often that an individual as well ensconced in a career, a way of living, as I am—with patterns of work, friends, companions, offspring, and so much varied experience always ready to be pulled into use—it is very seldom, in fact, that one may be attacked suddenly with such a feeling of futility. Of uselessness . . . which feelings must then at once and inevitably attack much more than an *individual* sense of usefulness. Again I was afflicted—as I had been before, hovering over the Rohandan scene, but such a different one—with existential doubts. It is not possible to be armoured against such feelings.

However, I pushed them away and instructed the crew to hover in the fast-invisible mode over Koshi itself.

I always like to examine a city in this way before actually entering it: one may often see at a glance its condition and probable future.

The first thing to be seen here was that it had experienced recent growth, that it bulged and spread out to the west in large suburbs of shining white villas and gardens. These covered more ground than the old city, which was earth coloured, and composed of densely crammed buildings from which rose tall cone-shaped towers. In other words, there was a disparity between the rich and the poor—a *punishable* disparity, to my mind. Gardens of an ornamental kind spread around the western suburbs. Market gardens lay to the south. To the east, the poor mud-coloured dwellings ended in the shabby-looking semidesert. This great city on its eminence in the plain had lost its vegetation almost entirely. The expanses of browns and yellows that surrounded it had little smears of green in some places, but dust clouds hung over the many roads and paths that ran into the city from all directions. I did not need to know more, and gave the order to set me down on the edge of one of the roads, which we could see were not frequented.

When this was done I experienced the usual exhilaration as I saw the spacecraft disappear like a soap bubble and I was alone and dependent on myself. Also, this was Rohanda, a planet with which I could not help but feel bonded. And I was already able to examine evidences of the "seasons" that were now part of Rohanda's nature: a cold wind blew hard on my back from the north, off ice and snow fields around the pole, so much more extensive than they had been. And the cold would intensify shortly, for it would be the time of the R-year when the northern hemisphere would be revolving on its tilt away from its sun. I was looking forward to experiencing the approaches to a "winter," something new for me.

There was no one on this road I had chosen. It was a minor road, unpaved, not much more than a dirt track, though straight and well ditched. Looking ahead at Koshi all I could see of the rich suburbs were a mass of trees in which I knew the houses were disposed. But the poor part of the town rose high, in a pattern of shapes I had not seen anywhere. Very tall and narrow conical buildings, twenty-one of them, all dun coloured and rather like certain ant heaps I had seen in my time on Isolated Southern Continent I, were crammed together, in a small space, looking as if their bases touched—yet already I could see low habitations, as if crumbling ant heap filled what space there was between the cones. I judged these tall buildings to be ten or eleven storeys high, and wondered at the reasons for building so tall when there was all the space any system of government could possibly need—unless this was the reason: tall tightly populated buildings are easily policed and supervised. So I speculated as I walked firmly in, keeping my eyes open for other travellers, for I wore my usual garb, basic Sirian, and carried over my arm a large piece of cloth that I had been advised I must envelop myself in as a female. I did see a group of individuals approaching, and wrapped myself completely in the black cloak, allowing only my eyes freedom. They were all men—that was the first obvious fact. Probably traders. And of a very varied genetic mix. I fancied I was able to see in them the high moulded cheekbones and wide-set eyes of the old giants, as well as the sturdy set of the natives, but this group of twenty or so were quite extraordinarily mixed, of several skin tones, and with grey and green eyes as well as the more familiar brown. They wore loose trousers, and baggy but belted tunics. I had seen variations on this theme so often, and in so many places, I was able to guess that these were not of the upper class who with quite remarkable uniformity everywhere in the Galaxy choose garments that are unsuitable for physical labour and for easy and unconfined movement: galactic nature is very much the same everywhere. But as I was thinking this, I remembered the garments of the Canopeans, which contradicted this rule.

There were no gardens on this side of the city. The road or track began to be bordered with many shacks and hovels, mostly of timber, and there were swarms of people, none of whom seemed to take any notice of me at all, neither offering greetings nor expecting any. Yet they all, like the travelling group of males, examined me closely and acutely, their eyes obviously skilled at getting a great deal of information in a curtailed glance: I knew that the inhabitants of this city were afraid, and compared what I was seeing with certain arrivals on our own Colonised Planets where our rule had become too harsh, and local officials needed to be checked.

This low huddling of rough buildings, crowds of poorly dressed people, children who I could see were ill-nourished, and an assortment of canines (which I had to resist the temptation to stop and inspect, since on none of our planets had we tamed a similar species) soon terminated abruptly as I reached the circular base of one of the very tall cones, which soared up above me into the blue sky with its floating white clouds that I had so often longed to see again. But I did not feel familiar here. There was a sharp tang of difference, of the alien, that was affecting me sharply, causing in me emotions that I was expecting: instability of feeling was a concomitant of *seasons*—so Klorathy's brief summary had warned me. And I felt, as I looked behind me into a sun that was sinking fast, and heard the cold winds creeping about among the hovels, a pang of melancholy that I did not like at all. Shaking it off, I plunged into the crowds. They were nearly all males. The figures shrouded like myself were presumably females. Even the female children were, after quite an early age, shrouded in this ugly black. I was conscious I was feeling *indignation*—this seemed to me a bad sign, and a most unwelcome sign of possible imbalance.

I was now among crooked streets and lanes, all crammed with people. There were open shops and booths, eating places, and so much noise I felt dizzy from it. The silences of space, in which I had been immersed, had ill prepared me for this shouting, sometimes screaming and quarrelling mob. And now I was seeing females *not* shrouded up. On the contrary, they were almost naked, much painted, bejewelled, and offering themselves freely. This degeneration was worse than I had expected, though of course it is a result of poverty everywhere unless severely controlled by legislation. . . . I realised I was straying through the crowds, as their pressure moved me, looking at everything, stopping to stare when I was able to hold my place in the press, and in every way behaving like a stranger. And in a moment I found my way blocked by a male, who stood firmly in front of me, obviously intending to keep me there. He was staring close into my eyes through the slit in my black sheet. I found him unpleasant. That is, specifically, there was something in him I was able to sense that was more than the alien, or the not-understood. He was of middle Rohandan height, a couple of spans taller than myself, broad and solid, and his skin, of a greyish colour, almost green, had the smooth cool appearance of stone. His eyes were opaque, oblong, without brows. He had no hair, as far as I could see, for he was wearing a square pull-on cap, ornamented with lumps of coloured stone, of a soft rich-looking material. His mouth was straight, almost to the ears, and only a slit. His clothing was a voluminous fur cloak. He put his arms akimbo, in a way that made me experience them as a fence or confinement, and stared closer and closer, the greenish eyes not blinking, and very intense. I realised he was trying to hypnotise me, and guarded myself. I was also noting something else: he wore heavy gold earrings of a certain pattern.

Among the artefacts I had been instructed by Klorathy to use as a protection were these precise earrings—but to be worn at certain times and in combination with other practices.

Earrings had been—and would be again—among the artefacts used in this manner. To ornament the ears can hardly be described as a rare thing; but I had long since concluded that the practice had originated in this way—and therefore must contain hazards.

I had exactly similar earrings concealed in a bag I had under my wrap, with the other specified objects. I had got to the point of wondering how I could conceal these if this evil—for by now I knew he was that—person captured me or was in a position to have me examined, when he said: "Very well then! I shall remember you!" and turned and vanished in the crowds. But he had spoken in basic Canopean, not in Sirian . . . altogether, I had been given a lot to think about. I concealed myself in a little porch and tried to decide how to proceed. The exhilaration that comes from having to pit one's wits against strangeness persisted, but I knew I had to find shelter quickly. I had been instructed to go "to the top of the third cone." And they were built together in a bunch! I was not going to risk my clumsy Canopean, and certainly not my Sirian, here: I left the porch and wandered among the odorous noisy throng, while the light left the sky, and flares were lit everywhere at angles of the streets and outside the eating places. This was a sad and to-be-pitied people, I could see, even more now the night had come, and they were taking their ease. They were drunken, often fighting, tense with deprivation, and the degraded females dominated everything, openly selling themselves, and retiring with their customers no further than into a doorway, or under a table. I had never seen anything like this scene, not anywhere. And still I did not know how to find the third cone. I tried to put myself back into that moment when I looked down from the spacecraft at the town, and had been able to notice, if there was one, a pattern in the cones—it could perhaps be said they were built in two very deep arcs that intersected: in which case I was near the third from the end of one of the arcs. I went inside, finding a cool pale interior: they used a very fine plaster, like a ceramic, to line their walls. A steep stairway spiralled inside the building: I went up and up, stopping continually to look out of narrow slitlike openings as the city opened below me, and the noisome hovels of the low town fell away, and the gardened suburbs, now shadowy and attractive with lights shining in the trees, came into view. Up and up . . . I thought that I would not easily make such a climb again, not that day—but when I reached the very top, I found a doorway that was curtained in thick dark red material, and on it a flake of writing ceramic that had on it the one word, in Sirian: Welcome.

I pushed the curtain aside and entered a large room, the half of a round: the circular top of the tower was bisected to make two rooms by a wall of the same finely gleaming plaster. This room was furnished pleasantly enough with low couches and tables and piles of cushions, but what I was looking at, after my first assessing glance, was—Klorathy. But it wasn't Klorathy.

That moment impressed itself on me sharply, and remains with me now. I often revive it, for a re-examination, because of what I learned from it—and still do.

It is not necessary for me to say again how intrigued I was, and had been, by Klorathy, how closely I attended to everything about him—what he said, how he said it. And so on. . . . No matter how often I had been annoyed or checked, or disappointed, I had never ceased to know that if I could understand him and his ways I would understand . . . well, but that was after all the point! And this preoccupation with him had been bound up, inevitably, with his person, how he looked, spoke, certain tricks of manner. I had unconsciously deemed these *Canopus*, associated a superior, and at the present time out of my reach, way of being with Klorathy's physical presence. His personality . . .

Yet in front of me was a man *not* Klorathy, who looked very like him, and whose smile and nod as he greeted me were familiar.

"I am Nasar," he said. "Klorathy told me you were coming, and asked me to see you have everything you want."

I was quite stunned. Believing he could have no idea why, I disposed myself comfortably on a low pile of cushions and accepted some wine.

What I have to say here, so as to make it unmistakably clear, is that I felt more than the dislocation that comes from misdirected and thwarted expectations. I was feeling a different kind of letdown.

It was a warning, and a strong one. This was not because of how Nasar *looked* or how he *behaved*—his courtesy was complete. But warnings were flashing through me.

And I suppressed them!

This was because of my awe of Canopus. Of everything Canopus stood for.

And yet all the time my after-all highly trained eyes were noting all kinds of discrepancies—seeing what I should be seeing, and then setting it all aside.

As I play back that scene, so as to examine it, there was everything there that I needed to prevent and save me from so much puzzlement and confusion.

There was a particular smile that appeared on the man's face, very briefly—only a flicker—of recklessness . . . carelessness. He had a way of suddenly letting out—and often inappropriately to what was being said or done—a short laugh, as if he were astonished at himself, and yet proposed to stand by what he found. He had a general air or manner that was familiar to me, for I had had often to deal with it—yet I chose not to put a name to it then.

So much for my perspicacity—or rather, for my readiness to use it.

We were not together for long. He showed me how to get food, if I wanted it, from the floor below, which was a foodshop for the building, opened a low door into the room next door, just like this one, which I was to use as a sleeping and private place—and having made his apologies, was ready to leave.

I was tired, but stimulated, and had hoped for more talk, or in lieu of that, to go out again into the teeming streets below. But he said that before I went out I must decide what role I was to play.

"In this charming place," said he, "there are three roles for a woman. One is to be a whore. One, the wife of a high official, or at least a trader or merchant. Or you may be a servant or working woman of some kind. You would not choose, I am sure, the first." The way he said this had a laugh behind it that I simply did not know how to take. "The second is out of your reach—for you are not here with a permit or passport and must conceal yourself. Therefore, I can only suggest that you pose as my servant. This would be entirely within the customs and mores of Koshi. What you wear indoors does not matter, though if someone arrives unexpectedly you must cover yourself up absolutely, but wear appropriate clothes underneath in case you are searched." He nodded at a chest and left. I found in it a plain blue skirt, baggy blue trousers, a long tunic. And that was the last I saw of Nasar for several days.

What had I expected?

That I should spend time with Klorathy, that he would instruct me, and would explain . . . all that I could not work out for myself, but felt continually on the edge of discovering.

I did not go out, but observed the town from my high vantage point, and from windows at many levels in the building. In the foodshop below, I excited notice. It was staffed by women wearing the same clothes as I did, short skirt over trousers, and the loose tunic; their hair tied in cloth. My unbound fair hair interested them: I was from the far Northwest, they said, and assumed I was a descendant of the survivors of the "events," which they referred to as "The Great Punishment." Some Adalantalanders had escaped somehow, had made their way east, and had helped to settle these great cities of the far eastern plains. They had a reputation for beauty, for wisdom—they were priestesses and shamanesses; and no fair or blue-eyed child could be born anywhere without being called "child of the lost islands of the great oceans of the west." But I was no true daughter of Adalantaland—I was too thin, my locks were too sparse, and my eyes were not sea blue. But my earrings, which I wore at certain hours of certain days, announced my true lineage, so these serving women knew: and they told everybody that the merchant on the top floor had as his serving maid a slave from the Northwest fringes. This I did not want, and wrapped my head thereafter so my "magic" earrings did not show, and tried to be inconspicuous, and took at one time as much food as was practical up the stairs so as to keep my visits few, though I wanted very much to talk with these cheerful slaves. For that is what they were. The females of this culture were truly enslaved, in that they did not know they were. They had never questioned that males should run everything, make laws, decide who should marry and how, and dispose of the futures of children. The dispossession of the true role of females had taken place so long ago they did not know it had ever happened. Their reverence for the old Adalantaland was all that remained to them of a real inkling of what females could do and be. And that had become "magic," and "witchcraft." Their highest ambition and possibility was to marry a man in a good position: or to give birth to sons who would prove themselves. I longed to study the warps and distortions in the female psyche that this displacement of their true function had caused: I wanted to study them in depth and in such a way that I could return home with a contribution to our Studies in Perverted Psychology. But first things first.

I kept myself private and retired to the windows where I could look north and see—so I fancied—the white beginnings of the icecaps, and south to great mountains where the snows lay again. It was getting colder daily, and I wrapped myself in my black cloth for the sake of warmth, and sat many hours quietly, thinking of the questions I was going to ask . . . Klorathy? Well, then, Nasar.

There were specific and definite things I wanted to know. It seemed to me that long ages had gone into my wanting to know them, that this wanting had fed a need that now could not any longer be put off.

And I imagined what would happen, how I would frame questions, how they would be answered, in all kinds of ways. And imagined, too, how they would *not* be answered, for I was already set to expect checks and delays.

One evening, when I had sat a long time in a window opening gazing over the rich suburbs and wondering who were the rich and powerful ones of this culture, and able—not all that inaccurately either—to picture them because of their victims and subjects I had seen in the streets, from the windows, and in the persons of the women downstairs in the foodshops; when I had watched in myself the melancholies and sadness that went with this "season" of the rapidly darkening days, so that there was less light in any day than there was night; when I had repeated in myself over and over again what I wanted to know, so that I could ask sensibly and well—in came Nasar, unexpectedly, and flung himself down on a low seat, opening a package of food he had brought from the shop below, and eating rapidly and in a way that I had never seen in Klorathy. He unceremoniously thrust a lump of some sweet stuff towards me and said: "Have some," and wiped his mouth roughly and lolled back, his hands locked behind his head, staring up and out at the sky that showed through the windows high in the ceilings. It was a cool sky, and clouds fled past. I was utterly overthrown again, because he was so similar to Klorathy.

I sat myself down carefully, and said to him, beginning my cross-examination: "Are you a relative of Klorathy?"

This he took as a shock, or a check. He set his eyes direct on me, and gave me his attention:

"Well, lovely lady," said he, and stopped. I remember how he briefly shut his eyes, sighed, and seemed to fight with himself. He said, in a different voice, patient, but *too* patient, there was much too much effort in it and he was speaking as from out of a dream or a trance: "We come from the same planet, Klorathy and I. We are all very similar in appearance." And there was, again, that flicker of a restless laugh—and then a turning aside of the eyes, a sort of painful grimace, a quick shaking of the head, as if thoughts were being shaken away. Then he looked at me again.

"Am I going to see Klorathy this time?"

"One Canopean is the same as another," he said, and it was like the ghost of a derisive quote.

"You are *not* like Klorathy," I said doggedly, surprised that I said it. And knew I had not meant it kindly.

He looked surprised, then laughed—sadly, I could have sworn to that—and said gently: "No, you are right. At this moment, at this time, I am indeed not remotely like Klorathy."

I did not know what to say.

"I want to ask questions of *somebody* . . ." and this was desperate. I was becoming amazed at myself—the tone of this interview or exchange was different from anything I had ever known. I, Ambien II, age-long high official of Sirius, with all that meant of responsibility and *effectiveness*—I did not recognise myself.

It seemed to me, however, that incompetent as I was being, he was arrested by me, and returned to something different from . . . I could not yet say to myself, simply, that he was in a bad, a *recognisably* wrong and bad state. I said that at this moment at least I could see something in him of Klorathy.

"Ask, fair Sirian." This I did not like but was able to swallow it—because of the element of caricature in what he said, the manner of it.

"First of all. I met a man on the very first evening I was here. I disliked everything about him . . ." I described him, physically, and waited.

"You must surely be able to work that out for yourself. We are under the aegis of Puttiora here. As I believe you were told. That was one of *them*. They know everything that happens. Who comes into the city and who goes out. But you passed their test."

"What test?"

"Obviously, you were of Canopus, and therefore you were not molested."

"I am not, however."

"They are an ignorant lot."

"Why do you tolerate their rule?" I asked, fierce, hot, incredulous. "Why?"

"A good question, fair Sirian. Why? I ask it myself. Every hour of every day. Why? Why do we put up with the nasty, stinking, loathsome, horrible . . ." and he got up, literally sick and choking, and went to the window and leaned out. From far below I heard the clamour of evening, and imagined the flare-lit streets, the poor posturing women, the sale of flesh, the fighting, the drinking.

At that point there was a very long silence. I could have, then, said things I did not until later. But this was *Canopus* and so . . . and when he turned a hunted haunted face towards me, and sighed, and then laughed, and then shook his head, and then put his face in his hands, and then flung himself down again, and yet was unable to stay still for even a moment, I said to myself only that this was a man disgusted by Shammat.

"Very long term, the perspectives of Canopus, you must learn to understand that," he said at last.

"And very long term are the perspectives of Sirius," I said, with dignity. For if there was one thing I understood, it was that . . . empires and the running of them . . . but he stared and laughed—he laughed until he flung himself back and lay exhausted, staring at the ceiling.

The thought was in my mind that this was a man who was in very deep situational trouble. And I suppressed it.

"Very well," I said, "for reasons of long-term development, you tolerate Shammat, you tolerate Puttiora and allow them to believe they are in control. Very well. But what are *you* doing here?"

"A good question, again, fair Sirian."

I said, "You do not have to call me that. I have a name. But it doesn't matter. What I want to know is, *what is the function of Canopus? What are you?*" And I was leaning forward, twisting my hands together, so that they cracked—all my limbs are thin and frail, and I sustain breaks easily. I was using enough strength to break bones. I sat back, carefully relaxing myself.

He was watching me thoughtfully. With respect.

"You are right to ask that question."

"But you are not going to answer it?"

At this he started up, leaning forward, gazing at me as if incredulous. "Can't you *see* . . ." he began—and then lay back again, silent.

"*See what?*" But he said nothing. "Why do you stop? Why is it that you will never answer? Why is it I always get so far and then you won't answer?"

He was gazing at me, from where he reclined. I could have sworn that this copper man, or bronze man, that bronze-eyed, alert smiling man was Klorathy. *But he was not.* The contrast was so absolute, and definite, to the extent that I said to him, not knowing I was going to: "What is the matter with you?"

He laughed.

And even then I didn't pursue it, for if I had done he would have answered.

He stood up. He collected himself. He smiled—oh, not at all like Klorathy.

"First of all . . . I have to tell you . . ." and he stopped, and he sighed. I saw he was not going to say it!

"I have to go," he said.

"Why? To work? They say you are a merchant?"

"I am a merchant. In Shammat land do as Shammat does. I am a merchant as you are my servant." He came close to me then and bent and put out both hands and touched my earrings. "Take care of them," said he, and sprang back, as if the touch burned him.

"Where are yours?" I asked.

"A good question. But they are on the earlobes of Shammat. They were stolen, you see. Or, more accurately, I got drunk and gave them to the earlobes of Shammat . . . very bad," he said. "Not good."

And he smiled in a way that frightened me, and left.

And now I knew at last that there was something very wrong with this Canopean. I was enabled to search my memory and come up with: the fact that this was a suborned, or disaffected, or rebellious official. I had seen it! I had had to deal with it a hundred times! This was Canopus gone wrong.

And I wrapped myself rapidly in my black cloth and I ran down those stairs after him, catching him halfway, and making him stop.

"Where are you going?"

"To visit my woman. I have a beautiful woman," said he. "Oh, don't look like that! Believe me, it is only those who understand nothing that look like that . . ." and he bounded down the stairs. I went after him, the alabaster walls of the stairs gleaming around us both, and we reached the dark street that was luridly illuminated and full of sweating shouting demented people. I grabbed him and made him turn. "Don't be a fool," he said. "Do you imagine we are unobserved?" He tore himself away. I did not listen, and went after him. He turned again and said in a low urgent voice: "I may be lost, but do you have to lose yourself, too? Be careful. . . ." And as we stood there, up came two of the same greenish-grey cold-eyed officials I had seen before, and one reached forward and wrenched down my headcloth to show my earrings, and a hand was already coming out to wrench them off, while another was pulling Nasar around by the arm, when Nasar said, "Punishment from Canopus!" and the one who had touched my earrings fell, like a stone, and the other ran off into the crowds. Nasar looked full at me, his amber eyes pained and sick, and said: "That cost us a good deal, Sirian, more than you know—get back upstairs. I may be lost, but why should you be?" And I took hold of both his arms, and asked him: "Very well, I have just understood . . . you have gone bad, you have gone wrong . . . I know the symptoms—yes, it has taken me long enough to see it . . . but come back, come back, Nasar . . . please. I demand it. You must. In the name of Canopus." Well, he came back up the stairs with me, the long climb of them, and when he was at the top he was ill and frightened. He had lost the inner power that for good or bad had sustained him in his encounters with me. He trembled, and was pale under his dark copper skin.

"What happened?" I kept asking.

I asked, and I pressed, and it was very late in the night, and the snow, a pale presence, filled the windows, and at last he said this: "Lady, I have been on this planet for twenty-five thousand years. Since before Adalantaland. It was I who taught that island and the peoples around it. I was here before the change of earth's axis and the birth of the seasons. It was I who taught—other cities and cultures you know nothing of. I have been *here, here, here.* Klorathy my brother has come and gone . . . there are those who visit, they come, they warn, they set the stones, they make the lines, they order, they align—and they go again if they are recalled to home, but I, I am a permanent official. And in my case they have made a mistake. Do you understand? I have gone very bad, as you say, Ambien the II or the III or the 97th. You come and go, too, I suppose? A sojourn on this planet and a little holiday on that? But I have been in this hellhole for . . . ages, ages, long ages. . . ." He muttered, and he swung his head, and he puckered up his face and sighed, and then leaped up and ran out of the door so fast I could not catch him.

It was a day and an hour when I had to perform the regulatory observances. I set out the objects on the rugs of the floor, arranged colours as they should go, put garments on myself in a certain way, adjusted my earrings, and observed the hour exactly, standing quietly there alone at the top of the great tower, enclosed in the snow's white hush . . . it was very difficult. I knew by the resistance of the time and the substance about me that I was contending with a great deal: many times had I performed these rituals, since the failure of the Lock, had performed them in this or that continent, and in several different manners, but never had I felt as if I, or the substance of something felt through me, was pushing against a resistance experienced as—evil. Felt as a heavy, dead weight. But stuck to my purpose, thinking of Klorathy, and that he had asked me here. *Why?* For what purpose?

I had just finished what I had been instructed to do, when the curtains of the door were yanked back, and the man I had seen on my first evening stood there. "Canopus," said he. "You are on sufferance here and that does not allow you to kill our officials."

What I was feeling as I stood up to face him surprised me: it was exactly the same tone or taste as what I felt when with Nasar. There was no mistaking that sensation, a resonance. I had told myself that Nasar had gone *bad*: but I had not gone on to understand what it might mean that he had been captured by Shammat, *was* Shammat.

I said nothing, but stood before him in my slight white robes, the luminous metal circlets on my upper arms, the metal band on my head of the same softly shining silvery gold, a metal foreign to Sirius, which I did not know, and my heavy golden earrings.

As he took in what I was wearing, his dull stonelike eyes stared, and he involuntarily took several steps forward. He was still wearing the golden earrings.

I was preserving a distancing and detached manner, while I attended to a large variety of thoughts and sensations. Speculations about Nasar continued. I was also thinking that this official ought never to have seen me thus accoutred and that he was at this moment fixing my image on his mind so as later to copy what he could; I noted, too, that he had not observed the patterns of colours, nor the scents, nor the stringed instrument on which I had been making the necessary sounds. I was right in thinking that he would be bound to believe these some sort of "female entertainment" and of no use to him. I was thinking that I did not believe the official punished by Nasar was in fact dead: more probably he was stunned. No authority of even ordinary sense uses greater methods of punishment or deterrent than are necessary. I was also concluding that my having to pretend to be Nasar's servant could not be for the benefit of the Shammat surveillance, but was necessary not to disturb the populace. More than all this, I was trying to decide how to behave in a way that would control him.

Before I could move he had again advanced, and now stood immediately in front of me: arms akimbo, legs apart. Seen thus, I had every opportunity for a full scan of this species, enabling me on my return to furnish the biologists with ample details. The most remarkable feature was the wide slit of a mouth, connected, I judged, not with alimentation, but with voice production: when he spoke next, I was able to see, as I had not when crushed in the street, that this slit seemed to vibrate, and the sounds came from his mid-torso. The way he spoke was resonant, giving a fuzzy sound to the words.

"Ornaments of this kind are not permitted in this city!"

And as his stone eyes seemed to swallow the artefacts, so that I was enveloped in a glitter of cupidity, I felt he was again trying some rather crude technique of hypnotism. But there was more to it: he was testing me, trying to elicit from me some kind of show of authority—was that it? Something he had been accustomed to find in Nasar? At any rate, I felt his triumph—and then, in myself, a weakness of fear because of this triumph in him. I knew that I had failed in some test he had applied.

My mind was racing. I turned from him casually, and moved away, my back to him, stood a few moments glancing out of the window, then sat down on a low chair. There are few places in the Galaxy where superiors do not sit, while supplicants or inferiors stand. As I sat, an idea flashed into my mind unrelated to the present situation—very clear my thoughts were, because of the aligning practices just concluded, and because of this situation of danger. "How long has it been," I enquired, "since this city was allowed to spoil its original design?" For I had understood that this city, *as it had been designed*, had consisted solely of the conical towers, in a certain alignment—probably interlocking arcs—and that the huddle of poor buildings around their bases, and the spreading new suburbs, were a dereliction of an original purpose. Memories of what I had been told of the ancient mathematical cities, speculations that were never far from my mind as to what their function was—these were in my mind, and my distance from this situation and this stone slab of a man was genuine.

His response was immediate: sullen, and this meant a genuine annoyance; cunning—which alerted me to say: "There will one day be an end to your cupidities and your despoilings."

He stood still. Very still. The heavy eyes seemed to glow. What I had said, not idly, but certainly not with any crushing intention, had made him remember past—warnings? Threats?

I remained where I sat, watching him. In my mind were two models of behaviour—one was Nasar, and everything that I felt was needed by this situation dismissed him. The other was Klorathy, who I understood as I thought of him would not regard this little servant of even the most horrible power with anything but—at the most—a detached dislike. So I said mildly, even with humour: "As for your colleague, he is of course not dead. He will recover, if he has not already . . ." and I rose again, as if dismissing him, and returned to the window, for I wanted to look around at these spiring towers with my new ideas in mind, and to imagine this city as it had been. *For what purpose?*

But I heard a humming, or vibration just behind me, and turning, there he was, that slit mouth of his thrumming: I knew now that that wordless sound had meaning, but knew, too, that I could not allow him to think I did not understand it. I leaned on the ledge there, and saw the towers dark against the pale falling sky.

"You are to come with me. I have authority. In this city I have the authority," he insisted, and I believed him: it was part of some agreement that Canopus had allowed.

"I shall change my clothes," I said.

"No," he said, slamming it out, and he again ate my headband, the armlets, my earrings, with his eyes. I remarked: "But it is very cold tonight."

"You have a cloak."

"I take it we must be expected at some very fine function indeed," I said, smiling. And his lips' rapid quiver conveyed to me that this was the case.

"I can only hope that you have a good reason to take me there tonight," I remarked, as I took up the great black cloth and enveloped myself in it, "for I had other plans. Canopus has work to do."

"I understand perfectly, perfectly," said he, hurried and placating, and I knew that while he had not expected that he would fail to get his way, he was at least relieved that he had got it: and was afraid that I might find some reason to give him the slip. And all the time everything about this creature emanated greed, so that I thought back to the visit, long ago, by the hairy avid Shammat-brutes: they were the same breed, different though they were. And I was not going to ask what he must be expecting me to know: Are there many different kinds on that Shammat of yours? Or are you from Puttiora itself? Well, I learned later he was from Puttiora: the cities of this plain were policed by Puttiora, and not by its subject planet Shammat—but that is part of another story.

We descended the long twining stairs, he coming close behind me, and I could feel the pressure of his itching want, want, want, all over me, his eyes like the touch of hands.

In the street we stood in a white storm, with dull lamps half obliterated at the entrances to streets and lanes. There were only the two of us. I was being chilled to stiffness as I stood, and the whine of the northern wind struck a painful fear into my bones: winter was fear, in this planet, and fear was the memory of sudden tempests of snow and ice that could wipe out a continent in a breath, of screaming winds that could tear water-masses and vast sea beasts into the air and whirl them around like dust. A square shape appeared in the white, an opening showed itself, and I got in, urged by my jailer, and found myself in a box furnished with cushions and a little oil lamp. I did not know at once how it was being conveyed, but soon thought it was by runner, for it was not the first time I had been carried in this way—the sign of a slave state, of a proud and ruthless governing class, wherever it is to be found.

The Puttioran smelled bad: it was a cold greasy smell. I of course checked this thought, knowing that mine was not likely to be pleasant to him: smell has always been the hardest obstacle to overcome in the good relations between species: in that nothing has changed! As I wrote the words beginning the account of my entry into the city of tall dun-coloured cones—which, alas, I could see nothing of from inside the jogging box—I was called to a delegation from one of quite the most pleasant of our Colonised Planets, and with the best will in the world, I had to leave the audience chambers on an excuse, for the smell that emanated from the otherwise quite ordinary and normal individuals, equipped as usual with "two legs, two arms, a head, a nose, eyes and mouth," as we say (but in this case it was a tail as well), was so appalling that I could not stand it.

The distance was not great. We stepped down on to thick snow outside a building that streamed light through pillars and from windows. We were outside one of the villas of the western suburbs, and this was a festivity of some kind, for I could hear music, of a kind I was ready to suppose an entertainment, though to my ears it was a high wail not unlike the whine of the gale. The box we had been brought in seemed to lift itself, and jerked away into the white: I could just see projecting handles, and dimly, four ill-clad beasts, who I hoped were being kept warm by the thick head hair that fell to the shoulders, which they freed from deposits of snow by continually shaking their heads. They vanished with the box into the snowfall.

I ascended wide steps beside the Puttioran, to a deep verandah that had many ornamented pillars, and braziers standing here and there. I was familiar with the affectation of governing classes anywhere for modes of their past, and knew that braziers were not the sum of their current technology for keeping themselves warm: the rooms at the top of the tower were heated by air that flowed in from ducts. Few individuals were on the verandahs because of the cold, but I saw they were in full festive dress by the fact that they were half naked.

I did not know whether it was on account of Sirius or of Canopus that I should strive for a good impression, but removed the poor black cloth in which I was muffled, and draped it over my right forearm in a way that I had seen in a certain history of custom from our early Dark Age: this manner of arranging an outer garment had signified rank.

I was being aided as I advanced through the graceful springing pillars by another historical comparison: a planet recently visited by me had preserved as a record of former times an area of villas similar to these, also set among vegetation—though of course I could see nothing of the gardens that I knew enclosed these suburbs.

The verandah was separated from the very wide and large inner room, or rooms, by curtains of thick many-coloured materials. I stood quite still in the entrance, in order that I might be observed. What I was observing was not unexpected: there were about twenty individuals there, all scantily clad, and with the unmistakable air of a ruling or privileged class taking its ease. They sat about on cushions, or on light chairs. Low tables were heaped with every kind of food and fruit. Around the walls stood about a dozen servers, almost naked young females and males, holding jugs and ewers of intoxicant. The lights were not braziers, but some kind of gas burning in transparent globules from pillars and walls. The stone floors had handsome rugs.

Their immobility was not because they were surprised at my arrival but because they had expected it and did not want to show —yet—whatever emotions or needs had led to my being summoned. For I could see that this was the case. There was no surprise shown by the Puttioran at my side. There were two others of this most unattractive species present, seated among the others, but not lolling or sprawled about—I was at once able to see that they were tolerated here, no more.

"Klorathy"—was there: Nasar, in this dim pearly light was so like Klorathy that for a moment I could not believe it was not he. But then he turned his head, and I knew at once his lateness in doing this was not because he had only just understood I had arrived but *because he was ashamed.* He had a studied and casual air, as he sat on a low square seat with his back to a pillar. He at least was not half naked.

In every scene there is a focus . . . a centre . . . and Nasar was not that centre here. Nor were the Puttiorans. At an arm's distance from Nasar, on a wide seat, which was not as low as the others, so that she looked down on her guests, sat a woman who dominated everything. She was exceedingly beautiful. She was more than that. I am certainly not talking of the aesthetic here, but of a sexual fascination, which was immediately and instantly evident, and which I had seen nothing to compare with for many ages.

Every breeding female has this quality, often briefly enough. But in certain conditions this sexual attraction can be concentrated and maintained by an effort of individual will, if the social circumstances permit. Of myself I can say that I am pale and blonde; but of her I can say only that she gleamed and shimmered. Her hair was of fine gold, elaborately dressed, with a mass of little waves and curls, and very fine plaits, like twisted gold wires, on either side of her broad, pearly, smiling face. Her eyes were grey blue and widely set under shining blonde brows. Her long white hands were displayed, unadorned, in her lap. White feet were in jewelled sandals.

On her bare arms were heavy gold bracelets made of repeated and interlocked V's, which very slightly compressed her flesh, in a calculated manner. Now these bracelets were of the exact pattern prescribed for previous practices set by Canopus, those that had been superceded by the "suggestions" sent to me before I began this visit. I looked quickly around again and saw that nearly everyone there, male and female, wore bracelets, earrings, anklets, or an association of colours that were *almost* accurate, for in each place I observed them, a pattern on a hem, or a design on a skirt, they had, as it were, slipped out of true—and now I understood why Nasar could not easily meet my eyes. Though he was in fact now rather sullenly gazing across at me, not so much defiantly as in reckless sombreness.

I understood a good deal as I stood there, smiling calmly. For one thing, what it was they wanted of me now: the three Puttiorans all wore the earrings of the current prescription—they and I wore them, not one of the others, and not Nasar. Who, of course, if he were being ruled by what had been prescribed, would not be wearing them at this occasion. Just as I should not, had I not been commanded and brought here in the way I had.

I saw that the eyes of every individual there glittered at the armbands, the headband, the earrings I wore, and as I wondered why the Puttioran who had fetched me had not simply taken them, realised that of course he must be afraid, or that is exactly what he would have done.

Still no one has moved, or made a sign of greeting. I took then a great chance, which made me quite cold, and inwardly confused for a moment: I stepped forward, with "Canopus greets you!" and glanced at Nasar to see how he took this, as I gestured to a girl servant to bring forward a chair that stood by the wall. This was a chair similar to the one used by the beauty, who was, I had decided, hostess there: I seated myself on her level, at a short distance from her and from Nasar, and clapped my hands without looking to see if this was being obeyed—a custom taken from another recent visit of mine—and when a goblet was presented to me of some crystalline material, was careful not to let a drop of it touch my lips, while I pretended to sip.

"I understood that you were from Sirius?" remarked the fair one, clapping her hands as I had done, and accepting a fresh goblet—this was to put me at my ease? To encourage me to drink?

This was the most dangerous moment of my meeting with these decadents. I could not afford to hesitate, and I smiled, merely, and with a rather amused little glance at Nasar, as to a fellow conspirator in a harmless joke: "If it has amused Nasar to say that I am, then why not?" And I laughed. And did not look at him, but smoothed my skirt.

He had now to challenge me. I knew that if he did, it would probably mean the loss of my life, let alone the ornaments they all coveted so much. I sat at ease, pretending to sip the intoxicant—pretty rough stuff, too, nothing tempting in it—and examining the scene quite frankly and with apparent enjoyment.

I cannot begin to convey how it dismayed and disgusted me.

The signs of a degenerate class are the same everywhere and always: I will not waste time in details. But I have seen them too often, and in too many places, and their perennial reappearance *can* only weary and dismay. The smiling ease, the cynical good nature that is so easily overturned when challenged and becomes a snarling threat; the carelessness that is the invariable mark of *easy* success; the softness of the flesh; the dependence on ease; the assumption of superiority over inevitable slaves or serfs or servants who, of course—everywhere and always—are their real and often evident masters . . . here it was again, again, *again*.

I had wondered often enough if on Canopus, or in her Empire, this rule applied, but as I was actually thinking that Nasar's presence here, subjugated and *used*, was an answer, he lifted his bronze eyes direct at mine and shook his head. "No," he said. "No, fair Canopean."

And he turned away, with an air so defeated, so angry, that I did not know what to do. But knew, at least, that I had survived a very dangerous moment. It would have been piquant, to say the least, to end my life here, on this degraded planet, with these demoralised creatures.

"Am I not to know the name of my hostess?" I asked.

"Your host is Nasar," she said, in a voice that I absolutely expected: it was lazy, rich, suggestive: her voice, just like her appearance, could make you think of one thing, one thing only,

and even if you had never experienced it. For I had not! I had read
of it all, certainly—I had made a study of pathology. But it had so
happened that my career in the Service had begun very young, and
that while our Empire has suffered periods when I might very well
have actually been at risk myself, I was always occupied well away
from the Mother Planet.

But sitting there in that gilded, amiable, pleasure-loving scene,
which had over it a sort of silky dew as if it were drenched in
ethereal honey, looking at the smiling glistening woman, it was not
necessary to have experienced it! I understood it all, and only too
well—because I was being affected as I sat there, trying to preserve
a correct, if not an official, air. For one thing, I ought not to be
wearing these artefacts, which were too powerful, even if they had
been put out of exact use by the fact they were not in alignment
with the other dispositions of the practice that had been disturbed
by the interruption by the Puttioran. For another, it is of course
not the case that to turn your back on an area of life is the same
as to abolish it! Often enough, and even with Ambien I, I had
understood very well what a seductive realm lay there, available,
just for the effort of saying: *Yes!* Of course I had known—been
aware of—watched for—guarded—that door, or entrance, which
watchfulness is in itself a way of signifying a disposition to enter
into something. This was what I was seeing. And what I was
understanding. Oh yes, the woman was magic! And as I thought
that word, I understood that she was a daughter of old Adalantaland; I remembered this full smiling ease of the flesh, the glisten—
but there and in that time it had a very different *function*. The
wonderful females of that island had been in a correct alignment—
or *almost*; of course I remembered how they had begun to slide
away: yet one could sense their oneness with their surroundings.
But this descendant of theirs had all the magnificence of the
physical, but in addition a witchery that had slipped out of its
place, had become sufficient to itself. As I looked at Nasar, tense
and miserable there in his low seat, and then at her, I did not have
to be told anything: I felt it. And I began to be afraid: it was a
very easy door to open, just one little step, one little decision—and
suddenly I found myself thinking of Klorathy as I had never done
yet: I was amazed and appalled: it seemed as if there, beckoning

me, was a smiling playful amorousness, which was certainly not
what I was in search for—in wait for—when thinking of companionship with Klorathy . . . with Canopus. And this lighthearted
amorousness was in itself an antechamber where I could very
quickly indeed descend to something very different. What I saw
there, in front of me now—nothing lighthearted about that! Nasar
was gazing sombrely at the woman's indolent lolling arm, and on
his face was a look of such pain that . . . but she was saying again:
"It is Nasar who is your host."

"I think not," I said smiling, as pleasantly as I could . . . and I
heard rather than saw the Puttiorans mutter to each other—or
rather vibrate together, a twanging sound added to the whining
repetition of the music that was working on my nerves as much as
the general atmosphere.

"Her name is Elylé," said Nasar abruptly. "This is her house.
And we are all her guests—aren't we?—your guests or your captives?" and he laughed, flinging back his head and pouring down
the fiery intoxicant.

"Her very willing captives," said a dark smiling lisping youth,
who had about him every sign of the spoiled rich. He rose from
heaps of cushions and sat by Elylé's chair, and, grasping her hand
with a rough painful movement, began planting kisses up and down
the forearm. She hardly moved, did not look at him—but at Nasar,
who had gone pale.

"Nasar," said she, in her soft beguiling voice, "is not as willing
a captive as you," and she looked at Nasar, with a laugh, challenging him—*willing* him. I saw there a truly dreadful struggle in him.
He was being drawn forward by her seductiveness, her frank and
open invitation, and at the same time he was fighting in himself
to resist her. Everyone in the room watched the struggle. And what
happened at last was that he gave a great gasp, leaned forward from
his seat, lifted her white arm, and having gazed at it with a shudder
that shook every part of him, kissed the hand, but negligently, and
even clumsily—so did the conflict in him manifest itself. He sank
back in his seat, staring in front of him, then took another great
gulp from his goblet.

He said harshly: "This desiccated bureaucrat of a Sirian is
shocked by us."

There was an indrawn breath and from the Puttiorans a louder thrumming. I could not laugh this off.

I said, "It is very clear that Nasar is not himself."

This was certainly obvious to everyone and saved me.

The youth cringing at Elylé's knees, his mouth on her forearm, now lifted his face to lisp: "We all want to know what that material is your dress is made of—fair Sirian!" He felt his daring, for he glanced up at the woman to see how she would take it—she frowned and withdrew her arm.

"My dress is made of Canopean crepe," I said.

"That is certainly true," confirmed Nasar: he was breathing harshly, and his eyes seemed fixed on the beautiful woman and the youth who, snubbed, was literally grovelling on the floor, his curly head on her nearly bare feet. And I could see it was all he could do to stop himself doing the same.

"Can I feel it?" asked a girl sitting near me. She wore a blue glittering skirt, but her breasts were bare, except for a pattern of jewels over the nipples. Her black hair hung down to her waist, she was dark skinned, dark eyed, very slight. There were no two individuals alike in this room: the genetic mix was very wide.

She got up, and bent to finger my dress. It was cut full, but was sleeveless—not so dissimilar from their style as to be a comment on it, but the fabric was one I had not previously been familiar with myself, rather like a fluent and supple metal. Glistening white, impossible to crease, it flowed through the fingers as you attempted to fold or settle it, and if it had not been so ample I would have been embarrassed, because where it did touch the flesh, it showed its contours—in my case, as Nasar had said, certainly "desiccated"; and it was a measure of how the atmosphere of this rich perverse villa and its emotive music affected me that I was full of wild regret that this was so, and that I was not like Elylé, whose very presence fascinated and drew and stung.

As this girl fingered my skirt, in a moment half a dozen others had crowded forward, handling first the stuff of the gown, and then their hands straying over my armlets and touching my head where the circlet gleamed. "What's this material?" they were murmuring, and asking each other, as if I were not there! As if I were some kind of a dummy on which these things were displayed. . . . And then

I felt the weight of the circlet lift from my hair and I was just in time to put my hand up to stop the thief slipping it off. I was being pressed down in my seat by the weight of thieving hands and fingers.

Past a cluster of heads bent all around me I could see Elylé sitting in her chair, longing to come forward and handle me with the rest, but her pride forbade it. Nasar had turned his head sharply, and was staring too at the scene, and I could see that he was alarmed for me. And I certainly was in great danger.

I stood up, and dislodged the greedy ones, so that they fell, and lay about on the floor laughing foolishly, drunk and helpless.

"Perhaps you could take off your bracelets and your headband," said Elylé, "and let us see them. I for one would love to see them closely." As she said this the tones of that indolent voice struck into me, so that I felt them in my senses as a pang, a song.

"No," I said. "I shall not do that."

She looked at Nasar—and this look's command I was able to feel in myself.

He sighed at the strength of the pressure on him: sweat started out on his face—and he said to me in a hurried angry voice: "Yes, take them off. . . ." And he added, "This is a command."

I cannot describe, even now, how this affected me. It was a command from Canopus: this, despite everything, was what it was. And from a man who was in appearance, even in manner—or some of the time—Klorathy, who I had been thinking of as one who might open doors for me, say to me what I longed to hear . . . and when he said, "This is a command," I was struck silent. What I was thinking was that I had been warned by Klorathy of this moment! *That he had known of it* . . . or of something like it that must present itself. And I was thinking, as I remembered Klorathy, his presence, his manner, *what he was*, that no matter how I suffered—and I was suffering in every particle of myself—I must resist.

"I have already said that you are not yourself," I said coldly. "Canopeans do not command Canopeans."

"But perhaps they do command Sirians," said Elylé and laughed her fat low laugh.

"Perhaps they do," I said, "but I don't know anything about

that. What I do know is this: these things that I wear are not ornaments. And those who use them wrongly will suffer."

Again I heard, or felt, Nasar struggle with himself. The sombre, sullen struggle went on, and his breathing sounded against the low fluttering vibration of the three Puttiorans, who had crowded up to me and stood close enough to snatch off what I wore—if they dared. And they still did not dare, and that was what gave me courage to go on. For I was reasoning as I stood there, my mind working as fast as it had ever done, that Nasar himself must have given warnings, even as he had weakly parted with these things as ornaments. . . .

"Is that not so, Nasar," I said, forcing him with my will to turn and look at me. He sat upright, his hands loosely held around his goblet—which was trembling, because he trembled. He looked at Elylé, who was smiling at him—and yet there was fear in her smile.

"Yes, it is so," he muttered at length.

And now there was a long pause, the scene again seemed to freeze, as it had when I entered.

I stood quiet, empty, my will on Nasar. The three Puttiorans, the grey-green stonelike men, with their dull eyes, and their fluttering humming lips, had turned to look at Nasar, and *they were waiting for him to make a sign* . . . it was a sign that had been agreed upon before I entered this place. I understood a great deal in that moment.

And again the moment stretched itself . . . and I looked, at my ease, from one face to the next . . . first the beautiful Elylé, Adalantaland's fallen daughter, and the besotted youth who had returned to slaver over her hand, and the others on the floor, silly and sprawling, and the almost naked servants, who were watching, with the mask-faces of servants everywhere and at all times—and what I was seeing struck me into a inner acknowledgement of something. These faces for that moment were all vacant, yet this was because within themselves they had been attacked by an inner questioning: they were lost, vague, dissatisfied, restless—they gripped their fingers against their palms, or bit their lips; their eyes roamed everywhere, they sighed, they twisted themselves, and they sat staring emptily.

Oh, I knew very well what I saw: it was a variation of the

existential question, or affliction—how could I not recognise something I knew so well, so very well, and in all its manifestations? Their clutching and sneaking and wanting after what I wore now— what Nasar had worn at other times—were nothing else but symptoms of that deep and basic yearning.

What I was thinking disarmed me. I felt as if I was on a level with them and no better, and had no right to withhold anything from them. If at that moment Nasar had said: "Canopus commands . . ." I would have handed over everything I had on.

But Nasar saved me, saved himself.

He was slowly struggling to his feet—the struggle was shown in the tenseness of heavy limbs, as if his longing simply to fall on the floor and put his lips on the smiling warmth of Elylé's flesh was weighting him—he did slowly straighten, and then, gasping, turned towards me.

"It is time Canopus left," he remarked, in a heavy dreamlike voice. I could see that if *she* spoke then he would simply fling himself at her feet and that would be the end of it.

"Yes, it is. And Canopus will now leave," I said. I put my hand at Nasar's elbow, afraid at this last moment that he would simply shake me off in repulsion because this touch was not hers.

"Nasar," she said softly, and the sound of it struck through me and I could feel him shiver.

"Come," I said softly. He gave a sort of groan and left himself in my hands. Gently directing him, I went with him through the parting in the gaily coloured curtains beyond which we could see the verandah with its exquisite pillars, the glowing braziers.

Just behind us I could sense the three Puttiorans.

We went to the edge of the verandah. On a long low bench one of the revellers lay sprawled, his cheek in his vomit—the sight of it seemed to strengthen Nasar.

"Be careful," he muttered, and we turned together to face the three evil ones, their hands outstretched for my headband, which was the easiest to take.

"It would kill you," I said coldly, and with contempt.

And *daring* to do it, I turned my back on them and at Nasar's urging ran down the steps into the snow, which was still smothering everything.

I could hear the feet of the Puttiorans scraping and slipping on the steps.

"I do not think you have understood," said Nasar, into the whiteness. "This lady is from the High Command of Canopus. You know what the agreement is."

I saw their stone faces looming vaguely in the white—and then vanish.

"Call a chair," said Nasar to them.

Again I saw the bearers shaking themselves free of the snow as they laboured running under the box-conveyance, but when we were in the box, Nasar and I, I had no time to think of them or of the Puttiorans, for now Nasar slumped back in the box, his eyes shut, breathing as if he were very ill, and shaking all over. Then his eyes were open and they stared, and from them poured liquid. Canopeans do not, normally, weep—that is far behind them. The fact that Nasar wept now said everything.

I remained quiet. I was bracing myself for what I thought would happen—and it did. When we were deposited at the foot of the great cone that soared above us into the whirling storm, the winds whining around it, there were the three stone men waiting for us.

"Nasar," I said, "one more effort; they are here."

Again he seemed to shudder as he took command of himself.

We descended from the box, and walked straight up to the three.

"You are fools," said Nasar, using contempt like a weapon.

"You gave us these," we heard, and saw the hands stroking the golden earrings on those narrow rims around their ears. "You gave us these . . ."

"Give them back," I said. "Canopus commands . . ." But they were running off into the white, for they weren't going to give up this fancied authority of theirs—for now I understand that this indeed was how they saw it. All the bits of gold and metal and buttons and bracelets—they believed them to be intrinsic and unchanging substance of Canopus and authority for themselves.

I saw Nasar staring after them, with the sombre anger that I was ready to believe was not only the characteristic of his subjection to this place but *his* characteristic and even, possibly, a Canopean characteristic.

And again, my thought was answered: "Oh no," said he, "that is not so. Believe me, fair Sirian, you must not think that, for your own sake . . ." and I saw *him* gazing at my earrings, my other appurtenances, and in such a way that for a moment I fancied myself back in the hands of the hungry ones in Elylé's house.

I walked swiftly away from him and started up the stairs. So we went up together, I first, he behind, up and around, and around, and around, until we reached the top.

I knew that I had by no means finished with the battle: and that more was to come. I was prepared to face him then, as we entered that half-circle of a room, whose windows were showing a grey daylight where snow whirled. But Nasar staggered forward and had fallen across piles of cushions before I was fairly inside. I put some coverings over him and retired next door where I sat quietly in a window opening to watch the day come, a grey-gold light behind the white whirl.

And what I was thinking then was not of what I was going to have to fight out with him but of those privileged citizens of Koshi in their soft-lit and luxurious rooms.

It will not, I am sure, come as a surprise to any of my readers that I was thinking of the problem Sirius has perennially had with a privileged class, which seems to re-create itself constantly and everywhere. I am sure there are those who have been wondering why I have not made the comparison more strongly before— particularly as I am known to have always been of the administrative party that has sought to check these privileged classes, when it has not been possible to prevent their emergence. I have more than once put forward the view that the possibility is we exaggerate the importance of this phenomenon. If a corrupt class can be expected to form, always and invariably, then this is as a result of, concomitant with, the strengthening and enlarging of a larger, and generally vigorous and active, class on which the effete ones float like scum on a wave. Has there ever been a society *without* its spoiled and rotten minority? Would it not be better simply to expect this, and to legislate limits to what cannot be prevented, rather than allowing fear of it to prevent any reforming efforts to be made at all—for that was what tended to happen. There was for a time—students of this particular sociological problem will be familiar with it—a very vocal faction putting forward the point of view that there is no point whatever in making revolutions (this was particularly strong after the rebellions on our Colonised Planets during the last phase of our Dark Age) because any revolution, no matter how pure and inspired, can be guaranteed to produce a privileged class within a generation. Worse; it was held that it was useless even to reform and reconstruct a society, for the same reason. This point of view certainly had the effect of causing a slump in morale, and a general pessimism, and had to be proscribed for a time because of this. Yes, we (that is, the administrative class) were indeed aware of the humour of the situation: that we were imposing the strictest penalties on the proponents of the viewpoint that the rulers (for we are certainly that) must not be attacked and criticised because our continual tendency towards corruption must not only be expected but cannot be averted: we were vigorously encouraging opposition and criticism, even to the extent, at one point, of actually setting up a party ourselves—secretly, of course—so alarmed were we at the pervasive cynicism and disgust. I myself was too well known a figure to be one of these individuals, but three of my progeny (not by Ambien I) took part, and so I had the benefit of their reports.

It is my view now, after what I am sure must be conceded as a pretty long and thorough experience, that there *is* nothing to be done to prevent an effete class; it can be postponed for a time, at the best. But it certainly can be circumscribed, and a difficulty in the way of such circumscription is always a too-violent, an emotional judgement of such—after all—weak and pointless people. There has never been a self-indulgent privileged class that has not destroyed itself, or allowed itself to be destroyed, almost as soon as it has come into being and grown, and flourished . . . temporarily.

But as I watched the snow fall there, with these thoughts in my mind, I was again wondering about Canopus: how did that great Empire deal with these problems? If they had them at all?—for we had never heard of them! And if they did not arise with them, *why not?*

I did not sit alone there for long. I listened for sounds on the other side of the dividing wall, for I had a pretty good idea that Nasar was in too poor an emotional state to rest, let alone sleep. I heard him moving about, clumsily and roughly. There was a silence for a while, but then I heard him enter from the stairs—he had been to the foodshop. He muttered, then he groaned. I believed I heard him weep.

I changed my garments, putting on my Sirian garb of the Colonial Service from some impulse, of which I was fully conscious, to stand on an exact and accurate footing with Nasar. I then asked if I might enter, and having repeated it and heard his "Very well then, come in!"—I went in. He was stretched out full length, on his side, head propped on his elbow. He was dishevelled. His eyes were red. So dejected was he that I could have believed him surrounded by a thick black cloud. He was certainly quite repulsive, and I heard myself mutter: "Oh! But he's so ugly!" So much for the outward form of an attraction! And I could not help remembering the "insect people" who were superior, so Klorathy said, and whom I found repulsive.

And he knew what I was thinking, for while he did not look up, he smiled briefly and bitterly. He said, "Help yourself if you are hungry." He had brought some sort of tea, and bread. I filled a cup for myself and refilled his, a service that he did not acknowledge, for he stared unblinking, seeing very little. I wondered briefly if I should seat myself low, like him; or put myself in a magisterial chair—for that there was going to be a confrontation I had no doubt. But in the end I took my cup to a window opening and looked out, which was what I wanted to do. I was able to see to the northeast, where the snow had stopped falling. And to the southeast, where it was retreating. The tall thin brown cones were reappearing from white obliterating clouds, and the cold fluffy masses seemed to pile themselves halfway up—but of course this was an illusion. Already around the bases of the towers now the snow had stopped falling, armies of small dark figures were at work making tunnels and runnels for themselves, and the huddle of the lower town, which had been blotted out by the storm, was reappearing under the efforts of this energetic swarm.

There was an idea—no, a memory—persistently presenting itself in my mind: this was that I recognised the black emotions that emanated from Nasar. Not so very long ago, one of our officials on Planet 9 had become demoralised after having been left there— so I thought, and so I put forward on his behalf—for too long. He had allowed himself to become a tool of an anti-Sirian party. I had been sent to adjudicate the situation. There was no doubt he was guilty, and I took him back to our Home Planet where, unfortunately, he was executed. I believed him capable of rehabilitation. He had radiated this same sullen explosive anger that, not being allowed to express itself outwardly, was as if the whole organism was vibrating on a strong discordant note.

I could see that Nasar was not able to keep still, but continually shifted position, how he jerked and twitched, how his eyes roved and glanced everywhere, how he sighed and then flung back his head, gasped, and again stared sombrely in front of him. But he was watching me, too, I could see that he was calculating—on guard, preparing himself. Was he planning to return to subjection to Elylé? If so, having felt the strength of it myself, I could understand it—understand it even as I shuddered.

"Quite so," said he suddenly. "But no, I shall not go back. I've been able to break it at last. And I suppose for that I have to thank you."

I was reflecting how, and when, he was able to know what I thought, as he went on: "But there is a price to pay, dear Sirius. And I am sure you will not be surprised to know what it is."

At this it came into my head that he was going to demand the prescribed artefacts from me: that I had by no means finished with that pressure.

"Exactly so," he said. "As you can see, I no longer have the things I need to protect me here . . ."

"You have given them away," I said—dry enough.

At which he leaped up, and began striding around and about the room, sometimes stopping and standing quite still, eyes staring, mouth fallen slightly open; then going on again, restless, discoordinated, *driven*—it was making me feel quite ill watching him, so I turned my back and looked out past the brown spires into the back of the retreating storm, and heard the winds whine and whisper around the grey sky.

"I have to have them," he said. "I have to."

"And so have I. I was invited here. I am here because of that. And I was given the things. And told how to use them. And I do not feel entitled to give them away."

"To give them *back*—to me—to Nasar of Canopus."

"I was told most specifically not to give them to anybody," I said.

I felt his eyes on me, and turned and he stood staring—trapped. That is how he felt.

And now I knew what he was thinking, and I said, "There is nothing to stop you from taking them. You are stronger than me. But then, Canopus has always been in a position simply to *take*."

I saw him shudder as if a black force had let him go, so that he could stand up straight, and breathe more easily.

"Thank you for reminding me," said he. Oh, not without humour—and I heard *that* note with enough relief! But he had spoken also with a renewal of responsibility. For he looked at me differently. "Yes, thank you. Thank you, Sirius." He stood, as if waiting for more.

I turned now and faced him fully. I was conscious of every sort of irony, and sorrow in this situation: I, in my garb of the top administration, but still of Sirius, and Canopus, our magnanimous superior, but in the shape of this criminal official. The word was taken up by him at once.

"*You* have criminals," said he smiling. "With us—we merely fall by the wayside." And he laughed out, genuinely; and the laugh changed, as it were, midway, and the haunted driven one was back, once again he was being impelled to stride around and across and back and forth.

"What do you do with your criminals, Sirius? What would happen to me, if I were one of yours?"

"I think you would be executed."

"Yes. That is what I thought. And suppose I agree with you and not with my own dear Empire? Suppose I think I ought to be executed?"

"You want to be punished?" I enquired, as dry as I could manage. And again I saw him straighten, the black weight on him lift. He said, just as dry: "Yes, and perhaps that is it. But Sirius, when I say that they have made a mistake, I mean it. I have not been strong enough for my work."

"Do you never get leave?" I asked. "They surely do not put you here indefinitely—not for the long ages you tell me you have been stationed here."

And now he came to stand by me, in my window embrasure, leaning against the inner wall, looking at me.

"I take it," said he, "that you are of the liberal party on Sirius."

"Yes, I am."

"Poor Sirius," he said softly, those dark-bronze, or copper, or amber eyes full and strong on my face. "Poor, poor Sirius."

Now this was quite unexpected, and I was thrown off my balance with him. We stood there, very close, looking into each other's faces. I was not now thinking of Klorathy, or of my search for his real friendship, or anything of the sort: I felt near, because of what Nasar had said, to some sort of mystery or understanding.

I waited until I could speak moderately, and said: "Why do you not simply go back home and tell them what you are saying to me."

"Because I have done so already."

"So you have been on leave?"

"Yes. But it was a long time ago—just after what these poor wretches call 'the Punishment.' But Sirius, to spend time *there*—and then to return here—do you know what that means? How one feels? How utterly *intolerable* . . ." and he struck off and away again, and began his despairing pacing.

"In short," he said, "it is not worthwhile to go home if one has to come back. And in my case I have to come back. That is what they say. This is my place. This hellhole. Shikasta the disgraced and the shameful one. *This.*"

"Rohanda is very beautiful," I said, with a sigh for my long stay on the Southern Continent, before the failure of the Lock. "No planet in our system is anything near as beautiful and as rich and as . . ." I was looking at the golden light in the grey sky to the southeast where the storm had now quite gone away. The brown cone nearest to this one showed the most elegant pattern of black markings all the way up, each touched with white: the snow underlined each window opening, and the symmetry and balance of the patterns gave me the deepest satisfaction; and that is what *Rohanda*—I was simply not prepared to use their niggardly little word for it—so plentifully did offer. A rich food for the senses—always and generously.

"Yes, it is beautiful," said he in a stifled voice, and he stood upright, eyes closed, his hand at his throat, and his eyes closed tight, quivering. He was thinking of Elylé.

"I understand," I said quietly. His eyes flew open: he gazed at me, sombre, but himself, and he strode across and bent over me, looking into my eyes. "Desiccated bureaucrat though I am, I understand very well. I wish I did not." And I could not prevent myself shuddering.

"Thank you," he said and went off again.

"I would like to know about this city—before it was spoiled."

He laughed, and with such bitterness. "And the other cities— before they were spoiled—because they are always spoiled, always, always."

"Always?"

"Yes."

"So then you have to make allowances for that?"

"Yes," he said with a sigh, the driven black one gone again, and he simple and *there* with me. "Yes. We make allowances. We know that if we build a city, or make a jewel, or a song, or a thought, then it will at once start to slide away, fall away—just as *I* have done, Sirius—and then—pfft!—that's it, it's over. *This* city, you say: the city of the twenty-one tall cones? And what of the city just there—can you see?"—and he pointed to where the storm had gone. I could just see a blur on the white horizon. "That is the city of the gardens. That *was* the city of the gardens . . ."

"And what is it now?"

"It is a city of gardens," said he, grim and savage, black and vibrating. "A gardened city. Elylé adores it. She has her place there, fountains and delights . . . Elylé, Elylé," he moaned suddenly, rocking, his hands up over his face.

"Nasar," I said sharply and he sighed and came to himself.

"You are going to have to give me your earrings," said he, coming up to me, taking me by the shoulders and peering into my face. The grip of those large hands bore heavily, and he felt me brace myself and he loosened them. "There's nothing to you," he said, incredulously. "A dry bone of a woman, with your judicious little face and your . . ."

"No, I am not Elylé," I said steadily. "Do you want me to be sorry for that?"

"No," he said simply, coming to himself.

"Nasar, is it that you want the earrings because you can stay here instead of going back home—and you have been ordered back home and don't want to go?"

"Exactly so."

"But wouldn't they—come after you and punish you?"

"No," he said, with his short laugh, that I now knew to associate with his inner comparisons between Canopus and what I made of Canopus as a Sirian. "No. What need of punishments? What punishments could conceivably be worse than *this* . . ." and he shut his eyes, and flung back his head with something like a howl—yes, it was like the howl of a desperate animal. "Ohhh," he groaned, or howled, "to *be* this, to have become part of it, to be Shikasta, to be Shammat . . ."

"You are not Shammat," I said, sharp and cold. And afraid.

"What do you suppose Shammat *is*, lady?" And he again marched and strode, and stopped, on his desperate course.

I had been given—I felt—another piece of my puzzle.

"Shammat is not merely an external tyranny?"

"Surely that is evident?"

"I see."

He enquired, really surprised. "How is it you have to ask?"

"I ask . . . and I ask . . . and I ask . . . there are questions I seem to ask over and over again. Yet I do not ever get an answer."

"But wasn't that an answer?"

I felt weighted with a half-knowledge, something too much, too painful, too dark—a long dark wail that was inward. And I could see the same on Nasar's face.

"This is a terrible place," he said in a bleak voice, as if suddenly seeing something for the first time—he who had lived with this for so long! Yet he was contemplating it again, anew. "A terrible place."

"Will you tell me *why*?" I said. "Please will you try and say. What *is* Shammat? That is what I want to know." And I added, "If I knew that, then could I understand Canopus?"

At this he laughed—a real laugh. "What is Shammat? Shammat is this—if you build a city—perfectly, and exactly, so that every feeling and thought in it is of Canopus—then slowly, the chords start to sound false—at first just slightly, then more and more—until soon the Canopus-nature has gone, it has slipped, it has fallen away . . . like me . . . and if you start again, and collect together, let us say, ten people and teach them Canopus—if you can, if you *can*—then that is all you can do because Shammat rises up and strikes back and for the ten of Canopus nature there will be ten times ten of Shammat. The ten you cherish, if they stand, *if* they stand, if they do not fall away like me . . . and if you say Love, then Love is the word, it is Love, yes, but then . . ." and he was muttering now, in a crazy, restless, wild desperation and misery, ". . . but then it is Love still but cracked, the sound false, then falser, and it is not love but wanting, oh Elylé, Elylé, Elylé the beautiful one, my beautiful one . . ."

"Nasar!" I stopped him and he sighed and came to himself. "Yes," he said, "Love the golden word does not sing her song for long here, before her voice cracks. . . . Love slowly turns down, down the spiral and then there is Hate. Each perfection becomes its opposite, that is Shammat. You ask what is Shammat—it is that if you say Love, then before long, it is Hate, and if you build for harmony, then soon it is quarrelling, and if you say Peace, then before long it is War—that is Shammat, that is Shammat, Sirius."

"And yet Canopus persists here. Canopus keeps this planet. Canopus does not jettison it. Rohanda is under your protection."

"That is our policy."

"And do you not agree with it?"

"No, I do not agree with it—but then, *I* am now Shammat, or at least for a good part of the time, so what does it matter what I agree with or not?"

"Tell me, you have been ordered back and you do not want to go?"

"Yes."

"Because you cannot face what you feel when you have to come back again?"

"Yes."

"And if I gave you the earrings and the other things . . ."

"Oh, the earrings would do, they would be enough," he muttered, desperate and evasive and savage.

"How could they be enough? You have certain exact and accurate practices, always changing as circumstances change. . . . Is that not so?"

He was staring at me, sullen, admiring in a way, but disliking.

"Very true."

"So if you are asking for the earrings, they cannot be to enable you to maintain yourself healthily here, but to give to Elylé. Is that it? Or is there something else?"

"There might be."

"Can it be that the Puttiorans, who have the earrings and who are making wrong use of them, are putting pressure on you to join them?" I heard my own voice, prim and scandalised—and incredulous.

"Something like that."

"You cannot conceivably be tempted by Puttiora?"

"Why not? If I can be tempted by Elylé—and more than tempted—do you realise I have been as good as her husband for—oh, I don't want to think how long . . ."

"Well, how long?" I asked, as the thought came into me that these creatures lived very short lives.

"Exactly so, Sirius. There is the additional torment that this absolute and incredible beauty is—stuff for a moment, snow on your palm. It is like being allowed to become besotted, drunk, *gone* into the perfection of a butterfly. Do you have butterflies on Sirius?"

"No. But I have seen them elsewhere."

"In Shikastan terms, I have *loved*—forgive the word—Elylé for a long time. In our terms, our time, I am drinking, drunk, *gone* into something that dissolves as I look at it, like wanting to possess a snowflake. Can you imagine the fascinations of that, Sirius?"

"Nasar, you should go home. And you should say all this—in the right quarters."

"And then?" he said—amused, I could see that; and in exactly the same way as I would be by a very young child.

"Very well," I said, "Sirian ways are not yours. But surely the problems of discipline are the same everywhere? You should obey orders, freely confess your derelictions, and take your punishment—but you say there isn't any."

He sighed, and began his pacing.

"And you should put forward your point of view—you should say that in your opinion the policy for this planet is incorrect."

He flung himself down again, on a pile of cushions, stretched his legs out, put his arms behind his head and watched me, with a smile.

"Canopus should argue with Canopus," said he. "Well, why not? It has never been done. But . . ." and he laughed.

"I do not understand why that is so amusing," I said. "But I have had a very great deal of experience with the administration of planets, and the personnel who administer them. I have always been an advocate of the policy that does not only allow, but insists on, the views of personnel being heard at all times. It is not possible for an administration that has to be centered on the Home Planet to remain *always* au fait with local problems. That is exactly how administrative policies get top-heavy and inflexible. If there is not a continual and active liaison between headquarters and the local officials—then in my experience, one can expect things to go wrong."

I have to record here that he laughed until I became very angry, but on behalf of Sirius, not of myself. For it was Sirius that was being criticised.

"Very well," said he, "I shall go back, as ordered. I shall demand active rehabilitation—for I certainly need it. I shall demand the right to put forward an opposition to existing policy. I shall say that this was on the advice of Sirius . . ." and he nearly began laughing again, but he saw my face and stopped. "I am sorry," he said, "I really am. But you simply do not know . . ."

"No, I don't know. But I would like you to go on. If your persuasions fail, and the existing policy stands, then . . ." I hesitated, and said: "I shall not attempt to conceal from you that Sirius would like all of Rohanda. We obviously have very different ideas from yours. Let us say, they are not so lofty! We could make good use of this planet for our experiments. We have made very good use of the southern hemisphere . . ." and here I had to stop.

I had forgotten, because of the superior and even commanding position I had had to take in relation with this Canopean functionary, that our part on this planet had not always been honestly played! Again I found myself in the position of hoping a Canopean was not able to read my thoughts, yet knew he did.

I made myself say: "Did you know that some of our experiments in the south were not always entirely within the terms of our agreements?"

"Yes, of course we know that."

He did not seem inclined to say any more. Because it was of no importance?

"That you would not always keep to the spirit, let alone the letter, of our agreements, was foreseen and allowed for."

I was angry now. And defensive. "What I can't understand is this: Canopus both allots this defective little planet a far more important role than we do—certainly you go to far greater lengths than we ever do—but at the same time you seem quite extraordinarily perfunctory . . ." and as I spoke, words flashed into my mind, and I received them with a sense of weariness. "I suppose you are going to say that what you do is in accordance with what is needed?"

"But what else could I possibly say?" he asked, genuinely surprised.

For some reason the insectlike people of their Planet 11 came into my mind: I remembered an infant that was a frail pink squirm held in milky semitransparent arms, surrounded by waving tentacles. And these loathsome things were higher in the evolutionary scale than I was, or at least very well regarded by Klorathy, and therefore, also, by Nasar. For me to approach "the Need" seemed to demand resources of tolerance in me that I could not believe I would ever have. And yet again we had reached, Canopus and I, a moment when an understanding had been on the verge of trembling into light. And then had gone again. Had been engulfed in anger, guilt, and in disbelief in my own capacities.

I did not know what it was I had *not* understood.

I heard myself muttering: "I don't understand, I don't understand."

"Poor Sirius," said Nasar, in the way he had done before.

"What will happen if you fail to persuade them?" I asked.

He stood up. He looked drained, and ashy and lustreless, all the energy gone out of him.

"I shall go home now. I shall take your advice. If I succeed in my application to question the Colonial policy, I shall say that in my view we should jettison Shikasta. I shall say that Sirius has put forward a serious request to take over Shikasta. If I fail, and the existing policy stands—and this is what will happen, Sirius, please do not expect too much—I shall, I suppose, have the pleasure of seeing you here again some time."

"Are you not permitted to request transfer to another planet?"

"I do not think that . . . but let us put it this way. Once I am there, and back in my normal frame of mind, I probably will not want to demand a transfer."

"I do not understand why not," I insisted. "And if you do return here, I hope you will suggest that you are not to be left down here so long without regular periods of leave."

He smiled again. It was gentle, and even appreciative and even—again—with a certain admiration. "I shall make your views known," he said.

"And what work do you think you will be assigned when you come back? If you do."

"What? Why, as always, I shall be sent to a new place—for of course it will not have escaped you that these cities of the eastern central landmass will soon be under sand?"

"No, it did not escape me!"

"Exactly so . . . and I shall either find myself in some dreadful city, which I shall regard, at *first*, as hell and torment, and then . . . perhaps it will all happen again? In any case, I shall set the current flowing, and guard the flow, and make checks to Shammat . . . all that, all that I shall do—as I always do! Or perhaps they will tell me to make another city, or a cluster of cities, like these—all perfect, perfect . . . until . . ."

"How do you go about creating your cities?" I asked—and again the word came to me. "Oh, according to *need*," I said. "Yes, but *how*?"

"I think I shall go now," he said. "If I don't, who knows what may happen! I shall even perhaps find myself back with Elylé—I wouldn't put it past myself, I assure you."

"How will you call your spacecraft?" I asked.

"I shall return—in another way," said he. "Goodbye, Sirius. And thank you. Look after your equipment—your earrings and the rest—they will be coming after it and after you, and when they find I have disappeared they may make that an excuse to take you physically. . . . Call your spaceship in and leave. That is my advice."

He ran out of the room, and after some time I saw him, a small dark figure, emerge from the base of the tower. He had taken no covering with him. I slowly understood. He was going to walk off into the great snow wastes and die there. This gave me food for thought indeed—it was the beginning of a new understanding about the ways of Canopus, their different means of going and coming, of "travelling," if you like. . . . I did not have time to think of all this then, any more than I had time to reflect on this long conversation with Canopus, in which there were so many openings for a greater comprehension. I was watching Nasar struggle forward. I could see from the low crowding white in the northeast that soon it would snow again. But long before it did, Nasar would be lost in the billowing piling masses. He would be dead very soon, I knew. He would not be found, I could be pretty sure, until the snow melted. That was when I could be afraid of the Puttiorans coming to take me in; probably on a charge of not reporting a disappearance, and even of murder—who knew what one could expect in a place like this! But the melting of the snows was a long way off. I had hoped to wait till the spring. I stood looking out at the scene that seemed crammed with white substance, and thinking that all that was water. How it would swirl and flood all around these towers when the season changed! I would stand up here in the little tip of this tower, and look down at brown floods—and then, so I believed, there would be a burst of vegetation. I had never seen anything like that.

I had no reason at all to doubt that when Canopus warned, they should be listened to. I did not want to have to face the Puttiorans, or even that degenerate smiling cruel lot—these gone-to-self-

indulgence classes are always cruel in their lazy insolent way. . . .
Then why was I waiting here? Why, of course, to meet Klorathy.

I had come here to meet Klorathy. . . .

I understood that I had met Klorathy. There was a mystery here
I did not expect to unravel then, but I knew there was one.

I decided that I would call in my hovering Space Traveller and
leave. I sent out the call, and collected my belongings. I found a
white hooded garment folded in a chest and huddled myself in it.
I did not want to be seen, a dark escapee against the snows, and
arrested.

Just as I was preparing to leave these high rooms at the cone's
tip, and descend to the street, I saw some writing sheets lying where
Nasar had been stretched before I came into the room.

His despair, his misery, his self-loathing, his conflicts, were written
there in broken, sometimes abusive or obscene words. I ran my
eye swiftly over them, leafing through the many sheets: there were
months of comment there. But on the sheet he had been scribbling
over, obviously, just before I had come into the room, was written:

I come again and again to the same thought. I may not be able to face
Canopus and my own nature now and the shame that will overwhelm
me when I contemplate what I have been here, but I have only to contemplate Sirius to be strengthened in the better side of myself: thinking
of Sirius I feel that perhaps I may at last force myself back to my duty.
How is it possible that an Empire can be so large, so strong, so long-
lasting; so energetic, so inventive, so skilled; how can it be so admirable
in so many ways—and yet never have any inkling at all of the basic
fact? They continue; they thrive; they fall into periods of decline; they
make decisions; they advance again . . . they let their populations rage
out of control, and then suddenly limit them to practically nothing.
And all this done according to a temporary balance of social forces and
opinion—*never* according to Need. This worthy and correct and competent official, who is no more capable of the shameful falling away than
I have shown I am only too capable of, is not able to take in anything
of what the *function* of Canopus is. What the *function* of Sirius could
be. Is that not a thought with enough power in it to make me whole
again?

That is what I saw written there. I put this sheet of brittle yet at the same time flexible substance—it was new to me—in my clothes, and in my turn walked rapidly down the stairs and out into the cold whiteness. It had begun to snow again, though lightly. I was not afraid I would not find the Space Traveller, only that I might be stopped first. I did see a couple of Puttioran guards at the base of the far tower, and I ran fast along the road I had come into the city on. It was hard to keep on the road. On either side were only faint depressions to mark the ditches. I stumbled on, wondering if Nasar was still upright and walking onwards, or if he had fallen and was dying. It was strange to think in this way: we did not expect to die! Not we of the Sirian Mother Planet who can renew our bodies almost indefinitely. Death was hardly a reality to us. And that Canopus should use bodies like an equipment of garments . . .

I had not run forward for long when I saw the soft glitter of the Space Traveller, and was in it and up and off the white thicknesses in a moment—soon below us the brown cones stood up out of the white coverlet, and above us was the Rohandan night sky crammed with blazing stars. I looked for our own dear star, which shed such a happy glow on our Home Planet, but I was bound for the southern hemisphere. We swept on, with the white expanse below us, and then over the great mountains that were white, too, and suddenly below us was the blue ocean. The experiments I was proposing to organise do not concern my purpose in this account.

And so I conclude my report of my encounter with Canopus in Koshi, of the cities of the eastern central landmass.

PLANET 3 (1), THE PLANET 9 ANIMALS

For a long time I was nowhere near Rohanda, but at the other end of our Empire, dealing with problems, mostly psychological, arising from the reductions of population. I did not enjoy this work, and if it were not that the problems were so taxing, and, often, dangerous to the Empire, I would have visited Rohanda for a personal inspection of the experiments that were being pursued there. But these were none of them of the class described as socio-biological, only small-scale laboratory work on genetic engineering.

It was not until the question arose of Planet 3 (1) and its future that I could with good conscience return home for the discussions on policy, and then look forward to a tour of duty on Rohanda.

The policy discussions were long and even stormy. Our decision not to acquire and develop further planets had been maintained. Planet 3 (1) was Planet 3's moon or satellite. Planet 3 was in active use. Its moon had never been developed, was almost entirely without oxygen: but it fell within the class of planets that are considered potentially the most useful and desirable, if their atmosphere can be adjusted. At the height of our Empire's expansion, plans had been made to force 3 (1), for it was plentifully equipped with all kinds of minerals. But as we pursued our deliberate policy of retraction and reduction, the search for new supplies of minerals became unnecessary. I think it is not far off the truth to say that we came to overlook 3 (1), even forgot it. Planet 3 itself, an adequately functioning place, was not concerned with it, except as to how it affected her gravitational situation.

The question of developing 3 (1) arose because there is always a latent hunger in our Colonial Service for the old days of expansion and development. I say this knowing I shall attract criticism, and cries of "Old Imperialist!" But why avoid the truth! It is my belief that very many of the ills and problems of our Service stem from this hunger. There is something in Sirian nature that demands, that flourishes, in situations of challenge, provided best by the takeover of a new planet, its problems, it regulations, its development. To *expand*, I maintain, if not normal for us (in the sense that is *right*) is at least the most agreeable condition. To monitor and police planets kept deliberately stable, and on a low level of energy generally, is *not* exhilarating, does not inspire and develop the members of the Service. If this were not true, why should we always have in operation so many schemes deliberately contrived to provide challenge to our Service?

No, the truth is that Planet 3 (1) came to our attention again because a large number of our personnel, particularly the younger ones, wanted to experience the sharp edge of difficulties, problems, hazards. Even dangers—for there is something quite different in quality between the dangers that have to be surmounted in establishing something new, and those faced in, let's say, a regular policing job on a planet that erupts in dissatisfaction or discontent because of a life level that is seen too clearly to be stagnant. I do not wish here to re-introduce metaphysical questions! It is far from my intention to stray into regions that are only too thoroughly explored by our social philosophers. If I mention that on many of our thoroughly stable and economically balanced planets we have deliberately—during some epochs—allowed the inhabitants to believe in dangers that are nonexistent, that is only because it is relevant here. We have invented threats from Puttiora, or from Shammat; caused rumours of possible cosmic hazards, such as approaching comets or unfortunate starry alignments; even provoked minor uprisings—all this to prevent planets from becoming dolefully sunk into What-is-the-purpose-of-it-all states of mind that, unchecked, can even lead to mass suicide.

At any rate, this was the main reason for our reconsidering Planet 3 (1), and it did not appear on the official list of reasons as released finally by our deliberating Conference. (It is my experience that this is a general rule, to be observed everywhere and in all kinds of situations: the *real*, the propelling cause of a situation or decision or change of policy is never mentioned at all, and must be sought for behind and buried under the peripheral ones.)

The reasons were listed as follows:

1 Planet 3 (1) is the only one of our Colonised Planets, or Planet's Planets, left undeveloped, or not made use of in some way or another.

2 To choose an analogy from the remote past, it is as if a well-run farm of the old kind allowed a single field to remain uncultivated. (Our younger members are particularly fond of these archaic and romantic comparisons—one may almost say that it is a cult with them.)

3 This planet, being so near to Sirius, would be more economical to use for its minerals than other mineral-rich planets.

4 Planet 3 has shown signs of the familiar moral stagnation and will benefit from the debates and disagreements resulting from the decision to bring its moon to life.

5 3 (1) presents new problems, and their solution will add to our stock of scientific knowledge.
6 There have been reminders from our personnel on Rohanda that our territories there are underused, and that parts of them are already overrun by peoples and races resulting from our previous experiments. The provision of an atmosphere for 3 (1) might be dovetailed into certain local conditions on Rohanda, as discussed at the Conference. (Details attached.)

I had a message sent to Canopus asking if it would inconvenience them to let us use part of their territory for a limited and definite time. I was not unaware of a certain duplicity here, if one was not to call it, simply, diplomacy; the point was that we did not know exactly how long we would need the territory. We wanted the highest possible mountains. Extremely high mountains covered a large area of the southern part of the central landmass. These had become higher still, and more extensive, during the internal squeezings and pushings of the planet during the unfortunate "events." We believed, through our espionage, that Canopus was not making much use of these mountainous areas. (Later we discovered this was mistaken.) But in any case, the message came back that they were not able to lend us these mountains or any part of them, and they "wished to draw our attention to" the very high mountain chains along the western edge of the Isolated Southern Continent II. Thank you very much! I thought; but of course we did have these mountains, and they were adequate for our purpose. One motive for at least attempting an occupation of their Great Mountain was that our reports indicated that Klorathy was or had been stationed in those parts. I had not heard anything further from him.
Nor from Nasar.
My experience with Nasar had gone into the background of my thoughts shortly after it ended. This in spite of an intriguing report of a conference on Canopus that had caused "great and unprecedented interest." It was a question of whether Rohanda should be entirely given up. "Top and Authoritative Policy" had been challenged. "The debate, which lasted longer than any previous debate, and which argued the very bases of Canopean colonial policy, ended in a majority vote in favour of the maintenance of

Rohanda." Colonial policy had been changed in a way that was unprecedented. "The disgruntled minority had put forward a suggestion which was adopted: that with the exception of those officials who had always been involved with Rohanda, service on the recalcitrant and burdensome planet would be voluntary: no one should be forced to sign up for a tour of duty." I translated these concepts, all very Sirian, into what I imagined would be nearer to Canopean ideas, in accordance with the conversations I had had with Nasar, and with what I had learned of the nature of Canopus. But a *fact* remained: there had been a conference on Canopus, as I had suggested to Nasar, to debate conditions of colonial service on Rohanda. (Their Shikasta.) He had laughed at the mere idea of it, but it had happened, nevertheless. But I had too little information. All this was not even secondhand: one of our officials, visiting Colony 10 for a routine exchange of information with their officials, had heard this conference mentioned in a casual conversation and had enquired about it, but without any sense of its importance, or its historic nature. . . . And I had to confess, thinking it all over, that perhaps it was *not* all that important. How was I to know the emphases Canopus must place on events, according to that "Necessity" of theirs! Because a disgruntled and disaffected—I hoped and believed only temporarily—official disagreed with a top-level policy, this did not mean that one had to take it all that seriously! Officials on my level had to consider this kind of thing all the time, and I took it as no more than routine. All the same, there *had* been a conference, and yet Nasar had laughed, and laughed, at the very idea of such a conference being possible. . . . I had to end up with this small fact, and abandon all other speculation.

The reason I did not dwell overmuch on my visit to Koshi was that it was all too much for me. That is the truth. What I had learned was a challenge to everything I was *as a Sirian official*. How could it not be? And yes, I was only too aware that to think on these lines—that I, Ambien II, might have ideas and intimations beyond my role as Sirius (I thought often enough of how Nasar had called me, simply, Sirius!) and was even beginning to separate off in myself these two entities, or ways of experiencing living—was, probably, treason. Treason of a kind. Treason to the Sirian way of looking at things. Yet who, and when, had ever shown any tendencies of this sort before? I could not remember it! When we (Sirius) had to face revolts on our colonies or disagreements about policy, these were always within Sirian terms, ideas, concepts. As for our famous "existential situation," this certainly did not go beyond Sirian boundaries. But, when I was with Canopus, inside Canopean thinking, it was Sirius itself that was challenged, its very bases, its foundations.

No, I certainly was not able to see myself as an alien to Sirius. For that was what it amounted to. Was I to put myself forward at one of our regular Conferences on Overall Policy and say—but what? That I believed Canopus to be altogether finer and higher than we were, and that we should go humbly to Canopus begging for instruction? Wrap it up as I might, that is what it amounted to.

I have already made it clear in this memoir, or account, of mine that our attitudes towards Canopus made that quite inconceivable.

Was I then—knowing this—to start propaganda work among my close colleagues and personal allies, such as the others of the Five, or Ambien I, or my offspring, with the idea of changing a nucleus that would (but how?) slowly change all of Sirius? The formation and cultivation of such "cells" of course was perennial and only to be expected by all of us when facing dissident planets and insurrectionary movements.

I might consider this, playing with the idea sometimes, but could not imagine myself actually doing it. There is such a thing as the art of the possible, and working with it. Well, it was not possible that I, with my position in the Empire, my experience, my temperament, should start what amounted to revolutionary cell-building!

What alternatives were there? I now have to state, categorically, that I could not envisage any alternatives. These were the possibilities . . . as I saw it. I did, dimly and distantly, see that Canopus itself might have ideas of its own. . . . I would entertain, sometimes, these rather visionary notions, and always when brooding about my various encounters with Canopus—where I had failed, where I had, in spite of these failures, learned. The practised and practising person that was Ambien II had to recognise facts, when I saw them. *Facts*, the more experienced one became, were always to be understood, garnered, taken in, with that part of oneself most deeply involved with *processes*, with life as it worked its way out. Facts were *not* best as understood formulas or summings up, but through this inward groping and *recognition*. Well, what I *recognised* in contemplating my relations with Canopus was some sort of purpose. It was unmistakable. To dismiss it, deny it, meant denying everything I had ever learned in my long career as participator in events. I could not dismiss it. But I could say that it was all too much for me. I postponed it. And for a very long time was busy with my work, which I was not enjoying, and which inwardly I was questioning and feeling sapped and diminished by, because of an ever-increasing sense of its futility (oh yes, treachery and treason, I know!), because of, in fact, the steady, unstoppable growth in me of that person or individual who was not "Sirius."

Who was—*who? Or what?* Canopus?

This was why I caused the request to be sent that we might borrow or lease their Great Mountains.

This was the cause of my disappointment at their refusal.

So! I was not to see Klorathy yet. . . . Very well then. I set myself to my task, and again pushed these thoughts to the back of my mind.

A map of Isolated Southern Continent II shows that rather more than a third of the way down the mountain chain is a lake high among the peaks.

What we wanted was to accustom a sufficient number of suitable individuals to living on sparse supplies of oxygen. It happened that we had, on our Colonised Planet 2, some high mountains, and on them were living a species able to function on comparatively little oxygen. But they had been established for generations. We needed flexibility, adaptability. After some thought, we chose a species from C.P. 9, a chilly, damp, dismal sort of place, whose nature was to match, phlegmatic and dour. We space-lifted 30,000 of them not to the highest peaks but to a plateau halfway up a mountain range that had sparse but adequate food, and a wet changeable climate. There we left them, under supervision, to adapt.

Meanwhile 3 (1) was being surveyed and prepared.

I visited there, I suppose it could be said, from curiosity, though there was not much on the place to feed interest.

It was arid, chilly, dusty.

There were semifrozen marshes, maintaining some sluggish lizards and frogs.

The vegetation was lichens, and a curious form of marsh weed that seemed half-animal. At any rate, while being anchored at one end in mud or slushy ice, the fronds, branches, feelers, crawled about all over the surface of the soil, sometimes even lifting and overturning stones and rocks, or burrowing down into mud, for the primitive insects and crustaceans. Sometimes these branches were half an R-mile long, and a single plant could cover a square mile. These animal-plants were a danger to our technicians, One was walking through what she believed to be quite ordinary, if unfamiliar vegetation, when the creature reached up with its "hands" or feelers, and tugged her over, and when she was rescued, it was only just in time, for the "plant" had already begun to dismantle her spacesuit, undoing screws and fastenings in search of the— obviously—delectable food within. This "plant" caused much excitement among our naturalists, it goes without saying; but as for me, I had a more localised interest in the place, namely, whether it would indeed be possible to change the planet's climate, as our experts claimed. It had one great advantage from our point of view: there was oxygen locked up in the soil.

This moon revolves about Planet 3 four times in its year, and spins on its axis once. Planet 3 is far from its sun, and is itself on the cold and lethargic side.

I left instructions to follow our experts' recommendations that thermonuclear explosions should be tried, with the aim of warming the planet, and returned to the settlement of our experimentees on the mountainside of Isolated S.C. II.

Enough time had passed for the first generation to have died out, and it was now a question of examining their progeny for signs of possible failure. None was found. Although they were existing on an oxygen supply of two-thirds of their familiar conditions on C.P. 9, they seemed to be thriving. I therefore took a decision: instead of giving them a further intermediate acclimatisation period, I ordered them to be transferred at once to as high as it was possible for animals to subsist. This was at over 15,000 R-feet, more than twice the height of their previous station, and the drop in oxygen level was severe, not only in comparison with that station halfway up the range but particularly in comparison with their Home Planet. The experts reported their lungs were already enlarging. I saw them established. It was now such an effort for them to accomplish what was needed that I ordered an abandonment of our usual policy and had housing installed for them. As it happened, it was possible to get this from a Canopean settlement on the Isolated Northern Continent—I was interested, more than interested, in how this happened. I was pondering about how to get this housing easily, for while we had settlements over the other side of the mountain range—this was not far, relatively speaking, from my settlement of the old days, in the time of the Lombis— it happened that we were short of suitable aircraft. It was at this moment that I had a message from Klorathy offering the materials I needed. I record that I merely noted that this was Klorathy, that he was at work so close, in the continent north of this one, and that he had known where I was. I noted it, and went on with my task.

I did not meet the fleet of their cargocraft as they arrived on the sea parallel with the mountains we were on, for I was convinced that Klorathy would not be there personally. The materials were lifted to the high plateaux by our craft. The settlement was soon in existence, double-storey wooden buildings, set out according to a plan that was found attached to the consignments of dismantled dwellings. I merely ordered this plan to be put into effect.

The Planet 9 animals were not the most attractive I have known! Again, they were of small build, not more than three to four R-feet. They were stocky, and their original hairiness was already enhanced, because of these cold heights they were adapting to. Very bright glassy blue eyes peered from under shelves of reddish fur. They had bred three or four or even five to a litter, but already were giving birth to only two or at the most three. They were strong, physically, but more importantly—as we believed—strong by moral nature. That is, they were not subject to emotional collapse under difficulties.

I watched these animals in their snowy valley lifted high up among those dreadful peaks, moving slowly in packs and groups, turning as one to face a new challenge—as, for instance, my appearance among them, or that of their supervisors. They stabilised their balance on long thick staves, and set their furry legs wide apart . . . the slow difficult turn of their heads, and the careful swivel of the cold blue eyes . . . the baffled glassy stare . . . all this was to see, or to fancy that one did, animals drugged, or tranced. I had seen this species on their Planet 9, where they are hardly a volatile or quick-moving kind, but at least did have some native liveliness. I was sorry for them, I admit. They had been told, on being rounded up for this experiment, that they were to accomplish a task of the greatest importance to Sirius, and that they would be honoured by the Empire if they succeeded: and what now remained in their progeny of this sense of importance was a feeling of having been *chosen*, or set apart. The supervisors reported that their instruction to their young was centred on their "special destiny" and their "superior qualities." All this was satisfactory.

Their high valley, with its beautiful lake, enjoyed three months of summer, when they were able to grow brief crops of a cereal we introduced from our Central Cereal Stocks that was able to flourish in high dry places, and to come to fruition within the three months. This was their staple, but they grew, too, various kinds of marrow and pumpkin. They kept some sort of sheep for milk and meat. But they were not able wholly to maintain themselves, so slow and difficult were their lives, and so prolonged their periods of snow; and so we supplied them yearly with additional foodstuffs, telling them it was an expression of the gratitude of the Empire. After all, it was not our intention to breed a species self-sufficient under any difficult circumstances, but to breed one able to stay alive in the early stages of the new existence of 3 (1).

I did not stay long on that trip. I had heard that the intermediary settlement, on the mountainside, had been visited by observers from a "kingdom" further north along the mountain chain, and that attempts had been made to kidnap some of the animals. Presumably as slaves. It was a slave state, of a particularly unpleasant sort. Further attempts would probably be made.

So went my reports. I then made a mistake. Believing that the extreme height of the new settlement would be enough of a deterrent, I did not order an increase in the supervisory force.

I ordered, however, a visit by spies into this "kingdom," and asked that their report should be sent to me where I would be on the other side of the mountain chain on the foothills above the great jungles that now covered so much of the continent.

I wished to visit Ambien I, whom I had not seen for a long time.

Ever since the unfortunate "events" on Rohanda, which had knocked the axis askew and caused seasons, involving changes of vegetation and weather of a sometimes spectacular nature, it had been fashionable for certain of the more advantaged of our citizens to spend holidays on both southern continents to observe these "seasons." Not only the well off; there were also excursions for officials of the more lowly kind, or even of ordinary citizens, particularly the elderly. In other words, there were two different sorts of visitor to Rohanda, for whom two standards of accommodation were prepared. My old friend Ambien I was put in charge of arranging the accommodation for the second class of our citizens and colonists. This did not mean more than a supervisory eye on the work of underlings. But he had indicated he would appreciate a chance to spend time in the better class of place, where I would join him.

As this most agreeable visit has nothing to do with this account of mine, I shall merely say that I flew down to a holiday settlement, from which one was able to see the high mountains on one side, and over the top of the jungles on the other, and where we watched the snows of the winter dwindle off the mountain ranges, and rush everywhere in fountains and torrents of sparkling water. Meanwhile Ambien and I caught up with news and gossip of what turned out to be—when we added it all up—fifty thousand R-years! We had in fact last met on this planet, on a joint mission connected with the inspection of our laboratories.

That meeting had seemed to us short enough; but this new one was even shorter, for the reports of our spies in the threatening kingdom reached me, and it was clear that something had to be done at once. An expeditionary force had been sent up into the mountains, and it had succeeded in capturing over 2,000 of the poor animals, whose future, judging from what I was finding out about Grakconkranpatl, was dark indeed.

Ambien I and I talked it all over, and I made my plans. Leaving him, reluctantly, I flew away from this holiday place, full of species

from every part of our Empire, all revelling in the sharp new
sensations to do with changing weather, the delightful emotions
associated with the "seasons"—which pleasures are to be found
only on Rohanda, or only to such a prodigal and always unexpected extent.

It was as a result of this meeting of ours, and what we observed
together of the reactions around us, that we recommended a team
of medical experts to visit the Southern Continents, to see whether
sojourns in places where the changes of the "seasons" were particularly marked could benefit certain psychological conditions, such as
melancholia, or an exaggerated dose of "the existentials"—an
irreverent name among the young for this emotional affliction. Our
recommendations were followed; a team of medical technicians did
explore possibilities on both continents; they agreed with our—
tentative—conclusions; clinics were set up on appropriate sites; and
it was not long before Rohanda became the most favoured place
for the treatment of these afflictions.

A side benefit was that a new branch or department of literature
resulted. It is categorised in our libraries as Effluvia of the Seasons.
I wonder how many now realise that this honoured, not to say
hoary, branch of our great literature originated in Rohanda with
that—now long-past—era of its use by us as a holiday station and
emotional-adjustment area?

GRAKCONKRANPATL

As usual, I began my investigation with an aerial survey. I had
to decide whether I wanted this to be noticed, and interpreted to
Sirian advantage. After deliberation I decided on minimum visi-
bility, choosing a surveillance aircraft that, if seen, could easily be
dismissed as the result of freak atmospheric effects. Whirling at
extreme speed, at the worst it would be seen as a kind of crystalline
glisten. I chose a day of high winds, fast-moving white cloud, and
bright sun, and hovered over Grakconkranpatl long enough for a
good survey.

I certainly did not like what I saw: for one thing, I observed our poor Colony 9 animals being sadly misused. I had to retire with my observations to my old headquarters in the foothills that once had monitored the Lombi and other experiments, for an opportunity for solitary thought.

What I had seen was this.

Descending through gaps in the mountain ranges, my eyes filled with the blue sweep of the ocean, below me was what at first glance could seem to be an assemblage of vast stone cubes assembled on a high place between peaks. The vegetation was heavy, a dense green, kept back from the piled stone by brief clearings showing the reddish soil. The massive cubes were of a dull greyish blue, the same colour as certain ticks I have seen infesting animals. These great blocks crammed and piled together were the city, and closer analysis showed they were built of uniformly cut stones, fitted together. Their lowering colour, their massing and crowding arrangement, gave an impression of hostility and threat, and even of great size. Yet it was not a large city. There were no gardens or green. No central open space, only a not overlong avenue, or narrow rectangle, that lay between two very large buildings, facing each other. These two opposing facades had no openings or windows. There were few windows anywhere, and once observed, this fact explained the sombreness and the threat of the place. The roofs, however, did offer some relief, for they were flat, and each was crowded.

I had never before seen a city like this, and if it had not been for our spies' reports, would not have been able to interpret it. The social structure could not easily be inferred from it. I knew this to be a wealthy culture with a large ruling class of one race, and slaves and menials of other captured races.

There was no sign here of rich and poor buildings, or rich and poor quarters of the city. Each of these vast blocklike buildings was a microcosm of the society, housing the rich and their attendants. The rich, as it was clear, lived on the top layers, where there were more windows, and on the roofs, which were equipped with awnings and shades and wind screens of all kinds. The slaves were down in the dungeonlike bottom layers where there was very little light. Life was never communal or public; there were no festivals or common amusements; no eating places, no baths, no shops.

Around this central city, the heart of Grakconkranpatl, on lower slopes, were the farms and the mines. These stretched in every direction for long distances. The farms were worked with gangs of slaves. They lived in heavy stone buildings, built in regular blocks. From the air they looked depressingly uniform. They were prisons. Even from the height of my observation craft I could see that where there was a cluster of working slaves, there were lines of supervisors, with weapons. I thought of our encampment in the heights where our Colony 9 animals were being acclimatised, and the regular patterns of wooden huts in which they were kept, and could not help a pang, wondering if they perhaps felt not very different from the poor wretches I could see slaving below me. But after all, our supervision was only for their benefit, to keep them in health and of course to prevent them from running away, which would do them no good. And our punishments were hardly of the kind I knew were used here.

All the same, I must record that I did not enjoy the comparisons I was being forced to make; and I suffered more than a few moments of attack from the existential problem.

At various distances from the central city, beyond the farming areas, were mines; the culture made extensive use of minerals. The same dark and forbidding patterns of barracks showed where the mines were. Down the mountainside from Grakconkranpatl ran an absolutely straight paved road, a dark grey streak through the lush forests. This road can only be described as insane. It made no concession to the terrain, to ups and downs or even mountains and precipices. Where there was a mountain it did not wind about it, but drove straight through. A long precipitous decline of several R-miles had been filled with rubble and the road taken over it. What it looked like was that some tyrant in a fit of hauteur had commanded: Make me a road straight to the ocean!

In fact I learned later that this was what had happened: hundreds of thousands of slaves had died in its making.

From my craft, I could watch long trains of transport animals with their loads of fish from the sea making their way up to the city on its high place. I could see that it was joined all along its length by smaller, equally straight roads, for the transport of farm produce and minerals.

I had to decide how best to present myself.

I was handicapped by not having experienced this particular type of society before. "Religions," of course, are to be found in one form or another everywhere. Only on Rohanda, due to the influence of Shammat—so I came to understand later—were theocracies common: that is, societies where the social structure was identical with the hierarchies of the religion. The ruling class was the priesthood, was hereditary, was all-powerful. The slaves were kept in order by the priesthood.

The root of my problem, so it seemed to me, was the degree of cynicism of the priesthood.

In other words, could they be frightened through "religion" or could they not? I studied the reports for accounts of their ceremonies and practices, and concluded that since—for Rohanda—they were well established, not to say ancient, having lasted for over a thousand years, and since this same ruling class had been perpetuated for so many generations, there was a likelihood that they in fact believed their repulsive inventions.

The practice on which this "religion" based itself was murder—ritual murder. This has always struck me as uneconomic, quite apart from its barbarity. One has to postulate a population organised to renew itself in excess of the needs of labour and breeding; or if not, then accessible to weaker cultures for the capture of slaves.

Not only were large numbers of unfortunate creatures "sacrificed" continually, the method was most disgusting. The heart was cut out while the victim was still alive. This had been going on, as I say, for centuries. This fact raises problems and questions that as an administrator cannot help but fascinate me, to do with the nature of what subject classes and races can be made to believe, or submit to.

The thought that occurred to me when I read of this practice was, of course, how had it originated? Memories of meetings with Canopus, reports from our agents, came to my aid. Canopus always and everywhere on Rohanda attempts to modify and soften the effects of Shammat by enjoining a moderation of the natural appetites, sometimes referred to as "sacrificing the heart." I concluded that this emotive and rhetorical phrase had, due to the continuous degeneration on Rohanda about which Nasar had been so eloquent, come to be taken literally. If this was the case, it seemed to me to indicate that Rohanda had, in the long interval since I had been involved there last, made a further step, and a large one, into brutishness.

It did occur to me that in a culture so addicted to murder, I might find myself a victim, but dismissed the thought: from our agents' reports I had concluded that erring slaves or captives from other cultures were sacrificed. In other words, I did not feel myself eligible. This was because situations of danger are so rare in our lives that I, like all of us long-lived administrative-class Sirians, had come to think of myself almost as immortal! Certainly death did not—does not—often approach my mind. And so I walked calmly and unafraid into the greatest danger I have ever experienced. This was not courage, but a result of the atrophy of the instinct of self-preservation.

I considered, and dismissed, plans for taking a large entourage. For instance, the inhabitants of Grakconkranpatl were all dark skinned; both rulers and slaves. A plan was for sending a craft down to the recreation settlements and asking for volunteers, from those races who were pale skinned and, preferably, with pale hair. I imagined the effect of a company of silvery ambassadors, arriving unexpectedly among those coppery or reddish people. Or, the opposite: I had often observed the impressive effect of individuals from C.P. 2: enormous black specimens, totally and glossily black, with cone-shaped narrow heads and long fine features. I imagined an entry of myself companioned in this way, but decided against this, too.

I toyed with a display of our crystal observation spheres, hovering low over the city, for long enough to be thought a permanent invasion, and then broadcasting loud and portentous messages, threatening them with destruction if they again raided our settlements.

But I have always been reluctant to use complicated or even untruthful means when something simpler would do.

What was the simplest of the means within my scope?

It was to go myself, alone. It was to demand to see the High Priest, alone. It was to tell him the truth: that this territory of theirs, on the slopes of the mountain ranges, was not at all, as they seemed to imagine, theirs, and under their rule, but under the overall sovereignty of "the Gods." Their astronomy was fair; they knew enough about the movements of the stars to match these with effects on crops and weather. They could be persuaded to make the step onwards to knowing that their superiors dwelled on the far stars: Gods. I would present myself as a God.

This was not untruthful, from the perspective of Rohanda.

I caused one of our agents to make a secret visit into the city, with a written message. I took care to use writing material foreign to Rohanda, and to choose solemn phrases to the effect that an Emissary from the Gods would visit them shortly, "from the skies."

I then left a good interval, so that this should become well absorbed, and took the opportunity to pay another quick visit to my dear Ambien I.

I was conveyed to Grakconkranpatl by a war machine specially summoned by me from the Home Planet. Our population-control experts had been instructed to design an aircraft that could intimidate by appearance. It was extremely swift, could hover, and shoot off in any direction, or land and take off very fast. It was absolutely silent. It was black, with a single dull-red eye on its body, which emitted greenish rays that in fact did have a temporarily stupefying effect on any living thing beneath. But its shape was the real triumph of the experts. This managed to suggest a heavy implacable strength and brutality. Nobody underneath it could avoid an emotional reaction: one was being monitored by a crudely punitive and jealous eye. This machine was very seldom used. The more sophisticated of our Colonised Planets were not likely to be more than irritated by it. Those of our planets kept backward, as for instance 24, where the transplanted Lombis were, would be too violently affected by it: the balances of their culture might be entirely overthrown. But for an occasion like this, it was admirable.

So I thought. I was right. But I should have ordered a fleet of them, accompanied them with threats, and not appeared myself at all. . . .

The machine set me down at such a speed that I had no opportunity to take in that the long oblong or central avenue was crammed, but in an organised and purposeful way. I was at one end of this avenue, my back to one blank frowning facade, facing down its length to its opposing building. The avenue was longer than it seemed from the air. It was narrower because it was banked with what seemed to be statues, or even machinelike beings. They wore straight dark grey tunics, to the ankles. Over their heads they wore hoods of the same colour, with only narrow slits for eyes. Their gloved hands held upright before them very long iron lances. Their feet were in heavy leather. They were five deep on either side.

It will already have been seen by the reader that these figures underlined and reinforced the theme of the buildings, with their featureless uniformity. Behind these guards stood in rigidly ordered groups the contents of each individual building—the living contents, in the shape of the members of a family group, or tribe, all wearing identical black robes, which covered them completely, leaving their faces bare. My first sight of the visage of this culture caused my physical self unmistakably to falter. It was a harsh, authoritarian face, remarkably little diversified, and with little difference, too, between the tribes or families. On their heads they each wore a certain style of stiff conical hat, in black felt. I was easily able to recognise this as having derived from one of the old and superceded special articles prescribed by Canopus to its agents. These privileged ones, the rulers of Grakconkranpatl, carried no arms.

Far ahead of me, at the end of the narrow grey corridor between these dark grey guards, and their black-robed rulers, was a massed group of priests, and theirs was the only colour on the scene. In scarlet and yellow, bright green and brilliant blue, these stood waiting under the blank dark wall of their temple. For these two buildings that stared eyelessly at each other were temples.

I understood, rather late, that this was a reception for me: and that the exact time of my arrival here had become known. This gave me food for thought indeed, since my decision when to come had been made two days before.

I was already aware that I had made a bad mistake. For one thing, I should not be wearing a slight white robe, that paid little homage to ceremonial. (I of course had on me the artefacts currently prescribed by Canopus, some concealed, and others in the shape of a necklace of Canopean silver, and heavy bracelets.) To these people, able to be impressed only by the grandiose, the emphatic, the threatening, I must be seeming like a leaf or piece of dead grass. Able, at any rate, to be crushed at a touch.

I walked slowly forward in a dead, an ominous silence. I could see the glint of eyes inside the oblong narrow slits in the dark hoods that hemmed me in; I could see behind them the heavy savage faces of the men and women of this horrid land.

I understood that my mouth was dry. That my knees were weak. That my breathing was shallow. Recognising these classic symptoms of Fear, which I could not remember having felt, I was of course fascinated. But at the same time I was analysing my situation. Very bad indeed, if they meant ill by me, as the atmosphere convinced me they did. I had told the aircraft to vanish itself well and it would not return without my signal. This would depend on my being able to preserve my Canopean artefacts exactly as they should be.

When I had got halfway along this living avenue, four figures detached themselves from the group of priests ahead. They were in black, the same robes as those of the patricians. These advanced swiftly towards me, and two came behind me and two went just ahead. I was impressed by their odour, a thick cold dead smell.

I knew now I was a prisoner.

When I was standing in front of the group of priests, in their vivid clothes, heavy with gold and jewels, the four escorts went back to join their family groups—each to an exact place. I was reflecting that in all that large multitude there was not one out of his or her ordered place, not one there by casual impulse, or who was watching, even, from the roofs. The slaves were well down in their dungeons, it seemed, for none was to be seen here. Yet at other times, so I learned later, when the sacrificial murders took place, the slaves were all herded out, and crammed into the narrow place between the five-deep bank of guards.

There was not a single individual in that city, on that day, whose whereabouts could not be accounted for, was not known by these dreadful cruel men and women whose faces I was studying as I stood below them, looking up. I said nothing. Silence is a potent weapon. Can be.

And so they had decided, too. Nothing was said by them. They stared contemptuously down at me. I outstared them, and even, sometimes, turned my head, as if unimpressed, and allowed myself to glance about.

On either side of the bank of brilliant priests sat a large animal of a kind unfamiliar to me, a feline, with a yellow hide marked with black, and large unwinking green eyes. At first I thought them statues, so still were they; then saw the lift and fall of breath as sunlight moved on glossy fur. These were not chained or restrained in any way. Beside each stood a tall strong female, skirted to the waist, naked above, but marked with many intricate patterns all over the flesh, using the breasts and nipples and navel as eyes. The animals kept their gaze on me. I realised I was in danger of being torn apart by those trained beasts. I therefore summoned up certain techniques that I had learned, and had hardly ever had the occasion to use. I caused them one after the other to lie down, their paws stretched in front of them: their eyes, no longer on mine, were directed out over the heads of the silent crowd.

I heard the slightest commenting breath among the priests, and momentarily in the ascendant, I smiled at them and said:

"I am from the star Sirius. Your Lord and Governor." I had spoken loudly, so that I could be heard at least by the guards nearer to me. I heard a movement among them. I knew that the priests would now have to act one way or the other.

The four black-robed ones closed in on me, and I was hustled by them into the midst of the priests. I could not then be seen from outside that group. I saw the harsh angry faces, reddish-bronze, with dense black eyes, bending down all around me. I was moved off by them into the low entrance of the temple. There was a smell of stale blood. The blood of this planet is a thick unstable substance, and its smell speaks of its animality. It was dark in the temple, except for flames high up near the unseen roof. I was hustled along passages, and then more and longer dark passages that were cold and musty—I was in the lower part of one of these great blocklike buildings, perhaps even being pushed along from one to another, and then another. We passed slaves, poor pallid creatures, who stared in terror at my guards and shrank away into some side passage. These corridors were lit at very long intervals with feeble lights on the walls. This was the underworld of the slaves. I was at last thrust into a cold and dimly lit place and left.

Alone. I was surrounded by cold blue-grey stone. It was not a small room, but was oppressive, because of its dimensions. I will say here that while Sirius even then was familiar with ideas to do with the relations between the dimensions of buildings and the psychological state of their inhabitants, we had—dare I say *have*?— not approached the understanding of Canopus in the field. It was a place designed to crush, belittle, depress. (These dimensions were in common use through all the levels of the buildings, even those in use by the ruling class. When I found this out, I concluded that this culture had been Canopus-inspired and had then degenerated under the influence of Shammat.)

The walls were of large slabs of squared stone. So was the floor. The ceiling was made to look the same, as it was faced with stone. The door was a single slab of stone, moving in a groove on invisible weights. There was no window. Two small oil lamps stood on a cube of stone that was the only table. A stone bench or ledge ran along one wall. This bluish-grey stone did not reflect the light. It was not stuffy: there was air coming from somewhere.

There was nothing in this room, or tomb, to soften or reassure. I decided therefore that my captors intended to threaten or even torture, and that I had been put here to lower my resistance.

I sat on the bench, as comfortably as I could, and entered into reflection on my situation.

First of all, and most important for the overall situation of Sirius, the exact timing of my arrival had been known: I had been expected. This meant a much closer acquaintance with our activities on this continent that we had known. One had always to expect some sort of espionage or at least a local curiosity enough to supply a certain amount of information, but the manner of my reception showed something well beyond this. No matter how I mentally surveyed my companions, our local staff, the members of our internal and external air forces, I could not find anyone to suspect. There was another thought that kept presenting itself: who was it that had always seemed to know what our movements and plans were? Canopus! Was I to believe that Canopus had supplied this nasty little kingdom with information about us? No, that was out of the question. Yet, here, in this area of possibility, was something that could not be dismissed. . . . I set it aside and considered my own present situation.

If it had been planned simply to kill me, to remove me as a threat, then this could have been done as I landed, or soon after, without this obedient populace knowing anything about it. The fact that I had been received by the entire priesthood—the upper class of this culture—and their guards meant that I was to be sacrificed publicly, probably as the central and even sole figure of an imposing ceremony.

I was beginning to feel very cold inside my prison. This, too, was not a sensation I could remember feeling—not to this degree. I noted my thoughts were slowing; my mental reactions were becoming as stiff as my limbs. There was an absolute silence here under this weight of stone.

If they were so well informed about our movements and intentions, why was there any need to interrogate me? . . . It was at this point I noted that my thinking was becoming too inefficient to continue and so I switched it off. Soon afterwards the great stone slab slid sideways in its grooves and a female entered. She was a slave. The reddish skin colour of this face was paler in her because of her long sojourn within these stone prisons. She was shorter and lighter in build than those great strong specimens, the ruling caste and their guards. But her face had the same brutality and I could see in her dulled brutish eyes that she would kill me at a word. She had brought in some dishes and jugs that contained quite an adequate meal. I told her that I was very cold. She stared, and did not seem to hear. She came swiftly to me, her black eyes not on my face but all over me, as if they were curious hands. And then her hands *were* all over me and I thought she was going to take my protective necklace and bracelets. I could see that she was afraid of this exploration of my person, but could not resist it. Her face showed an uneasiness not far off terror, and her eyes kept flickering towards the open doorway. Yet she felt my hair, ran thick fingers up and down my arm, and then bent to peer right into my face, and my eyes: this was the oddest sensation, because it was the colour of my eyes that fascinated her, the shape of my face, and I might have been inanimate for all the interest she had in my intrinsic self, in anything my eyes might have been saying to her.

Then she abruptly stood straight and turned to go out. I said again that I was cold and again she did not respond.

Perhaps she was deaf. Or even dumb.

Although I believed there might be drugs in the food, I did not hesitate to eat and drink, and without any real concern for the results. This was partly because of the frigid slowness of my mental processes, but partly because of what I have already mentioned. My inbuilt unconquerable belief that I was *immune*. Not eligible for death!

Yet I was certainly able to consider, and even with an appreciation, that I was likely to be murdered in this ugly little city on this inferior little planet. It was a *fact* that I kept supplying to myself, as something that had to be taken in. But I could not.

Between my functioning being, the familiar mechanisms of Ambien II, senior official of Sirius, member of a race that did not expect to die, except by some quite fortuitous event, such as a meteorite striking a Space Traveller—between that state of consciousness, and the real urgent apprehension of the fact: *You may very well be murdered at any moment*, there was really no connection. I literally could not "take it in." I wondered what it would feel like to "take it in" so that my whole organism knew, understood, was prepared. What would it be like to live, as these unfortunates did, not more than four hundred to eight hundred years, depending on their local conditions—no sooner born than ready to die? Did they feel it? Really *feel* their impermanence? Or was there something in the nature of the conditions of living on this planet that imposed a barrier between fact and its perception?

I pursued these thoughts, or rather, allowed them to float through my mind, or—perhaps even more accurately—observed them to take shape and pass, while I ingested foodstuffs that I hoped would soon warm me.

Soon there came in another female.

Once again I am faced with that problem of hindsight. The female was Rhodia. To try and put myself back into my state of mind before I knew who she was, without distortion, is not easy.

But I can say accurately that at once I was saying to myself that she did not resemble the slave who had brought the food. She was dressed in the same clothes, long loose dark blue cloth trousers, and a tunic of the same, which was belted with leather, and hung with various keys. She was a wardress or jailor. She was larger in build than the other, and her red or red-brown skin was lightened by lack of sunlight, like the other. But I at once felt an ease in her presence, to the extent that I was warning myself: Be careful, it might be a trap. She was not, as I was already seeing, of the same race. Or not of the same sub-race. Same in general style or pattern— skin colour, build, with the long black hair—she nevertheless had an aliveness that at once set her aside. She stood immediately in front of me, this handsome, alert female, and her large black eyes were full on mine. And remained there, as if expecting or request- ing an exchange. I did smile at her, even while I was telling myself that it was the oldest trick in the world—the amiable jailor. She had over her arm a length of dark blue woollen cloth, and this she unfolded to display a warm cloak, in which I was thankful to muffle myself. Then she grasped me by the arm and assisted me to rise, knowing that I had become stiffened and lumpish. This firm confident touch was quite unlike the avid, brushing touch, like a snake's tongue, of the other inferior wardress. She walked me, gently enough, to the door, and then assisted me through it. By now my responses were blocked and confused. Everything in me that told me to like this creature was being chided and set aside by me. She felt this, for her hand fell away from my elbow and I stumbled on by myself along the low dark corridors, all straight, all lit by the same regular minor gleams of yellow light at long intervals, all of the same regular blocks of dark stone. Somewhere above me was the heavy sunlight of this region, were the great peaks capped with snow. But it was as hard to take in, to really believe that fact, as it was to believe that this woman might easily slide a knife into me.

After a long walk, turning with monotonous regularity at sharp angles from one corridor to another, the lights on the walls suddenly increased, there was softness under my feet—and I saw coloured rugs and carpets, and the walls had hangings on them. Abruptly, we stopped. Apparently facing a blank wall. She pressed down a lever that projected from the wall, and another great slab of stone slid silently back. I was in the entrance to a brightly lit room that had windows in it. This alone nearly overthrew me—being in ordinary daylight again. Seven tall men, in the black cloaks I had already seen, were seated behind a long wooden table. An eighth stood by a window half turned away, looking out. Again, I have to disentangle what I later learned of the eighth man and what I felt then. Then, I saw at once he was not of the same race as that of Grakconkranpatl, nor of my wardress, who was standing just behind me. He reminded me of those Shammat pirates who had visited me such a very long time ago, the shameless thieving ones. He was, however, taller than they. He was more finely built. His skin was pale brown, as theirs had been. His eyes were quick and brown. His hair was profuse, curly and reddish, worn long on the head, with a neat strong beard. He was the old Shammat type much refined. Compared to the seven, in their heavy black, with their brutish features, their long black eyes that conveyed coldness and deadness as much as they did avidity and lust for power, he seemed infinitely better, even reassuring. And it was as I stood there, my eyes turning for relief to this eighth man, that I heard a breath from behind me: "Sirius, be careful." This sound floated into my mind, as if it came from not now and here but from Koshi, or from the spaces between the stars. I could not believe I was hearing it, and even thought I had imagined it . . . when I slightly turned my head, the woman was a few paces behind, and her face was immobile, even indifferent.

And I was still waiting there, in front of these coldly observant men, all eight of them, now that the one by the window had turned to stare, too. And as yet nothing had been said.

One of the men rose, came over to me, his cold gaze assessing my hair, my skin, my light brittle build, and whipped off the dark cloak, and, gripping my upper arm, pushed me forward closer to the seven so that I stood close against the table they sat along, one, two, three, four, five, six, all so alike, copies of each other, so little variation there was between them. And the seventh stood behind me, and lifted my hair in his large hands, so that he could feel it and show it to the others, and then lifted one of my arms, and then the other—both bare, now that the enveloping cloak lay discarded on the floor. Then he slid the bracelets up and down my arms in a way that showed he wanted to take them from me, but, leaving them for the moment, he began to unhook the necklace of Canopean silver. I was surrounded by his cold unpleasant smell and I felt faint, but I said calmly:

"If you take these things from me, it will be the worse for you."

I saw the eyes of all six of these rulers—priests and tyrants—turn towards the one who lounged still at the window, showing his superiority to them and the scene by his affectation of half-indifference, sometimes watching what went on in the room, sometimes observing some events out of my sight on the central avenue that, presumably, was not now lined with the guards. He now glanced at them, and nodded very slightly—such a minimal gesture was this that I could easily have believed it had not occurred, was it not that it had its effect: the hands of the man who stood behind me no longer fumbled at the catch of the necklace.

Was this eighth man, then, the tyrant who called himself the High Priest? How otherwise was he in a position of supereminence?

Under my robe, I could feel the girdle of starstones, which was the third object given me for protection by Canopus, lying tightly around my waist, not a few inches from the covetous one behind me. I was conscious of the smooth clasp of the gold band around my left thigh, which was the fourth of the talismans.

If the priests had not summoned me to take these things, or to interrogate me, why then was I here? The thought strongest in me was that it was the eighth man who had demanded this confrontation. But why?

Again, I was standing there, no one speaking, the eighth man gazing apparently indifferently out of the window, six of them ranged one beside the other opposite me on the other side of the long narrow table, six pairs of black eyes staring at me. I do not remember any other species who has struck me with such unpleasantness as these did: if they had been simple brutes—that is, a species still totally brutish, or one just lifting itelf away from brutishness—they would have been more tolerable. But they were a long way from running about on four legs or tearing their food with their fangs. It was the end of a line of evolution I was seeing; one that had taken its path into this cruelty and narrow caste interest and was frozen there.

It came into me that there were two different interests at work here: those of the eighth man being different from the seven, but they did not know it.

One of the men got up, pushed down a lever that slid stone panels across the windows, extinguishing daylight, and I found myself standing in a beam of brilliant light that fell on me from above. All around me was quite black, and I stood illuminated. I knew then that this was a rehearsal for some ceremony: they wished to see how I would look to an assembly of, probably, slaves as well as the ruling caste, when I stood before them, bathed in light, in one of the temples, before the priests cut the heart out of my body.

A moment later, the stone window panels had slid open again, the light had been switched off, and I was being wrapped in the heavy cloak by the woman, and then taken back along the passages to my room.

There she left me, without other communication.

I sat alone in the awful silence, and now my mind was full of Nasar. I was reliving my exchanges with him before I left Koshi. So strong was my sense of him that when the door slab slid back and the same woman stood there, I was thinking still of Nasar, and it was with difficulty that I forced my mind to take her in. Again I was telling myself that one did not trust jailors, while I was contrasting this simple direct presence with the men I had been taken to stand before. The seven men—yet I was seeing the one at the window as apart from the others and as better than them, even while I remembered the whisper: Sirius, be careful. I looked into this woman's strong dark eyes, and she gazed straight back at me.

It was as if my mind was trying to open itself, to take in something . . . but after a long silence, she put down on the stone bench a bundle, which I saw was bedding, and she said: "Try to sleep." I believed I heard the word "Sirius," after that admonition, but she had gone. I lay down on the stone slab wrapped in heavy woven material, and lay awake, very far from sleep.

Now, looking back, I can see very clearly two strands, or factors, in my situation. One was the eighth man, he who reminded me of the Shammat thieves. And the other was Rhodia. The bad and the good. The two potentials in my situation. The two currents that are in every situation if one learns to recognise them! *Now* it is all very clear.

Then I lay and thought of Nasar, and sometimes of Klorathy, and hardly at all of the eighth man.

In what I supposed to be the morning of a new day, the first slave came again, with food for me.

I sat wrapped to the chin in all the coverings there were, my hands around a bowl of hot meaty liquid, for warmth. My mind was ringing with Nasar! Nasar!—to the extent that I was beginning to judge myself mad. When the female Rhodia came in swiftly, and stood before me, I stammered out "Nasar" before I could stop myself, and then stared at her, as if expecting her to explain.

She kept her eyes on mine for a long interval, as she had done before, and then said, "You must give me your talismans, Sirius."

I did not move, and she said: "When they come and ask for them, you will say that you have disintegrated them to keep them out of the wrong hands."

"I have no such skill," I said. All this while our eyes were engaged, and my mind felt again as if it tried to enlarge, yet could not.

"No, but there are those who have."

"And these—criminals know this?"

"They know it."

As I unwound the thick cloths around me, it was with the strongest of feelings of identity with this woman. The thought that I did wrong to trust her was faint now. I held out my bared arms to her to slip off the heavy bracelets. I slid the band down off my thigh and gave it to her. I stood to unlatch the girdle of stones from my waist. I bent my head so that she could undo the necklace. These articles vanished into the voluminous folds of her clothing.

"And now for a time you will be very weak," she stated. "You are unarmed against Rohanda. You must guard yourself in every way. It will not be for long."

Not knowing I was going to say this, I said: "This is a very strange place to find you in."

And *she* said: "And it is a very foolish place to find *you* in, Sirius."

I was breathing the name Nasar, again, as she reached the doorway, and she turned, swiftly, and said, "Yes." And was gone.

I could feel the weakness of not being protected. My mind seemed to dim and fade. I sat quietly holding on to what she, or *he*, had promised, that it would not be long.

Soon two of the black-clothed men, tall knifelike men, came and said: "Give us the things!"

They were bending over me, their alien black eyes consuming me, and my senses weakened with the odour of them.

I said, as Nasar had told me to say: "I do not have them. I disintegrated them, so that they should not fall into wrong hands."

At this their faces distorted, rage convulsed them, and their hands dragged off my coverings and were all over me, finding nothing. They stood up, looking at each other—so alike they were, so dreadfully alike, it was as if individuality had been engineered out of them. Then, without looking at me, they strode out and the stone slab closed the entrance.

Now, feeling my mind's strength ebb away, I simply held on, held on.

When Rhodia, or Nasar, came in, she had a cup of some drink, which she made me take, and it did restore me a little.

Then she sat by me on the bench, and, rubbing my hands between hers, said: "You will have to do absolutely everything I say. When you find yourself lifted up on the sacrificial place, and a green light shines on you, call out, as if in invocation, 'Death to the Dead . . .' and then fling yourself backwards. You will be caught." And she was already up and away to the door.

I whispered: "Canopus, why are you doing this?"

She said, low and hurried: "You saved me. Though you did not know from what degradations. So now it is my turn to save you." And the door slid to.

I felt the weight of the cold dark misery of that place come down over me, and wondered how it must affect those who were not protected, as I had been, by my talismans. My mind kept darkening, as if it were full of mist that thickened, but then thinned again; and I was repeating to myself over and over what I had to do.

And it all happened quickly. Into my cell crowded the dark priests, any number of them, and I was hurried along corridors in a press of people and then up some steps, and was inside one of the temples. It was massed with slaves at the lower end, standing in ordered ranks and companies, each with their guards. I caught a glimpse of our poor Colony 9 animals, chained together, lifting their hairy faces and bewildered blue eyes at what they saw at our end of the temple. The black-clothed ones, males and females, were in their ranks on either side of a great reclining statue of stone. Where its belly should have been was a hole, and from it came the smell of stale blood. Oh, the smell of that place! That in itself was enough to quench any sense I retained. Behind the evil statue —for its visage was horrible, an evil face above gross swollen limbs— was a high plinth. On to this I was pushed, and stood there swaying and faint. I saw before me the squat dark interior of this temple, with its stone gods, I saw the massed slaves, I saw the priestly caste who used and fed off them—all this bathed in a ruddy ugly light that suffused the place. A savage wailing began from the black-clothed ones. It was a hymn. I was holding on to my senses, but only just. . . . I could imagine what it was *they* were seeing—a white wraith, or phantom, with its glittering fleece of hair, in a white wisp of a dress, on which red light flickered . . . and then the light on my hands turned green, there was a green where the blood glow had been. My mind told me that this was a signal, I fought for the words I had to cry out, at last they came to me—as I saw a knife raised in the hand of a priest aimed for my heart, I called out, "Death to the Dead . . . Death to the Dead . . ." There was something else I had to do, and I could not remember. The knife was still held above me, its blade glittering green. I jumped backwards off the plinth, fell into something that yielded and then gave way altogether. I heard a clang of stone on stone above me. There were people around me and they were lifting me and carrying me. My part in this escape having been done, I slept or went into a trance.

And yet it was not a complete oblivion, for I was conscious of urgency, of flight along low dark passages, and of Rhodia's voice. And I was talking to her, asking questions, which were answered, for as the dark in my mind lifted, and I began to see that we were coming out from deep underearth places into light, the information I had been given was making a clear enough picture.

Rhodia was not a native of the priest-ruled city, but of Lelanos, which was not very far from here. Not far, that is, in distance. . . .

She had caused herself to be captured and made a slave. Her capacities had quickly raised her to a position of trusted wardress of captives who were to play a leading part in the sacrificial ceremonies. Many were the unfortunate ones whom she had guarded, cared for, and seen lifted up on the plinth above the blood-filled stone god. No, she had not been able to save any of these, not one of the important victims, though she had managed to spirit away a few, not many, of the lesser slaves. Her task had been to position herself ready for my capture, so that she could save me. *She . . . she . . .* I was making myself use this word, as I saw a dim light begin to fill the passages we fled along, and as I saw *her*, Rhodia, this strong, tall, handsome female, running along beside me where I was being carried in the arms of a male slave. I had to say *she*, think *she*— yet in my half-trance or sleep, in the almost complete dark of the deep earth, I had been able to *feel* only Nasar, his presence had been there around me.

What is that quality in an individual so strong, so independent of looks, sex, age, species—independent of the planet "he" or "she" originates from—that enables one to walk into a completely dark room, where one had not expected anyone to be, and to stammer out—a name! It doesn't matter what name! Nasar. Rhodia. Canopus.

Yes, it has happened to me. More than once.

But it has only to happen once for it to become impossible ever after to do more than salute an appearance, or the distinctions of a race or a sex, while recognising that other, deeper truth. I had known this unique and individual being as Nasar, the tormented man in Koshi. And so the associations of my brain made me want to name her "Nasar." Had I met this being first as Rhodia, then other names would come just as reluctantly to my tongue.

The light was growing stronger, and I kept my eyes on Rhodia, reaching out with my sight, as if there was some truth there I could not grasp. She was Nasar, and she was not; he was Rhodia, but he was not . . . whatever *was* there inside that female shape was deeply familiar to me. But beyond this puzzle was something else. There was a bleached look to her, and she had a pallid and even repelling aspect at moments when the light fell more strongly at the angle of a passage. I wondered if she had been struck by lightning, or had some disease. . . . In the dungeons, and in the room with the eight men, I had not seen her clearly, either from the dimness of the light, or because of pressure from anxious thoughts.

So disquieting did I find these glimpses of her that I tried to turn my attention from her, and instead reviewed what I knew about recent events so as to make some kind of coherent picture.

Rhodia's main concern, when I was taken prisoner, was to make sure that the Canopean talismans should not fall into their hands: very evil use would have been made of them. For, in spite of all their efforts, Grakconkranpatl had not once managed to steal any of the articles that had, for this time, Canopean effect.

Her second concern—and I was expected to understand and to agree with this order of priorities—was to get me away. She had caused the priests to believe that I had powers they would be wise to fear. They believed I had made the ornaments vanish by use of these powers. But they had not been in one mind, the group of Overlords, or Chief Priests, whom I had seen: they had almost decided to take me out of their city and leave me to make my way back to my own kind as I could—if I could. But I had actually been seen arriving "from the heavens." They could not cause the memory of this event to vanish from the minds of their enslaved peoples. So it had been given out that I was an enemy, drawn to the city, and into their hands, by their cunning powers. Enemies were always publicly sacrificed. If I had simply vanished, never to be seen again, this could only weaken the powers of this caste, who ruled by fear. So in the end it had been decided to cut the heart from my breast, in the temple, as had always been done. But Rhodia had strengthened their doubts.

When I was pushed up on to the plinth they were all apprehensive. There was a point in the ceremony when the priests shouted and sang to their "Gods" that they were the Dead, identifying themselves temporarily with the sacrificed ones who would almost immediately in fact be dead: the victims were in some ambiguous and rather unsatisfactory way—to a rational mind—the same as those who murdered them. My call, Death to the Dead, condemned the entire priestly caste. Behind the idol was a stone that moved on levers, used for purposes of trickery and illusion in the ceremonies. As my threat momentarily froze the priests and then made them run away from where I stood bathed in the unexpected green ray, Rhodia and her accomplices turned the stone, and pulled me down into the rooms underneath the temple proper. This was the most dangerous part of the escape, for of course those clever priests were not likely to remain confused for long. It was, for a few moments, speed that had to save us. There were passages under the buildings of the city, running everywhere below the tunnels used by the slaves. These were complicated, and none known to all of the priests: a tyranny is always self-divided, always a balance of competing interests. It was this that saved us, the jealous knowledge of mutually suspicious sects. But Rhodia had learned every one of the passageways. As our band fled deeper and further, the guards of the priests were running parallel to us at times, or above us, and they might very well have come on the right turning by accident and encountered us—but Rhodia knew of a very old and disused system of tunnels, made long ago by slaves who had tried to dig their way to safety and had been caught. Once we had found the entrance to these we were safe.

We found ourselves on the side of a high mountain, in a little cleft among rocks, screened by bushes. Far below us was the priests' dark city. And I saw those poor slaves who had come with us fling themselves down on the sun-fed earth and kiss it and weep. And when they lifted their faces, of that faded red-earth colour, to the sun, I fancied that I saw health come into that starved skin even as I watched. And as Rhodia watched, standing aside, waiting for them to be past their first convulsion of delight.

She caught my questioning thought and said to me: "These are the slaves I was able to talk to, and who I was able to trust."

It was an obvious, a simple, thing to say. She could have said nothing else! Yet it struck me so painfully then, the strength, the inexorableness of the laws that govern us all. Down in the chilly dim prisons under the priests' city, slaves who—some of them—could remember nothing else, having been born there, had been able to respond to some quality that they—recognised? *remembered?*—in a fellow slave who was better than they only in as much as she was able, so it must often have seemed to them, to torment them, stand in authority over them. . . . But they *had* seen, felt something in her, listened; and because of some—chance?—qualities in themselves, had been found reliable. Trustworthy. And so it was they who now kissed the earth on the free mountainside, and lifted their pale faces to the sun. For the first time in their lives, for some of them. It was a thought enough to chill the heart—*my* heart that, if it were not for Rhodia, would now have been lying in a pool of blood in the idol's hollowed-out belly. And she knew what I was thinking and smiled. And for the first time I caught from her a physical memory of Nasar, and his derisive angers. It *was* Nasar, for that moment, sharing with me an appreciation of our grim necessities . . . so strongly *there* that I could have been back with him at the top of the tall cone with the snow flying past.

And then I saw her quelling the emotions of her charges, and urging them to their feet, and pointing out over the slopes of the mountains to the north. For they were to go one way into the forests, for safety, and she and I another. When they had gone off, some fifty or so, turning to smile and hold up their arms to her in thankfulness and farewell, she came to me and, rummaging in the folds of her garments again, produced the ornaments and told me to put them on. As I did so, first the band on my thigh, and then the girdle of cool starstones, and then the bracelets, and lastly the necklace, it was as if my mind cleared, my thoughts steadied, and even a short moment after my old state of mind had been banished by the secret strengths of the ornaments, it seemed as dreadful and inconceivable a place or state of being as the dungeons of the city now seemed. I looked at Rhodia with clarity and steadiness of thought and saw her straight. Again, my thought was that she was suffering from some horrible disease, like a leprosy. She had a faded, drained look, as if she had been dusted with ashes. I had not seen anything like it before. The face, the hands, what was visible of her arms and legs, were all dried up, and had a shrivelled look, as a corpse sometimes does. And the hair on her head, which by race was a vigorous glossy black, had white in it.

She saw how I stared, and she said: "Sirius, you are looking at the physical aspect of the Shikastan Degenerative Disease."

"Rohanda has become so decadent?"

"Now, by halfway through their lives, and sometimes even sooner, they start to show signs of decay. This is a process that accelerates generation by generation. They have even forgotten that this is a recent thing with them."

I could not at once recover from the horror of it. I was trying to imagine what it must be like for these unfortunates, trapped inside their enfeebled defective bodies, and I was wondering if it were not possible for Canopus, with their knowledge of the techniques of how to discard bodies at will, to aid the poor creatures.

And she sighed, and then gave her short characteristic Nasar-laugh. "There are other priorities. Believe me. We have other, and most urgent, things to do."

"Necessities," I said, meaning to joke with her.

And she acknowledged my intention with a smile, but said, "Yes, indeed, Sirius—necessities!"

And on this familiar note we began our journey eastwards through the valleys and passes of the mountain chains along the coast. We went up and we went down, but it was without haste. We were not in danger, she said. This was because "our greatest danger is also our protection. On this occasion." And when I pressed her to elucidate she gave me a long strong look from eyes that I saw had around their black pupils colourless edges, the tax of Rohandan age—a look that made me think of the whisper: *Sirius, be careful!*—which seemed to sound, now, all the time, somewhere in my deepest self. She said only: "*Your* greatest danger. *Yours*, Sirius." And would not say any more on that subject. Though she talked willingly and at length about the city we were going to.

We walked for several days through thick and pleasant forests. We did not hurry. I got the impression that this pace was for my benefit. So that I could absorb—instruction. From her. From Nasar. From Canopus. I did not mind. I was in her, their, hands. Very different was my state of mind now from my angered self-esteem when I had had the chance to be with Canopus, in the person of Klorathy, in those faraway days of the unfortunate "events." I was trying to listen. To adjust. But now, looking back, I see that I was trying over and over again and in every way I knew to find out about Canopus itself, its organisations, its ways of managing itself, its planets—and while I did this Rhodia patiently returned the subject to Grakconkranpatl, to Shammat, and, several times, to the eighth man of those priests. It was not, I see now, that she repeated his name, which was Tafta, so that Tafta recurred through our talk, but that she kept bringing me to points and places where I had to think of him. He was strongly in my mind. I could feel his presence there. Just as, wrapped shivering in my stone cell, Nasar had rung in my mind, so that the name could not help but come to my tongue, so, now, as we walked through those magnificent forests, the great snowy mountains at our backs, the feeling or sense of that man kept coming back. I found myself thinking of him, and what he was, when I recognised his particular and unique pulse in my mind: disturbing, harsh, yet nothing near the cold evil of the priests.

And when she brought me back to this point, Tafta, the smiling, handsome, and enigmatic savage, it was always with the long dark stare of warning that I recognised.

LELANOS

We were able to look down on Lelanos from a height—and what a difference from the other city! The same bluish-grey stone was used, but lightened with a glistening white quartz and thin bands of red, so that the place had a lively charm about it. As I moved about Lelanos in the days that followed, I often thought I had glimpsed a pattern or even several interlocking patterns in the way the buildings were set out, but I never grasped it wholly, and this was one of the things that I omitted to ask Rhodia, and then it was too late. At any rate, to view it from above, there was variation, and informality; there were no frowningly dominant buildings; no temples; no threat of stone, and rock, and earth being used to imprison or weight the tender—and so brief—flesh of Rohanda.

And from what I had heard from Rhodia of its governance, there was nothing to fear from it.

This was its history. On this site, a small plain ringed by low and friendly mountains, had been several tribes of creatures at that level where their physical needs ordered their lives, and these needs had not been given a religious or "higher purpose" recognition. In other words, they were considerably lower even than the Lombis before their culture was disturbed by our use of them. They fished, hunted, ate, mated, slept.

Nasar caused himself to be born into a family that retained enough of the remnants of "an ancient and high knowledge," as they put it, to see in this girl something superior. The family was a well-regarded one among a dwindling people living far to the north in the narrow peninsula that separated the Isolated Northern and Isolated Southern Continents—this land bridge, or channel, had often been under water, completely cutting off the Southern Continent, but the "events" had lifted it high above the ocean, and subsequent minor "events" had not succeeded in submerging it. There had flourished a Canopus-inspired culture that had degenerated, and these fast-vanishing people were all that remained. Their memories of the "ancient knowledge" were equated with female dominance, for a variety of reasons extraneous to this account. Rhodia was well treated, and when she told her parents of her needs, was given a company of the physically most striking young males and females of her people to go with her, and she travelled southwards looking for a place and race that would respond to her instruction.

It was easy to imagine how these handsome visitors must have struck the tribes. Rhodia's people were a tall, broad, red-brown type, with large dark eyes, and flowing luxuriant black hair. They had all the ease of manner and confidence of their past high culture. The tribes were of a slight, shorter kind, with a dark brown skin, small black eyes, sparse coarse black locks. The new arrivals wore handsome coloured cotton clothes; the tribes wore skins. The "Gods" were able to instruct them in a thousand skills undreamed of by them, and to cut it short, within a couple of their generations, but while Rhodia's people were still youthful, there was a large, expanding city that had been set up according to her instruction, but was governed by themselves. All the visitors but Rhodia had returned to their own people. Rhodia was considered, still, a "God," but lived as they did, had married one of their males, and her children were not set apart in any way from the other citizens.

Lelanos was governed like this.

It was a democracy, elective. There was no written or formal constitution, since Rhodia had taught them that some of the worst tyrannies in Rohandan history had had "constitutions" and written laws with no purpose except to deceive the unfortunate victims and outside observers. There was no point in constitutions and frameworks of laws. If each child was taught what its inheritance was, both of rights due from it and to it, taught to watch its own behaviour and that of others, told that the proper and healthy functioning of this wonderful city depended only on his or her vigilance —then law would thrive and renew itself. But the moment any child was left excluded from a full and feeling participation in the governance of its city, then she or he must become a threat and soon there would be decay and then a pulling down and a destruction.

I was much interested in this, because of what I, Sirius, had observed, and often: when we took over a planet and ordered its rule, we always imposed a constitution that seemed appropriate to us; and this was safeguarded by every sort of threat and punishment. But never had any rule imposed by us stayed for long the same, without falling into anarchy or rebellion.

There were three safeguards used by Lelanos. The first was the governing body itself, which made the laws. This was elected by general suffrage, every person over the age of sixteen becoming eligible both to vote and to take office. Each officeholder had to lay bare his or her life to the examination of a body of citizens separately elected by the citizens. This scrutiny was to prevent any individual benefitting from office, and to see him or her dismissed at the first evidence of any falling away from high conduct. What these officeholders might not do included the use of servants— there were no slaves—who were treated in any slightest detail differently from members of their own households; the improper use of sex by either male or female—that is, to dominate or degrade; and luxurious or greedy behavior. The individuals voted on to this Scrutiny, for so it was simply called, were considered the best and most honourable of all Lelannians, and to serve Scrutiny was the highest office.

The second safeguard was an independent judiciary, to keep the laws made by the governing body. The members of this arm of the State, too, were continually watched by Scrutiny, and their behavior was expected to be as beyond reproach as that of the rulers.

While it was not considered undesirable for an individual suited for the work to be re-elected, even for the whole of a lifetime, onto either the governing body or the judiciary, the citizens who staffed Scrutiny were not allowed to serve more than one term of four years, though they might after retiring from Scrutiny serve either on the judiciary or the governing body.

The third safeguard was a jealously kept law that the currency used to facilitate the exchange of goods should never be allowed to acquire a self-breeding value. That is, the coins used were only and always to be used as a means of exchange and nothing else. If any individual or body of individuals were to fall into debt, then no interest could be charged, and the debt itself must be abrogated at the end of seven years. Rhodia had caused to come into existence a body of instruction, framed as tales and songs, to enforce the message that if once "money" was allowed to become a commodity on its own account, then the downfall of Lelanos could be shortly expected, because she or he who charged "interest" would shortly control the supply of goods and of labour and a ruling class would become inevitable. The songs and stories were based on the histories of innumerable cities and cultures in Rohanda, where the means of exchange had become king. Over and over again, so Rhodia said, Canopus had laid down laws and instruction forbidding the improper use of money, and yet never had this been prevented for long. Shammat was too strong in these unfortunate ones who could never retain excellence.

"And does this mean," I enquired of Rhodia, "that Lelanos can be expected to fall away?" For, walking towards it, and then into its outer suburbs, I was struck with the manifest health and sanity of the place, the absence of poverty and deprivation, the real and inbred democracy that ruled here—for one may very easily see its opposite in any place, in signs of servility, fear, deceitfulness.

And Rhodia said only: "You will see for yourself."

She had a small house towards the centre of the place, in a group of them set around a small square. She lived there alone now, for her children had grown and left. The house had two small rooms on an upper floor and two on the ground floor. She had lived in it since the city was built, and had resisted all pressures on her by her children to move into a larger house—and when she told me this, her eyes met mine with a mordant amused glance I remembered from Koshi. Oh yes, I was being told quite enough to make me suspect that my arrival here was at a point in the city's fortunes before a fall, or decline: and in the next few days it seemed to me that Rhodia was doing everything to impress on me, not only the charm, the health, the good sense of this place, but, at the same time, what was wrong with it. And I could not help wondering why she did . . .

Looking back I see that everything conspired to put me into a high (or low!) but at least irrational and emotional condition. First of all, the contrast between this lovely civilised city with its horrible opposite across the mountains. Within a few days I had been taken from one to the other, and they illustrated extremes of what was possible on this planet: I had experienced, was still experiencing, within myself, these two extremes. And there had been the un-hurried walk here, with Rhodia, or Nasar, and the way this presence —this Canopean reality—seemed to explore and challenge my deepest self. And there had been something else. I had traversed a zone of forest in no way different from any other, but this had in fact been the barrier zone between the Lelannian territory and that of Grakconkranpatl. For many centuries the evil and preda-tory city had been kept from attacking Lelanos because of rumours set afloat by Rhodia and then sedulously kept up that there was a zone or band of forest completely surrounding Lelanos that, if invaded or infringed, would result in the most savage reprisals. Lelanos was a villainous place—so the rumours went—feeding on flesh and blood, ruled by a self-perpetuating oligarchy that would lay in ruins any attacking city. Every kind of chance or even con-trived incident or event was pressed into service to give credence to these tales. When I heard some of them on our way to Lelanos, from a terrified tribesman who had been fed all his life on stories of the cruelties of Lelanos, I felt my whole self powerfully affected. The shiverings and shudderings of the poor wretch as he described Lelanos the horrible showed how skilful had been the work of Rhodia and her associates. This propaganda work, and nothing else, had kept Lelanos safe. The clever and cunning priests of the city that really was wicked, using every kind of deceit themselves, had not been able to penetrate the disguise of Lelanos . . . and there was something as disturbing here as there had been in the sight of the band of thirty freed slaves who of all the innumerable slaves of Grakconkranpatl were the only ones able to free themselves by use of some inward recognition of reality, of the truth. Standing on a slender tower in magically charming Lelanos, looking out over forests where I had travelled, knowing what they were and how they were seen by those outside Lelannian borders—this was enough to set me shuddering in something not far off awe at the strange capacities for self-deception of the Rohandan mentality. And awe was not an emotion that I easily accommodated!

No, I conclude now, but was not dispassionate enough to do so then, the sojourn in the cold dungeons, the deprivation of my protective devices, close contact with the Canopean—all this had unbalanced me. And still Shammat rang in my mind and pulled me towards it—towards Tafta, who was working on me powerfully, though I did not know it. I was beginning to react away from Rhodia. I found myself watching this strong old, or elderly, female, with her simple directness, her honesties, and I was seeing in them callousness, indifference to suffering, a refusal to use powers she certainly must have, as Canopus, to relieve the lot of these Rohandans.

It is a strange thing that I, Ambien II, after many long ages of a Colonial Service that supervised the continual and often—as we had to know—painful adjustment of innumerable species, cultures, social structures, the fates of myriads of individuals, could now suffer as I did over this one city. For never had a culture seemed more valuable to me than did Lelanos, never had one been felt by me as a more remarkable and precious accomplishment, set as it was among so much barbarity and waste and decline. I found I was wrung continually with pity, an emotion I literally at first did not recognise for what it was, so strange was it.

I would wander about the streets and avenues of this place, sometimes with Rhodia and sometimes by myself, and everything about these people hurt me. That they should have been brought to such a pitch of responsibility and civil awareness in such a short time . . .

and from such unpromising material, merely a few barbarous tribes living only to keep alive . . . and that they should use each other with such alert and lively and free kindness . . . and that all this was the achievement of poor wretches who were so far gone with the Rohandan Degenerative Disease that hardly a whole or healthy specimen was to be seen among them . . . and that every one of them, almost from middle age, was struck as if with an invisible withering blast, leaving them enfeebled and bleached and shrunk with "ageing" . . . and that . . . and that . . . there was no end to the sights and sounds that could inspire me to pitying anger, to the need to protect and keep safe.

Rhodia watched all this in me, and I knew she did, and I was by now in the grip of a resentment against her. Against Canopus. Yet I did, just occasionally, gain the most faint of insights into my condition and was able to match it with Nasar himself, in Koshi, wrung with conflict, and with the pain of this place, this unfortunate Rohanda. Or Shikasta.

A great deal that I saw later was very far from me then. For instance, there was my casual, almost careless, approach to the priests' dark city, my allowing myself to so easily be taken prisoner. How to account for that? For never before, not in any planet, had I behaved in a comparable way. I saw after it was all over, and my subjection to Shammat was past, that there had been a softening and a slackening all through me, long before my descent to Rohanda on this visit, and this was due to my low spirits and inner doubtings because of the work I was having to do, and for so long.

And that was another thing: we might congratulate ourselves as we liked on the order and good sense on the planets we governed, with their minimum well-fed, well-cared-for populations, their willing submission to our rule, but it had been a very long time indeed, it had been long ages, since I had seen a culture anything like as lively as this city Lelanos. No, something had gone out of our provenance, our Empire—I had known it, sensed it; but not until I had been brought here by Rhodia was I able to see what it was that had been lost. This place had some kind of vitality that we lacked. A deadness, a lack of inspiration was afflicting us, Sirius. . . .

And why had Rhodia brought me here at all? All she had to do was to send me with guides back southwards to our Sirian stations.

Yet here I was, with her, with Canopus, in this city. A city that had reached its perfection, and was about to sink . . . *had* begun to sink away from itself.

And I could not stand the thought of it! I could not! I found that I wished to raise my voice and howl in protest, to cry out, to complain to—but to whom? Rhodia, the now willing and dutiful servant of Canopus?

There was a morning when she and I sat together in one of the little rooms at the top of her house. We had been taking a meal of fruit and bread. We were not talking: talk between us had become difficult.

The sun came in through window openings in the brick walls, and lay in patterns on woven and coloured rugs. It was a scene of such simple friendliness and pleasantness.

I was looking in hostility at Rhodia, knowing she knew it, and yet I could not prevent my critical feelings. She seemed to me stubborn. I was seeing in her, as she sat quietly on her cushions, hands folded in her lap, looking up into the blue of the Rohandan sky, a stubborn and difficult woman who was refusing me, or something, or some demand. I felt towards her at that moment as I had done with Nasar in Koshi, when he rebelled, or half rebelled, or struggled against his inner rebellion. And I was not able to tell myself that this time the case was opposite.

She looked straight at me, with one of her full steady looks, and said: "Sirius, I am going to leave you."

"Well, then, you are going to leave me! And you will leave this poor place, too, abandon it to its fate."

"There is nothing that can be done to arrest the laws of Rohanda," she said, "or indeed, the laws of the universe. They are worse here, that is all. We see them on Rohanda exaggerated and displayed, but there is never anything that can stay the same. You know that from your own Empire! Has there been a single culture you have established that has not changed and fallen away?"

I looked into her eyes—I had to—and agreed that this was the case. But not willingly, not with grace.

"The best we can do is to set up something that approximates to the good, for a short time. This I have done in this city. And now it is time for me to go."

"You have finished your task for this visit?"

"Yes. For this time it is done."

"I have to thank you for rescuing me, Nasar."

"As you did me."

She stood up. I saw she was weary, holding herself up only with an effort.

"You'll be glad to go," I said, sullen.

"I am always glad to go," she said, on the old grim note. "Yes, I shall never, I sometimes believe, come to terms with it—the striving and striving to make the good and honest thing, and then—and so soon, so terribly soon, it is done, it is finished, it has become its own opposite."

I saw her face ravaged, for a moment, with pain. Then it was clear again, patient. She contemplated some future I was trying to guess at.

"Be careful, Sirius," she said. "You are in very great danger."

"Why did you lead me into it?" I was angry, angry and resentful.

"You have to know it," she said. "You are a stubborn one, Sirius. You are not of those who can be told a thing, and absorb it."

"Well," I said, sarcastically, "tell me, do you have hopes of my surviving this danger?"

She turned her face full towards me, and smiled.

"If not this time, then another," she said, and this struck me again with the idea of her callousness, her indifference.

And *she* responded to this in me with: "Sirius, rebellion is of no use, you know. That is what you are now—rebellion, the essence and heart of *no, no, no.* But against what are you rebelling? Have you asked yourself? When you run about this city gazing at its people as victims and the abandoned—*who* is it that has abandoned them and what is it that governs their good and their evil? To rebel against an Empire—Sirius, you punish that quickly enough, do you not?" And she held my eyes with hers, insistent, till I nodded. "Yes, you do, and very harshly! There is little pity in you, Sirius, for those who rise up against you. But when you, or I, rebel, protesting against what rules us all, and must rule us all, no one imprisons us, or kills us in the name of order and authority. Yet order and authority there are. We are subject to the Necessity, Sirius, always and everywhere. Are you thinking, as you sit there sulking and angry and bitter at what you see as the waste of it all, that you may change the Necessity itself? By your little cries and complaints? Well? And what did you say to me when I was biting my hands and howling like an animal, in Koshi? Do you not recognise a disobedient servant when you see one?"

As she spoke, into the stillness of the morning, there came a sound of shouting, and distant anger. This was something I had heard often enough on other planets, and often, too, on this one, but I had not believed it possible I might hear it here.

"Yes," said Rhodia. "When a place, or a person, begins to fall away, to descend from itself, to degenerate, then it is a quick business. It is inherent in this planet, in the states of mind it engenders, that we tend to see things, patterns of events, conditions, in terms of balances of force and energy that are already past and done. The high time of Lelanos is done with, Sirius. And be careful. Fare well. We shall meet soon enough. We shall meet again here, on Shikasta, the unfortunate one . . . *unfortunately*, we shall meet . . ." and she accompanied this last "unfortunately" with the ironic Nasar smile that oddly enough comforted me and made me laugh.

She went quietly out of the room, and down the little stair. Outside a throng of people rushed past, with weapons of all kinds, screaming, shouting, raging. I heard "Death to the Tyrants, death to Rhodia, death to the Oligarchy . . ." And as I stood looking down, I saw Rhodia walk out from the door of her house into the mob. They screamed abuse as they saw her, surrounded her, struck her down, and rushed on, leaving her lying dead on the sunny bricks of the roadway.

Such was the disorder in the city that her burial was a matter of throwing her with the other victims of the riots into a communal grave. And it was how, I felt sure, she would have wanted it. I wished I were not there. I had no protection here now, I was known as her associate, and it was impossible to disguise my appearance. But soon Rhodia's death had affected me into a state of noncaring, indifference: thus I was pulled down further away from my proper levels of thought and responsibility. I walked a great deal about Lelanos; and for me it was a ritual of mourning. Not for Rhodia, or Nasar, but for a perfect thing. I could not tire of what I saw. Each city, anywhere, has its unique note, and that of Lelanos was unexpectedness and variety gained by the ingenious use of its materials. There was its setting, a wide plain or plateau, ringed with mountains but not closely enough to oppress. The plain was not flat, but was full of change and unevenness, and the trees were of many tones of a rich full green. Oh, the green of Rohanda, the infinite ranges of its greens, its wonderful green! Those of us who have not known such a planet must find hard to imagine the charm and interest that resides always in the colours of vegetation of this kind. And the "seasons" that had resulted from the "events" caused even wider changes in colour and texture. This Rohandan plain was—alas, one may not say *is*, it has been through many metamorphoses since those far-off days—one of the most beguiling I have seen. And the city seemed to grow from it, was its spirit, its expression. Anywhere in Lelanos one might walk, seeing only the rich shining greens of trees and grass, with glimpses of buildings that astonished and caused a need to smile, even to laugh—there was always the hint of fantasy or even of self-parody in Lelanos. One longed to hasten, to come on this half-seen building, but did not, because of the pleasures of waiting, of lingering . . . and then there it was, and you *were* smiling, and laughing: at its best, in Lelanos, a smile was never far from any face. This was the architecture of the smile. The building in front of you was not large, though one might find, once inside it, that there was more space than you could believe possible. Not large, but then size was not what it spoke of. It was made of clouds, perhaps? Coloured bubbles? It looked like a thunderhead building itself up, up, rapidly, in a clear but electric sky. Glistening white puffs and balls and shafts underlay the dark blue-grey stone of the region, which balanced in light globes or cubes on it, as if the snowy crystal had given birth to these darker shapes, which in their turn sped up again, burgeoning and unfolding, as summer clouds do. The red stone was used in the lightest of touches, for instance in their symbol for the lightning flash—these buildings were all a reminder, a celebration, of the natural forces that gave them life on this planet. And beyond these airy fantastic buildings, which yet spoke so accurately through stone of the *necessary* (so that I felt I was being enabled to glimpse that "need" of the Canopean levels of thought), were others, but placed not in rows of an obvious order, but so that walking among them they opened and showed themselves, or became concealed, as if one were to walk through sky—as if these earthbound creatures had actually flown through their skies. Air and sky were brought near to them in Lelanos. I cannot express the lightness of spirit, the cheerfulness that the place induced: and I thought of the dreadful weight of threat and punishment expressed in the same dark grey stone over the far mountains. Through this happy city thronged the tall, sinewy, almost black race, a quick-witted, smiling, subtle people, and beautiful to look at, with the same sharpness of colour in them as their city, loving to wear the brilliance of feathers from their forest birds or multihued and vivid flowers in their clothes or in their hair.

As I wandered there I saw a class of children, seated on bright green grass, their dark glossy skins and coloured clothes making brilliancy and light, but their faces were sullen and they stared at a woman who was a teacher from the time of the city's health. She was asking them to comment on the rioting and destruction that was taking place now continually, to comment on it from within the spirit of their inheritance. She had a weary look to her, and seemed even distraught—and this was from lack of comprehension. She did not know what had happened or why it was happening. And as she stood there, appealing to them, one began to shout, and then another: "Death to the Oligarchy!" And they were up and away and racing off into another part of Lelanos where, soon, we could hear shouting and screams. And then smoke rose slow and steady into the blue air.

The teacher came slowly towards me. She stopped, and I saw the reaction I had become accustomed to. I was so amazing to them that their good manners could not prevent incredulity, then repulsion, at my white skin, my shreds of pale hair. "If this is your doing," she said, in a low bitter voice, "then be proud!" And then, surprising herself, she spat at me. She looked horrified—at herself, and hurried away. I saw crystal drops of liquid splashing from her eyes on to the shining black of her arms.

I understood that I was in danger of being killed like Rhodia, but I was unable to care. I went off in the direction of the now thickly rising blue smoke, which seemed, in its up-pouring, rather like another form of the buildings. Crowds were hurrying in from all parts of the city. Nothing had been set on fire before.

And soon I was in a vast crowd that was sullen and silent, standing to watch one of those graceful stone fantasies pouring dark smoke from every opening, and then it seemed to shrink, and then dissolve, and it collapsed inwards in a burst of smoke. And now an angry roaring went up from everywhere, and the focus of the crowd having gone, they surged about, and looked for some other thing to absorb them. Those near me were staring hard, and muttering. I was becoming surrounded by ominous people. And then I saw, almost as if I had expected it, and as if nothing else could have happened, Tafta—and he was making his way through the throng. He was wearing the garb of Lelanos, loose blue trousers, with a belted tunic of the same, which I was also wearing, though it could do nothing to disguise me. He, too, could not be taken for one of them, being broad and brown and thickly bearded, but he was determined, and full of authority, and so they fell away from him—briefly, but it was enough. He took me by the arm, and pulled me out of the crowd, not running, but quickly enough. We had soon left them all behind, and were hidden from them by the curve of a crystal globule, in which there was a low round opening.

This was some kind of public building. The interior shone more softly than its outer dazzle. It was like being inside a blown egg, dimly white and quiet. But we went on deeper into the building, so as not to be seen at once by someone entering, and climbed high through the globes and cubes till we came out on a small flat roof, from which we could look down on the city. Smoke rose still from the fallen building. We were high enough for the crowds below to look small and easily manageable—this was a frame of mind familiar to me from so many hoverings above places, cities, herds, tribes, crowds. The space beneath one's craft, everything within the span of one's personal vision, seems under one's control, and even contemptible or at least negligible. I have had often enough to note this reaction and to check it. Yet we were not so high that there were not still taller shapes of white and bluish stone around us where we could shelter, unseen.

And that was the setting of my encounter with Tafta. We were there for a long time, all that day, and on into the night, and I shall give a summary of what was said, what I understood.

First, it is necessary to establish my emotional condition—though that is hardly the kind of statement with which I normally preface a report! Tafta, who when he had been "the eighth man" had struck me as an acceptable barbarian, compared with obviously evil priests, was now seeming to me a savage, but a not-unattractive one, compared with Rhodia, of whom I was thinking with reluctance, as if this was a duty. I did not want to think of her at all. There was something intractable, stubborn, even meagre about my memory of that elderly female. As if she had refused me something that was my due, and which I had earned: yes, this was a recurrence, in a milder form, of my old reactions to Klorathy. It was as if she were determined to keep herself out of my reach and would *not* let me encompass her with what I was convinced was a reasonable demand. I felt thwarted by her, refused.

And now, by contrast, here was this Tafta, about whom she had warned me. He was her enemy, the enemy of Canopus. And therefore of Sirius. But here I was sticking, in my thoughts. She had said that we had been enabled to escape from that dreadful city because of our enemy—that meant he had helped, or at least allowed our escape. She had said . . . and implied . . . yet *not* said . . .

Tafta was doing everything to win me—I could see that, of course, but did not dislike this, or even resent it—provided he kept at a good distance. The physical presence of the creature, this great hairy barbarian, glistening with crude strength, affected me as if I was being threatened by the smell of their blood, or at least by something too hot, too thick, too pressing. As he leaned towards me, where he sat in his characteristic swagger on a low seat—this little patch of roof was used for sitting out on—and smiled, showing the great glistening teeth of a healthy animal, and compressed his features in a smile that was like a snarl—even so, I found myself reassured. The snarl, after all, was only what *I* saw, with my experience of these lower species: it was their expression of friendliness: the shining white teeth, like the exposed teeth of the lower animals, meant I need not expect attack. The light almost

colourless eyes surrounded by fringes of yellowy hair were not unfamiliar to me: these eyes were to be seen even among the favoured
class of our Home Planet. Provided I was able to hold off in myself
a strong reaction to this animality, I was able to regard him steadily
—and to regard myself, too. I was not unconscious of the contrast
between us, and of how he must be seeing me, Sirius, in the light
of our long history of domination of Shammat. What I was thinking most strongly was that this almost overpowering vitality of his,
which he was using like a weapon, was at least not a symptom of
decline as were the inner doubts and dryness that was afflicting
our Empire. At least this one was not likely to let his magnificent
confidence be assailed by any existential confusions! And when he
spoke to me of what I, Sirius, could do here, in this city, to prevent
its decline, I found myself unable to stand up to him. That is the
truth.

He was speaking to me as if he, Tafta, this enemy of Sirius, had
somehow become the voice of my most inner feelings. As if he
had laboured, with me, devising my last tour of duty in our outer-
most planets, asking himself *why*, and *what for*, and *what next*. As
if he wandered, with me, through Lelanos, inwardly grieving for
its imminent overthrow.

I had hardly to speak! As the day passed and the blue went
out of Rohanda's sky, I was feeling that this enemy was myself. As
if some part of my mind, or inner self, had been occupied by this
Tafta without my knowing it. And long before the Rohandan sky
had filled with its stars and I had signalled a private greeting to my
own home, I had agreed, at least by silence, to the following:

That I would put myself at the head of the government of this
city. That he, Tafta, would maintain me in power for as long as I
needed to restore Lelanos to its former balance and health. That I
would set up a governing body with his aid, of the best individuals
to be found in Lelanos. And that when all this was done, I would
either stay as ruler, or queen, or whatever I wished, or leave—and
he would see me safely to my own part of the continent.

He told me I might now return to my room in Rhodia's house,
without fear, since I was "under his protection" and that he would
meet me again next day for further discussion of "our plans."

I spent the night seated at a window, star-bathing, as if I were already safely home. I was immersed in my plans for the re-establishment of Lelanos.

And next day, when I walked quite openly and at ease through the green spaces to the same airy building, and went up to our little platform among those stone symmetries, my mind was at work on management: the exercises and uses of management.

He was not there as he had said he would be. I did not think anything of this, then. I was considering the causes of the falling away of Lelanos, among which Rhodia had indicated was the failure to maintain the independence and integrity of money. Well, that was easily put right! An enforcement of the law . . . if necessary an enforcement by the power of Tafta's troops . . . the strengthening of the Scrutiny, and its powers . . . perhaps Tafta should be made a member of the Scrutiny . . .

Tafta did not come at all that day. I felt as if I had had something snatched from me: and I was again full of grief on behalf of Lelanos, the deprived—the deprived of *me*, and my expert and benevolent guidance. But as I waited there on my little platform among the snowy and bluish cubes and spheres, the deep blue of the Rohandan sky enclosing the lovely scene, I looked down on little people far below, and it was as if I held them in my protection; as if I was promising them an eternal safety and well-being.

It is not that I am proud of this: I have to record it.

By the end of that day, I was in the sort of mood where, had I been on my own ground, within my own frame of understanding, I would have had to watch myself so as not to punish unjustly. I was feeling about Tafta as about a delinquent servant. That night, my contemplation of our stars was hazed, I seemed not to be able to find their shadow within myself, and at the back of my mind, where the shores of Sound begin, I could hear the warning whisper, Sirius, Sirius, Sirius, and I was shaking my head as an animal does when its ears are full of irritating water. Sirius, Sirius—and I shook my head so as not to hear the echo of: Be careful, be careful, be careful.

I was late going to my high watching place next day, and it was from calculation, and when I reached it, Tafta was there, and bent in a gesture of submission that I had always previously found slavish. He applied his furry lips to my hand, and then glanced up from this humble position with a winning glance and a baring of his white teeth. "My apologies," he said. "But it was for the sake of our cause."

And that did begin to shake me out of my illusion. He stood before me, all confident physicality, all glisten and shine, the sun warm on his whiskers and the smooth curls of his head, his brown skin where you could see the red blood running underneath shining, too. This type of animal, when overheated, produces a greasy secretion to cool itself: the exposed areas of his skin, cheeks, brow, nose, arms, hands, even his ears, were beaded with globules of liquid. It had a salty smell. And yet there was something in me even then that said: this is health, this is vitality, you need it!

He told me that his absence was due to his having to bring in from outside the city the troops that would guard us. And to his having to organise their safety and their shelter. And he said that on the next morning he would come to my lodging for me and we—he and I and the guards—would make a public display of ourselves through Lelanos, to the place of government of the city and its environs, where we would be installed as rulers. This was not at all as I had been imagining events. But meanwhile we were standing on the very edge of the little snowy platform, overlooking the whole plain and its focal city, and he was flinging out his arm and saying: "It is yours, all yours. And together we will restore it and make it everything it was." There was such a glossy insolence about him! He could not stop the triumphant grimace that showed his teeth, he could not control his glances down at me, as if he had already swallowed me whole, and finding me negligible, was about to spit me out again.

And yet my head swam as I overlooked Lelanos, and I was promising it in a silent passionate bond with it: "I will protect you, I will guard you, I will keep you safe." And the warning whisper, Sirius, Sirius, was not more than a low hissing from a long way off.

Again he kissed my hand, and I descended, he following, and I went to my rooms, and—but now I was thinking. Thoughts that had been far from me crowded in.

Who was it who had warned the priests of the time of my arrival in the other city? Not Rhodia—though she *had* known what was going to happen.

How was it that this gallant ruffian had made his appearance in Lelanos only *after* Rhodia's death?

And how could I explain that Shammat was now so ready to devote himself to the restoration of sweet civilisation and order, when I had so recently seen this, their servant, at work, of the kind to be expected of them, with the dark priests?

How was it . . . but it was as if two forces were at war in me. I did not want to hear warnings from deep within me, or remember Canopus. I wanted with all my *present* self—the self brought into being by Shammat—to rule this city, and to strengthen my inner feebleness by *doing as Canopus did*. And I was already thinking of how, when Lelanos was itself again, balanced under the care of the Scrutiny, I would leave here and find other tribes, descendants perhaps of the Lombis, or subsequent experiments, and build, as Rhodia had done, a perfect and lovely civilisation, using all my own age-long experience, and what I had learned from Rhodia, here.

Next morning I waited quietly for Tafta, my mind already beyond the—so I thought—unimportant formalities of the day, dwelling on future plans and arrangements, when Tafta walked in, saw me standing there in my ordinary Lelannian clothes, flung over me without asking a cape of fur, which smelled of the poor animals that had been killed to make it, and pressed me to the door, his arm at my back, to stop me sliding away. He was grinning, triumphant . . . outside were company after company of Shammat soldiers, the nastiest, most brutish types you can imagine. Tafta pulled me in front of them, a harsh thumping music started up, and I was being marched along the leafy ways of Lelanos, a captive of Shammat.

And unable to escape. My mind was darting frantically around the possibilities of escape. My whole self had been shocked back into sanity, into sense. Behind me came, singing—if that is the word for it—the Shammat contingents. Beside me strolled, grinning, Tafta. Those people who came out of their houses or ran along beside us to see what this impossible and inconceivable visitation could be were beaten back with swords, with cudgels, with knouts

—and our path was lined with poor wretches who lay bleeding, or tried to crawl away to safety.

That is how Ambien II, of Sirius, one of the Five, came to be marching into the gay and colourful building that was used to house the governing bodies of Lelanos, at the head of a Shammat army; how I came to be made ruler of Lelanos, with Tafta.

When the brief and ridiculous ceremony was over, Tafta announced that he would take me to my "palace"—there was no such thing in Lelanos—and I said that I would return to my own lodgings. It was at this moment the illusion, or spell, that had been on me finally dissolved, and left me looking at a half-animal adventurer, who had no idea of the dimensions of the forces he was challenging. He could not stop me. Not unless he made me a prisoner then and there and ended *his* illusion. He was living in some dream of glory and grandeur, with his own city to rule, backed by Sirius, whom he could manipulate and use in his, Shammat's, eternal battle with Canopus. So he had seen it. So he still saw it; looking into those shallow almost colourless eyes of his, I could see his thoughts swimming there, for my Sirian intelligence had come back to me—I could see, in the cocksure, but absurd, postures his limbs fell into that he was dreaming of an Empire that would match that dreamed of by Grakconkranpatl. Suddenly, I was able to see all kinds of things.

He might have been able to find out by subtle reasoning when I was to arrive in the other city, but he had *not* known that Lelanos was peaceful behind its forbidden zone, and not a tyrant. He had not dared to challenge Canopus by entering Lelanos, until Rhodia was gone. And he did not know that our forces could crush anything he or the evil city across the mountains did any time we wanted—that if they were allowed to survive, it was because it did not matter to us.

And because, of course, Canopus, inexplicably, allowed them to survive—but this was deep waters for me, and I was far off understanding.

I said to this little upstart that I would take myself back to my lodgings and he did not stop me. It was because he did not care. He had got what he wanted—to be ruler of Lelanos.

Well, I could tell myself that if he was a tyrant who would bring the place to ruin very fast, then this was no more than Lelanos would do for itself, could not prevent itself doing. I had hastened an inevitability, that was all.

I left him there lolling in the graceful council chamber, ruler of Lelanos, among his savages, whom he had been to fetch the day before from where they had been feasting and roistering in the forests, not daring to enter the city—I left them, and went to my lodgings, where I sat up and thought, and thought, through the night.

The low and sibilant song of *Sirius, Sirius, be careful*, was very strong, and it drowned out other thoughts, until I bade the song be quiet, for it had a valedictory sound. And it was quiet, for I had no need of it now that I was restored to myself. Except for my shame. My incredulous shame . . . how easy it had been after all, for Shammat to win me over. And with such slight powers at his disposal! No more than a minimal use of intuition, as in the case of my first capture, constant brooding about Canopus, envy of Canopus, hatred of Canopus, had brought to Shammat some of the least and most lowly of Canopean skills. How easy, then, to flatter me, by speaking through my weaknesses. How easy to take me over. And now it was all done with, I could hardly believe it had happened and that I had succumbed—yet I had to believe it, and, by extension know that I could easily be lost again, and that I might easily have not recovered my own good sense this time—for if it had not been for the low sweet song of Sirius, Sirius, set into me by Rhodia, by Nasar, by Canopus, to remind me of what I was, I might easily be lolling there with Shammat now, ready to tyrannise poor Lelanos.

When the morning came, I walked out of my lodgings into the empty street and away from the city. I reasoned that Shammat would be drunk this morning, and in any case he would not care. He could use the legend of the white goddess, or priests from afar, or any such formulation, to strengthen his claims to power there. For as long as it lasted. Why should he come after me? He might know, using the pitiful little powers he did possess, where I was, approximately, in the forests to the south of the city, but did he want an unwilling captive, one who would not grace his rule, but must be drugged, or beaten into submission? Sirius willing was one thing. Sirius sullen and subversive could do nothing to help him.

Besides, he was afraid of—not me, but Canopus. Shammat might control this planet—Canopus admitted this. But Shammat controlled it only within limits Canopus set. Drunk with power, with inglorious confidence, as Tafta might be, he could not choose to challenge retribution.

He had gambled to his limits when he had told the dark priests I would be an easy capture. He had wanted two things. One, to take from me the ornaments that he knew had some sort of talismanic power—Shammat with or without Puttiora were always trying to get their hands on the articles powerful at any given time. But he also expected to be able to use the situation, for he had been waiting, having partially gained the confidence of the priestly caste, to gain total power over them, and to rule Grakconkranpatl. He knew that Canopus was somewhere close, for he could sense the strength there, but he never guessed it was Rhodia the wardress who watched and knew everything he did. And when the priests, afraid of me, afraid that one faction might use me to strengthen its position and win power over the others, decided to sacrifice me, and he sensed that Rhodia—or someone—would rescue me, he did not give the alarm, for he was a gambler by nature, always ready to see where any new twist in a situation would lead him.

He would not follow me. I knew this, having thought it out carefully all through the long night.

And so I walked steadily south, by myself, and had many pleasant solitary days, and even some adventures (which I have published elsewhere, for the entertainment of our young people), and at last I reached one of our outposts, from which I could send a message for an aircraft to come and fetch me.

And so ended my descent into Shammat-nature. Ended, at least, outwardly. But inwardly it was a different matter. It is not possible to become a subject of Shammat, even temporarily, without being affected, profoundly, and for a long time, in every fibre of oneself.

When I reached our headquarters for the supervision of the Colony 9 animals, I spent a short time restoring my inner balances. I was now viewing my recent psychological overthrow with amazement as well as apprehension for a possible recurrence. When I thought of the woman Rhodia it was with admiration, a feeling that I was able to take refuge in the thought of that strength of hers—

or his! And I now could think with abhorrence of Tafta, whom I had even liked, for a while.

It had to be decided what was to be done with the slave city, Grakconkranpatl. I thought long and hard about this. Easy enough to blast the whole place out of existence. But there was no way of preventing another just as bad coming into being. And looking at it from the overall view (which after all it was my responsibility to do), these indigenous cultures—if it was accurate to call cultures native when the origin of their genes lay so far from Rohanda, in such distant planets—were useful to us. Some of them provided social laboratories without any effort on our part. I decided only to rescue our 2,000 captives, and sent five cargo planes, with ten armed craft for support. These flew back and forth over Grakconkranpatl for a sufficient time, and then the cargo planes descended at the prison farms where the animals were working in chains. The 2,000 were returned to the settlement in the high peaks. It was felt that their sojourn in the lower areas, and then a re-introduction to the harsh conditions, would strengthen them and further their adaptability. And so it turned out.

As the future of these animals does not concern this narrative further, I will summarize. The controlled explosions on Planet 3 (1) did not affect its atmosphere in the way it had been hoped. The crawling plant-animals were destroyed, however. This did not seem to be likely to change the planet's atmosphere in any way, but some of our biologists complained that we had destroyed a unique and irreplaceable species. The usual arguments took place: "You cannot make an omelette, etc." against the "Storehouse of nature." An amount of oxygen was locked up in the soil and rocks of the planet; we did not know how much. Thermonuclear explosions with a different intent took place. The oxygen content of the atmosphere did significantly increase. We shipped the Planet 9 animals from their high, oxygen-starved station in the mountains to the low oxygen-starved air of Planet 9. About half succumbed, but this was felt to be better than expected. We introduced at the same time a large quantity of different kinds of vegetation at the lichen level, and marsh plants, and types of seaweed—all with the idea of adding to the oxygen. A fuller account of this experiment will be found in the appropriate place. The planet, in fact, did slowly come to life, and within five hundred S-years was in a condition to allow the exploitation of minerals. But it was and is a chilly, phlegmatic planet, where everything is slow moving, small, dank. It was interesting to see what happened to the Planet 9 type. They became smaller; their fur became more like scales, or lichens; they laid eggs that they carried in a pouch under their tails until they hatched; and they were amphibious. They became useless for physical work of any kind. Their function remains slowly to increase the oxygen content. The exploitation of the planet has to be carried out by technicians and labourers who work in strictly controlled conditions for short periods.

The success of this experiment influenced how we set up our stations on the Rohandan moon.

A necessary word about my state of mind. I remained on Rohanda for a considerable time after my experience as a captive. I recognised that I had been in an unhealthy and dangerous emotional condition. I knew that this was not a new thing: its origin was due to the situation of Sirius itself. I felt that I should do something about it, change myself in some way—at least not remain as I had been: capable of such foolhardiness and almost cynical indifference. But time did not seem to improve me. Discussions with Ambien I led to no more than assurances of mutual support, and declarations that we understood each other's metaphysical situation: for my mood was not confined to myself, and the briefest of exploratory conversations with others of our Service revealed how general the unease had become.

What slowly hardened in me was a feeling of resentment, or at least puzzlement, over the behaviour of Rhodia, or Nasar. *Why* had I been led into such temptation? For what purpose? I had succumbed, had freed myself—or, rather, had recognised in myself the implanted reminders of Canopus, which were the means by which I saw my situation and could free myself. But what had it all been for?

And this thought, or emotion, was directly linked to, fed by, an astonishment, a sick angry disbelief that Shammat—was so paltry! *Who* was, *what* was, this power that held Rohanda in thrall? Tafta was an insignificantly nasty half-animal who had acquired some minor capacities that allowed him petty tricks. He was not more than crafty and cunning. Evil I *had* seen in the cruel priesthood. What relation did Tafta have to these evil ones? Had he created them or merely tolerated and used them? Could the progeny of an unpleasant, mildly disgusting, unimportant nastiness become so much worse than its progenitors? What I was feeling became—as it crystallised out so that I could look at it—something like this: if Nasar had arranged for me to become tempted by something really wicked, like the dark priests, a total and thoroughgoing beastliness, I might have found some point in that! But to have succumbed to Tafta was humiliating. Yes—it was my pride that was speaking; and I was even half aware of it. What it amounted to was that I was annoyed with Canopus for not arranging for me a more profound evil! They had rated me low because of matching me with such a petty wickedness. I felt insulted! And yet my reason told me that I had been proved not to rate any greater nastiness than Tafta! After all, I had succumbed, even though briefly. I had not been immune to petty nastiness and ambition. Yet I could not imagine myself ever wanting anything the priesthood of Grakconkranpatl could offer me: nor feeling anything but revulsion for them. . . . Was I then to understand, from my weakening towards Tafta, that the beginnings of an immersion in evil must always start with something easy, paltry, seemingly unimportant? Was this what Canopus had been teaching me?

All these thoughts, and many others on these lines, conflicted in me and at length I found it all too much, and I shut a door on them. Enough. I had been proved to be gullible and feeble. I knew it. I was not going to deny it. I flew away from Rohanda, with a dissatisfaction in me I was not equipped to handle.

This dwindled into a dry sorrow, which was not very far from the "existential malady," or so I found, when subjecting it to my dispassionate judgment.

I was away from Rohanda for some time.

The experiments being undertaken there, less biosociological than strictly scientific, laboratory stuff, did not interest me much. I followed the progress of only one. The atmosphere of Rohanda is 80 percent nitrogen. Yet its mammals subsist on less than 20 percent oxygen. The idea was to breed an animal capable of living on nitrogen, or at least a mixture of nitrogen and oxygen. Many and ingenious were the experiments, which had to end because all of Isolated S.C. II was overrun by an empire ruled by Grakcon-kranpatl and Lelanos. This was an uneasy alliance. Alliances between two partners equal in strength and with much the same aim in my experience have to be unstable. They last only when one is in a generously tutelary relationship with the other. Our history is in point. Lelanos had become as horrible a place as the other. The Lelannians mated freely with the race of dark priests, whose main feature had been a heavy uniformity of ugliness, and this match had produced a type of very strong, but more flexible and varied people, who adopted the "religious" practices of their former enemies and terrorized the entire continent. The new cross dominated Grakcon-kranpatl and used the former priestly caste as slaves. Thus had the new state of affairs come into being where the two cities had become allied in evil.

But I was not disposed to concern myself much with Rohanda. Affairs elsewhere in our Empire seemed more important. When I got a message from Canopus, inviting me to a discussion "on the present situation in Rohanda, with particular attention to the Isolated Southern Continent II," I at first ignored this order. For it was one. I then was sent a message signed by Klorathy, of whom I had never ceased to think, who was always at the back of my mind, even when I was much occupied elsewhere. What he said was that "the present situation in the continents under your control is disadvantageously affecting all of Rohanda."

Now, I was quite aware that both the Southern Continents were populated by warring, savage, degenerated tribes. But when we had wanted the use of these two continents for—mostly—experimental purposes, it was not in my mind that our responsibilities should also be altruistic. I saw no reason why Sirius should not simply leave Rohanda altogether. Canopus was welcome to both Southern Continents. Nor did my reports indicate that the state of affairs in the northern hemisphere was much to the credit of Canopus. If our uses of Rohanda could not be described as having led to an improvement of the place, then the same had to be said about Canopus.

So I saw things then.

I was reluctant to accede to Klorathy's invitation, because it was to discuss a squalid and unsatisfactory planet full of brutes who could be relied upon for only one thing—to kill each other on one pretext or another at the first opportunity.

If Klorathy had sent me an invitation to visit him on Canopus— yes. Or to discuss other planets that concerned us—yes.

I was disappointed. I felt as if I had been waiting, perhaps only half-consciously, for the development of an unfulfilled friendship, and then been offered a participation in a dreary task that by definition could not succeed. I sent a message to Canopus that I could not meet Klorathy, "though I might be able to find time later." There was no satisfaction for me in this gesture. I felt only an intensification of my aridity. But a task that I knew I would find difficult and absorbing was waiting for me at the end of the Galaxy. As I prepared to leave, I was again summoned to a top-level conference. It concerned Rohanda, or rather, her moon. It had of course been known to us that Shammat was established on this small and unpleasant planet. Now it appeared there were new developments. I appointed someone to represent me at this conference, turned my mind away from Rohanda—and found that as I went about my preparations for leaving, possibly for a long time, it was as if, again, my ears were being filled with an insinuating memory. *Sirius*, I heard, *Sirius, Sirius* . . . and I could not free myself of it. Waves of this insidious whispering came up in me, so that I could hear nothing else, and ebbed, leaving a silence that I knew was waiting to be filled with *Sirius, Sirius*. In Nasar's voice. In Rhodia's. And in Klorathy's. And in voices I had never heard but knew I would. I stubbornly ignored this call, or tried to, making my mind dwell on problems distant and different from Rohanda's and found that no matter what I did, the whispering grew, so that I would find myself standing quite still, some task forgotten, listening.

THE LELANNIAN EXPERIMENTS

I told the Department that my mission must be postponed. I sent a message to Klorathy that I was going to Rohanda, and ordered the Space Traveller to set me down near our old station.

We had maintained this post, though it had several times fallen into disuse, and twice been destroyed by earthquakes. It was repaired partly through sentiment: I had been so usefully happy there. Now I promised myself a short space of freedom and thought, in solitude, for Klorathy would need time to reach me. For one thing, he would have to enquire from my Home Planet where on Rohanda he could find me . . . so far had I forgotten what one might expect of Canopean abilities!

I walked by myself up to the little group of buildings among low foothills, the towering ranges of the western mountains at my back, a good way to the south from where I had done the same, going towards Lelanos, and as I approached thought they did not look uninhabited. Had the Lelannian tyrants then taken this Sirian station for themselves? If so, if they had lost all fear of Sirius, then they had fallen very far away from any sort of understanding. I was preparing in my mind how to deal with an emergency if I found one, as I entered the first one of the buildings, an airy set of rooms similar to those I had once, so pleasantly, lived in: it would be easy, for instance, to summon the Space Traveller, which was already stationed just above me, and visible as a silvery glitter.

There was someone sitting, back to the light, across the room. I knew at once that it was Klorathy. Though, of course, it was technically impossible that he should have got here in the time since my message went out. This meant that he had known I would be here, in this place, well before the message did go out, and even before I had decided myself. . . . I was absorbing this as I went towards him saying: "This is Sirius."

"I am an uninvited visitor, I know," said he; and I left the remark unanswered, meaning him to feel that I was making a point. And went to sit where I could see him clearly. I had not seen him since the experience on their Colony 11. It is of course a not uncommon thing to see, on this or that planet, within the Canopean aegis or within ours, an individual one recognises, so that one goes forward to say: "Greetings, Klorathy," or Nasar, or whoever it might be. But then one sees it as a *type* one has recognised, a species, a *kind*—and what then looks back from inside this known shape is an individual quite strange to one. It has always been, to me, a disturbing business, to be with this *shape*, which is that of a remembered friend or associate: and to match gestures, glances, mannerisms, that are so close to those that are, in memory, the property of this or that person. What absolutely individual and unmatchable entity is it that is *not* here? And, conversely, this other experience: when one encounters the species, type, shape, equipped with *roughly* similar manners and ways, and it *is* the remembered individual. This was Klorathy. I had known it was he, the moment I saw him, a shape against light, all his features invisible. Yet this was not the identical Klorathy. He had chosen to inhabit a physical equipment almost the same as his last. Presumably it was useful, being strong, healthy, and—I deduced—a good all-purpose type that would adapt easily to any planet and species without too much remark. For instance, he would not be likely to choose *my* physical type, which in fact always calls forth remark, and often uneasiness, if not worse, except on my own originating planet.

I had long been considering the Canopean ways of re-juvenation and re-issue. I have given a good deal of my time to this problem since. And I want to make the point at this time and place that I consider we, Sirius, would do well to master these other techniques.

There is nothing we do not know about substitution and prosthetics. We replace parts of the body as fast as they wear out. I do not think there is an organ or a tissue in me that was Ambien II in pre-Disaster time, let alone even what the Canopeans call the First Time. There is nothing left even of what made up my being when I was whirled about the skies during the "events." Even the ichor in my veins has been replaced many times. But these transplants and transfusions are costly in time and patience. Yes, I know that the argument will be, as usual, that a vast quantity of admirable technicians would be put out of work; that many skills and techniques would become redundant. But this is a question that falls under the heading of the existential problem, question, or dilemma. If we have answered that, in all other fields, by always accepting advances in knowledge even at the cost of falling populations, as classes of work become obsolete, then it is consistent for us to consider whether we should adopt the Canopean ways of self-perpetuation. How simple to "die"—and to take on new physical equipment. After all, it is not even necessary to go through the tedious business of having to endure infancy and childhood—they have learned to bypass all that. How pettifogging and even pedantic the Canopean attitude to outworn physical equipment makes ours look! We patch and replace, and transplant, and preserve—they throw an inefficient body aside and step into a new one without fuss, sentimentality, or regret.

Klorathy had inhabited three different bodies since I had seen him last. And he told me that Nasar was at that time down in *our* Southern Continent I as a very small brown male, a hunter, bringing a species up to a new height of knowledge about its position in relation to "The Great Spirit." Which was the formulation suitable for that place.

Klorathy told me this in a way that meant it was a rebuke—a rebuke to us, for our negligence. We had no stations on that continent then.

And so we two engaged in, if not conflict, at least disagreement, and from the very first moment.

I was with Klorathy for fifty R-years; and I will sum up the essence of our being together thus: that he was there to bring me to a new view of the Sirian usage of the planet, a new view of ourselves altogether. And he was prepared to go to a great trouble . . . from the start I was wondering what sort of importance Canopus could possibly be attributing to it all, to designate Klorathy, one of their senior Colonial officials, to my tutelage for such a long time. Of course I did not fool myself that this was an individual matter. No, it was Canopus and Sirius—as always. But I recognised that I was in a familiar position. Nasar . . . Klorathy . . . or whatever names they might be choosing to use, whatever shapes they wore, when with me, were—I had to accept it—instructors.

And Klorathy sat there patiently with me in that pleasant airy room, where we looked out together over landscapes I almost was able to match with what I remembered—and talked.

When I had lived here during the best time, in the days when I thought of Rohanda almost as my home, what I saw from the foothills was savannah, a pleasant, lightly-treed country broken by valleys and plains of grass. All was different now: it was rain forest. Climatic changes of a dramatic kind had caused vast rivers to flow, and their many tributaries ran through enormous trees, which made a canopy of foliage it was not possible to see through. We looked at vast expanses of leaves, leaves, always leaves, the tops of trees that shimmered and moved under a heavy and uncomfortable sun. It was not at all the bracing and invigorating place of my memories.

There was nothing now in this continent pleasant to hear about. Klorathy was making certain that I *did* hear, and, as I have said, with the intention of making me feel it all as a responsibility. I shall never forget how, through those days of preparation—as he clearly saw it—I was held there by him, held by his determination, that I should not be allowed to escape anything of the truth. Sometimes, evading the necessity of looking at him, I gazed out into the hot steamy perspectives of green that were so often drenched by sultry rains: but otherwise I sat regarding him, Klorathy, taking in and wondering at the authority of this person who never demanded, never enforced, but who had only to be there, be present, be himself, to make of what he said a claim and something that had to be attended to.

The situation through the continent was this. While the Lelannians had become a tyranny that controlled the old Lelannian and Grakconkranpatl territories that, because of their position, also controlled the long isthmus that joined the Southern Continent to the Isolated Northern Continent, acting as a barrier to the movement of peoples, everywhere else was evolving a fairly uniform species made from the escapees and mutants from our—by now— very numerous experiments, crossed with that kind of borderline semi-ape that is so often the predominant animal on certain types of planet. This cross was not dissimilar to the Lelanos type before it had degenerated. In appearance they were a lithe, slightly built, tallish people with the common ranges of colour from light-brown to almost black, long straight black hair, black eyes. They were hunters, and gathered plants from the forests. That their genes, which held memories of origins in other places where agriculture was understood, had not spoken in them here was not surprising: this was a sparse population, with no need to grow food. They were in strict harmony with their surroundings, at that stage where no act, or intention, or thought, could be outside the mental and emotional frames of reference forming their "religion." The Great Spirit, here, as Nasar was teaching on the other Southern Continent, was in everything they did: they lived within the sacramental, or—as I attempted to joke with Klorathy—according to the Necessity. Our relations were not easy. (I see now that this had to be so, representing as we did, and *do*—I must insist—Empires on such different levels.) But we did joke, were able to use this ease between ourselves. Klorathy evidently could not see my, admittedly, minor and perhaps clumsy jests as worth more than the slightest of smiles; yes, said he, these people indeed lived within the ordinance of the Necessity. Or rather, had done, before they had been overrun by the Lelannians. They were now slaves and servants from the extreme south of the continent to the isthmus. Everywhere they worked mines and plantations, or provided the meat for the ritual murders of the Lelannian religion. They were also material for experiment. This surprised me, and I had to sit and hear, and at very great length and in detail, of the development of the master race into technicians who saw the animals that surrounded them as controllable and malleable and available for their purposes not only *socially*, that is, within the limits of sociological malleability, which after all was a viewpoint that as such, and in itself, I could hardly criticise, since we—Sirius—had always seen this as the foundation of Empire, the basis of good government. But they had gone further, used any living being they ruled, on any level, as the stuff for experiments of a most brutal nature. No, although I did have my uncomfortable moments listening to Klorathy describe the practices of these overlords, I could say to myself that never had we, had Sirius, done unnecessary, or cruel experiments. Of course, experimentation of the physical, as distinct from the bio-sociological kind, is necessary and so permitted. But after all, it is always done, with us, within the limits of *our* necessity, even if this is sometimes only a local need . . . so I fatuously argued with myself as I sat listening to Klorathy, during these conversations that I was already seeing as a preparation. A deliberate, calculated preparation for what was to come. Oh, Canopus never did, never has done, anything that has not been calculated, foreseen, measured, and this down to the last detail, even when the plan is such a long-term one that . . . I have to state here again that we—meaning Sirius, and I say this knowing the criticism I risk—are not able to comprehend the Canopean understanding of what may be long term, or long foreseen. Yes, I am saying this. I am stating it.

I am insisting on it. . . . If I may not do this, then my attempt in writing this record, or report, is without use.

This small example, which I am describing here, consisting of Klorathy's use of the situation in this continent at this time to instruct me, Sirius, contains many aspects of Canopean planning, foresight, patience. Even as I dwelt there, in that old Sirian station, day after day with Klorathy, I knew that he had calculated that I would *need* this period for adjustment, for the absorption of what he was presenting to me.

When I knew he wanted me to accompany him on a long and certainly dangerous journey to see for myself what he was describing, I resisted. Not because of the danger. I was acquiring very different attitudes to my own extinction! Once I would have regarded "death," of the kind now obsolete among us, as a calamity, certainly as a loss to our community because of my vast experience. Now I was thinking that if I was worth a survival of physical extinction, then what there was in me to survive, would—*must*. And I was thinking, too, that if we were caught and killed by these truly horrible animals, the Lelannians, I would be in the company of Canopus, who regarded "death" as a change of circumstance. No, I was resisting because of my old lack, or disability: I was not being given what I felt I was due! In the past I had sulked, or allowed myself to become impervious to what I might be learning, because Klorathy's attention was not being given to me alone. Now, when it *was* being given to me alone, or rather, to me as Sirius, I still felt neglected, insufficiently appreciated, because it was only a journey among these savage Rohandans that was being offered. I would have been prepared to stay in the little station in the foothills, overlooking the long reaches of simmering rain forest, listening to what Klorathy had to tell me—even though he talked only of Lelanos and Lelannians, and their habits, and not ever of Canopus itself, which I longed so much to hear about—taking in what I knew was an education of a sort far larger than I was then equipped to understand. When Klorathy spoke, his words came from Canopus, were of the substance of Canopus—that I did know. But he was putting a term to this experience of ours, which on one level was so easygoing, even lazy, and demanding that we should go forth, into something else.

There were various ways we might travel. One was to summon my Space Traveller, and to descend, the two of us, as representatives of Sirius—they would not know Canopus, the real and true power!—and demand to see what we wanted. Or we could pretend to be emissaries from another part of Rohanda, "from across the seas." Or we could announce ourselves as from the Northern Continent, and the fact that the isthmus was closed would add to our—we hoped—mysteriousness. It was not possible to purport to come from another city in the Lelannian system, for it was a monolithic and all-pervasive tyranny, and knew everything that went on everywhere.

The problem was my appearance: I at least could not hope to remain unremarked.

The alternatives were put to me by Klorathy, in his way of leaving me free, so that I had to consider them, and then offer my choice to him for his acceptance. I chose descent by Space Traveller, as the easiest. He did not at once disagree, but kept hesitating, as he made suggestions, or the beginnings of suggestions, waiting for me to take up trains of thought for myself. I soon saw that to appear, suddenly, "from the skies," and after such a long time during which the Sirian surveillance had been forgotten, would be to disrupt the social system totally, and in ways that ought to be calculated, weighed, planned for—in the Canopean manner. Planned for even when the subjects of this consideration were such an unpleasant kind?

Yes, indeed, I had to accept it. What I was being given was a lesson in Canopean viewpoints—very far from ours.

No, we were not to use the easy way. In the end it was decided to be visitors from "over the seas." Prompted by him, I brought forth from within myself the advantages—and they were all inside a Canopean scope of time. The main one, from which the others flowed, was that even these ugly tyrants would be open to information or instruction from "over the seas," for their legends kept references to such beings. Not by chance: some visiting Canopean had no doubt made sure that these legends would contain such memories.

This journey of ours through the Southern Continent was a long one, and there were many aspects to it that unfolded themselves as we went, that sometimes became clear to me only later. Are still, in fact, showing new facets, when I contemplate that time. I submitted a full report on this journey, which is still available. There is nothing untrue, or even evasive there: on that I must insist. But I must urge, too, that it is possible, and indeed often inevitable, that one may report events as fully and honestly as one knows how—and yet find oneself up against a check, beyond which one may in no way pass. This barrier is the nature or state of those for whom the report is made. Their state *at that time*. Preparing this report, with one's mind on those who will receive it—the words are chosen for you, the frequencies limited. As one's mind goes out to touch, or assess, those who will take it in, one knows that only so much of it *can* be taken in. But that later, perhaps, much more will be found. I wonder if those of my fellow Sirians who have read so far—and, as I have already said, I can guess only too well the nature of some of their emotions—might care to look up that old report of the journey. I feel that both those who saw it all those ages ago, and those who read it now, for the first time, may find there a great deal that can amplify this present account of mine.

We dressed ourselves as differently from the current Lelannian mode as possible: they expressed their hierarchic society most fully in their clothes, which were elaborate, stiff, and ornamented. We wore simple robes, and made sure that the current protective devices were well concealed; though we believed that all memory of such things had been forgotten.

Klorathy took me straight, not to the new capital but to a main research centre.

It was situated well away from areas of habitation, was guarded heavily. The actual appearance of the place was not dissimilar to our research establishments that had been in past times quite plentiful over this and the other Southern Continent: this fact did give me some unpleasant moments, and I wondered if our practices had been noted by the ancestors of this present breed, and copied. I did not mention my suspicion to Klorathy, who, however, as it passed through my mind, said only: "May I suggest that we reserve all comment and comparison until *after* our journey is done?"

The station consisted of laboratories of various kinds, and compounds and camps for the retention of the experimentees: a local tribe.

When we arrived in the place, and said that we were "from afar, over the long blue seas"—a phrase which was part of their heritage of song—they showed a disposition to worship us, which we discouraged, asking to be shown examples of their technical knowledge.

Their awe was a disadvantage, because it made it difficult for them to produce simple answers to straight questions; but we could see enough without that.

These currently ruling animals seemed to have inherited the worst of the two originating breeds. The heavy slablike uniformity of the Grakconkranpatls remained: there was a truly extraordinary lack of variation in feature and build. Any lightness or quickness was derived from the subtle vitality of the old Lelannians, but this had degenerated into mental dishonesty and capacity for self-deception, which showed itself in their faces and eyes as shiftiness, evasiveness. It is truly astonishing how a characteristic may become deformed into its opposite under the pressure of degeneration.

Experiments then in progress at that station included the following:

In order to find out the capacities for endurance and perseverance of their subject animals, they had built a very large tank, with slippery sloping sides on which it was not possible to find a purchase. This was filled with water. About a hundred particularly healthy and strong tribesmen had been selected and put into this tank to swim there until they drowned. All around the edge of the tank researchers stood with stopwatches in their hands. Others guarded the instruments with which they were measuring the pulse rate and breathing of the experimentees: from time to time an animal would be selected, pulled out of the water, and tested, and then, in spite of cries and pleadings, would be flung back in again.

The teams of researchers, as they tired, were replaced. Astonishing feats of endurance were performed. It was not the most pleasant of sights. Though it was certainly interesting to see the differences between the swimming animals. Some, when they were thrown in, suspecting the nature of the experiment, at once allowed themselves to drown. This tendency was regarded as a measure of intelligence. Some cried and begged to be taken out. Some panicked and clung to others so that one might see two or three or more drown at a time, sinking during their struggles. Others were silent and conserved their strength and swam around and around and around, regarding their masters on the edges with a look in their eyes that—I have to record for the sake of truthfulness—I had seen in the eyes of some of our subject races . . . the Lombis, for instance. Some, seeing others weaken, went to support them knowing that their own ends would be nearer. But a few swam on for several days. And even when they seemed half-conscious, swam on, and on, until at last they sank. To stand on those high banks, while some of the unfortunate animals scrabbled and clutched at the slippery slopes beneath me, calling out for aid—I soon found this too upsetting, and suggested to Klorathy that we should leave.

There was another experiment to measure strength and endurance. They had a large cauldron under which were piles of wood. The cauldron, from which it was impossible to climb, because the sides sloped inwards, was filled with water. Into this they put, one at a time, males, females, children, and lit the fires, and slowly heated the water. This was to measure the different rates at which the experimentees succumbed to the heating water. Again the differences were remarkable. A few managed to stay alive until the water was nearly at boiling point. (This part of my account will be more fully appreciated if the reader equips himself with a basic knowledge of Rohandan chemistry.)

In a third experiment they transplanted limbs and organs. It was unpleasant to see all this work being done on techniques that had not only been in use with us for so long but were already becoming superceded—though we did not (do not yet) appreciate that. Yes, I am making this comparison quite soberly.

The monsters created by their crude techniques were, I suppose, not without interest, when I was able to quell my—by then soaring —indignation. The mammary glands of some females had been grafted on their backs. Others had them on their thighs. The sexual organs of males were transferred to their faces, so that the organs for eating and progeniture were adjacent. This caused severe psychological maladjustment, which they found, surprisingly, of interest. I saw a child that had had legs grafted on to its hips! And we were told that this unfortunate at least would have an adequate future, for it would be used as entertainment for the ruling classes: it was able to revolve itself on these four legs as on the spokes of a wheel. The technicians did seem quite pleased to be able to reassure us when they could—as in the case of this cartwheeling child. They did not enjoy causing pain, they insisted. But they believed that the experimentees, being of an inferior kind, did not feel physical or psychological pain as they themselves did. I have not before encountered this trick of the mental processes—at least not since the very early days of our science, when there were tendencies to assure ourselves of the invulnerability of our experimentees.

At least Sirius can say that not for many long ages have we been hypocrites . . . I said this then, to Klorathy, who merely repeated that we should wait for the end of our journey to make comments.

Before we left that place we were taken on a tour of the compounds. They housed several hundred tribespeople: males, females, children. Long sheds contained tiers of bunks in which they slept. These were built of concrete because, as was explained to us, the animals were thus more easily protected from vermin and kept clean: the interiors of the sheds, and the animals, were hosed down once a day with water that had chemicals in it. Some animals took cold and died of this treatment: the hot steamy climate disposed them to respiratory diseases. They were fed from large pots filled with porridge made of a cereal introduced by us long before from our Planet 17. They were made to do exercises twice a day, because unfit animals were of no use in research work. There was a prison and punishment block for offenders, and a small hospital for the sick. The compound was surrounded by tall fences, and guarded heavily. As we made our tour, a male tribesman stood forth, holding up his hands palms out—in their gesture for entreaty. As the guards went forward to club him back among his fellows, I asked them to let him speak. He wanted to make a petition. He said that many of the experiments being made on them were unnecessary, because the information needed could be gained by simply asking them— as for instance, as to abilities of endurance compared among individuals. In their native habitat, before their subjection, their own traditions told them that there had been an extensive and rich knowledge of the nature of their physiques, and of their mental processes. They had used a medicine based on plants and on psychological understanding. Also, they had known how to live in and with the terrain in such a way that this was not damaged.

The poor fellow came out with this in a rush, because of his fear of being checked, looking all the time at me, begging for my protection. He stood naked there before us, his features marked with the signs of long imprisonment, but he had a self-respect that was impressive. This "inferior" race was obviously, and at even the most cursory inspection, superior to their masters—particularly in the honesty and straightforwardness of their understanding and means of expressing themselves.

He said that at no time had the Lelannians ever asked the natives about what might be known by them, and which could be used generally, to benefit everyone. Never had the Lelannians been prepared to listen, though the natives had continually tried to offer their knowledge, their expertise . . . but the Lelannians were not prepared to listen then either—clubs and whips descended; soon the poor fellow was lying senseless in his blood, and the group of technicians who were showing us around showed indignation at the "impertinence" and then went on with the self-satisfied stupidity that was their characteristic, to say that "these animals were always up to their tricks." I was seething with indignation, not only because of the injustice I had witnessed but because of the waste of it all. I was thinking that never had Sirius—at least, not since our civilised time began—gone into a planet and destroyed the precious knowledge of its inhabitants, the irreplaceable knowledge—for only those who have been evolved from the earth and air and liquid of a planet can know its real, its innermost, nature.

But Klorathy stood silent by me. I knew him enough to understand that a tightening of his face showed he was suffering. But he made no sign, only turned to go. And we made our way through the packed masses of naked tribespeople, all beseeching us with their eyes and holding up their palms to us, afraid to speak, but taking this opportunity to make their cause known to those who—they could see—were not Lelannians.

Before we left the place we had to endure a long feast at which we played our parts. The feast was nauseating. The flesh of the natives and other animals was its main feature. The technicians of this place were glad of an excuse for a feast, we could see: they saw themselves as sophisticates banished for long tours of duty in a backwater, and longed to be returned to the capital.

They made speeches every one of which congratulated themselves on their brilliant experimental work. It did not cross their minds to think we might not admire them as they admired themselves.

And next morning we thankfully left.

News about the appearance of "the great ones from over the waters" had preceded us to the capital. We were received with much pomp and ceremonial. Again, the priesthood ruled, but the ruling caste did not consist only of the priestly families, as had been the case in old Grakconkranpatl. The division showed at once as we proceeded between two ranks, on one side the priests in their gorgeous robes and jewellery, flanked and buttressed by the soldiery; and on the other the privileged families, in colourful clothing and jewels, as charming and infantile as such indulged castes always are. No soldiers on their side! No guards, even! And no need of either, for they were the willing captives of the ruling priests. I shall not describe our visit to this capital city any further—there were no experimental stations there. But I shall mention the architecture. When the Lelannian and Grakconkranpatl states mingled, and Lelanos dominated, taking over the priesthood, the dark, blocklike, ominous, Grakconkranpatl style was used for all administrative buildings, prisons, hospitals, punishment centres. The light, fanciful Lelanos ways were used for housing and places of entertainment. Strange it was to see these extremes so juxtaposed.

We spent some months in the capital. Slowly I saw that Klorathy needed this time to find out whether these brutes were capable of regeneration. The process, for the most part, consisted of listening. Or he probed, lightly and skillfully. Sometimes he made experiments of his own—but so slight and subtle were they that at first I did not notice what he was doing: I had to learn to be able to observe what went on. He would test their reactions to this idea or that, by suggestions, or even mild provocation. He would implant a new idea into a group and then wait to see how it would become processed by their particular mentation. I was not equipped to understand how he was reacting to what he found in them. But I was able to see that he was increasingly sombre, and even—it took me some time to be able to admit to myself that the great Canopus was capable of such emotions—discouraged. But there was soon no doubt of it: he was containing a dry and powerful sorrow, and I was able to recognise what I knew myself so very well and so intimately from such a long immersion in it.

This stay in the capital is fully dealt with in my old report.

By the time we left, in spite of Klorathy's attempts to prevent us becoming cult objects, focuses of useless awe, that is what we had become. We had to forbid, absolutely, ceremonies in which droves of unfortunate natives were designated as "sacrifices to the Gods." We insisted, as far as we could, that such practices were regarded at least "over the long blue seas" as unnecessary—it would not do to suggest to these self-satisfied ones that they were barbaric and primitive. When we left we travelled accompanied by priests, who performed their repulsive ceremonies at every opportunity; and by some of the youth, who saw no shame in describing themselves as "playpeople."

The experimental station we visited next was similar to the other in appearance. The experimental subjects again consisted of the local tribesmen, but they also used some other kinds of animals, notably carnivores. They preferred to use the natives, on the ground that these were nearer to themselves in physical structure. Also that they had done so much work on them comparisons could more usefully be made.

At this station Klorathy made an attempt to persuade the technicians into asking the natives in a systematic way for information about their medicine. He spoke of places "beyond the waters" where an advanced medicine was used, based on local balances and earth forces, on the rhythms of the stars, on the disposition of exactly placed and planned buildings, and on the use of plants. This "medicine" was more than curative or preventive: health was considered as a result and an expression of the exact sciences, used by a whole society, taught to every individual in the society. Health was being in balance with the natural forces of—the Galaxy. Yes, he went so far. And, yes, I was all ears. For this was what I had wanted to know. He was talking about the Necessity, even if in this guarded and indirect way. That much I did recognise. But as usual I was being disadvantaged by my emotional reactions. How was it that this precious information, the real secrets of Canopus, of the Canopean superiority, was being given to these debased Lelannians. How was it, that when I had wanted, and for so long, to hear him talk in this way, it was not I who was addressed . . . it took me a long time, not until after we separated on this occasion, to see the simple fact that after all he had been speaking to me, since I was there. To Sirius. . . . And he had not been talking to the Lelannians, that is, if one was to judge by results: for they could make no use of what they heard. They did *not* hear. They *could* not hear. I have never before seen so clearly and simply illustrated that law of development that makes a certain stage of growth impossible to an individual, a people, a planet: first, they have to hear. They have to be able to take in what they are being offered.

Throughout the main occasions when Klorathy was with these top-level priest-technicians, they sat apparently all attention and respect, but their faces showed always the self-esteem that was their curse, the mark of their incapacity. The ground of their nature was this conviction of superiority, of innate worth over other species. Klorathy was not able to shake it.

This was true of nearly all. There were in fact a few of them who did absorb the intuition that there was something here they could learn, and they came to him secretly. And he instructed them as far as he could. When we left this station, they accompanied us. Our escort was now an extraordinary mixture of officials and priests, the frivolously curious, and these serious students of his ways of thought.

The third station was of particular interest, and the work there could have thrown light on the nature of the processes that had Rohanda in their grip—if the Lelannians had been capable of understanding them. The station researched the Degenerative Disease that caused the "ageing" that I had first seen—but still only in a mild form—in Rhodia. Since that time, this expression of Rohanda's falling away from earlier excellence had accelerated. The term of life was half of what it had been in the old Lelannian days. A hundred and fifty R-years was the norm now. And "ageing" began at the end of the stage of physical readiness for mating and reproduction. There was a dryness, a shrivelling, and, soon, a wrinkling of all the skin casing. The hair lost its colour and became spectral and pale. The eyes, too, lost colour. Hearing, sight, touch, taste—all the senses—became blunted, or ceased to operate. The processes of mentation were affected, sometimes to the point of imbecility. There were compounds full of local natives, all over a certain age, and these were being tortured to give up the secrets of "ageing."

An interesting fact was that the natives were viable much longer than the "superior" race. They remained energetic and flexible in limb for longer, their hair kept its colour often until death—their pitifully early deaths—and their teeth often remained comparatively excellent. Also, there was less mental confusion. This, Klorathy said, was because of the natives' closer bond with the natural flows and forces, as compared with the Lelannians, whose ways were mechanical and imposed by arbitrary law or by whim; because they worked physically, which the "superior" ones were proud not to do; because the stuff of their genetic inheritance did not include any contribution from Shammat and Puttiora.

It was at this stage in our journey that Klorathy informed me nothing could be done for the Lelannians. They were beyond improvement. He asked me—in that way of his—what I thought should be done in this situation, but asked, too, that I should take my time thinking about it, "putting aside my emotions."

When we were back in the Sirian post in the hills above the rain forests, we sat together, as we had before our long and difficult journey, and we talked. I was impatient for him to come to a conclusion, to "sum up"—a favourite Lelannian expression. But he was in no hurry and for many days, and then months, our experience was allowed to, as it were, ferment between us.

He was at particular pains to make me think about the Lelannian experiments, the Lelannian attitudes towards themselves as experimenters and researchers. I was by then reluctant to do this. I had been so sickened and disgusted at what I had seen, and my inability to change anything, that I wanted only to put the whole experience out of my mind.

He said that the Lelannians, living in a rich and fruitful continent, blessed by the climate, and by every natural resource, had little need to work hard and to sustain themselves. That even if they had, they provided themselves with abundant slaves and servants who did all their unpleasant work for them. Leisure was their inheritance. It was, as the Shammat observers saw, their means of being kept in subjection, because it rotted them: the right amount of sloth and ease would keep them Shammat's. Too much would make them useless. Shammat had influenced them towards their experimentation. Apart from a very small administrative class, who increasingly left this work to slaves trained for this purpose—who could be expected shortly to seize power for themselves, but that is another story—the ruling race as a whole occupied themselves with the increasingly refined techniques of research. There were not enough genuine avenues of enquiry to occupy everyone, and therefore the experiments became more bizarre, extensive—useless. And more and more unfortunate animals of other species were sacrificed.

Their attitude towards themselves, that everything that surrounded them was their property, to use as they wished, meant that the delicate and invisible balances of force and power were increasingly disrupted. The two Southern Continents, the Sirian responsibility, were wildly out of key, were unbalancing the already precarious Rohandan cosmic economy. There had been a time, at the beginning of our journey, said Klorathy, when he had believed it might be possible to arrest the brutalisation of these Lelannians, to make them see the natural balances of earth, rock, vegetation, water, fire, and the infinitely various and differing species of animals, the creatures of earth, of water, of air, as irreplaceable and distinct, each with its part to play in the invisible cosmic dance. But it had become clear that the innate self-esteem of the Lelannians was too strong.

And now we had come to the culminating point of our encounter, Klorathy and I: Canopus and Sirius.

He was making, in fact, a complaint. If one could call this long process of journeying together for the purposes of my instruction, and these long discussions, during which he never insisted, or demanded, but only demonstrated—a complaint. The differing roles of Canopus and Sirius, our different weights and emphases in the cosmic scale, made these conversations of ours have the effect of criticism and—on my side—of resistance.

Why had we neglected these Southern Continents?

Because they had not seemed worth our while.

But we had asked for them, had done more, had insisted on having them?

At the time we needed them. (And, of course, we were not going to let Canopus get away with anything—ridiculous and petty though this attitude was. And is.)

What were we going to do now?

The point was, Rohanda was not of much interest to our Empire. Not now. It had been relegated, with other planets, to a position of being possibly useful again, in the future. Not all my persuasions, if I decided to take this course, would make Sirius actively exploit Rohanda again. It was too overrun with inferior species, too problematical—and there was Shammat, whose rule was established everywhere. Apparently with Canopean permission, and *that* was more than we could understand.

I said to Klorathy that there was nothing we, Sirius, could do for Rohanda.

"You will not then, I am sure, be resentful if *we* interest ourselves in your territories?"

"You are already! You have been for some time. I am not saying that anything you do is harmful, far from it. I am sure that without your intervention everything would be worse. But it is hypocritical to ask for permission for actions you have already taken."

"Never without your knowledge." At this we exchanged smiles: he was referring to the extensive and admirable Sirian espionage systems.

"But now, in my view, definite and prompt action is needed in Southern Continent II. As is being done in Isolated Southern Continent I. By your old friend Nasar, among others."

I allowed him to understand that I did not care, would be happy to leave it all to him.

"Tell me, Sirius, now that you have seen everything and thought about it, what, in your opinion, is the right thing to be done?"

I exploded, out of long months of indignation and revulsion: "I would call in our fleet of Flame Makers and destroy these squalid little animals."

He was silent for a long time.

"You are shocked, of course," I said.

"No. I—we—cannot afford to be shocked. We have in fact destroyed cultures that have become corrupt."

"I am surprised that the great Canopus should use such means."

"Or surprised at our admitting it?"

"Yes. I suppose that is it."

For we certainly would not have admitted it, in similar circumstances.

"But when we have been forced to use such means, in order to keep our balances within measure, then these have been small local cultures. A city . . . a group of two or three cities . . . even a few particularly damaging individuals. At this very time, in the area of the great inland seas . . ." and he seemed distressed, in pain ". . . we are being forced to take certain steps. . . . This is not always the most pleasant of tasks, this Shikastan assignment."

"No. It is a horrible place."

"But you are actually suggesting we should destroy all life over a whole continent?" he asked reproachfully.

"They should be treated as they treat others."

"A hard rule, Sirius . . . tell me, have you ever reflected that our behaviour influences theirs?"

This came too close to certain private thoughts of mine, and I exploded with: "The native tribes may be sympathetic enough now, harmless, but you know as well as I do that given opportunity they will become as bad as the Lelannians. That is *why* this is such a nasty planet."

"It is not the fault of the planet."

"That way of thinking is not within our scope, Canopus," I said, looking at him as forcefully as I could, hoping that he would—at last, as I *then* saw it—begin to reveal truths, secrets, Canopean expertise.

"Why isn't it, Sirius?"

This silenced me. He was saying that I had admitted our inferiority and that he was challenging its inevitability.

"Why? . . . and here we are," he added, in a low, reproachful voice.

"Very well then, what do you think should be done?"

"I propose that we space-lift all the Lelannians away from this planet."

"Where to?"

"Why," he said smiling, "to Shammat, of course. Each to his own."

I laughed. "There are a million of them!"

"You are rich, Sirius. You have large fleets. You are in the habit of transporting populations from planet to planet. And you suffer from underemployment."

"It is absolutely out of the question that I could get Administration to agree. They would not waste so many resources on such an inferior species."

He was silent for a while. "Sirius, very often a great deal of time, effort, and resources are spent on 'inferior' species. Everything is relative, you know!"

I did not choose to "hear" this. Not at that time.

"You are also very rich, Canopus. Are you telling me that you do not transport populations from planet to planet?"

"Yes, I am telling you that. Not for the reasons you do, at least. Very rarely. We have a very finely balanced economy, Sirius. Exactly and delicately tuned. And if we were to undertake to transport a million animals from here to Shammat, then this would impose a strain on us."

There was a great deal of information in this, of the kind I wanted so much to have from him—about Canopus and its nature. But I was too disturbed at that juncture to take it in.

"I tell you, it is not possible for me to arrange it."

"Not possible for one of the five senior administrators of the Sirian Colonial Service?"

"No."

"I appeal to you. It may surprise you to know that your economy is more flexible in certain ways than ours."

"I am sorry."

"Then we shall have to undertake it."

I attempted to joke in the face of his evident disappointment, and even worry. "A million all at once will certainly impose a strain on Shammat!"

"It might keep them busy for a bit, at least. And I must confess it does give me some pleasure, unworthy though it is, I am sure, that these Lelannians will become slaves now in their turn. Shammat is short of labour at this time."

"I share your feelings."

"Will you help us perhaps with the task of rehabilitating the tribes?"

And now I did hesitate for a long time. I did feel in the wrong about refusing our aid in the matter of the mass space-lift. I was feeling lacking generally in relation to Canopus—hardly a new emotion! But I also could not understand why he, or they, should concern themselves with this trivial nastiness.

"Why?" I demanded. "Why take so much trouble?"

"It will be useful for us—for everyone—for the whole Galaxy, if the tribes are enabled to return as far as possible to their old state. They will be returned to their own territories, and encouraged to resume their former simple lives in balance with the environment. Not taking more than they need, not despoiling, not overrunning their geographical areas, or laying waste. Before the Lelannian conquest this continent was in harmony. We shall see that it becomes so again."

"And for how long?" I enquired, making him face me on this.

"Well, not forever, certainly. No. That we know."

"Why?—oh, don't talk to me of the Necessity!"

"There is nothing else, or less, I can talk to you of."

"Then do so," I cried, excited and peremptory. "I am waiting. I feel always at the edge of things, and you never come to the point."

At this he looked, at first, faintly startled, then grieved, and then—as if he had determined to use this aid—amused.

"Sirius, you are indeed hard to please."

I was angry. I was angry because of knowing I was in the wrong. I even knew *then* that this was why I was so fatally angry. I rose to my feet, unable to prevent myself, and said: "Canopus, I am leaving now."

"I shall not prevent you!" said he, in an attempt to remind me of our old ironical understanding of the real situation.

"Very well, you can stop me if you want. But you won't. Perhaps I would even be glad of that—if you would simply, and once and for all, do something unequivocal."

And now he laughed. He laughed out, shaking his head with comical disbelief. This finally enraged me. I ran out into the open, summoned the hovering Space Traveller, and turned to see him in the doorway watching.

"May I perhaps give you a lift? To your Planet 10, perhaps? I shall be passing it."

"I shall be staying here for a while."

"Then goodbye."

And that was how this encounter of ours came to its conclusion.

Once again, distancing myself, it was with relief. I was simply not up to it! It was all too much! And, as I approached home again, I found myself muttering: "That's it then—it's enough!" And: "Very well, if that's how you want it!" But what these defiances actually meant was something I soon discovered, after I reported back and started to re-align myself with the work I had interrupted, for I found my mind was at work in quite other ways.

Recently I was scanning a history of that time in connection with a different subject, when I came across this: "Checks and restrictions were imposed on our experimental and research programmes; and as a result the numbers of animals licensed for use fell sharply."

In this dry sentence is encapsulated what I am sure must have been the hardest effort of my career. I did not depart for the borders of our Empire. I did not apply for leave—which I was entitled to. I did not do, as Klorathy wanted, anything about our responsibility for Rohanda. But what I did engage myself with was a fight to force us, Sirius, into a different attitude towards our subject populations, and particularly as regards their use as laboratory material. This battle is by no means over. As I write this, different factions of opinion are still engaged.

Large-scale experiments of the biosociological kind are in progress —the kind that one of our wits has summed up as: *What if we . . . ?* In other words, populations are subjected to this and that stress, or the planets of planets moved about—all that class of thing. And I am far from claiming that this does not cause suffering.

Of course it does. I do not believe that it is useful—as some of our technicians still do—to say things of this sort: "These creatures are of so low a mental development that they do not know what is happening to them." Yes, I certainly was of their company—once. I like to think that it was a long time ago. It will not have escaped the speculation of the more sensitive reader that my—perhaps unnecessarily full—account of the Lombis was for a purpose. But it is not possible to avoid such disturbances of a Colonised Planet altogether. What would then be the purpose of colonising one? No planet is welcomed into the Sirian system without careful thought and planning and, as I have said, at this particular time our expansion is suspended.

To be part of the Sirian whole is to be part of progress, development, an attitude of "one for all and all for each!" Sacrifices have to be made by everyone for such an ideal. I want to make it clear, here, at this point, that I do not demand the total abolition of all social disturbance—that would be to demand the end of Sirius itself—Sirius the Mother Planet, herself daughter of the great star Sirius, and sister to her two siblings—Sirius the glorious, with her wonderful children scattered so felicitously through the Galaxy. Of course, I cannot mean that, cannot want that . . . I want no part of the sentimentalism that says that "Nature has its rights!" "Each in its own place!" Or "Hands off . . ."—whatever planet is in question: to mention a few of the more popular current slogans. No. It is the duty of the more evolved planets, like the great daughter of Sirius, to guide and control.

But that is a very different thing from using not hundreds, not thousands, not even millions, but billions of animals of all kinds and types of genera and species in cruel and unnecessary experiments. As we used to do. For a very long time. For not millennia, but for long ages. I say *unnecessary*. I use the word knowing how this goes straight to the point of the argument, the disagreement. *Necessary for what?*

At the time of my return from Rohanda on that trip, two-thirds of all the technicians throughout the Empire were employed on experiments on various kinds of animals. These were of every kind, from the mild to the horrific. In some there was concern that the pain suffered by the animals should be kept minimal. In others there was no concern at all. But, as often happens, the debate that started, and then raged—the only word for it—as a result of my efforts, was centered on the pain suffered or not suffered, and how much, and how it should be regulated. What was not discussed then—and what to my mind has not been adequately recognised since—is the question of the actual use of the animals at all, our attitude to them, what right we have to arbitrarily take them and exploit them according to our current needs. And this question, which to my mind is the real one, is rooted in another, much deeper: what is a genus *for*? What is its function? What does it do? What part does it play in the cosmic harmony?

It will be seen that I approach here the Canopean formula, or tenet, or habit of mind: *according to the Necessity.*

It is also, of course, linked with our existential situation or problem. And much more fundamentally than on that level where we had to face the truth that something like fifteen millions of our most highly trained technicians were without an occupation. Without a function. Which is what we did have to face as the controversy raged, and resulted in public opinion changing to the point where it could not tolerate any longer the mass torture—the accurate word—the mass and unnecessary torture of billions of living creatures. If we, Sirius were—are—to decide, at last, what we are for, what our function is, then it follows that we have to wonder at last what these lower animals are for.

Well, a great many of us are now pondering just this question . . .

The fifteen million technicians, finding themselves without a use, were retired, according to our custom, on to planets of their choice, to live out the remainder of their lives in honour and peace. And, of course, to join those who have leisure to devote themselves to our basic, crucial, quintessential problem. Most of them died off very quickly. This always happens when a class of workers finds itself obsolete.

None of this happened without bitterness, emotional and mental conflict, and even—in some planets—rioting and social disturbance. It will almost certainly strike present-day students unpleasantly, and surprisingly, to know that some of the slogans under which these old battles were fought included: *What we have, we hold.*

Might is right. Victory to the strongest. The ends justify the means. The function of the inferior is to serve the superior.

Our entire administrative class was threatened. As for my own position, I had to face a long period of near-ostracism. That I was wrongheaded was the least of it. It was only with great difficulty that I avoided being sent off to Adjustive Hospitalisation. Yes, it was put about that my mentality had been affected by sojourns in inimicable climates on unpleasant planets—Rohanda being chiefly blamed. And in some moods I even found myself agreeing with my critics. It was not always easy to see Klorathy's influence on my life —on (I insist) Sirius—as unambiguously good.

What I have put down here can give only a hint of what lay behind those words: "Checks and restrictions were imposed . . ." etc.

While all this was going on, I had no word from Canopus, though it can be imagined how much I thought of things Canopean, and of my friends. Yes, I thought of Klorathy and Nasar thus, although it was never without strain. The strain that the inferior must feel in coming into contact with the superior. I hope that this statement will not earn me, again, a threat of Adjustive Hospitalisation!

It was on the day that the law was passed in our Legislature, restricting the use of animals for research, that this message came from Klorathy. "And now I am looking forward very much to meeting you on Shikasta's planet shortly. Our co-operation is desirable during the period of the deepening crisis on Shikasta."

ROHANDA'S PLANET

I feel that there is no need for me to describe my reactions to this.

I did think, and seriously, about whether I would return a message suggesting a date for our meeting, but the fact remained that Sirius had decided not to involve itself further with Rohanda. I therefore did nothing, reflecting how past experience indicated that if Canopus had decided on something, then this tended to come to pass. I had again made plans to take up my interrupted work, when I was instructed to go to Rohanda's planet and deal with a crisis there. I went, unsurprised that this had happened; and expecting to meet Nasar or Klorathy.

The situation on this moon was at that time as follows:

For a long time Shammat's base there had been small, only used as a way station for its personnel and as a fuelling depot. Then, as conditions on Rohanda steadily deteriorated—as Canopus saw it—and improved, from the point of view of Shammat, the emanations that Shammat elicited and used became too plentiful for previous means of transmission, and an accumulator was set up. This needed a permanent staff of technicians. These were of Shammat's dominant class who demanded high standards in living conditions, which amenities were soon being used by their workers on Rohanda for ever-longer periods of recreation. What amounted to good-sized settlements came into existence. These were underground, because of the peculiar conditions of this moon, vulnerable to bombardment from space because of its lack of atmosphere, mostly from an asteroid belt that was the remains of a former planet. It was at that point that we placed our own personnel there, to keep a close and permanent watch on Shammat, who soon had gone further, and was engaged in extensive mining operations. Neither Canopus nor ourselves objected to this: we were not short of minerals of any kind. But now Canopus, too, established itself in an observational capacity. No hostilities of a physical sort occurred between Shammat and the two superior powers—for Shammat was too afraid of us both. But while contact took place continually between ourselves and Canopus, of a formal kind, Shammat shunned us, and we were only too pleased to have it so.

From this time onwards, Rohanda was visited continually by spacecraft of all kinds, mostly Shammatan. The Canopus influence was more indirect: I have hinted at some of their means of coming and going. They seldom used physical craft, and when they did, it was with discretion, or with a deliberate intent to instruct the current Rohandan dominant species in some necessary way. The Shammatans, on the other hand, were using their spacecraft with increasing indifference to the effect a sight of these vehicles might have on the populations. They had had underground settlements on Rohanda itself for a long time. From these they came and went, using every type of craft, quite freely. And they used, too, under-water craft. They took from Rohanda supplies of foodstuffs un-available on the moon, and easier to fetch from there than from Shammat itself. They took, often, fresh water. They also kidnapped Rohandans from anywhere there were species that intrigued or amused them. These became pets on the moon or were sent back to Shammat itself to entertain the ruling caste. They were taken off vehicles on the oceans, or from isolated places. As can be imagined, folklore and fantastic tales of all kinds were the result; but while "sightings" of Shammat craft had taken place over millennia, and particularly recently, the populations of Rohanda did not know what it was they were seeing. Though legends of every branch of the dominant species contained stories of "higher beings," these were always associated with "flying serpents" or "flying lizards" and so on, according to local conditions, and their technology had not yet developed to the point of recognition.

I must record at this point that on the Rohandan moon were, too, representatives of three other planets in this solar system. They had established there small observation posts, because of their concern about the increasingly discordant emanations of Rohanda, which threatened their own balances. This was a recent develop-ment. I shall say no more about it, because it does not concern my present theme. But my dispatch to this moon was because of alarm felt by the highest Sirian levels that perhaps the three planets might be tempted to become allied with Shammat, thus upsetting our alignments of power. Having surveyed the scene thoroughly, I sent back a report that in my view conditions on Rohanda's planet were stable. I did not, however, leave the place at once, though this type of underground shelter never has suited me, no matter how well and flexibly the atmospheres are adjusted. It was not long before Klorathy arrived. He was again in a different, though similar physical housing. He greeted me with: "If I am not particularly welcome, this is at least a not unexpected visit, I see."

And we achieved good fellowship on this note, though I was determined not to give way to his demands.

Again there was a period when we simply sat together, establishing some sort of communion whose nature he understood and was exactly adjusting, and which I at least was able to recognise.

The following exchanges will convey the nature of our many and prolonged conversations during this meeting on Rohanda's moon.

"Sirius, you made undertakings, which you have gone back on!"

"I do not remember that we ever promised to engage ourselves with Rohanda in perpetuity!"

"Promises do not have to be verbal. By the fact that you involve yourself in a situation, becoming affected yourself as you affect it—that is in itself a promise."

"You announce these laws to me with such authority!"

"Canopus did not invent the Laws. Have you not observed for yourself that if one disengages oneself from a process arbitrarily, then all kinds of connections and links and growths are broken—and that you yourself suffer for it?"

"Very well, then—yes, as you speak, it seems that I do remember seeing this myself. Very often when you say things of this kind, I might object or deny or refuse—and then later, on reflection, I see the truth of what you say. But I can only repeat that I do not decide Colonial policy." And I asked, "Who is it above *you*, then, that makes laws?"

And he laughed at this. "Laws are not *made*—they are inherent in the nature of the Galaxy, of the Universe."

"You are saying that we have to learn how to observe these laws in operation?"

"Yes, Sirius, yes, yes."

"You are a great one for lost causes, I think!" And he smiled wryly. "How long have you spent with me? How many long ages of effort? And suppose that at last I do begin to see for myself something of what you mean. But I am one small individual in a vast Empire. Do you know that I am already known as a bit of a misfit, an eccentric, someone who often has to be tolerated? I have been threatened with all kinds of mental re-processing—yes, of course you do know. And you are not likely to regard as important the fate of one . . ." I had been going to say "one individual" but could not since I had been overtaken with the falseness of what I had said. "All right, then . . . but suppose you have changed me, suppose you have given me some of your nature—what do you expect of the

Sirian Empire?" As I spoke, I was thinking that in fact I had caused the controversy over the misuse of animals, then at its height . . . and this thought, as it were, stunned my mind and . . . I came to myself later, not knowing how long, for I had been somewhere deep within myself, in thought.

And again: "Why is it you want my help? You, the all-powerful Canopus!"

"We are spread very thin at this time in Rohanda."

"Because it is now policy that service on Rohanda is voluntary and there are not enough volunteers?"

"There are volunteers, but the turnover is very high. It is hard to maintain our links with Shikasta. Very hard. And getting harder with every millennium."

"You want me to go back and try and persuade Sirius to take over responsibility for the Southern Continents again?"

"Yes, we do."

"Although our rule is so much less effective than yours? Although we, Sirius, cannot give to a situation what you can give?"

He said gently, with a diffidence that was rooted in his nature, and that I have seen very seldom in my career: "If you will consent to act with us, so that we can influence through you, then perhaps things can at least be ameliorated. Maintained. Prevented from getting worse."

"Why, why, *why*? What is the purpose of your concern?"

"Sometimes we have to take things on trust!"

"Are *you* taking things on trust?"

"Do you imagine that it could be otherwise? Sirius, this Galaxy is vast, is infinitely various, is always changing, is always beyond what we can see of it, in whatever little corner is our home."

"To hear you call Canopus a little corner is—not easy to understand. Can it possibly be that just as I watch *you*, Canopus, while I strive and strive to understand—because I have to admit this, though of course you know it already!—is it possible that just as this is my relation to you, then so is your relation to—to . . ." and my mind faded out, into its depths.

And again: "You have never told me *why*! Do you really have no inkling at all of why such care should go into these . . . these . . ."

"These murderous half-apes?"

"Or worse." And I could feel how my mouth was twisted with distaste and dislike. . . .

And he, looking embarrassed, was *not* looking at me, but away.

"Oh, very well, very well, then! But you cannot possibly be saying, Canopus, that to an outside view, an objective view, *yours*, Canopus, the inhabitants of Sirius, or at least some of us, the lower kinds of our Empire, strike you as repulsively as Rohandans strike me?" And, as he did not reply, I cried out: "That cannot be! You do not take into account the efforts that have gone into our Empire. How we have striven and tried and even when we have failed, have tried again! You do not seem to notice the excellence of our Colonial Service, the concern we show for the good of all, or how individual officials sacrifice themselves for their charges! If we have made mistakes—and of course we have—we have always tried to right them. Do you not give us any credit for the long periods of peace and prosperity under our rule, at least on some planets or for a time? Yes, I know it seems as if there is something deeply rooted in the very nature of things that must work for the over-throwing of everything that is, no matter whether it is good or bad, so that nothing we set up can be trusted to last, but is that the fault of those who try and try again to . . . to . . ."

"To *what*, Sirius?"

"We are not as bad," I said stubbornly. "We are *not*."

"As?"

"As *them*, the Rohandans. Or as Shammat."

"Did I say you were?"

"But as you sat there and I was talking I had such a vision of us, of Sirius, of our greatness, and it seems to me suddenly that all it is—is a mirage. A shadow of greatness. And not very different from what I see when I . . . no, I am *not* going to equate us with Shammat. I can't bear it. I cannot stand . . . what we are," I concluded with difficulty.

"But it is not what you will be."

"So you say, Canopus."

"And now I want to show you something." He indicated that I should sit on a low seat near to him. I could not help hesitating. It is always risky, too close a physical contact between those of different planets. Often enough, I have seen my own proximity badly affect others, even to death. It is one of the first things taught us of the Colonial Service: "Never go near the inhabitants of another planet without being sure how your differing specifics may interact." I had not been within touching distance of Klorathy before: had been careful not to be.

THE HORSEMEN

As I sat beside him, I felt the same strain, on the physical level, that I knew on the mental level, when I was endeavouring to follow him beyond my own natural limits. But he took my hand firmly and as he did so said, "Look at that wall, do not let your eyes close." This I did, and saw on the wall, quite as clearly as one does with ordinary vision—but as it were distanced and speeded up, so that what I was seeing was both exactly accurate, a true representation of actual events, and yet encapsulated, and simplified —a series of pictures, or visions, that drew me forward into them so that it was almost as if I was more a part of the events I watched than a spectator of them.

I was looking down at Rohanda, towards the east of the great central landmass, and rather to the north. This was not far from the area where I had met Nasar at the time of my visit to Koshi and where, before that, I had been tossed about the skies during the "events." This region had been desert for millennia, then had become fertile again as the climate shifted, been deep desert where layers and layers of old cities lay covered, and was now a vast region of grassland. Looking down it was an ocean of grass, broken by mountains and hills where there were some trees. Great rivers crossed it, but it was a dry and harsh land where a few nomads moved with their horses.

Around the areas of the great inland seas, and all over the plateaux of the southern part of the central landmass, and around the great mountains and on the eastern parts of the landmass, were many different cultures and social groupings infinitely complex and various and rich, and at every conceivable level of civilisation.

And as I watched, these little scattered groups of nomads multiplied, and covered all the vast plains, and there was a climatic change, and the grasses were replaced, here and there, by dust and drought, and the horsemen burst outward from their heartland to the east, and to the south and to the west and all the points between, threatened the rich civilisations that bordered them— and then, loaded with booty, fell back again, and, because the winds were blowing differently and the grasses were covering their plains, stayed where they were bred. Besides, they were weakened by their conquests and, for a while, spoiled. And again the civilisa- tions on the edges of their enormous grassy homelands flourished and prospered and multiplied—and, as is the way (I was going to say of Rohanda) of our Galaxy, fell, and were overrun by local conquerors and remade themselves . . . and again the hordes on the grassy plains multiplied and covered them, seeming from the dis- tance at which I was watching, or seemed to be watching, like swarms of insects that darkened everything . . . and again the winds blew dust instead of rain, and the horsemen massed them- selves and then sped outwards east and south and west, and this time went further, and threatened more, and despoiled more—and returned home, as before, carrying gold and jewels and garments and swords and shields and weapons of all kinds, and as the grasses grew up again covering all those vastnesses with their soft green or golden shine, they stayed at home. But while these spoils of war amused them and even though they fought for them, they remained as they were, people of the horse. They were very hardy, and brave, and they could live from their herds of horses and needed nothing else for months at a time, and their use of the horse for skill and cleverness has never been equalled, before or after. And the fame of these terrible peoples who could appear without warning at the edge of a valley full of rich farms, or on a city's walls, covered all the central landmass, so that even in that area that Canopus calls the Northwest fringes, which was at the very edge of the landmass, and at that time full of barbaric peoples who were so far away from their great ancestors the Adalantalanders that these weren't even a memory, were a savage fringe to the civilisations that lay to their south—even there, in black forests and swamps and in the misty isles of the extreme northwest, tales of the dreaded horsemen kept children awake when they should have been asleep, and even a rumour of their approach sent whole peoples running for cover.

Meanwhile, on that area that lies immediately to the east of the Southern Continent I, which had previously been forested and green and very fertile, and since had become desert and semidesert, like so much of Rohanda, had arisen a religion, the third of those emanating from the region of the great inland seas, similar to one another, each succeeding one confirming its predecessor—though of course their exponents fought for dominance, claiming superiority. This third variation of the local religion had created marvellous and rich and complex civilisations that tolerated—at least to an extent and as far as is possible for Rohandans—the previous variations and also all kinds of other sects and cults and idea-groupings. There was prosperity, the development of knowledge of cosmic matters, and a precariously maintained peace. I could not have enough of gazing at these pictures of this amazingly intricate and affluent culture. And then, as I watched, the nomad horsemen arose from their grassy breeding places and overwhelmed everything I looked at, but everything, so that nothing was left but smoking cities, and charred fields and mounds of the slaughtered. The horsemen chased after every fleeing thing, even domestic animals, and killed them. From the northern half of Southern Continent I to the far east fringes of the main landmass remained only a waste of ruins. I cried out, I came to myself sitting on the Rohandan moon by Klorathy, and I looked at him with passionate appeal and reproach.

"All!" I said to him, "Nothing left; is it possible that such an accomplishment can be wiped out, just like that?"

"Yes, indeed it is possible—and it nearly happened."

"So what I saw was not the truth?"

"It is what will happen—unless . . ."

"Unless I help you?"

"I need your help. I keep telling you so. It is a strange fact, but everywhere in the Galaxy when the weaker look at the stronger and the more powerful, what they see is self-sufficiency, easy capacity, an effortless ability—very seldom something that is indeed stronger, but only if it receives aid, support, a continuous and maintained regard of a certain kind, to enable this strength to function."

I said nothing for a long time.

"Well," I said, "I have a long leave due to me at home, and I shall take it now. It is without precedent—the way I propose to spend my leave! And as a matter of fact, how? What do you want specifically?"

"You shall be the ruler of a small realm, on the western slopes of the Great Mountains. And you shall confront the horsemen from the plains."

"And you?"

"I shall be the general who commands the army of horsemen who will have overrun everything, leaving nothing behind but death— and who then stand at your gates ready to slay you and your people and lay your kingdom waste."

"And Nasar?"

"He, and others, will be there."

"Very well."

I sent the appropriate messages home and put myself into the hands of Klorathy.

To voluntarily submerge myself in that story of murder and destruction that I had watched to its last detail was not the easiest thing I have done. One moment I was poised above, still a spectator, with Klorathy, and the next it was as if I had been swallowed by the brilliancies and multitudinous detail of that mountainous kingdom where Queen Sha'zvin still ruled, waiting and watching while the cruel horsemen came closer, destroying everything they found.

It was not without interest, learning this Canopean technique of occupying a mind for a brief and exact purpose. The Queen, a vigorous and handsome woman in middle age, the widow of a much-loved husband who had been killed in her youth, fighting during an earlier campaign against the horsemen, was standing high at the windows of her palace, which overlooked the walls of her city, gazing down a narrow ravine where the horsemen would have to come. Her mind was alert, though anxious; and occupied with the surveillance of a thousand administrative details. To enter that mind was not to overthrow it, or to supplant its own intelligence— rather to remain a spectator, and rather to one side, in readiness for the moments of decision. And so, too, Klorathy was doing a hundred miles away, with the general, Ghonkez.

Queen Sha'zvin was not aware of my entrance into her being, except as an increase in her anxiety. It was an experience more powerful than I had expected. I did not lose my Sirian perspectives, the Sirian scope of time and space. But I was inside, too, this civilisation's view of itself as all there was of the known world—for on its edges were, to the north, the threatening horsemen, to the northwest, very far away, dark forests full of barbarians whom these people scarcely accounted as human at all, believing them not much more than beasts—and from their point of view, accurately—while beyond what was known and understood, in the Southern Continent, were, again, barbarians useful for trade and as slaves. Nothing was known at all of the Isolated Northern Continent and the Isolated Southern Continent. The world as understood by this great and powerful Queen was, though it stretched from one end of the main landmass to the other, circumscribed indeed, and the stars that roofed it were understood only—and to limited extent—by their influences on their movements . . . on *our* movements . . . an odd, a startling, a disturbing, clash of focusses and perspectives encompassed me; and as for the historical aspect, this queen knew the story of her own civilisation and some legends, mostly inaccurate, of a "distant" past, which to me, and my mind, was virtually contemporary with her.

She was feeling, as she stood there—part of a scene drenched with sunlight and with the vivid colours of Rohanda—that death lay just ahead not only for her but for her people. Death had already ended so much of what she knew. This kingdom of hers lay among the passes and roads that controlled the territories to the south, to the east, and to the west. The horsemen had already devastated everything to the west. For hundreds of miles there were nothing but ruins and corpses and the stink of death. She looked over her kingdom that as yet was all richness and peace, and the wind brought to her nostrils the news of corruption and of spoiling. The horsemen were encircling her to the south—there, too, the principalities and the kingdoms lay smoking. To her east, high in the mountains still remained some small safe valleys—for how long? Beyond them, on the other side of the Great Mountains, the horsemen ravaged and plundered and killed. She had survived so long because of this position on a small plateau encompassed by rocky and precipitous mountains. The horsemen of the plains did not love high places and rocks and fastnesses where, looking down, their heads swam and dizzied. They had left her and her people to the last.

Her land maintained five hundred thousand people. It was, had been, a place of contentment and order and harmony. She had seen herself as one blessed by God—such were the words she used—since her rulership had experienced none of the misfortunes that she knew well enough came sooner or later to all kingdoms. Now she ruled three times that number. Men, women, children, fleeing from the horsemen, had begged for refuge. She had taken them all in. Where a household had had ten people, now it had thirty. The smallest hut and shelter was crammed with refugees from hundreds of miles of devastated country. There was very little food. The wells were so low that water was limited to a few mouthfuls a day. Over this fair city of hers, all markets and pleasant buildings and lively streets, lay a silence. Often had she stood here, for the pleasure of watching her people—but now there was little movement, and no cries of buying and selling or greeting, no singing or laughter. Silence. They all, as she did, awaited death.

This scene I had noticed, as the sweep and scope of the terrible invasion had been shown to me by Klorathy, but now, there was a variation—a great hammering and clamour at the western gates of the city. The Queen turned to face, so she believed, the horsemen, looking to see them appear on the high walls. But they were not there. A messenger came running, breathless, pale. "There are more refugees from the west—about ten thousand—they have made their way here and beg your aid."

The Queen stood silent. She was thinking that now, in this decision she was going to make, she would pay for all her long years of pleasure in the equilibrium of her rule, where she had never had to make a decision out of the pressures of a hard choice. She was about to say that she would not open her gates, because these ten thousand would drag her city into famine tomorrow instead of its possibly lasting another week, and it was her duty as custodian to . . . but I caused her to say, instead, "Admit the leader of these people. For the time being bar the gates to the others."

"They are dying of thirst and hunger," said the man who had brought the message.

"Take them enough food and water to keep them alive, no more."

He ran off, and shortly entered a young man, who ordinarily would be handsome, strong, and full of vitality, but now was gaunt and faint with famine. He put out his hand to hold himself on the painted arch of the entrance, and at the sight of his condition, Queen Sha'zvin filled a cup of water and took it across to him, and held it to his lips. He took one swallow of the precious liquid, and looked her in the eyes and said: "We beg your mercy, great Queen."

I was saying to myself Nasar, Nasar, Nasar, knowing it was he, though nothing in his *appearance* said so. And now I was in control of this Queen's mind and her decisions: Sirius and Canopus commanded, and Canopus was racing towards us at the head of a myriad brutes ready to destroy everything they could see.

"Among us are savants, wise men and women, poets, geographers —those who have been saved from the devastation by Allah for purposes in the future. Take them in, and quickly, for it will not be long before the Mongols appear."

The Queen said, smiling: "These precious ones will die almost as quickly inside our gates as they would outside them!" And I said, or made her say: "But bring them in. I will give the order." She clapped her hands, and called the order to an attendant, who ran off.

We three stood together in the silent city, in the high rooms of this delightful palace, the death-smelling breeze stirring the embroidered hangings, and clinging in an unseen miasma on the surfaces of walls, pillars, the brilliant tile work of the ceilings.

"You will buy time," said Nasar, "in this way. You will go out to the northern wall and stand there, alone, facing them as they ride up the ravine."

"They have been slaughtering women all the way from China to the dark forests of the northwest and down to the southern seas."

"Ah, but we will be aided, just a little, for just long enough, in an illusion, great Queen."

"It will have to be a strong one," said she, smiling—and I, now, had retreated to the back of her mind. For the course of events I had seen projected by Klorathy was altered: I had seen nothing of this: what was happening because of our intervention.

Nasar, revived a little by the swallow of water, but still staggering as he went, descended the stairways of this lovely building, so soon to be ruins, and arrived in the open square below the palace as the people he had brought across the deserts of the west came in. They, too, could hardly stand. They were an army of ghosts, and phantoms. And yet they were to live, a good many of them.

The Queen divested herself of her dagger, her ornaments, and, wrapping herself in a dark cloak, walked along the northern wall of her kingdom as the first horseman came chasing up the ravine.

Flights of arrows were already on their way to her when the leader shouted an order. These men who could shoot at full gallop as accurately as from the ground rested their bows on their horses' necks. There was not room in the narrow ravine, dark between its rock edges, for more than a few hundred of them. They were gazing up to the sunlit walls of this famed city, where there stood a single figure, a woman, confronting them steadily and without moving at all.

As they looked, it seemed as if rays of light dazzled around her. Their ideas of deity did not include an illuminated female figure, and they were only temporarily stayed. They were riding steadily nearer, and higher, and soon, as the gates of the city swung back on a signal from the Queen, they saw the city itself, in its gardens and orchards and fantastic variety, a scene of plenty and deliciousness that had never failed to inflame these men—whose measures of worth were all related to the hardships and endurance of their symbiotic relationship with their herds—into a rage to destroy and afflict. Yet as they looked, every tree and plant and flower seemed to dazzle with light that was like a million minute rainbows. The woman on the high wall, the gardens, the buildings, all shone and dazzled, and from the watching horsemen there rose a deep and anguished groan. Their leader shouted to them that they were faced with demons; and the massed horsemen in their close leather tunics and trousers and caps, emanating a smell of sweaty skins— their own and their beasts—sent up, too, the smell of fear as they jostled back down the pass again, in the shades of the evening.

Sending back fearful glances they saw high above them the red sandstone walls, and the woman there, motionless, surrounded by a dazzle of light.

They made a camp at the foot of the escarpment, and their cooking fires seemed to burn with otherworldly lights. But then their fear became anger, and after that, derision. These were not cowards, these men. They could not remember ever staying their hands before. Besides, not all had seen the enchanted city in its halo of iridescence. Even those who had, now doubted what they had seen. Their General Ghonkez maintained steadily—as his troops, who were not accustomed to subservience and blind obedience, but only to following orders whose sense they could understand, and who increasingly shouted criticisms at him—that they had done well to wait there through the night until the morning came and they could again ride up the pass and face the city in the plain light of day.

When these horsemen again jostled up the pass to the city, it was in a mood of savage anger against their general. The gates of the city were still open. They rode inside the walls like avenging devils and found only what they had seen in a hundred other places —an intricate and rich and comfortable web of streets and markets and gardens, which they felt they had to obliterate. No radiant mists of light surrounded what they saw and they burned and destroyed as they rode. But there were very few living creatures. A dog sitting at the door of his empty house. Cats sunning themselves on sills in dwellings where humans had gone. An old man or an old woman who had said they would stay behind, since their days had been lived through and it was enough. These the horsemen killed.

And when they reached the palace, they found Queen Sha'zvin standing alone in her rooms and they killed her. They then turned on their General Ghonkez and slew him, so that we two lay side by side, in our deaths, as the palace burned down around us.

Meanwhile, Nasar had led away long columns of people out of the eastern gates of the city. Not all had had time to leave and these were killed. And then, suddenly, and out of season, a blizzard descended, and the horsemen were stopped. They knew blizzards and cold from the terrible winters of their northern plains. But they understood nothing of the treacherous snowdrifts and the ice masses and the murderous winds of the mountains. They rode away down into the plains to wait until better weather, so that they could chase the refugees into their high fastnesses and kill them all. For they had sworn to leave no one alive in all the lands they raided. But the winter came and blocked the way. Thousands of the fleeing ones died of cold and deprivation but most did reach the high sheltered valleys. When the spring came and the snows of the passes melted and the way was open for the horsemen, they did not come. There were rumours of an enchantment and of dangers from demons. Their killing of their general had put a curse on them—so it was said. And they had heard that none of the refugees had survived their ordeals in the snow.

But among those who did survive were enough with the skills and knowledge of their destroyed civilisation to instruct others. Those who came to be instructed were the descendants of these same horsemen.

And that was how I, Ambien II, and Klorathy, and Nasar, together with others who have not been mentioned, took our roles in this drama. And this was not the only one. In two other sequences of events, at that time of the cruel horsemen, did we three play our parts, altering enough of the pattern to save a few here, preserve a city there, and keep safe men and women equipped with the knowledge of the sciences of matching the ebbs and flows of the currents of life with invisible needs and imperatives. These were scientists. Real scientists, armoured by their subtle knowledge against all the wiles and machinations of Shammat.

Klorathy and I sat together in the Sirian moon station. I had just rescued him from slow death in prison. Nasar had made me captive to save me from being executed, and had secretly released me. I had been one of the raiding horsemen. Klorathy was a deposed judge. Nasar was a female slave from the heart of Southern Continent I, who had risen to be the manager of a large household belonging to an indolent and tyrannical princeling.

A monitor showed that above us on the moon's surface it was night, and very cold. Rohanda was hidden from us, being between us and the sun.

Klorathy clapped his hands, and on to the blank wall came a map of Rohanda—the continents and oceans laid flat. Klorathy went to stand beside it. With his finger he outlined that part of the main landmass that had been afflicted by the horsemen. Holding me with his eyes he outlined it again—slowly. I knew what he wanted me to understand: that all those centuries of invasion and destruction were being contained within the shape his finger had traced. And he expected me to make, too, comparisons with Sirius, our vast Empire.

"Very well," I said.

"The horsemen have terrorised this part of Rohanda for centuries, and the fear of them is imprinted in the innermost nature of all the peoples of this region. Yet soon they will have been absorbed into what remains of the peoples they conquered. And civilisations will rise and fall, rise and fall—until quite soon, a race will come into being—here." And he ran his finger down the edge of the great landmass. "Here, in the Northwest fringes, in these islands, in this little space, a race is being formed even now. It will overrun the whole world, but all the world, not just the central part of it, as with the horsemen of the plains. This race will destroy everything. The creed of this white race will be: if it is there, it belongs to us. If I want it I must have it. If what I see is different from myself then it must be punished or wiped out. Anything that is not me, is primitive and bad . . . and this creed they will teach to the whole of Shikasta."

"All? The whole world?"

"Very nearly."

"Shammat being their tutor?"

"Shammat being their nature. Do you want to see what will happen?" And he stretched out his hand to make a gesture that would summon the stream of pictures, the moving vision, that had showed me the wave after wave after wave of the Mongol threat.

"No, no, no—or not yet." And I covered my eyes.

He returned quietly to his seat near me.

"You want our help?"

"Yes. And *you* need our help."

"Yes," I said. "I know it."

I could hear through the earthy walls of this shelter the grinding and shuddering of machinery: Shammat at work in a crater not far away.

"When I go back home now, I shall say only that I have chosen to spend my leave here. I shall not be questioned about this choice: but my reputation for eccentricity will be added to. I, Sirius, shall not be able to say one word to Sirius of what I have experienced with you . . ."

"Of the *work* you have done with Canopus . . ."

"Very well. Of the work we have done together. Because Sirius would not be able to understand one word of what I said. Only Canopus can understand me now."

"You are lonely, Ambien!"

"Very."

He nodded. "Please do what you can, Sirius."

Before I left this moon, I instructed my Space Traveller to fly low all over the sunlit side. The Shammat mining operations were evident everywhere. Their settlements were mostly underground, but in places were to be seen their observatories and laboratories. In the craters, some of them many R-miles across, their machinery laboured. It was ingenious, but none was unknown to me. Shammat the thief did not initiate; it sent spies into the territories of others, and copied what it saw.

A vast machine like a segmented worm whose segments could be fitted together in various ways was the kind they used most. One of these could be a mile or more long. Inside it were workplaces; temporary living places of labourers and technicians; and the extremities of a segment could be fitted with excavating devices. Some sucked in earth and sprayed it out again. One I hovered low over looked for all the world like the dragon of the Rohandan mythologies, with its spray of dirt emitted from its "mouth." Others looked like starfish sprawling. They were a most ingenious type of machine. Flexible, so they could climb and clamber and balance; of any desired size, according to the number of segments fitted; very long, traversing difficult terrain and becoming bridges or tunnels as necessary; easily kept in repair, since an individual segment was so quickly replaced—these "crawlers" had been evolved by us for use on inhospitable planets that were rich in minerals. But so adaptable and multifunctional had they proved that they were employed for purposes far beyond mining.

As I sped away, I was escorted by a dozen of the wasplike Shammatan fighter craft. This was an act of impudence that in fact I welcomed. It would strengthen my hand in the efforts I was now about to make at home: I had to persuade our Colonial Service that our active presence on Rohanda was necessary to us.

THE FIVE

As one will, I formulated in my mind all kinds of approaches to the problem, but soon understood that none was suitable: again and again, bringing to a situation or a person the framework of words, ideas, already formulated in my mind, these as it were fell apart, dissipated like a mist when the sun falls on it. I saw, then, that there was something wrong in my assessment of the situation. I even wondered if my mind had been affected by my excursions into the Rohandan reality; I half believed I had become more Canopean than Sirian. All kinds of doubts and weaknesses assailed me.

Meanwhile, colleagues were referring to my "leave" on the Rohandan moon in a careful nonjudgemental way. I knew it was not possible for them to have any inkling as to what I had really been doing; and could not decide what it was they suspected that made them treat me like a—well, yes: I had to accept it: I was being handled in the way we use for those about to be summoned to a formal court of enquiry, or even arrested. Meanwhile discussions went forward for, again, my long interrupted work on our borders. I concluded at last that something was at work in the situation that I was severely misinterpreting.

Time was passing. I had not raised the subject of Rohanda. Tempted to let the subject slide away from me yet again, I made myself remember undertakings to Klorathy. At last, not knowing what else to do, I summoned a meeting of the Five.

The Five, of whom I am one, run the Colonial Service. This fact everybody in the Empire knows. That we implement policy made by our Legislature is known. That this policy is influenced by us is known. What is not understood is the extent to which we influence policy. I shall simply state here, without softening it, and as a fact, something that contradicts the Sirian view of itself; our view of ourselves. We Five run the Empire, govern everything, except for the details of the lives of our elite class. That does not concern us in the slightest! This elite of ours does as it pleases. Within limits. *Our* limits. I have already said that there has to be an elite: legislation will not prevent one coming into being, or do away with one when it has. And as little as we, the rulers of Sirius, are interested in the affairs of these darlings and charmers, so are they interested in what we do. There is a law that no formal framework of an organisation, or a society, can affect. Or not for long. It is that those who do the work are the real rulers of it, no matter how they are described.

We Five embody the governance of our Empire. That is what we *are*. And have been since the end of the war between ourselves and Canopus.

I took a risk in summoning only the Five, and not the extended council of the planetary representatives. Whatever decisions the Five came to, would stand. If it were to be a meeting of the Thirty, I would have a right of appeal to the twenty-five who sit listening to the case we present, without taking part in the discussion, and who are available for precisely this purpose: to set aside our decisions for varying periods, according to their importance and severity, while we Five are instructed to re-consider.

The meeting took place as usual. Since the appearance of each one of us Five is familiar to every Sirian citizen from infancy, I shall say no more, beyond remarking that the extraordinary nature of the circumstances did make me conscious of the dramatic aspect; I found myself, as we took our seats, looking into the faces of these colleagues of mine, with whom I was, and am, so close, with whom I worked through the millennia, who make up, with me, a whole, an organism, almost an organ of the Sirian body. And, feeling my closeness to them, I was at the same time anguished, being so distanced from them, so alien in part of myself, because of Canopus. I sat looking at one face after another, all so different since we come—by policy—from different planets, and wondering how it was possible that we could be so close, so *one*—and yet I could at the same time feel set apart from them.

The meetings of those who know each other as well as we do have no need of rules and an order. Often enough we have sat silent together until agreement has been reached, and separated without a word being said.

I wondered, to begin with, if this was to be such an occasion.

At last I addressed them: "You know that I want us to agree on a reversal of our policy towards Rohanda."

Four faces said that they had expected me to take up the argument in a more developed way.

I said: "I am having difficulty. The reasons that I think are conclusive—I do not know how to put to you."

Silence again.

Then spoke Stagruk from Planet 2.

"Since it seems recent experiences have distanced you from us, to the extent where we do not know how we each think, I shall sum up our thoughts."

This pained me—and they, too, were suffering.

"First. There is no advantage to Sirius in Rohanda. As an experimental field it is valueless, because of the overrunning of every part of it, and because of the mixture of races and even species . . ."

"The latter largely as a result of our intervention."

A pause. I had introduced, and so soon, a note foreign to us.

"We shall have to accept that you see things differently. Shall we continue? Since there is no advantage to us, it must be that there is an advantage to Canopus." A pause. "Canopus is our old enemy."

I sat silent, looking at them all in enquiry, because of how this had been said.

Up and down through our Empire, Canopus is talked of in, if I may say so, pretty stereotyped ways. These are the ways used always for the strong, the threatening—the superior. That is, when not implicit, as, almost, a background to our lives, Canopus is mentioned with a laugh of contempt, a sneer, a jibe, or at least with that hardening of the countenance and voice that means a subject is taboo from serious enquiry. Among us, among the Five, this tone was not used, of course; it would be more accurate to describe ours as that due to a senior partner who has won the position by unfair means. But the word "Canopus" had been spoken without any of these undertones, and almost as an enquiry. The word fell between us, lightly, and our eyes met over it.

"Canopus was *once* our enemy," I said.

"You have just spent a long—a very long—leave, with Klorathy."

"On the Rohandan moon."

"The attractions of which we do not believe responsible for the quite inordinate time you were away."

I looked at each of them, slowly one after another, so that they might read, if they could, the truth in my eyes.

It seemed I had failed, for Stagruk said: "For us to re-engage in Rohanda means to re-open the debate about our function as an Empire. About whether we maintain our present minimum performance or whether we expand again. It will mean training technicians to operate in the two Southern Continents. This will be of necessity a difficult and expensive training because of the appalling situation on Rohanda. There will be, almost certainly, loss of life among them. This will again re-inforce the questionings among us —it is absolutely essential for us to realise that if we do as you say, the very least we can expect is an inflammation of the Existential Question—and to a dangerous point. That is our view, Ambien."

I sat, absorbing the news that this had already been fully discussed among them: *they*, as four, had discussed one, me, Ambien. My distance and alienation from them, my ancient friends and co-workers, was such that I could have given up then. If I had not been thinking of Klorathy.

I was conscious that my continual reliance on him, in thought, was creating, or continuing, or reminding me of—I did not know which—a feeling that was becoming stronger as I sat there. For through this talk of ours a silent word reverberated: Klorathy, Klorathy, Klorathy.

I said: "It has long been policy that I should cultivate an association with Klorathy."

At once Stagruk said: "For *our* benefit."

This was a threat. And yet—there are threats and threats!

A situation can contain a threat—and then it doesn't matter

what is *said*: a group of individuals in a room swearing eternal brotherhood are eating the wind, if the *situation* they are in contains threat to them. And vice versa. Here there was no doubt—on the face of it—that there was a threat. I knew the calm judgemental expressions on the faces of these colleagues of mine very well. They were using this look because they believed the situation demanded it. And yet . . .

At the back of my mind my thoughts were racing: not yet has Canopus wanted something, when it has not happened! A request became a fact, even if I seem to have done nothing to further it. Everything that has passed between Sirius and Canopus, re Rohanda, between Klorathy and myself as Sirius and as Ambien, is insisting now, in a thousand voices, that what Canopus wants will come to pass. The worst that can happen is that these dear colleagues of mine will punish me in some way, but this will not prevent a Sirian involvement in Rohanda. This is because *we are already involved*, and in a way that Canopus needs—for the education of Sirius. A decision has already been made. And therefore: the threat that is present here and now is only to me . . . and, since my fate is of no importance, there is no real threat present.

While I considered all this, we were silent again—and whirling about among the other thoughts was that it was not possible that what I thought did not affect them, with whom I was so close. *With whom I made a whole.*

Feeling that these words had already been said, or thought, or existed somehow, I said: "It is my belief that this association has always been for our benefit. And planned to be so."

This was, if you like, treason. But it was putting into words what had been implicit among us all for a long time. This is where Ambien II, a Five, had, if you like, "gone wrong." And long ago.

I felt a great relief, a relaxing all through me and through us all. A climax had been awaited, had been reached—had gone past.

They were all looking at me, and not in hostility. Curiosity, perhaps, but not of an urgent or pressuring kind.

"You have not once mentioned Shammat," said Stagruk.

"No."

"Shammat is not a threat, in your belief?"

"Shammat apparently controls Rohanda. And her moon.

Shammat is prowling and working and busy from one end of Rohanda to the other. And yet this is with the permission or at least the tolerance of Canopus. Who could stop it tomorrow."

"And you believe we have to take all this on trust?"

"Yes, I do."

I knew then that they were going to agree. Canopus, working on me, on my nature, had also worked on them—without knowing it. They had watched me involved with Canopus, had wondered, had speculated—and their innermost selves had been touched. As I understood this I felt close to them in a way I had not before. And I do now.

"It is all good," I said. "Believe me. It is for our good. For the good of . . ." I had been going to say, for the good of Sirius, but found myself saying, ". . . the Galaxy."

"Very well," said Stagruk. "We will agree. You will take charge of the new policy. You will be responsible for the training of the personnel. And for liaison with Canopus. And you will announce, and then control, the ensuing debates on policy." And then she added, with a smile, "May I suggest that the public reasons you give for this change of policy, on behalf of us all, include the threat of Shammat on Rohanda, and the possible need for us to start mining on the Rohandan moon."

"You four have decided on mining that moon?"

"We are, after all, going to experience considerable difficulty in changing the policy for the entire Empire. Will you mind our pointing out that your new—alignments—at times seem to make you rather remote from our Sirian realities? Some kind of face-saving formula is essential."

I laughed, of course. And mostly with relief. But we all stayed where we were, looking close into each other's faces.

"Why can't you tell us, Ambien?" said Stagruk, suddenly, in a voice both hard with pride and reproachful. "Surely you must see how we feel?"

And I said, in equal pain and conflict: "How can I? Don't you see? It has taken—oh, so long! And so much reluctance on my part has had to be overcome. And everything I have learned from them has been bit by bit and slowly, so that I never even knew I had changed so much until I came to sit here with you . . ." And then I wept. It was a long time since water had spurted from my eyes, like the most primitive of our populations. And they, too, my old companions, showed signs of relapsing into the older ways.

The situation was so unusual for us all that we were not as disturbed by our reactions as we might otherwise have been.

This is what happened in that council meeting that later was recognised by everyone as a turning point, the beginning of a new orientation, for Sirius. Of course, at the time, that this was so was implicit in everything we said, and what we did not say. But none knew how far-reaching the changes would be. Even now, as I write, the importance of that meeting is still being re-assessed.

I shall now make two statements, without elaboration.

The first is that I have not again met Klorathy.

The second is that a very great deal of effort went into the change of policy that had to be made before I could actively and openly take my place identified in the eyes of the whole Empire as "Rohandan Ambien." Ambien I aided me behind the scenes during this campaign.

Meanwhile, I was thinking deeply and privately about what it was Canopus really needed from us. These thoughts could be shared with no one, not even Ambien I.

Again, I shall not overload the narrative with detail. The attentive reader will be able, I am sure, to understand my reasons for this or that decision.

I did not make arrangements for large numbers of technicians to establish themselves on Southern Continents I and II. This would have amounted to an armed occupation of these territories. Both continents were already being overrun by the white invaders from the northwest fringes: Klorathy's prophecies were being proved true. Both vast territories were being conquered by the most savage brutalities, and indigenous peoples and races were being wiped out or enslaved. The rule was everywhere that of force, of compulsion, of tyranny. Shammat, or its spirit, was absolutely dominant. And there was another thought: to equip our forces on a large enough scale to subjugate, or at least to control, these continents would be to undertake more than Canopus was doing in the northern areas. And it would mean teaching our technicians ways of war that we were forgetting—*learning* to forget as a deliberate and strict policy. We had our armed forces, yes; but these were small, and kept for special and particular occasions and tasks.

What I did was to have trained a restricted number of carefully selected personnel, all from Planet 11, who were of a similar build and height to the average Rohandan, and of a dark colour—that is, similar to the subjugated ones on both continents. Being of the subject races meant they would be more policed and watched; yet even so they would be less visible than if they had been chosen from among our white peoples. These were trained in surveillance, and the arts of exact and accurate assessments of social and political situations. Yet, although so few, they were able to monitor everything that went on in these continents. I am going to make the claim here that there have never been, anywhere, such expert and tactful spies as these.

And such self-sacrificing ones: their dislike of this unpleasant, and often heartbreaking, work was such that none was expected to do more than a tour of duty consisting of ten R-years.

But when they returned, the effect of their experience was very great: what they had seen of the extremes of suffering, cruelty, social disruption, was conveyed in all kinds of ways to our populations; and as a result, the whole subject of how an Empire should, and could—but not necessarily *did*—behave was debated in a new way. And this effect of our acceding to the Canopean request has by no means been exhausted. I make a point of mentioning this, because it is sometimes forgotten where and why the sudden renewal of self-questioning originated. And it is since that time that there has been a small but persistent—and powerful—undercurrent of interest in Canopus, its ways, its *function*. Yes, that is a word, on the lips of so many of our young, that dates from then.

To try and dismiss such a strong new way of thought as "treachery," or even slackness of moral fibre, does not, in my view, show enough insight into our *deeper* social processes, and those that will, I am sure, ultimately prevail. I am saying this in the conviction that I am speaking for very many more of our more senior individuals than have—as yet—expressed themselves.

I made an investigatory trip through both Southern Continents when our skeleton staffs were well established. I was always on the lookout for Klorathy, believing that the relationship established on the moon would have a continuance on that same level. It was not that I had formulated something precisely probable in my mind: more that my emotional self was demanding some kind of food. Of an infantile nature. As I was soon coming to see it. I looked, too, for Nasar. But reflection told me that both these Canopean officials were more likely to be at work in the north, once they were assured that we had taken over at least an adequate, if minimal, responsibility. In fact, it was obvious I would not run into either— after what Klorathy had told me of their being so stretched. Obvious once I had reflected!

It was Tafta I saw.

TAFTA

An advanced kingdom had been established for a good long time —Rohandan reckoning—in the mountain chain along the western coasts of Southern Continent II. This was at Stabilised Level 4, Galactic Scale. Invading whites from the Northwest fringes had by treachery overcome this state, and laid it in ruins, for the sake of the gold that filled its treasure-houses. From one end of this kingdom to the other, nothing was to be seen but corpses, ruined crops, and burning cities.

I had summoned my Space Traveller to a long stretch of sandy coast, and was waiting for its descent. I saw a column of males with mules and horses coming from the foothills, all laden with gold in every shape and form—bars, bags of dust, ornaments, the stripped-off coverings of official and sacred buildings. These men were as if intoxicated: I recognised easily the characteristics of indulged greed. Then I saw them all, about three hundred or so, at an order from a leader, put down their burdens and gather in a great circle. Standing rather above, on some grassy dunes, I was able to look down into the circle. Tafta was there. He was the commander of this plundering expedition. He was dressed as they all were, in coloured tunics, belted, over knee breeches. He was hung about with knives and weapons of all kinds. He swaggered and laughed. I was comparing this animal with the one who had approached us, in the time of the Lombis. And with the Tafta who completed the destruction of the first Lelanos. He had refined, in the sense that physically he was less animal; there was an obvious worsening, too, in another way, which I could not easily define. Impudence, rascality, had always been his nature: the attributes of the thief were his inheritance. But there was a new savagery here, quite distinct from the physical, a quality of the moral self. He was sickening to look at: this band of thieves were revolting. They did not even have the easy animal attractiveness that Tafta had had when I had lost myself into the temptations of easy power.

I saw that three men had been roughly flung into the centre of the ring. Three others were equipped with instruments of punishment. They were heavy sticks, to which were fixed nine thin tough ropes. Those who were to be punished were tied to stakes, their backs facing the punishers. Tafta, his hands on his hips, legs apart, swaggered there, grinning.

He raised his hand, and dropped it, and the whips hissed as they descended into the exposed flesh. Screams, groans, which held a note of surprise: the degree of pain felt was unexpected.

Again Tafta raised his hand and dropped it and the flails descended. I expected perhaps two or three strokes. I had never seen such coldly practised brutality. The groans and cries made the air quiver. The smell of blood sharpened the salt of the sea. It was a late afternoon, and the sun was sinking. A gold spread of cloud, gold edging the ridges of the waves, a wash of gold over the sands, and over the scene I was watching. And that hand rose, the palm facing out at shoulder height—and fell, and the whips came down and the shrieks went up. The watching circle of men was silent, watching in terror, their attitudes expressing how they, like me, counted each stroke by the sympathies of their own flesh. And the whistling flails came down, and down . . . the men being flogged sank as bushes or swathes of grass subside under flames.

And then the groans ceased. But the whips went on. And on. The punished ones were three bundles of bloody rags slumped by the stakes.

Tafta let out a shout. The company of pirates turned their backs on what they had been forced to watch, and shouldered their loads of gold. They made their way to boats tied to some rocks. A vessel with sails awaited them. The beasts they had used to carry these loads were being left on the shore to die or save themselves. I signalled my Space Traveller to wait, and walked down, past the butchered men, to the crowd of thieves. They all became immobile when they saw me, their jaws dropping. It was their silence that caused Tafta to turn, with brutalities already on his lips, before he even knew why they were silent.

There was a moment of indecision when he saw me. Then a grinning confidence puffed him out and he swaggered forward. He made a deep bow, lifting off a broad hat that had jewels in it, and was about to take my hand to kiss it. But while he hid his fear at my look, he did not lose his ease.

We looked at each other, across the small sandy space that separated us.

"Tafta," I said, "were you punishing those men because they disliked the savagery of your behaviour with the Indian kingdom? Was that it?"

From the men around him arose a deep assenting moan, which was at once stilled at his look. And in a moment they had recovered their air of greedy confidence.

"One day, Tafta," I said, "there will be an account made. There will come a time when you will suffer as you now make others suffer."

Again the minutest flicker of indecision, and then his swagger was back. He smiled. This handsome coarse brute smiled, and strengthened the cocky thrust of his shoulders. And I was looking at this stage of the creature's evolution, holding in my mind the stages of what he had been, and crying out to Canopus in my mind, Why, why, *why* do you allow it?

"It must be a long time since you were on Rohanda," he said. "It is mine. Mine from end to end."

"No, Tafta, it is not. And you will see that it is not."

He let out a guffaw, which was easy, even indulgent, as if I were an inferior in mentality. This was the change in him: and, looking at him, seeing this in him, I glanced around at his company and saw the same in them. It was conceit. They were all thickened and stupefied by it. Their intoxication was of many strands, and conceit was as strong as their greed.

I walked away from them back to the small eminence on which I had been before, and stayed watching as they put themselves and their loot into their boats and rowed themselves out to their winged vessel. Oh, yes, it was aesthetically very pleasing, this galleon of theirs: I had not before seen sailing craft at this precise stage of technology. And the scene was beautiful, as the light faded, leaving the dark acres of the ocean, crisping with light from a thin slice of moon. The Rohandan moon, which was my next assignment.

Having made sure the poor wretches at their stakes were in fact dead and having called to the mules and horses to follow me from off the beaches into the forests where they could find food and water, I took off for the planet's planet.

Since I had been there last, considerable changes. The Shammat stake was still the largest and had been spreading rapidly. Mining operations were predominant. Everywhere the crawlers could be seen at work in the craters, and new craters were visible. That was on the surface: underground, we knew, every kind of technological operation was in progress. But we, Sirius, had placed ourselves all around the perimeter of the Shammat area in an arc on one side: Canopus had done the same on the other. Our crawlers were plentiful, some of them the largest we had, five or six miles in diameter. We were mining; and we proposed to make use of what we produced: but let me put it this way: I have never seen in one of our operations so great a proportion of *visible* effect to what was actually produced. And Canopus had placed vast domes, and manned them and armed them. Shammat was therefore contained, and knew it.

Visible, too, were the observational towers of the three planets, and the pylons used by one of them to anchor their aircraft. The moon was now furiously active, but the inhabitants of Rohanda were only just beginning to develop instruments capable of seeing this.

I made sure that our policy of friendly co-operation among the three planets was being maintained, and paid a short visit to each station myself.

After consultation with the Canopean station, I ordered a Demonstration, first class, over the surface of the whole planet. It was interesting to me, underlining certain developments, that it was so long since we had had to use any such show of force, that our Mother Planet was hard put to it to raise enough craft and personnel of the required kind. But at length thirty-seven Battalions of our largest and most impressive machines, built for precisely this purpose, appeared all at once from space, hovered everywhere over the surface of this moon, swept repeatedly around it, hovered again, and departed in clouds of luminosity especially developed for this kind of effect. Yet, remembering Tafta, this new unreal confidence of his, I found doubts in myself. And I was dubious, too, about my reaction when I returned home. Which I then did, getting there not long after the return of the special Battalions.

The Four called me to a meeting.

The personnel were now returning as their tours of duty were completed, from the two Southern Continents, and what they were reporting of their experiences had caused a furore prognosticated by these experienced ones. Never had our Mother Planet even imagined anything like the pointless, barbarous treatment of the peoples of these continents by the invading ones, the Northwest fringers. They had not believed such cruelty could be. . . .

I shall now take the liberty of making a short observation. It is that a certain law clearly to be observed on Rohanda is not exactly unknown elsewhere. There, a geographical area, or nation, would criticise another for faults it committed itself. To such lengths was this tendency developed in the last period of Rohanda that this planet, at this time, has become the exemplar for us, and descriptions may be found plentifully in our technical literature. But for my own part I must say I have never been more amazed as when observing full-scale, all-global conferences on Rohanda, where all the nations hurled accusations at each other for practices that they were apparently incapable of seeing in themselves.

My colleagues and I were facing a first-class crisis—not immediately evident as one, but with the potentialities of social ferment that could affect everything.

And my request for the thirty-seven Battalions, and the resulting re-organisation and rapid re-training, had not gone unobserved by our people.

What was Rohanda, why was she of such importance to us, that so much disturbance was being allowed on her account?

We, the Five, sat together, now Four and One, as on the last occasion, and they wanted to know if I had seen Klorathy again. I said I had not, and that that was not the point. But how could I expect them to understand what had taken me so long?

They waited, regarding me in an expectation not untinged with anxiety. They were feeling, even if they had not formulated this, that their destinies, Sirian destinies, were in other hands. That this had always been so, they did not suspect. Nor could I easily think along these lines, even now.

They were waiting for me to say something as simple as "I believe this Canopean bond will benefit us in such and such a way."

At last, they demanded, having heard of the developments on the Rohandan moon, if I proposed to send a report to Klorathy. This was because they wished to read it and to assess our relationship from it. I said I did not believe a report was indicated yet.

This ended our meeting. I can see now their faces, turned as one towards me, and feel their fretfulness, their distrust. I don't blame them: I have never done that! In their places I would have been, I would have done, the same.

SHAMMAT

I was summoned back to the Rohandan moon. Fighting had broken out in the Shammat territory: civil war on Shammat was being reflected here. It was ground fighting. All over their territory were explosions that made new craters where their underground dwellings and factories had been; and wrecked crawlers, their limbs torn off, sprawled over the workings of the old craters. That the factions had not yet dared to make an aerial attack seemed to us a sign that they had not entirely lost a sense of their position. We took no chances; another show of our strength was arranged over their battlefields so that they would not be tempted to forget our presence, and that of Canopus. The details of this war do not concern this narrative.

On Rohanda was a similar state of affairs. That planet was now into its Century of Destruction, with the first of its global wars.

Most of the fighting took place in the Northwest fringes, where the nations tried to destroy each other over the question of who was to control—mainly—Southern Continent I. This war combined the maximum of nastiness with a maximum of rhetoric. It was a disgusting war. I caught glimpses of Tafta. Even more inflated with self-esteem than he had been when I had seen him last, he was at work inflaming national passions, as "a man of God," the term given to the exemplars of the local religions. First on one side, and then on the other, he announced God's support for whatever policy of mass destruction was being implemented. I shall not easily forget his evil unctuousness, his face all inflamed with sincerity, as he urged on the poor wretches who died or were wounded and crippled in multitudes.

My recall to Sirius was by the Four, who wanted to know "what Canopus thought it was doing"—allowing such carnage on Rohanda. They believed I had been meeting Klorathy and that for some reason connected with my inclination towards Canopus, was not telling them so. I could only repeat that I had not met Klorathy, nor had "instructions" from him; but that for my part I was disposed to trust in the long-term purposes of Canopus. This was not a happy meeting; and I was relieved to get an urgent message from Rohanda. The Shammat war on the planet's planet was at an end; the faction that had won on Shammat had imposed itself there, too: it was a matter of indifference to us—for nastiness and baseness there was nothing to choose between the factions. Tafta, the Shammat representative on Rohanda, had been compromised by the civil war in such a way that his personal position on Rohanda was weakened. It was known to us that on his return home he might face arrest or assassination. This was possibly not known to him.

The destructive processes on Rohanda were hastening to a conclusion. The second global war was in progress. Again, this had originated in the Northwest fringes, as an expression of national rivalries, but had spread everywhere, affected every part of the planet. It was this war that weakened, finally, the position of the white races; they had dominated the planet from end to end, destroying every local variation of culture and civilisation as their technological needs dictated.

The changes in the balances of power made by the second war are fully documented; but the details of these local struggles—which after all was all they were, looked at from any reasonable perspective—did not concern me nearly so much as the lessons that could be drawn from them and that could be applied to our own problems.

I was watching the changes in the sets of mind throughout our own Empire, on our Mother Planet and on the Colonised Planets. Every planet had different attitudes and ideas, which were stubbornly defended, always passionately, often violently. And each took in new facts and ideas at a different rate. I did not at first understand that this was my prime preoccupation: it was one thing to have seen that to cause changes in the Sirian Empire was a long-term aim of Canopus, and that I was their instrument—I have done my best to chronicle the slow, difficult growth of my understanding—but to comprehend a process fully, it is often essential to see the results of it. And this is true even for skilled administrators like the Five.

What I was doing during this period, which turned out to be a short one, was to stay quietly in my quarters thinking. It occurred to me that it was a very long time since I had done anything of the kind. I have been almost permanently on the move, or stationed on another planet. But it was not only my remaining at home that was unusual: I understood that the state of my mind was one I did not remember.

It was when the other members of the Five had been to see me, separately and almost furtively, and with that apologetic air caused by not understanding fully why one is doing something, that I began to comprehend. For one thing, I have only too often observed that this type of apology easily becomes irritation and then, very quickly, worse . . .

We had seldom visited each other in this way. Our formal meetings were necessary for the records, and so that citizens' groups could have reassurance for their anxieties by actually watching us at work in the council chambers. *We had known what we were all thinking, were likely to think, had formed something like a collective mind. . . .* The uneasiness of my visitors was partly because they did not like the necessity they found themselves in, to come to my quarters so as to find out—but find out *what*? They did not know!

Each of them arrived with this aggressive and embarrassed manner, and then enquired most solicitously after my health. Which I assured them was, as always, excellent. The visits were all the same. We agreed that we were seeing Sirius in ferment, beliefs and ideas held for millennia being thrown out, new ones being adopted. When this upheaval was over—and as usual during a period of tumult it was hard to believe it could ever be over—there was no means of foreseeing what our Empire would have become.

Our talk then turned to Rohanda. "Paradox, contradiction, the anomalous—when a planet is in a period of transformation, these are always evident. Well then, in your view, Ambien, what is the most important of these? Important from the point of view of illustrating mechanisms of social change?"

"First of all, I am not equipped to talk of the real, the deep, the really fundamental changes that are taking place." I said this firmly, knowing it would exasperate. But looked my visitor calmly in the eyes, insisting that I had to say this. And when it was accepted, with good grace or not, I said: "But as for the immediately evident and obvious paradoxes, I would say that it is that Rohanda has perfected techniques of communication so powerful that the remotest and most isolated individual anywhere can be informed of anything happening anywhere on Rohanda at once. There are millions of them engaged in these industries to do with communication. Through the senses of sight and sound and through ways they do not yet suspect, each Rohandan is subjected day and night to an assault of information. Of 'news.' And yet never has there been such a gap between what this individual is told, is allowed to know, and what is actually happening."

"But Ambien, is this not always true, everywhere, to an extent at least?"

"Yes, it is. For instance, if a Sirian were to be told that our Empire is run by a Dictatorship of Five, he would laugh or call the doctors."

"I am not talking about that, Ambien—and I don't like how you put it. If we are dictators, then when have there been rulers so responsive to the needs of their subjects . . . so compassionate . . .

so concerned for the general good. . . . Very well, you look impatient, you look as if I am quite ridiculous—we all of us recognise that we Five no longer think as one. You have your own views . . . but I was not talking of any specific problem we may have. I was suggesting that what *can* be taken in by an ordinary individual is *always* behind the facts."

"It is a question of degree. But are generalities useful at this point? This dangerous and crucial point? Very well then, let me put it like this. When what the populace believes falls too far behind what is really going on, then rulers do well to be afraid. It is because a mind, individual or collective, can be regarded as a machine. From this point of view. Feed in information too fast and it jams. This jam manifests in rage—riots, uprisings, rebellions."

"Which we are seeing now throughout our Empire. All kinds of new ideas fight for acceptance."

"But how many more are there that are not yet seen at all? But you don't want to talk about the particular. Very well then, though in my view we—*you*—are making a mistake. We ought to be talking about the Sirian situation. And about *our* situation. We ought to be thinking of ways our populations can be told: you Sirians, you, the Sirian Empire, have been ruled by an Oligarchy of Five, and this fact does not fit in at all with what you have been taught . . . oh very well then, let us stick to Rohanda. I shall make a very general observation. We all know that the central fact in a situation is often, and in fact most usually, the one that is not seen. We may say even that there is *always* a tendency to look for distant or complicated explanations for something that is very simple or near at hand. I shall say that as a result of watching the mental processes on Rohanda, I have concluded that they do not understand an extremely simple and basic fact. It is that each person everywhere sees itself, thinks of itself, as a unique and extraordinary individual, and never suspects to what an extent it is a tiny unit that can exist only as part of a whole."

"And that is a really new idea for you, Ambien? Ambien of the Five?"

"Wholes. A whole. It is not possible for an individual to think differently from the whole he or she is part of . . . no, wait. Let us take an example from Rohanda. There is a large ocean vessel of a new and advanced design. It is struck by a lump of floating ice and instantly sinks, though it has been advertised as unsinkable. They appoint a committee of experts—individuals, that is, of the highest probity and public admiration, with the longest and most efficient training possible in that field. This committee produces a report that whitewashes everyone concerned. But this same report, studied only a few years later, strikes a new generation as either mendacious or as incompetent . . . well?"

"You occupy your mind with the minuscule! It isn't what we expect of you."

"It seems to me that the minuscule, the petty, the humble example is exactly where we can study best this particular problem. What happened in the interval between the first report and the reassessment of it?"

"Change of viewpoint."

"Exactly. An assortment of individuals, identically trained, all members of a certain class, came together on a problem. They were already members of a group mind—together they concentrated into a smaller one of the same kind. They produced a report that could not have been different, since they could *not* think differently. Not *then*. That is why one generation swears black, and the next white."

"But you, Ambien, are surely proof that a group mind is hardly inviolable—or permanent!"

"Ah, but here is another mechanism . . . what we are seeing are only mechanisms, machineries, that is all . . . let us consider these group minds . . . these little individuals making up wholes. Sets of ideas making up a whole can be very large, for instance, when they are occupying a national area, and millions will go to war for opinions that may very well be different or even opposite only a decade later—and die in their millions. Each is part of this vast group mind and *cannot* think differently, not without risking madness, or exile or . . ."

Here there was a moment of consciousness, discomfort, sorrow—which I dissipated at once by going on.

"Yes, you said that I have been at odds with you and for a long time, and that this fact proves I am wrong. But what is the mechanism, the machinery, that creates a group, a whole, and then develops a dissident member—develops thoughts that are different from those of the whole?"

"Perhaps this individual may have been suborned? Influenced by some alien and unfriendly power?"

"If we are going to allow ourselves to think like that, then—"

"Then *what*, Ambien? Tell me. Tell *us*. We are ready to understand, don't you believe that?"

"It is a mechanism for social change. After a time . . . and it can be a very long time indeed; or after only a short time . . . as we see now on Rohanda, where everything is speeded up and sets of ideas that have been considered unchallengeable can be dispersed almost overnight—after a period of time, short or long, during which the group mind has held these sacred and *right* ideas, it is challenged. Often by an extremely small deviance of opinion. It is characteristic of these group minds, these wholes, to describe an individual thinking only very slightly differently as quite remarkably and even dangerously different. Yet this difference may very shortly seem ludicrously minor . . ."

"And so we all hope, Ambien."

"But there is a question here, it torments me, for we do not know how to answer it. This deviant individual in this group—he or she has been unquestioningly and happily and conformingly part of this group, and then new ideas creep in. *Where do they come from?*"

"Well, obviously, from new social developments."

"Thank you. Oh, thank you so much! That's settled then, and we need think no more about it! May I go on? When such a deviant individual becomes too uncomfortable for the group mind to tolerate, various things can happen. Commonly, expulsion. Labelled seditious, mad, and in any case wrongheaded, he or she is thrown out . . . yes, yes, we all agree that in our case this would be a pity. Talking generally though, this individual may start an opposing group having attracted enough people with similar ideas—no, I am *not* threatening you. Can we not talk about this with less personal reference? Can we not? Yes, indeed, I am concerned about our ancient association, indeed I am anxious for my personal safety— but can you not believe that brooding about these questions I am

still Ambien II, who have with you administered a vast Empire
for so long? Thank you! This deviant individual may influence
others of this group, this mind, to think differently, when the
entity will split into two—and I do not expect this to happen in
this case. No. What has caused me to think differently from you
has affected, I believe, only myself . . . no? We shall see! No, I am
not threatening! How can it be a threat? *We are not in control of
these processes.* We like to think we are. But they control us. You
don't like that thought! We of the Five don't like to think that all
this long time we have never been more than straws in a current
. . . but may I go on to suggest another possibility for this deviant
and so irritating individual? If he or she is not expelled, or does not
expel herself, but remains, contemplating her position, then a certain train of thought is inevitable. She has been part of a group
mind, thinking the same thoughts as her peers. But now her mind
holds other ideas. *Of what whole is she now a part?* Of what invisible whole? It is surely not without interest to speculate, when
feeling isolated, apparently alone, on the other little items or atoms
who with her are making up this other whole . . . this line of
thought doesn't interest you? And yet surely I have been seeing
indications that it does, it interests you very much—and in fact
perhaps *your* speculations in this realm are why you are here, visiting me, just as the others have done . . . you did not know that
the others have all been? Odd, that! *Once* we would all have
known, we *did* all know what the others did, and thought. What is
happening to us? We don't know! That is the point! Are we going
to be like the Rohandans, quite happy to use social machinery without being prepared to examine the mechanisms that rule them?
Are we quarrelling? Does our disagreement have to be seen as such
a threat?"

"We are not hostile to you, Ambien. You must not think that we
are. Not to you personally."

"When have we ever seen our relations with each other as
personal? Well, I am delighted to have your *personal* good wishes,
of course."

"I must go. Can we send you anything? Do you need anything?"

"I am not ill! I am not, as far as I am aware, under arrest? But
thank you, no, I don't need anything, and I have occupation enough

with what I am thinking. I think day and night about group minds and how they work. Do you realise that one may present a fact as hard and bright and as precious as allyrium to a group of individuals forming a group mind, one that is already set in a different way, and they cannot see it. Literally. *Cannot take it in*. Do you understand the implications of that? *Do you?* Well, thank you for coming to see me. Thank you. Thank you."

During this period I had not heard from Klorathy, nor had there been any official communication between Canopus and Sirius. When the other members of the Five had concluded their visits to me, a message arrived addressed personally to me. "Perhaps you would consider making a visit to the Isolated Northern Continent."

The Four had seen this, and had directed it on: normally a message for an individual of the Five is not intercepted.

I informed the Four that I was again visiting Rohanda, but they made no comment. Not knowing what I was supposed to be doing, I instructed my Space Traveller to hover over the Isolated Northern Continent, at the highest altitude possible for observation. I was not alone. The skies were full not only of craft originating on Rohanda, but of the observational machines of Canopus, Shammat, the three neighboring planets. A Canopean Crystal, Shammat Wasps, and ten of the Darters evolved by the three planets: they often shared their technology.

I was looking down at the continent, in an idle nonfocussed way, remembering the other guises and transformations I had seen it in, when the Canopean Crystal floated down and lay in the air in front of me. It was in its most usual shape, a cone, and as it hung point down among the charming clouds of that atmosphere, with the blue of the atmosphere beyond, it was most attractive, and I was admiring it when it moved off, slowly, and I followed. I did not understand this lesson, which I assumed it was, but only watched, and enjoyed—as always—the aesthetic bonuses of this planet. The Crystal became a tetrahedron—the three facets of it I could see reflecting the landscape of these blue and white skies—then a globe. A glistening ball rolled and danced among the clouds. I was laughing with the pleasure of it, and even clapping my hands and applauding . . . it elongated and became like a drop of liquid at the moment when it falls from a point. But it was lying horizontally, the thin end in front of us. This exquisite drop of crystalline glitter was thus because of the pressures of the atmosphere, it was adjusting itself to the flow of the jet stream, we were being sped along by the air rivers, and the Crystal had become a long transparent streak. My craft was almost in the end of the streak, and for a few moments we seemed almost to intermingle, and what delicious thoughts sang through my mind as we saw the rivers and mountains and deserts of the landmass beneath through what seemed like liquefied light. My guide was changing again, was showing how it had to change, and flow, and adapt itself, for all the movements and alterations of the atmosphere we were submerged in like liquid moulded this Globe, or Rod, or Streak, or Fringe. . . . How many shapes it assumed, this enchanting guide of mine, as we followed the flowing streams of the upper airs of Rohanda—how it evolved and adapted and shone! —but then dulled, so it seemed as if a lump of dullish lead lay there, sullen in a chilly and yellow light, but then lost its grey, and took in a sparkle and a glisten again, and seemed to frolic and to play, and yet again became serious and stern, with an edge of hardness in it, all the time a flowing and an answering, and an astonishment, but then, my mind lost in contemplation of this Crystal that seemed to have become no more than a visible expression of the air currents, I saw it had stopped, and had become the shape of a drop that points down. Its narrow end was directing my attention below. What was it I was supposed to be noticing?

I hovered there near the monitoring Crystal and saw again how the edges of the continent were being pressed and squeezed up into its mountain folds, how the deserts lay and spread, how the great forests of other times had gone, and realised that I was seeing something extraordinary. A grid had been stamped over the whole continent. It was a mesh of absolutely regular rectangles. I was seeing a map, a chart, of a certain way of thinking . . . this was a way of thought, a set of mind, made visible. It was the mind of the Northwest fringes, the mind of the white conquerors. Over the variety and change and differentiation of the continent, over the flows and movement and changes of the earth—as vigorous as that of the air above, though in a different dimension of time—was this stamp of rigidity. Cities, towns, the larger mountains, the deserts, interrupted it: but over rivers and hills and marshes and plains lay the grid, this inflexible pattern. It was a pattern of ownership, a multiplication of the basic unit of the possession of land. I had not noticed it before: previous visits of surveillance from this height had been before the new conquerors had inflicted their ways of thought on everything: I had seen how the growth and unfolding of the material of the continent displayed itself in surface contours, and in the disposition of its waters and its vegetation. But now, between me and the language of growth and change was this imperious stamp. This pattern. This grid. This print. This mint.

Now I knew what it was Canopus had wanted me to see, and I looked towards the Crystal, for some kind of directive. I would have liked to leave, and to be allowed to take my attention from this depressing and miserable map—the mind of Shammat. But still it hovered there, silent, changing its shape at every moment, demonstrating the possibilities of a fluid communication . . . and then it was lifting up and away, was a great drop of glittering water from the black depths of space, and it hung there, this infinitely various and variable and flowing thing, this creation of the Canopean mind, it spoke to me, it sang to me, it sent messages of hope, of the eternal renewal of everything, and then it again elongated itself, and ebbed up and fled back to its station high above Rohanda, where it was a mote in sunlight, a memory of itself.

And so I was alone again. I wondered if I had seen all that I was meant to see, and if I should now return home. I thought of how I would speak to the Four of the messages I had been given, and of how they might receive it . . . but then reflected that I had not seen the western coasts of this continent during this present phase of Rohanda, and I directed my Traveller accordingly.

I was set down at the top of an immensely tall building in a large city. From there I could see the deserts and mountains inland, and the ocean on the other side. Beneath me the city itself was hardly visible, for it was filled with a poisonous smoke, and the buildings emerged from the fumes like islands from water.

I deliberately curtailed this survey since I knew I was being invaded by emotions not felt by me since my sojourn in Lelanos: these were because of the contrast between what these animals had made of their technical achievements and what they in fact were doing. But it is a story unfortunately not rare in our annals;

and I will simply state that this *was* my state of mind—dangerous to my equilibrium. I left the top of the building and went down into a room in the heart of the building, a public room, constructed in such a way that it could only adversely affect the mental processes. In it was a machine for the transmission of "news." Visual transmission, and consisting only of brutalities and savageries of various kinds.

Of the real situation of the planet nothing was being coherently said: there were glimpses, references, all kinds of half-truths, but never the full picture.

Then I saw Tafta. On the screen of the machine was Tafta, and he was on a platform in a hall that was full of people. He was superficially different in appearance from how I had last seen him as the black-clothed, war-inciting priest. His physical being had not much changed. He glistened with health, was rather fleshy, and he emanated a calm, self-satisfied conceit. His garb was that now worn everywhere over the planet, as if it had been ordered by a dictator —but these animals have never been able to relinquish uniforms. He wore blue very tight trousers of a thick material, which emphasized his sexuality, and a tight singlet.

He was resting one buttock on the edge of a table, swung one leg, and smiled easily and confidently down at his audience.

Tafta was now one of the senior technicians of the continent, and his task was to answer questions put by this disquieted and indeed frankly terrified gathering. He was a world figure, as an apologist for current technology. For some years he had enjoyed a reputation as an intrepid critic of governmental and global policies to do with the uses of technology, and had written several works of fiction, of that category where social possibilities of the day were given expression in a popular form. This type of fiction was both challenging and useful, in that it gave the populace opportunities to examine potentialities of technological discoveries; but also anodyne, because the mere fact that sometimes appalling developments had been displayed in print at all seemed to reassure the citizens that they could not happen. At any rate, Tafta illustrated the social law—so often seen, and of course causing me, because of my own position, much private alarm in case I might fall victim to it—that to the extent an individual has been a deviant from a group, a set of ideas, a "received opinion" of some sort, and then his own deviant opinions becoming "respectable," ousting or questioning the former standards, so that he as an individual has ceased to be a threat, but on the contrary has become stabilised in the new orthodoxy, then to the same degree he may be expected to misuse, scorn, and ridicule the new uprising generation of "freaks," of "eccentrics," of nonconformists.

I shall not detail the set of attitudes that on this occasion he was defending, but they were all to do with the despoiling of the planet, the damage being done by technology, poisoning, fouling, wastage, death. He was reassuring his questioners, and this easy, affable, smiling, democratic fellow, the very embodiment of successful adaptation, was deeply reassuring to them, or at least to most. And of course that this was so was not an accident.

There he sat, informally posed on the edge of the table, one leg pleasantly swinging, as if his exuberant vitality could not help expressing the sheer invincible joy of life in this way, the bright candid blue eyes beaming over his full healthy beard, and it occurred to me that he did not look all that different from the pirate whom I had watched plundering the continent south of this one. And he smiled. How he smiled! His smile was a most powerful instrument . . .

As a question was put to him from below, in the hall, the smile was adjusted: he adjusted, minutely, ridicule, scorn, contempt; but it was the mildest and almost careless ridicule that he was using to demonstrate the questioner's foolishness or stupidity.

And he was, similarly, mildly and almost carelessly sarcastic. An individual stood up to demand reassurance about something or other, and he would, as he listened, adjust that smile and adjust the tone of his voice—exactly. Perfectly. What a performance Tafta was giving! I could not help but admire it. The social mechanism he was using so well was that social law that most Rohandans could not bear to be ridiculed, to be "out of step." It was too uncomfortable to them to be outside the current group mind, and they were easily manipulated back into it.

Ten years before, the questions being asked had been different: in the meantime, many of the possibilities dismissed by Tafta or a similar spokesman as absurd had become fact. In ten years' time, the questions being asked today, and being so subtly ridiculed, would have been answered by events. . . .

By the end of that "conference" and the "discussion period," Tafta's bland well-mannered contempt had succeeded in making his audience seem absurd and silly-minded little people, and most had a crestfallen look. But others, a few, had an air of stubborn self-preservation.

I left the scene and went down into the street, as much to escape the imbalances being caused in me by this unpleasant building as to rid myself of the sight of Tafta. It took Shammat—I was thinking—to make of good humour a quality to be suspected and distrusted.

In the street I was not conspicuous, for I was wearing the uniform, the thick tight trousers and a singlet, and my face was daubed thoroughly with paint.

Tafta soon sauntered towards me, smiling.

"Were you watching?" And he let out a guffaw, which reminded me of the beach, the three whipped wretches, the buccaneers.

"I was indeed."

"Well, Sirius?"—and I have never seen such a triumphant sneer. There was nothing in this vulgarian, all crude contempt, of the urbane gentleman of science I had just been watching.

"It is not Sirius," I said quietly, as I had done before, "who is master of this planet."

But while his gaze did meet mine, it was only with the surface of his attention. He was enclosed in his conceit, and his pleasure at his cleverness. And yet, as this boasting animal swaggered there, laughing, I knew that what I was seeing was—defeat.

"Tafta," I said, "you are very sure of yourself."

"We have just had a directive from home," said he. "From Shammat. Shammat of Puttiora . . ." And he laughed and he laughed, because the planet Shammat was now master of the Empire of Puttiora, and he was identifying himself with this mastery. "The directive was to test the degree of imperviousness among these Rohandans to the truth of their situation. And I have tested it. And believe me, Sirius, it is absolute."

"You are wrong. It only seems to be so."

"If any leader of any nation of Rohanda stood up and told them the truth, the full truth, of their real situation, do you know what would happen? They would not believe him. They would kill him. Or lock him up as a madman."

"So it seems now."

He was looming and swaggering above me, smiling and ascendant, drunk with power and with confidence. And, just as had happened so often before, his great brown hairy hands came out, one on either side of my head, where my allyrium earrings hung. His fingers itchingly stroked the things, while his eyes glittered. But he had forgotten their purposes. . . . And, as I remembered how much he had forgotten, how far he was from any real understanding, I felt some strength come back into me, and this repelled his leeching and sucking at me. His hands fell away.

"What pretty earrings," said he, in a different voice, a half-mutter, thick and dreamlike, and into his eyes came an anxious look.

"Yes, Shammat, they are."

Now we stood at a distance from each other. He seemed to shrink and diminish as I watched him. He was now only the poor beast Shammat, the doomed one, and I was sorry for him.

"Tafta," I said, "it was foolish of you to follow that order from your Home Planet. Very foolish."

"Why? What do you know . . ." As I walked away from him I heard him come running after me, and felt his hot carnivorous breath on my cheek.

Without turning I said, "Goodbye, Tafta."

I heard him cursing me as he stood there impotent on the street's edge. And then he was coughing and gasping and retching in the fumes of the machines. And so I left him.

I bought myself a mask of the kind worn by these unfortunates in their streets, to protect themselves from the poisons manufactured by their machines, and which often made them blind, or ill, or silly, and I went walking around and about that city, unable to bring myself yet to summon my Traveller, for I was thinking of Klorathy, of Canopus. I wanted—I am afraid this was the truth— some sort of reassurance; for while I had been showing firmness and confidence with Tafta, I could not help feeling myself undermined by the familiar dry sorrow at the waste of it, the dreadful squandering waste of it all. I remembered Nasar and how he had learned to contain his pain on behalf of this sad place, and I was thinking of the things he had said, and how much I had learned. I was wishing I might see him again. How much it would reassure me simply to see him, and to exchange a few words. What would he be thinking now, my old friend Nasar—my old friend Canopus?

CANOPUS

I was on the edge of the city, looking at a building, and thinking that it pleased me. It was simple enough, a dwelling place, and built of the local stone. There was nothing remarkable about it, yet it drew me. It was built on a small rocky hill that rose clear from the city's dirty fumes. I saw that on the steps stood a young man, wearing the familiar uniform of tight trousers and a singlet, but I could not see his face, for though he was turned towards me, he was wearing a mask. Nasar, Nasar, was ringing in my mind, and I said aloud: "Nasar, I am sure that it is you."

We were like two snouted creatures, and he took off his mask, and I took off mine. We went higher up the hill, to be more above the fumes, since our eyes had at once begun to redden and water.

"Well, Sirius?"

"Did you build this place? Are you an architect?"

"I am an architect among other things."

We stood looking at the building, side by side. It was really very pleasant. The horrible dissonances of the rest of the city seemed to disappear, and only this house remained.

"Those who live here will be sane?"

"*I* am living here. I suppose I am slightly saner than most," said he, on the familiar Nasar note, and I laughed.

"Ah, Canopus, but why, why, *why?*"

"Are you still asking why, Ambien?"

"Don't you?"

He hesitated, and I recognised in this something I knew well: he was not able to communicate what he was thinking to me, Sirius. I was not up to it! He said: "Ambien, has it not occurred to you that there are useful questions, and those that are not? Not at all! Not in the slightest degree!"

"It is hard to accept."

"Won't you accept it from Nasar—who knows all about useless rebellions?" And he laughed again, looking into my eyes, so that we remembered our time together in Koshi.

"Perhaps I am not strong enough for that truth."

"Then so much the worse for you. And we none of us have any choice . . . or do you want to remain of those who make up any kind of solution or answer for themselves, and take refuge in it, because they are too weak for patience?"

And I could not help laughing, thinking of the long ages of his patience.

But as I laughed, I began to cough, and he was coughing, too.

He put back his mask and so did I. Again, two snouted monsters, we faced each other, Nasar and I.

"Ambien, listen to me."

"When did I ever do anything else?"

"Good. After watching us at work for the long time you have been involved with us, are you still able to believe that we deal in failure?"

"No."

"Remember that then. Remember it."

He made a jaunty little gesture of farewell, and went up the steps into his house.

I then left Rohanda, without going back to its moon.

The Four were waiting for me.

This time it was not possible to put them off. They had to have some sort of information.

After a good deal of thought, I dispatched this message to Klorathy. (We always used their term, Shikasta, for Rohanda in such exchanges.)

Private letter sent through the Diplomatic Bag,

AMBIEN II *of* SIRIUS, *to* KLORATHY, CANOPUS

In haste. Have just been looking through our reports from Shikasta. In case—which is unlikely, I know—you have not got this information, Shammat called a meeting of all its agents in one place. This in itself seems to us symptomatic of something long suspected by us—and I know, by you, too. Conditions on Shikasta are affecting Shammatans even more than Shikastans, or affecting them faster. Their general mentation seems to be deteriorating rapidly. They suffer from hectivity, acceleration, arrhythmictivity. Their diagnosis of situations, as far as they are capable and within the limits of their species, is adequate. Adequate for certain specific situations and conditions. The conclusions they are drawing from analyses are increasingly wild. That Shammat should order this meeting, exposing its agents to such danger, shows the Mother Planet is affected; as much as that the local Shammat agents should obey an obviously reckless order.

This condition of Shammat and its agents, then, seems to us likely to add to the spontaneous and random destructivity to be expected of Shikasta at this time.

As if we needed anything worse!

Our intelligence indicates that you are weathering the Shikastan crisis pretty well—not that anything else was ever expected of you. If all continues to go well, when may we expect a visit? As always we look forward to seeing you.

Shortly after this, I was called by the Four, who had of course read this and discussed it.

"Why is it that you do not tell us what has really happened between you and Klorathy?"

"Between Sirius and Canopus."

They were not so much annoyed at this, as alarmed.

I had a vision of *our* mind, the mind of the Five—five globules or cells nestling together in a whole, and one of them pulsing at a different rate. And the Four shrinking closer while the one, me, vibrated more wildly, because of the space around it.

"You tell us nothing, *nothing.*"

"I tell you everything I can."

"Ambien, you are going to have to tell us. Because if we cannot produce, as a whole—we as the Five—a consistent and convincing reason for our activities on Rohanda, then we are all threatened."

"You have the remedy," I said, looking at each in turn, steadily.

"But we obviously don't want to use it."

"Do you really imagine that all I have to do is to find a formula, a set of words, some phrases strung together—and then you would nod your heads and say: Oh of course, that's it! and then you would release them to the Empire and everyone would be happy?"

This meeting, I have to emphasise, was at the height of the debate, which still continues, and threatens to destroy our foundations.

What foundations?

What uses, what purposes?

What service? What function?

At length I said to the Four that to explain to them as they wanted would mean my talking for a year or writing a book.

"Well, why not write a book, Ambien?"

I saw that many purposes would be served by this.

"It comes hard to an old bureaucrat, to write a history of the heart, rather than of events," I said.

The jokes made between those who have been very close and who are so no longer are indeed painful.

They sent me on extended leave. In other words, I am under planet arrest, on Colonised Planet 13.

I would do exactly the same in their place. In my view the institution of the Five, now—I hope, temporarily—the Four, is the most valuable regulator of our Empire. It should not be destroyed. I make a point of saying this, hoping that my millennia-long service and experience will not be entirely dismissed.

It is hard for me to be confined to this one planet, accustomed as I have been to range at will through the Galaxy, but I am not complaining. I feel it is a privilege for me to be allowed to write this account of what I know is a unique experience.

To think of Rohanda gives me pain, though I try to comfort myself with Nasar's last words to me.

If I have learned so much that I never expected, what more can I hope to learn and understand, providing I am patient, and do not allow myself to ask useless questions?

> This is Rohandan Ambien, Ambien II
> of the Five, from Planet 13 of the
> Sirian Empire

DIRECTIVE FROM THE FOUR,
TO THE SIRIAN MOTHER PLANET
AND ALL COLONISED PLANETS OF THE SIRIAN EMPIRE:

Attention! There is a document in general circulation that purports
to be the work of Ambien II, formerly of the Five. That this so-
called memoir has never been printed and therefore shown to be
approved is evidence enough that it is not authentic, to those who
use their judgement. We wish, however, to emphasise that this is
a crude invention, and the work of unfortunates who wish to
subvert the good government of our Empire. Ambien II, after her
long and valued service to our Empire, succumbed to a mental
disequilibrium, due to an overprolonged immersion in the affairs
of the planet Rohanda. She is under treatment, and we her colleagues are confident that in due course she will be able to resume
her duties, even if only to a restricted, and less taxing, degree.

LETTER FROM AMBIEN II TO STAGRUK:

I have seen your Directive. I can see that with the turn events have
taken, and the danger of a revolution in every part of our Empire,
you Four had to take some such action. I have received your kind
messages about my health. Yes, thank you, I am well, and I have no
need of anything. Of course, I cannot help craving a real participation in affairs. Old habits die hard! Meanwhile, it is a consolation
to me that—not for the first time, as you know!—I receive visits
from each one of you separately. These are a great pleasure to me.
I like to feel that my experience is even now being put to use in this
indirect way. I reflect on the fact that you all assure me of your
personal support, and your sympathetic understanding of why I
took the steps I did to make sure my manuscript reached general
circulation, even in its somewhat archaic form. I agree with you
that unpalatable facts have to be released to the populace in
measured and often ambiguous ways. Was it not I who first introduced this view? I reflect, too, that this rapport between us old

colleagues may stand us all in good stead yet when—as you will, I am sure, agree seems more and more likely to happen—we all find ourselves together in "corrective exile" on this quite pleasant though tedious Planet 13.

A NOTE ON THE TYPE

The text of this book was set in Electra, a Linotype face designed by
W. A. Dwiggins (1880–1956). Although a great deal of Dwiggins'
early work was in advertising and he was the author of the standard
volume *Layout in Advertising*, Mr. Dwiggins later devoted his prolific
talents to book typography and type design and worked with great
distinction in both fields. In addition to his designs for Electra, he
created the Metro, Caledonia, and Eldorado series of typefaces, as
well as a number of experimental cuttings that have never been issued
commercially.

Electra cannot be classified as either modern or old-style. It is not
based on any historical model, nor does it echo a particular period or
style. It avoids the extreme contrast between thick and thin elements
that marks most modern faces and attempts to give a feeling of
fluidity, power, and speed.

This book was composed by The Maryland Linotype Composition
Co., Baltimore, Maryland. It was printed and bound by American
Book–Stratford Press, Saddle Brook, New Jersey.

Typography and binding based on a design by Camilla Filancia.